# Virus-C

The Change Chronicle Volume 1

By

## Major Ursa

Burlington, Vermont

Cover Art by Green Dragon

Copyright © 2024 by Ursa Books

All rights reserved. No part of this publication may be reproduced, distributed, or transmitted in any form or by any means, including photocopying, recording, or other electronic or mechanical methods, without the prior written permission of the publisher, except in the case of brief quotations embodied in critical reviews and certain other noncommercial uses permitted by copyright law.

Onion River Press
89 Church St
Burlington, VT 05401
info@onionriverpress.com
www.onionriverpress.com

ISBN: 978-1-957184-83-8 Paperback
ISBN: 978-1-957184-84-5 eBook
Library of Congress Control Number: 2024921937

# Acknowledgement

This book is for all the heroes in my own life. For my great grandfather who never let his blindness or the occasional telephone pole stop him from living or being happy. For all the times he stirred my ketchup with his finger to make it taste better. For my father who served his country with honor. He faced bout after bout of cancer with courage. They were incredible role models for a young boy and later as a man. They were not the only heroes in my life, but their impact is beyond measure. Welcome to the team, Amber. Your inputs were awesome.

Thanks again GD for all your hard work.

# Author Note

A world, especially a place of fantasy, needs to have a beginning. Inevitably, someone asks about the history of the world. Questions about my writing are my greatest weakness. All of the short stories in Tapestry of the World came from questions asked by my friends or grandkids. "What is it with Shorty and squirrels? It makes no sense." And thus, was born All Good Things Come with Squirrels. Sometimes it is hard to stay on track with the current book because a question pops up and I have to write another story. Tapestry of the World II is up to seven completed stories, and I am not even ready to start writing it.

And so began Virus-C. The bard in the Short Path spoke of the destruction of the world by the mages of science. I had baited a hook sure to catch a question. And now, instead of writing the second book of Becoming Heroes, I am trying to answer the question, "What was the Great Change?" The answer was in the back of my brain. I knew what had happened, but I had to find a way to tell the tale. Who would be the heroes and who would be the villains? And of course, who would be the fools?

The world I imagined was a world of change, conflict, and chaos. It was a world that I knew well because I was living in it. And so, Virus-C escaped from my mind and onto the page. It was the first book that I did not know in advance where it was going. But finding the clues wasn't hard. They were all around me. If the pages of this book feel too real, they are not. It just feels that way. And to prevent the inevitable question if you make it to the end of the book... Yes, I had my COVID shots.

## *Disclaimer*

*This is a work of fiction. Unless otherwise indicated, all the names, characters, businesses, places, events and incidents in this book are either the product of the author's imagination or used in a fictitious manner. Any resemblance to actual persons, living or dead, or actual events is purely coincidental.*

# CONTENTS

Part I Gain of Function .................................................................... 1
Part II Containment Breach ........................................................... 51
Part III Outbreak ........................................................................... 159
Part IV Epidemic .......................................................................... 299
Cast of Characters ........................................................................ 353

# Part I
# Gain of Function

**Chapter 1
Out of China**

Dr Anita Caufi entered her office at the National Institute of Allergies and Infectious Diseases. It was just after six a.m. She hated coming in this early, but it was the only way to avoid the traffic around Bethesda. It was either come in at the crack of dawn or sit on the beltline for hours. All of her years of hard work, all of her achievements, and she was still forced to get up early and slog into the office.

At least the office was a nice one on the top floor. The view from her window was incredible. She had all the comforts befitting the head of the Institute and the Chief Medical Adviser to the President. She glanced at her desk. It was state of the art with a touchscreen computer built into the marble desktop. The desk was an expensive work of art. It was perfect except that, as usual, her inbox was overflowing. Even with a secretary and three administrative assistants, she still spent the first two hours of her day pushing paper.

Her ritual morning complaining was interrupted by the ding of the automatic coffee maker in the far corner of the room by the picture window. The machine began to gurgle and the enticing smell of hazelnut wafted through the room. Anita pulled off her winter coat and hung it on the back of her door. Then she headed for the best part of her morning. A large mug sat upside down on a towel beside the pot. She picked it up and waited for the pot to fill. As soon as the coffee maker went silent, she began to pour.

She lifted the mug to her nose and breathed in deeply. The anticipation was almost as enjoyable as the first sip of her morning nectar. Anita turned to stare out the window as she drank. The sky was still dark at this time of the morning in early December. The darkness above was a stark contrast to the NIAID campus far below. The roads and parking lots were ablaze with the lights of too many cars. But that was life in the DC area. She drained the first cup and turned back to the coffee maker for her paperwork cup.

She placed the second mug of coffee on its coaster and relaxed into her chair. She glanced briefly at the monitor inset into her desktop. There weren't any emails in her urgent folder. Sighing, Anita reached for the top folder in her overflowing inbox. One schedule, four status memos and three appraisals later, her inbox didn't look any better. The coffee in her mug was now cold. She was about to top it off when the next item in her box caught her attention.

Three printed pages stapled neatly in one corner rested at the new top of her inbox. The logo for the World Health Organization was at the top of the first page. In her opinion, the WHO was a waste of time and dollars that she would gladly put towards her own projects. But she was not the President and she didn't get to make that particular decision. The question was why anyone would think she cared which catastrophe the WHO was predicting next?

Anita stared at the pages until her curiosity overcame her desire for hot coffee. She picked up the update and leaned back in her chair to scan it. The first page was all a rehash of known outbreaks in Africa. There was nothing she wasn't already aware of and definitely nothing she was concerned about. When she flipped the page, a single line highlighted in pink stared back at her. The location immediately caught her attention.

*Wuhan City, Hubei Province, China*

Anita felt her heart race. She began to read. The WHO was tracking a new viral outbreak. Chinese officials were denying it, but the death toll was rising. Details were sketchy because the WHO only had a small contingent on the ground so far. Anita did not need their assessment to know what had happened or what was coming. The stupid bastards had lost containment. She knew without a doubt that this was her project. She had to minimize the potential backlash of this screw-up before word of this hit the media.

She dropped the report into the shredder behind her desk and pulled out the burner phone she kept in the desk for emergencies. She stared at the cheap Android screen as the phone came to life. This had to be done carefully. Opening the text message screen, she entered the first phone number and a single line of text. "VC breach. WR Hospital 11 am, 2B214." Then she pressed send. She sent the exact same message to two other numbers. She would not compromise her team by linking all three people in the same message.

Anita placed the phone on her desk and stared at it. There was one more player, but she wasn't sure about bringing him into this yet. No, she decided, this was not the time to be hesitant about things. She needed to know what cards she had to play if things went as bad as she was expecting. Picking up the phone, she typed and sent the same message a fourth time.

Looking at her watch, she discovered it was nearly 7:53 in the morning. Walter Reed was close. She had time before she needed to leave for the meeting. Rising, she took the burner phone and headed to the door. Outside her office, a well-dressed young man sat at a desk. Anita composed herself. Her voice was calm and professional when she spoke, "Denton, please clear my calendar for the rest of the day. Something just came up."

The young man looked up from the touch screen inset into his desk. "Yes Ma'am. Is there anything else I can do?"

Anita relaxed a little at his response. Denton was competent and would not pry. Good staff like him were hard to find. "Yes, please arrange for a car to pick me up. I need to be at Walter Reed by 11 o'clock. Thank you."

Anita was already moving to the elevator when he replied, "Yes, Ma'am" a second time.

The executive elevator arrived moments later. Anita stepped inside and pressed the button for sub-basement three. She waited as the elevator dropped quickly to the lab level. The doors opened into a sterile white hallway lit by flickering fluorescent lights. She stepped from the elevator and walked down the hall to the biolab entrance. She pulled a blank pass card out of the pocket of her business suit and used it to open the lab door. It would not do to have her own card traced to this lab. She walked across the room to a sign with bright red letters that read "Warning: Bio-Hazardous Materials."

The container below the sign was a high-tech device meant to safely collect and store cultures from many of the diseases and infections her staff were trying to cure. Many of those specimens were highly contagious.

Anita placed the burner phone into the waste receptacle and closed the outer door. Then she stepped on the lever to activate the suction. There was a whooshing sound as the phone was drawn into an airtight receiving chamber. A second later, she heard a click as the upper chamber sealed. As soon as the system verified that there was no chance of contamination, another more powerful suction pump kicked in. With a thunk, the phone dropped into the BFL-3 containment chamber. At some point, the chamber would be pumped into an incinerator many levels below. The toxic waste from all of the labs would be burned to ash. Even the smoke from that fire would be filtered sixteen times. Each of those sixteen filters would eventually be decontaminated. NIAID did not allow breaches.

With the phone disposed of, she headed back to her office to keep up appearances. That meant emails and paperwork until it was time for the meeting.

———————————

John Boboden stood in a maintenance hallway two levels below Walter Reed Army Medical Hospital. He glanced over at the sign on the wall beside the rather plain wooden door in front of him.

> *Room 2B214*
> *Building Maintenance*
> *Conference Room*

It was the last place one would expect some of the most knowledgeable virologists in the country to be holding a secret meeting. He approved. The game they were playing was dangerous enough. They did not need to call attention to themselves.

He reached for the doorknob and opened the door. The voices inside immediately went silent. Stepping into the room, John examined the two men and one woman seated on the cheap conference room chairs. These were the key players on Dr Caufi's covert project team. He ignored them and closed the door. John pulled one of the cleaner chairs into a corner and sat down. The other three went back to speculating on the reason they had been called to such an unusual location on short notice. John did not care. Their work had nothing to do with his project.

At precisely 11 o'clock, the door opened again. A thin older woman in a light grey business suit stood in the doorway. The Senior Medical Advisor to the President looked as sharp as ever despite her nearly 78 years. Her hair had gone grey years before, but Anita had accepted the signs of her age with dignity and grace. She was a master at working people, but today her face had a hard edge to it. John knew instinctively that something was seriously wrong.

She stepped briskly into the room and closed the door behind her. She strode to the end of the table and turned to look at her team. "We do not have a lot of time, so I am going to keep this brief and to the point. The idiots at Wuhan lost containment. Our project is loose and, apparently, they were successful at enhancing it."

John watched as the faces of the three underlings went pale. The woman was the first to regain enough composure to ask, "How bad is it?"

Dr Caufi shook her head. "I don't know yet. The WHO is just setting up. The CCP is, of course, denying everything. My guess is that it has already transitioned outside of China."

The younger of the two men, the one John thought was probably Caufi's financial wizard, asked, "What do you want us to do?"

At least they asked intelligent questions, John thought.

The doctor's expression was stern. "Make sure there are no records anywhere that lead back to us. I don't want to be explaining to the American people why we were doing gain-of-function research in

China. That is for you more than anyone, Charles. Make sure a money trail does not exist."

The younger man nodded. "Yes, Ma'am."

The three sat straighter waiting for additional orders. Anita sighed and motioned towards the door. "Go. There is nothing else any of us can do. Make sure our tracks are covered."

John sat silently as the three rose and shuffled out the door. He waited until they were gone before taking a small black box out of his pocket and setting it on the table. He pressed a button on the side of the box. Small LEDs flashed, first red then yellow and finally green before he turned to face his nominal boss. "We are secure now, Anita. Why did I spend over an hour on a helicopter just to hear you tell them to make sure their pants were zipped up properly?"

Anita pulled out a chair and looked down at the seat. She reached down and brushed something off the chair before taking a seat. Then her brown eyes snapped up to meet his. Her gaze was hard and unrelenting. "This is going to get bad, John. I need an ace in the hole. Your research is my best hope."

John leaned back in his chair and studied her. "The President won't authorize what I am working on. You know that."

Anita smiled for the first time since entering the room. "He is up for re-election in less than a year. He won't be President much longer."

John considered her words. "You seem rather confident of that fact."

Anita nodded. "Even if the coming pandemic doesn't cost him the job, there are others who are working to ensure he loses the election."

"So, why am I here?" He asked.

As always, her reply went directly to the point. "I need information. Have you made any progress?"

John considered how much to tell her. The work she had authorized was far from legal in the United States. It probably wasn't any more acceptable in ninety percent of the world. Finally, he nodded. "As you know, none of our previous test subjects have survived. It was not the serum itself that killed them. The problems all arise during the transformation process. None of the changes have been viable until now."

There was a slight twitch of the doctor's lips at the words 'until now.' The rest of her expression did not change as she asked, "And now?"

John sat back and checked the device sitting on the table. The green LED was still lit. It did not detect any surveillance of the room. "Patient 1WR27M received a standard dose of serum D2Y33. Five days later, he began to change. The process took over a week to complete. He lived."

There was eagerness in her voice this time. "Why did it work this time?"

John sighed. "Hell, I don't know Anita. The new serum? Something unusual about the subject? It is too soon to tell. We have been studying him for three days now. Basically, since his change stabilized. Even when the testing is finished, we still might not know anything. I don't even know if an autopsy would tell us anything. You are looking for answers that we just don't have."

"Give me something, John. Anything is better than nothing at all. At least tell me about the test subject."

John nodded. "The subject was a marine corporal with stage 4 cancer. We found him in a VA facility on the border of Vermont and New Hampshire. He had no family, no connections and little chance of surviving. He volunteered for an experimental treatment. He really wants to live."

Anita leaned closer. "But he is alive? He survived the change?"

John sighed. "Yes, he is alive, but he is not human anymore. He is over nine feet tall and weighs close to 700 pounds. This kid was smart, Anita. He was a disciplined soldier. Now he has the intelligence and self-control of a small puppy. He is incredibly strong. I saw him put his fist through a steel door. And he has serious anger management issues. He is dangerous. I need elephant tranquilizers to keep him sedated."

Anita's fascination was obvious. "How did he grow so big, John?"

John was growing frustrated. Couldn't she see how wrong this was? "I have no idea, Anita. Magic? It makes no sense for an unconscious man on an IV to grow like that. What he has become isn't good and you can't put a positive spin on it, Anita. This isn't the success story you're looking for."

Anita rose from her chair. "Maybe not, but it is a step in the right direction, John."

"I am not so sure, Anita. My team has nicknamed him the ogre. I don't think this is what we wanted to achieve."

She came to stand before him. "I need you to keep going John. This may be the only way to save the human race."

He shook his head. "I am not sure that we can. Test subjects aren't easy to come by, especially ones that won't be missed."

Anita walked to the door. She turned back to look at him. "If Virus-C gets as bad as I think it will, you will have more test subjects than you know what to do with. Keep up the good work, John."

He watched the door close behind her. When he was sure she was gone, he whispered, "Is this really to save lives, Doctor? Or is this another of your political ploys?"

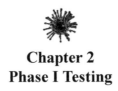

# Chapter 2
# Phase I Testing

***The New York Times***
*Virus-C spreads to Europe*
Jan 24, 2020 7:52 p.m. ET --- China's public health crisis has taken its first steps on the path to becoming a pandemic. Three confirmed cases of Virus-C were detected in France ...

    ***New York Post***
    *First case of Virus-C confirmed in New York City*
    Mar 1, 2020 8:15 a.m. ET. --- The first case of Virus-C in New York City was confirmed Sunday to be a man in his early 40s ...

***Washington Post***
*Virus-C now a global pandemic*
Mar 11, 2020 11:09 p.m. EDT --- The National Institute of Health announced that the World Health Organization (WHO) officially declares Virus-C a pandemic ...

    ***Washington Post***
    *Europe implements travel bans as Virus-C cases surge*
    Mar 13, 2020 12:07 p.m. EDT --- Concerns about the Virus-C pandemic rippled across the globe, as countries close their borders in an attempt to slow the ...

***Washington Post***
*White House launches $7B program to speed Virus-C vaccine*
Apr 10, 2023 9:07 p.m. EDT -- President Ondald has signed an Executive Order establishing "Operation Warp Speed" ...

Dr Anita Caufi sat in the back row in the White House press room. Her face was calm and composed. Inside, though, she was seething. Here they were in the middle of a pandemic - the most exciting crisis in her entire career - and she was relegated to sitting behind a bunch of corporate toadies who just wanted to suck up to the President. Instead of being front and center to lead the country as its expert on infectious diseases, she was being treated as a spectator while that conceited old man put on a dog and pony show with his rich cronies.

So, instead of making recommendations to the public on how to stay safe, she sat and watched as President Ondald introduced CEO after CEO. Each of them was given an opportunity to talk about how their company would support the President in his effort to develop a vaccine. She was surprised the fat old man had even bothered to introduce her near the end. Could this day get any worse?

---

John Boboden pressed a button on his new desk. He watched as a panel slid down to hide the television from view. The President's press conference hadn't told him anything he did not already know. At least his boss had seemed pleased to get the free publicity. Well, that and a hefty share of the $7 billion in vaccine funding. That was one of the reasons that John's project had been moved from Cambridge. His old lab was going to be used for vaccine testing. This new lab was nice, if a bit isolated.

John stared down at the three folders stacked in the middle of the desk. Unfortunately, there were other reasons that his team had been transferred to this remote location. Two deaths on the containment level had been deemed unacceptable by management.

He opened the top folder and began to read. The first page was titled

Autopsy Report -- Kevin Mafrin -- Age 27

John remembered the big security specialist. Kevin had been several inches over six-feet-tall. The man had been solid muscle. Until the containment breach eight days ago, John would have sworn that there was nothing the big man couldn't handle. But now Kevin was dead. His friend wouldn't be smiling over a round of beers anymore.

He continued reading the autopsy report. Cause of Death: Blunt Force Trauma. Was that the correct phrase for a blow that shattered eight of the twelve ribs on the right side of a man's chest? The blow had sent bone fragments through the lung wall and other shards of bone to lacerate Kevin's liver, gallbladder, and pancreas. The medical examiner wasn't even sure that was the blow that killed Kevin. The creature they called 'the ogre' had hit Kevin a second time, caving in his skull and snapping his neck. Then again, did it really matter which blow had killed his friend?

It was something that never should have been allowed to happen. 'The ogre' had been in isolation. Powerful sedatives were being pumped continuously into the ogre's body. That body had been locked in a Class 2 secure room with the best magnetic lock money could buy. Apparently, John's precautions had not been enough.

John flipped to the next page and scanned the death certificate. The cause of death here was very different. On this document, Kevin had been hit by a tractor trailer while changing a tire on the side of the interstate. The accident had been classified as a hit and run. The State Police were still searching for clues to the identity of the driver or the rig.

John sighed and closed the folder. He opened the second folder. This was the case file for Corporal Andrew Malone. He spent a few minutes reading the corporal's performance evaluations. Malone had been a good marine. He was well liked by the men in his unit. He was not the kind of man to beat someone to death in a silent hallway.

Malone's evaluations were, in most respects, exemplary. But at five feet, four inches tall and only 145 pounds, Malone had not fit the image of what a Marine was supposed to look like. He had served with distinction in the Gulf War where he had been exposed to something nasty. The cancer had taken what little body mass the soldier had. All Malone had ever wanted was to be as big and strong so he could be a proper Marine.

In a way, John and his team had given the dying soldier everything he had wanted and more. When the serum had taken over, Malone had nearly doubled in height and gained over six hundred pounds. Malone had also been cured of his stage 4 cancer. Achieving those dreams had come at a steep price; Malone had lost his self-control and, to an extent, his humanity. The creature that had come out of the transformation was powerful enough to take on a tank, but it no longer cared about protecting others. Malone had become the proverbial super soldier out of comic books, except that he now hated being told what to do.

What was left of the soldier Malone had once had been died during the change. It had taken nine armor piercing rounds to kill what he had become. There would be no official autopsy of the ogre's body. The remaining organs and tissue were scattered across a hundred labs in petri dishes and under microscopes. The company wanted to understand why he had been the first to survive the serum.

John set the second folder aside and opened the final folder, labeled "Forensic Analysis." He flipped through the pages until he reached the one labeled "System Failures." This was the data that concerned John the most. He wanted to know what had gone wrong. He needed to know if it was really his fault.

Malone's monstrous body had been hooked up to one of the most advanced intravenous pumps money could buy. The pump not only administered the sedative they used to keep 'the ogre' unconscious; it also had a built-in biometrics system that measured the medication levels in Malone's bloodstream. The pump even had internal diagnostic circuitry to provide a warning before a system failure. So many safeguards and none of them had worked.

According to the diagnostics, the pump had encountered simultaneous critical faults in nearly every one of its subsystems. According to the manufacturer's specs, such a failure was impossible. And yet, it was not the first pump to fail unexpectedly while attached to Malone's body. It was just the most costly failure to date.

On the next page, John found that the security door whose specifications exceeded those of most bank vaults, had also suffered numerous software failures. Instead of keeping Malone in his prison cell, it had reset itself to factory defaults and opened. None of it made any sense. Only John's insistence that there be a human in the loop had prevented Malone from escaping into the main complex and possibly onto the streets of Cambridge. His friend had been on duty that night. Kevin had sounded the alarm and then engaged 'the ogre.' Kevin had gone down quickly. His killer joined him in death moments later.

John sat there considering his options. He had to tell Anita that her test subject had been killed. They had known that they could not risk keeping the creature alive for long, but they needed to learn more before they were forced to kill it. They had hoped for another success before they destroyed the one they had lost control of. That particular gambit had cost a good man his life.

With a sigh, John dropped the folder onto his desk. He reached into his top drawer and pulled out a single piece of paper filled with phone numbers. John ran his finger down the page until he located the next phone number in Dr Caufi's burner list. He keyed the number into his own burner phone and began to type.

Dear Amazon Customer, The item you ordered, 1WR27M, has been discontinued. To receive your refund of $735, please log in using the link below. As always, Amazon thanks you for your business. https://www.amazon.com/JB/1WR27M Thank you, the Amazon Team

John pressed send and sat back to wait for instructions. The answer to his message was not long in coming. The angry response he was expecting didn't come.

Jerk. Stop texting my phone. You are as likely to be Amazon as I am to be the tooth fairy bringing you four shiny quarters. Now stop bothering me.

John stood up and began to pace in front of his desk. What was Anita Caufi up to? And who or what were the 'four quarters' she was sending him? But there really was only one thing Dr Caufi would send him at this juncture. John wasn't sure how he felt about that answer.

John took the battery out of the phone and dropped it into the classified waste. His people knew what to do with it. Then he headed for the door to make sure everything was ready for a delivery. He suspected he would need four beds in the medical ward very soon.

## Chapter 3
## Lab Specimens

Dr Alfred Morrall entered the isolation ward and slotted his air hose into the receptacle by the door. The solid steel connection was flash heated to 400 degrees Fahrenheit. The connector was then rapidly cooled to below freezing before his environmental suit allowed any air to flow into his suit. The process did not take long, but his suit was already getting warm by the time the air began to flow. Thankfully, the air-conditioned air quickly pulled the sweat from his body.

He reached up and tapped the control beside his left ear. This turned on the external microphone. The sound of the four ventilators filled his helmet. His excitement grew as he listened to the steady thrum of the equipment. So many new test subjects were an unexpected treat even if none of them were in good shape. All four of the new test subjects were in the final stages of Virus-C. They had been acquired from a New York City hospital that was already over capacity. The hospital had been frantically looking for a place to transfer some of its terminal cases.

Making the four just disappear from a well-known hospital was far easier than it should have been. But from what Alfred had been able to piece together, the hospital had been already losing track of corpses for weeks. Even if one of his new 'volunteers' was missed, everyone would just assume they were another misplaced body. With so many of the dead already stored in refrigeration trucks, it would be easy to overlook these four.

Alfred hummed happily as he approached the first bed. Subject 1NY42F was a middle-aged woman from Queens. She had contracted the virus one week ago. Virus-C had invaded her body at a record pace. Alfred scanned her chart. Ah, he thought. She was diabetic. That probably accounted for her rapid decline. Because of her diabetes, she was not eligible for one of the experimental treatments. Luckily for her, he didn't have any restrictions on who he gave the serum to. His serum would kill the Virus-C in her system, but he wasn't sure if she would survive the transformation. He picked up the pen hanging from the clipboard and annotated D2Y34 on her chart. Then he placed a 1 in the box for Containment Cell.

The second bed also held a woman. Subject 2NY22F was younger and seemed healthy. He considered giving her one of the more aggressive serum variants until he noticed the marks on her thigh. He bent so that his face plate was close to the scars. He sighed. Needle tracks. None were recent, but she too would be high risk. He lifted the pen and marked her chart for D2Y35 and placed her in Containment Cell 4.

Alfred perked up when he reached 3NY17M. The boy had been strong and fit before contracting Virus-C. His youth made him an excellent candidate for Alfred's latest variant. But Alfred needed to be sure.

He scanned the chart. The young were normally more resistant to the virus. Why had the boy gotten so sick? The explanation was there in his chart. The boy had contracted the virus during surgery. One of the boy's wisdom teeth had been impacted. During the surgery to remove the tooth, someone on the surgical team had infected the boy. His subject's bad luck was an incredible break for Alfred. He was unlikely to get such a specimen again. The boy was exactly the kind of subject he needed to test the latest creation. He marked D3Y01s on the boy's chart and ordered the boy placed in Containment Cell 3.

The final subject was an older man. According to the chart, 4NY62M was a history professor at a local New York college. Alfred shook his head. Did anyone really take classes in ancient languages by choice? Aramaic and Hebrew? Both languages seemed a colossal waste of time. Alfred had not even enjoyed the Latin he had been forced to take.

The man appeared to have been healthy before the virus. From the look of his legs, Alfred assumed the man had been a runner before he came down with Virus-C. Alfred reached for the pen and then hesitated. This was a rare opportunity to run an experiment within an experiment. What affect would age have on the new variant? It might be some time before he got four guinea pigs at the same time again. Alfred smiled as he wrote D3Y01s on this chart as well. He placed the professor in Cell 2 next to the boy.

Alfred began to hum again as he began to prep the four needles. He could have let his staff give the injections, but this was one of Alfred's favorite parts of his job. It was his way of providing a personal touch to his work.

By the next day, all four patients were off their ventilators. The improvements in all four were phenomenal, but Alfred kept them sedated anyway. He disliked dealing with people if it was at all avoidable. That was especially true of whiny patients who wanted to be told that everything would be alright. Better that they sleep. They would be a lot less trouble that way.

As he suspected they would, the women's bodies began the transformation too soon. Alfred stopped his visits to the Containment Cells at that point. He had staff and security specialists to deal with those who underwent the change. After what happened in Cambridge, Alfred had no intention of taking unnecessary risks.

The older woman had died less than a day after she began to change. The younger woman had lasted seventeen hours longer. As had happened before, both women's transformations never finished. Whatever they had almost become was not viable. Alfred ordered a full tissue analysis and closed their files.

It took almost a week before the boy and the old man showed external signs of the transformation. But it had not been a boring wait; the two men's blood work had been fascinating. The new variant had done something unexpected. It had bonded with the Virus-C molecules and used the virus to penetrate the cell wall. The effect was unintentional, but its benefits were evident as soon as the men began to change.

Both men's vitals remained stable as the process took hold of their bodies. That had never happened before. This time, the transformations proceeded at a less frantic rate. None of the tissue samples Alfred examined showed the normal signs of damage that had been evident in early variants. The only analogy Alfred could come up with to describe the effects of the D3Y variant was that of seduction versus rape. The D3Y was coaxing the subject's cells into making stable changes.

While the data was encouraging, Alfred was far from happy with his analysis. Both subjects had been given the same serum. Their transformations should follow similar paths. And yet, their DNA changes were radically different. If their changes continued on their present course, neither man would even be the same species in the end. Alfred wasn't even sure they would end up in the same genus.

---

John Boboden looked up in surprise when the door to his office opened without warning. Dr Anita Caufi stood in the doorway with an intent expression on her face. He could see his secretary standing just behind Anita looking confused and apologetic. John rose and came to greet his guest. Anita's grip was firm as she shook his hand. John motioned to the table and chairs in the corner of the room near the coffee maker. As he closed the door to his office, he whispered, "It's all right, Trish. It's not your fault."

John turned to stare at his unexpected visitor. Why would the Chief Medical Advisor to the President risk a visit to this facility? He moved around her chair to stand next to the coffee maker. "Welcome to our facility, Anita. Would you like a cup of coffee? Sorry, all I have is black. If I had known you were coming, I would have picked up some hazelnut."

Dr Caufi shook her head. "No, thank you though. Coffee and helicopter rides don't mix well at my age. No bathrooms on the small, fast model."

John poured himself a cup and sat down across from her. "Is it a good idea for you to be here? I thought you wanted deniability."

A scary looking grin crossed her face. It reminded him of the smile horror movie monsters made just before swallowing the hero whole. "Why John, I am not here. I am sitting in my office doing a live radio interview with NPR. They had some questions about Virus-C and wanted my expert opinion. I am sure you can catch a rebroadcast later today."

John raised his cup to his lips to cover his momentary confusion. He took a sip and swallowed. "Then I guess I should ask what I can do for you?"

Anita placed her hands on the table, slowly intertwining her fingers. "I want to see them, John. Dr Morrall's reports have me curious. The metabolic data is intriguing. More importantly, I need to understand how the serum inhibited the Virus-C. Alfred says they aren't just cured, they are immune."

John set down his cup. The coffee didn't taste good anymore. "We lost half of the test population already, Anita. And we still don't know if either of the other two will be sane when they wake up. And Dr Morrall has absolutely no idea what they are becoming."

It bothered John that those facts did not seem to bother the medical doctor sitting before him. Anita's voice was patronizing as she replied, "All in good time, John. We are talking about the future of the human race. There are bound to be a few losses along the way."

John thought back to the deaths in Cambridge. It was all he could do to suppress his outrage at her words. Somehow, he kept his face composed. "Of course, Dr Caufi. Let me escort you to the observation room."

Anita rose from her chair and moved towards the door. "Don't trouble yourself, John. Alfred is waiting for me. I already asked your security chief to take me down to meet with Alfred. I only stopped to say hello and let you know that I am arranging more specimens for Alfred. So many hospitals are looking for places to dispose of their overflow. Finding test subjects has never been easier. I will be in touch."

John stared at the door, wondering if there was any chance he qualified for an early retirement.

---

Dr Alfred Morrall stared at the monitor as he zoomed the camera in on 3NY17M. The boy's long, dark hair had all fallen out the day before.

So had his eyebrows and his scraggly mustache. The boy had even lost his eyelashes. That had been interesting, but it was nothing compared to what Alfred was recording now. Alfred had not expected new hair follicles to form at all, let alone that hair could grow this quickly.

Alfred checked the clock as he focused the camera on the boy's face. The new hair was coming in a coppery red color. The eyebrows had come in first, long and bushy. A thick rug of body hair had shown up next. Now Alfred was watching the creature's beard, and mustache literally sprout before his eyes. The hair on top of its head had gone from stubble to shoulder length so quickly that Alfred had not been able to record it. He had been better prepared when the beard had started to grow.

Alfred had gotten the camera focused and a timer set as soon as he noticed the creature had a five o'clock shadow. The copper wisps had thickened and curled as they covered the creature's face. Alfred gaped as the 'beard' began to crawl down 3NY17M's chest. The hairs did not stop their advance until they reached the subject's navel.

Alfred stopped the recording then and stared at the timer in amazement. The beard had only taken 53 seconds to grow nearly two feet. Alfred's raised his hand to the back of his neck. He began to knead the muscles there as he fought to understand what he had just observed. With the recording stopped, the camera automatically zoomed back out so he could see the subject's entire body, which was now covered in copper curls.

Alfred jumped when a firm female voice asked from behind him, "Is everything all right, Dr Morrall?" He had been so caught up in his work that he had forgotten that he had an important guest arriving soon.

Alfred spun to see his benefactor, Dr Anita Caufi, standing just inside the door of the observation room. He quickly composed himself and answered, "Hello, Anita. Yes, everything is fine. There have been a few unexpected developments, but nothing that endangers the specimens."

Alfred watched with trepidation as the woman who controlled the future of his research crossed the room to join him at the observation window. She stared down at 3NY17M. Her tone was curious, which Alfred took as a good sign. "This one seems a bit more human than the creature in the Cambridge lab. Tell me about it."

Alfred stepped up beside her at the window. "This subject was a 17-year-old male of Hispanic descent. Based on the markings we found on his arm, we believe he was involved in one of New York's many gangs. Since receiving the serum, his body has shrunk from 70 inches in height to 49 inches. At the same time, his mass has nearly tripled. As near as we can tell, his bone and muscle density more closely resemble rock than they do flesh and bone. The hair that covers his body is a recent development."

Anita turned to meet his gaze. "How recent?"

Alfred swallowed hard before replying, "The full beard came in the last several minutes."

He expected her to argue, but her only comment was, "Interesting."

He watched as her eyes darted to the darkened windows at both ends of the room. Those two rooms had been sterilized and shut down after the deaths of the two female subjects. She simply ignored both darkened spaces and faced the remaining window that looked down into Cell 2.

Alfred followed her as she walked to the second lit window. "And this one?"

Alfred cleared his throat. "This subject was a 62-year-old college professor."

Alfred paused as she raised a hand to point at the naked figure lying on the bed below. "That is not the body of an old man, Alfred. His skin and features resemble those of a student, not those of an elderly professor. His complexion is rather pale, but that is not unusual for someone with his light blond hair color."

Alfred stared down at the specimen lying on the table below. "I can't explain the way his body is regenerating his cells any more than I can explain his pointed ears." At her frown of disapproval, Alfred added, "Yet."

She turned back to the window to stare down. "I assume this one received a different variant than the other specimen?"

Alfred shook his head. "No, Dr Caufi. Both injections came from the same serum sample."

"Are you sure? No chance your staff made a mistake?" She asked.

Alfred stammered. "I… I am sure. I like to administer the serum myself. Both syringes were drawn from the same vial."

Anita nodded thoughtfully. "I see." Her foot began to tap as she considered how to approach the topic she came to discuss. "I was told that they are now immune to the virus. Is that true?"

Alfred felt himself begin to sweat. "In a manner of speaking, Anita."

Her face hardened. "Explain."

Alfred's gaze grew distant as he considered his response. The interaction of the serum with the virus had not been planned. "I needed a different mechanism to get the serum past the cell wall so it could interact with the host's DNA. Earlier variants damaged key chromosomes as they breached the cell membrane. I modified the carrier virus that we used to distribute and insert the serum into the cells of the host's body."

Anita nodded. "I understand the basic process, Dr Morrall. What exactly did you change in this variant?"

Alfred sighed. "I wanted the delivery of the serum to be less aggressive. I changed one protein sequences in the delivery virus. It was only supposed to prevent damage to the nucleus of the cell. I thought this approach would improve the survival rate during the transformation."

Anita studied him as she asked, "And what was the result?"

This was a line of questioning Alfred had hoped to avoid. He tried to sound confident as he pressed on. "The new sequence caused the delivery virus to target the Virus-C in the host's body. The serum essentially highjacked Virus-C. The world's most dangerous virus became little more than a delivery service for the serum. Virus-C's ability to penetrate the cell membrane now facilitates delivery of the serum. After the serum enters the cell, Virus-C becomes essentially inert."

Anita shook her head. "You were hasty, Dr Morrall. What you did could have gone very badly." Her gaze turned back to the subject lying on the hospital bed below the window. She asked, "Is the serum ready for additional testing? Perhaps on a larger scale?"

Alfred chose his words carefully. "There are still some small adjustments I need to make and test."

Anita turned and walked to the door. "How many specimens do you need, Alfred, to test your adjustments?"

He sighed. "The space in this facility is rather limited. If these two continue to survive, I can only handle five more subjects here. If they allowed me to use the facilities at Cambridge too, I could study another five there."

She nodded. "Fine. I will arrange for you to get access to your old lab. Start getting things ready. I will be in touch. If you can show me some useful results, Alfred, I can get you access to a much larger facility and more staff. Do not disappoint me."

Alfred nodded nervously as she opened to door. She paused at the open doorway to study him again. "Wake them up, Dr Morrall. I need to know if they retained their humanity or not."

The door closed and she was gone. He sighed in genuine relief. His work would be allowed to continue.

## Chapter 4
## Phase II Results

Miguel Sanchez slowly became aware that he wasn't dead. Not only was he alive, he felt better than he had since before his cheek grew to the size of a small melon. His mouth didn't hurt at all now. His only complaint was how fuzzy his brain felt. He was having a hard time focusing. It was like being drunk without the beer or the hangover or the headache.

A random thought cut through the fog in his head. The surface below his back was hard. This could not be his cot at the Banda. It also wasn't his bed at Mama's. Those beds were both very soft - just the way he liked them. Or at least the way he thought he liked his beds. Strangely, the unyielding surface below him seemed more comfortable than anything he had ever slept on before. The hard bed raised an important question... Where the heck was he?

Miguel, no he corrected himself, only Mama called him that anymore. He was now a full member of a gang, a Banda. His new family had given him a new name, Herrera. It was his job to repair or make tools, weapons, and even armor for the members of the Banda. He had always been good at fixing things and he liked working with his hands. Now his skills had a purpose and that was something he had needed badly. The Banda might even send him to a school so he could learn about cars and engines. Life was good now that he had earned his place. His new family would keep him safe.

Again, he wondered where he was. He opened his eyes. The room he lay in was large and dimly lit. He tried to sit up but found that a heavy strap across his chest held him down. His arms and legs were also strapped to whatever he lay on. He turned his head to study his prison. The room was strange. No, he realized, something was wrong with his eyes. The colors were all wrong. Everything he could see was in shades of blue or red. Instinctively, he knew the blue was cold and the red was warm. But, he did not know how he knew that.

Herrera tried to remember how he had gotten here, but there was nothing in the room that jogged his memory. His last clear memory was of pain. The right side of his face hurt to touch. Somehow, he had made it to Mama's apartment. He remembered Mama taking him to a free clinic. It was all that she could afford. A man in a blue mask said the tooth had to come out. Later that afternoon, they had put a needle in his arm. The pain and everything else had gone away.

He thought he remembered waking up after the surgery. His face had still hurt, but the pain had been different. Mama took him home in a cab. She had put him in his old room on his nice soft bed. He remembered coughing and being cold. He had been thirsty, and it had hurt to breathe. He remembered strange dreams and men's voices. Had Mama said he was sick? Herrera wasn't sure. And now he was here. Wherever that was.

Herrera did not hurt anymore. He drew in a deep breath and felt no pain. In fact, he felt stronger than he ever had. He had always been small for his age. He was not a fighter like the others in the Banda. They had taken him because he was so good at fixing things. He did not care why they had accepted him. He only knew he did not have to be afraid anymore.

He wondered how strong his bonds were. Herrera tensed his right arm. The strap holding his arm groaned in protest. He felt the muscles in his arm flex. He knew he could break free if he wanted to, but was it a good idea? Herrera relaxed his arm muscles. He did not know how it had happened, but he actually had muscles now. It was a new feeling and one he liked a lot.

As he relaxed his arm, Herrera's hand came to rest on the thin pad that he lay on top of. He ran his fingers over across its surface and over its edge. There was a steel table beneath the pad. His fingertips caressed the smoothness of the metal. Thoughts came unbidden into his mind. The steel was about a quarter of an inch thick. The large flat piece of steel had not been forged by hand. The surface grain was too uniform. No smith could have worked such a large piece without leaving at least some blemishes on its surface.

Where had he learned so much about steel? Herrera had never had the opportunity to take classes on metal working. They did not teach classes like that at the schools he was allowed to attend. Yet despite the lack of training, Herrera knew those random thoughts were correct. He wondered what he could make from that piece of steel if he had some tools.

His thoughts turned from the steel to the empty room around him. How long before someone came for him? He was hungry enough that he didn't care what he ate. He would even consider eating something from McDonalds. A smile came to his lips. Mama would never forgive him if he did that.

---

Jacob Dror sat in a library that was larger than any he had ever been in. It was huge. He was surrounded by shelves that reached up towards the vaulted ceiling that stretched across the library. Images gazed back at him from different places around the room. Each image was painted in only a few colors, but they were masterpieces nonetheless.

The images were not of his faith, but Jacob recognized them anyway. Osiris and Isis were the most prominent, but Seth and some of the other Egyptian gods were represented as well. Jacob forced his eyes away from those fierce visages to study the shelves around him. There were no books that he could see. The shelves were filled with scrolls.

The room was so familiar and yet, Jacob couldn't remembers visiting it. Then it came to him. One of his favorite professors had been obsessed with ancient Egypt. Professor Donnally had kept the same poster on his wall the entire four years Jacob had attended New York University. The poster had shown the artist's conception of the Great Library of Alexandria. Jacob knew then that he was dreaming. It had to be a dream because the Alexandria library had burned to the ground over 2000 years ago.

In his dream, Jacob was seated on a stone bench before a large table. A papyrus scroll had been unrolled on the table so that Jacob could read it. Both ends were held open by small stones carved in the image of Anubis. The dream was so realistic that Jacob leaned forward to see if he could read the scroll.

Two sets of ancient script spread across the page, each flowing from right to left. The symbols might have been mistaken for the same language, but Jacob knew better. He had studied both tongues since he was a small boy. He had first seen both scripts in books at the synagogue. They had captivated him. His love of the ancient languages led him to New York University as a young man.

Jacob had wanted to be an archeologist. He wanted to explore the history of his people. He had planned to spend his life traveling from one set of ancient ruins to the next. Or he had until he had met Beth. Beth had not been interested in travel. She wanted a family. So, Jacob had become a professor - adjunct faculty at several New York colleges. Instead of exploring, Jacob had taught the two languages he loved to anyone that was willing to learn them. Beth had died giving birth to their first child. Their son had died that day too.

Jacob had never considered going back to archeology. Travel meant not being able to visit the cemetery where Beth and little Samuel were buried. Years passed and students became less frequent as people seemed less and less interested in history. But Jacob continued to teach. His students were all that he had. He had taught until recently when he became sick. A student had unknowingly given Jacob that strange new virus. The doctor said Jacob's age made him more vulnerable. As he got worse, they had made him sign a release so they could put him on a ventilator. He signed it knowing he was going to die. He did not mind as long as they buried him with his family. Jacob was tired of being alone.

Did dying people dream? Jacob wasn't sure. Perhaps the scroll was important. He leaned forward and began to read. The scroll was unusual. There was no story or message. Both lines were the same sequence of words, one over the other. It was almost like a translation guide except that the order of the words made no sense. At least not to him.

As he read, Jacob noted that two sets of runes appeared to glow. They stood for light and sleep. Why those two words he wondered. He could almost feel the brightness of those words burning their image into his mind. Jacob closed his eyes, but then he could still see the glowing runes. Jacob reopened his eyes, but the scroll and the library were gone.

Jacob found himself in a dimly lit room. His vision was sharper than it had been in years. He could see the gleam of metal walls. A small observation window was set high in the wall across from where he lay. He was no longer in the over-crowded hospital. This room was much larger and there weren't five other patients crowded in around him. The ventilator was gone now too. Jacob wasn't dead. He actually felt good. No, it was more than that. He felt better than he had in years. All of the aches and pains that came with 62 years of living were gone now. The knee he had damaged while running did not hurt either. He felt young again.

Jacob tried to raise his left hand to run his fingers over his body. But his arm was strapped securely to the table. So was his other arm and both of his legs. The restraints seemed a bit excessive. Didn't they realize how often a man his age needed to go to the bathroom? There was no one in the room to ask for help. His desire to be free grew with each passing minute, but no one came.

The window high on the wall seemed to stare down at him. Was someone up there watching him? If so, what were they waiting for? But the space beyond the window was dark. For all he knew, he was the last living person in the world and he could not move. If only he could see what was behind that glass. If only there was light. Then he saw the words that had been burned into his memory by the dream. One of them had meant light. Jacob whispered that one small syllable, "ore."

It made no sense. Light blossomed behind the window. He saw movement as dark figures in white coats scurried around behind the glass. The one small light in Jacob's room went out. Somewhere, an alarm began to sound.

---------------------

The room echoed with the sound of someone pounding on his door. Alfred cursed and raised a hand to rub the sleep from his eyes. Couldn't they give him a few hours of sleep?

The security chief's voice came through the door. "Dr Morrall! You are needed down on the observation level. We have a problem!"

Alfred rolled over and sat up. "Give me a moment to get some clothes on!"

The pounding stopped. Reaching down, Alfred grabbed the jeans he had worn the night before when he had gone to the small bar an hour down the road. His dirty shirt lay crumpled next to where the jeans had been. Pulling it over his head, he slid his feet into the old slippers he wore around his room. It wasn't a professional look, but he did not care at. Alfred glanced down at his watch. It was 3:48 in the morning. "This had better be important," he muttered.

He ran his fingers through his thinning hair as he walked over and opened the door. An impatient looking Chief Barreau stood right outside. The security chief spun and began walking down the hall. Alfred had to hurry to match the man's long strides. "What the hell is going on, Chief?"

Barreau hit the button for the elevator. "The team was monitoring both of the subjects per your orders. There was more of that strange static on the monitors, but nothing we aren't used to. Then there was an unexplained burst of light in the observation room and every computer and monitor in the room failed. Your pets are awake and, for the moment. We can't do anything but watch them through the glass."

Alfred cursed and pushed his way into the elevator as soon as the doors opened. "Where are the damned techs? I am sick of these equipment failures."

Barreau followed him in as Alfred swiped his badge and punched the elevator controls.

Barreau reached up to tap the earpiece in his right ear. "Techies are there. They are already swapping out equipment. Apparently, whatever that light was, it overloaded the circuit boards. The computer nerds think it was an EMP burst."

The elevator doors slid closed and the car began to descend.

# Chapter 5
# Efficacy Analysis

*New York Times*
CDC Recommends closing the nation's schools
Jan 6, 2020 12:01 p.m. ET --- The Center for Disease
Control recommends closing all K-12 schools due to
Virus-C. A similar recommendation for colleges is ...

*CNBC*
First human trials of the Virus-C vaccine begin next week
Mar 16, 2020 --- A potential vaccine to prevent Virus-C
will begin human trials early next week ...

*USA Today*
Virus-C impact on economy may devastate many businesses
Mar 30, 2020 --- In addition to loss of life, Virus-C's casualty
list now includes a growing number of businesses as retail,
entertainment, and vacation industries close. Many never to ...

*CNBC*
Nine cruise ships stranded at sea with nowhere to go...
Mar 31, 2020 --- According to Secretary of Transportation's office,
nearly 30,000 passengers are stranded at sea due to Virus-C
outbreaks on board. The following vessels are currently ...

*NPR*
Virus-C death toll hits 100,000 in U.S.
Apr 22, 2020 --- While losses in the United States
are staggering, U.S. losses are still much lower
than in many nations across ...

*Wall Street Journal*
Global food crisis triggered by Virus-C
May 13, 2020 --- Food prices skyrocket. Shortages escalate

*as produce rots in the field. Workforce shortages impact farmers, meat processing plants, and warehouses ...*

Anita glared at the stacks of action memos sitting on her desk. Not every pandemic problem had a medical solution. Why was everything coming her way? She lifted the pile on the right and dropped it back into her inbox. Supply shortages, businesses failing, people out of work. She was a medical doctor, not some Harvard business wizard. What did they expect her to do about the economy?

Her hand strayed to the papers on the left side of the desk. She slid them to the edge of her desk and let them drop into the blue recycling bin. School closures, unemployment reports, riots, and social drama. It was a damn pandemic! People's lives were not going to go back to normal anytime soon, if ever. It was not like the pandemic was her fault. If the Chinese hadn't lost containment, none of this would be happening.

Anita turned her attention to the final stack of reports. Death totals, new variants, test results that were far from where she wanted them to be. The vaccine appeared to be effective, but they needed better than seventy-five percent. She needed at least ninety percent to get more money out of congress. They might do better if Ondald would just stay out of her business. The President was a businessman. He needed to stop distracting her research teams with press conferences. She really doubted there was anything he could do to reassure the American people.

What she needed to secure her reputation was something fast that made people actually immune to the virus. Her team had played with the data from that idiot Morrall. But none of the viral sequences he had identified seemed to affect Virus-C. She was fairly certain the sneaky little bastard had left something vital out of his reports. The only way she was going to get anything out of Morrall was to play his little game.

Anita opened her file drawer and pulled out the latest report from John Boboden. The two subjects were awake. Both were psychologically stable. The memories of both males were intact. Neither was causing a problem. The only real issue appeared to be a rash of technology failures. She had warned Boboden that there had better not be another containment breach. His two guests needed to stay alive and out of the sight.

Morrall had done as she asked. It was past time to keep her promise to provide more test subjects. She needed at least ten people infected with Virus-C. Anita pulled the recycle bin closer. She rummaged in the papers until she found the list of current outbreaks. She scanned the pages looking for someplace where the hospitals were over capacity.

Her fingers paused and a smile came to her face. This was almost too easy. A bunch of college students had contracted the virus while on vacation in Florida. Now Georgetown University Hospital was stacking patients in the hallways. She would be a local hero if she helped them get back down to capacity. No one would care if a few of the college students got moved to a private facility in western Massachusetts.

Anita reached for a burner phone at the back of the file drawer. Maybe this would help her get the information she needed out of Morrall.

---

John ran his fingers across the massive oak table. Despite its age, the wood's grain was still deep. The table was solid and strangely real in a world that did not make sense anymore. And as insane as the world had become with the advent of Virus-C, his own project was an even greater assault on the stability of his world.

He glanced at the man sitting to his right. Dr Alfred Morrall was fidgeting with his glasses. John was not sure how he felt about his chief scientist. Morrall might be a genius, but he was an unfeeling one. The doctor showed little concern for his test subjects. Morrall considered them little better than lab rats. Granted, all of his patients had been terminally ill before they were selected to receive Morrall's serum, but even the dying deserved some dignity.

John realized he was probably being a fool. It was long past the point where he could make moral objections to the doctor's research. John knew that most of the things they did in his lab were against the law, but then it hadn't always been that way. They had begun with the goal of saving lives. His team was supposed to cure some of humanities deadliest medical conditions. John wasn't sure what they were trying to do anymore. Somewhere in the last five years he had crossed a line between helping people and using them. Could he ever find a way back across that line so that he could stand the man he saw each day in the mirror?

There was a clatter on the floor near his feet. A pair of eyeglasses lay near the toe of John's right loafer. Morral's fidgeting was growing more pronounced. John reached down and snagged the glasses. He studied the doctor as he handed him his glasses.

There was a sheen of sweat on Morrall's forehead. The doctor's fingers trembled as he took his glasses and began to open and close the arms over and over. Morrall was using enough force to bend the frames. John looked back down at the table as he considered what he had seen. Was the man who manipulated the world's most deadly viruses afraid? If so, of what? This was only an interview with one of their recent successes. There was no reason for Morrall to be this nervous.

The man they were meeting was 62 years old. He had not been an imposing man even before the change. Jacob was even smaller after the change. Chief Barreau of security was standing by the door. Jacob just wasn't that dangerous. Morrall's response seemed out of character. John had watched the doctor examine each of the five new patients just that morning. He had not shown any sign of nervousness then. John struggled to piece the puzzle together. Why was Jacob a threat? He did not even have Virus-C anymore.

Then John realized what was different about this interview. Jacob wasn't unconscious and strapped to a table. Dr Alfred Morrall would finally be forced to look into the eyes of one of his experiments. John wondered how long it had been since his chief medical officer had been held accountable by one of his patients.

John leaned back in his chair as he considered what this said about the man sitting next to him. Nothing good, John decided. But was he any better sitting here beside the doctor? John hoped so.

The final man in the room was nothing like either of the men sitting behind the table. There was neither fear nor guilt evident on the face of the lab's Chief of Security. Michel Barreau stood like a statue near the door, his grey digicams merging into the wall behind him. The digicam pattern blended so perfectly with the deep grain of the grey cinder blocks that Barreau could almost disappear anywhere in the lower levels of the lab. John liked the man. He trusted the Chief's calm demeanor, his strength, and his skill with the taser that hung just inches from the man's right hand.

There was a soft rap at the door. Before John could speak, Barreau's quiet voice said, "Enter."

The door opened and a woman in digicams stepped back to reveal one of the few people to survive Dr Morrall's serum. No one, least of all Dr Morrall, could explain why Jacob and little Herrera had survived or if they were still human. The two men's DNA said no, but John wasn't so sure that science was right this time. Were both men a species unknown to planet Earth or did the definition of human just need to be expanded? There were too many unanswered questions. Rather than answer those questions, they were about to inject Morrell's serum into another batch of people not knowing what the change would do to their young bodies.

The Chief pulled out the chair next to him and motioned for Jacob to sit. The man that entered looked more like a teenager in his jeans and t-shirt than he did his actual age of 62. Jacob's eyes met those of Dr Morrall. John could detect no anger or resentment in that look. Jacob only seemed curious.

John watched with curiosity as Jacob lowered himself into the chair. John had seen pictures of the dark complected man that Jacob had once been. Jacob's Jewish heritage had been evident in his coloring and features. But that had been before the change. The new Jacob was four inches shy of his original six-foot height. His dark skin had turned pale with what John thought of as a golden hue. Jacob's dark hair had gone steel grey with age. Now it was the palest yellow that John had ever seen. His eyebrows, slightly higher near Jacob's pointed ears, were the same pale yellow. Jacob's dark eyes were now the blue of a cloudless summer sky.

Jacob allowed John to study him without complaint. John flushed as he realized how rude he was being. Jacob grinned and brough his hands up onto the table. The fingers that laced together were almost delicate. Jacob gave John a sardonic smile as he said, "Hello, John. I take it this is not the meeting where you tell me I am cured and that I am free to go."

Something snapped on John's right. One of the arms of Morrall's now broken eyeglasses bounced across the table towards Jacob.

John suddenly realized how badly this meeting was about to go. It wasn't Jacob that John had to be concerned about. It was his own medical officer. John pushed aside his own reaction to Morrall. Using his calmest senior manager tone, John replied, "I'm sorry, Jacob. There are things we still need to understand about your response to the new treatment. I am afraid we need to keep you here a bit longer for observation."

Jacob nodded. "I won't complain, John. Your doctor did save my life after all."

Alfred's fear was clear as he whispered, "What the hell are you now?"

Jacob gave a soft chuckle. "How would I know, Dr Morrall? I have no idea what you did to me, I was dying of the virus. I was ready to join my wife. Now I am what you made me. Don't you know what I am, Doctor?"

John laid a calming hand on Morrall's arm. Then he smiled at Jacob. "You are a very intelligent man, Jacob. We were hoping you had some idea what you had become. The changes caught us all by surprise."

Jacob's right hand rose to push the hair back from the side of his face. A slender finger traced the point at the top of his ear. Then a playful grin crossed his lips as he stared directly into Morrall's terrified gaze. "Based on the ears, I think I may be a Vulcan now. Do I have green blood too, Dr McCoy?"

Despite the sudden tension in Morrall's arm, John began to laugh. "Sorry, Jacob. I have seen the lab results. Your blood is as red as my own. Scotty will not be beaming you up anytime soon."

"Damn," Jacob replied. "That would have been really cool."

John felt the tension leave Alfred's arm, so he released it and placed his hand back in his lap. "Your changes are very different from the other trial we ran. Do you have any idea why?"

Jacob shook his head. "Herrera and I are nothing alike. Herrera is what my wife would have called a fire plug. That boy is all muscle. I had assumed your Doctor gave us a different cocktail. Sorry, I wasn't conscious when he drugged us."

Morrall's voice was harsh as he banged the table with his fist. "I prepared both injections myself from the same vial. There were no errors in your treatment."

Jacob shrugged. "Then maybe the changes are random, Doctor. This isn't my area of expertise."

Morrall muttered angrily, "Science does not work that way, fool!"

John snapped at Morrall. "Enough, Alfred!" When he turned back to Jacob, the calm returning to his voice. "I am only asking your opinion, Jacob. You went through it. You have spoken with Herrera. Do you have a theory?"

Jacob stared down at his hands. He studied the fingers that still did not seem to be his own. He remembered some of the dreams that still haunted him from when he was sick. He also remembered the power he had felt when he had spoken the word from the old tongue. He had only used the old tongue that once. What had happened had scared even him. He had only learned later that the light had somehow caused a lot of damage. Jacob had told no one about what he had done. Nor would he.

After a time, John prompted again. "Jacob?"

Those blue eyes met John's. Jacob's voice was soft as he said, "Maybe the answer you seek isn't found in science, Mr. Boboden. Maybe something more powerful is responsible."

Morrall rose from his chair. "Bullshit! Religious mumbo-jumbo isn't a part of this. I created this serum, not your ancient god." Morrall walked around the table and opened the door. He looked back. "This is a waste of time, John. I have some real work to do." Morrall stepped out the door and slammed it behind him.

John shook his head and turned to apologize to Jacob. John heard the man muttering softly to himself. "Do not lean on your own understanding. In all your ways acknowledge him, and he will make straight your path."

Somehow those words seemed profound and John wasn't sure how to respond. Finally, he asked, "Do you have any other ideas, Jacob?"

Jacob was silent for a moment and then asked, "Have you considered that the difference might be within your test subjects? Maybe it is their own spirit that controls the change?"

John was unsure what to say to that response. It was the Chief that asked the next question. "What do you mean by their spirit?"

Jacob turned to stare up at Barreau. "Maybe spirit is not the best word. Their desires, their will to live. Maybe your drug helps people become what they truly want to be."

The notion bothered John. Like Morrall, he wanted to believe in a repeatable, scientific solution. If Jacob was correct, this wasn't science and the cure could be more dangerous than the disease. Again, it was the Chief that spoke. "And you, Herrera? What did you both want to be and why are you different now?"

Jacob shrugged. "I don't know the answer to that really. Herrera wanted to be more than just a boy in the gangs. He wanted to make things and fix things. He wanted to use his hands and his mind to create. Whatever he is now, he is very talented. The things he can carve from a bar of soap, they're incredible. Me, there are parts of the ancient tongues I still want to learn. My Hebrew is among the best in the world. I wanted to master Aramaic the same way. I wanted to be more than just an old man teaching classes no one wants to take anymore."

John considered Jacob's words before asking. "And the two women that died?"

Jacob shrugged. "I don't know anything about them. Had they given up on life? Did they have dreams? Or a desire to be more than they were? If not, that may be why you lost them."

John nodded, "Thank you, Jacob. I will give your words some thought."

Jacob rose from his chair. His movements were graceful like those of a dancer. He looked at John. "I know you will never get the answers you seek with just the two of us. But there are answers that man is not supposed to have. I hope you are smart enough not to do this to anyone else. Your doctor and his scientific magic are dangerous. What you seek is not worth the risk."

John felt his muscles tighten subconsciously. There was a sharp intake of breath from the slim figure beside the door. "Oh, John. You have already done it haven't you? How many more people did you let Dr Frankenstein experiment on this time? Did you stop to think what they might become before you did this thing to them?" There was concern in Jacob's eyes as he continued, "I pray to Yahweh that you can control what they become."

Those words burned themselves into John's heart. He closed his eyes and spoke. "Goodbye for now, Jacob. And thank you. I hope we can speak again some time."

John heard the Chief escort Jacob from the room. He sat there for a long, long time considering the choices he had made since taking this job. He considered the college students he had watched Dr Morrall inject with the newest serum earlier that morning. He wondered where this would all end.

# Chapter 6
# Crisis Management

***Washington Post***
*Ondald raises concerns about mail-in voting fraud*
*Aug 3, 2020 — The debate over voter safety vs. the risk*
*of voter fraud move to the courts. Proof of identity vs.*
*claims of discrimination rage as both parties ...*

> ***Newsweek***
> *More school closings as Virus-C evolves*
> *Aug 12, 2020 — American students hope of returning*
> *to school for the next school year fade as new variants ...*

***The New York Times***
*Bendi Calls for national mask mandate*
*Aug 18, 2021 4:30 p.m. — President Elect Bendi calls for*
*a national mask mandate as he tries to avoid shutting down ...*

> ***The New York Post***
> *Ondald's campaign stumbles after positive test results*
> *Oct 7, 2020 — WASHINGTON — President Ondald announced he*
> *tested positive for Virus-C. He is suspending public appearances*
> *...*

***Los Angeles Times***
*2020 campaign over: Bendi elected 45th President of the Unite States*
*Nov 15, 2020 — President-elect Robin Bendi won the race after days*
*of waiting for mail-in ballots and multiple recounts in key ...*

Dr Anita Caufi smiled as she closed out the CNN tab on her browser. It was finally over. Days of waiting for ballots to be delivered by an overwhelmed postal service. Recount after recount that only delayed the inevitable. None of Ondald's ploys had worked and now that pompous windbag had lost. The best part was that Ondald had never seen it coming. He had been thoroughly beaten. If it wasn't so funny, she might even have felt sorry for him. Ondald had been so full of himself just a couple days ago and now all he had left was his pathetic cry of election fraud. If the old man only knew the true extent of what had happened.

The future looked so promising now. Two more months and Ondald would be out of the White House. All the respect that was her due would be hers again. Bendi was not one to pretend he knew more than the medical experts did. The President Elect had shown outright fear of the virus during the final months of the campaign. She intended to use that fear to influence his decisions. Bendi should readily accept most of her recommendations. If not, she was sure he would be susceptible to a number of the ploys that Ondald had refused to give credence to.

She was counting on the new President being willing to fund several of her research projects. She just needed to pitch them as efforts to end the pandemic. She still had a lot of prep work to do, but two months should be plenty of time to get everything ready for the man who wanted to rule the world. And when that world fell apart around him, she would be there to offer her support.

Anita carefully considered how to grow her power base. She was going to need a bigger staff and someplace to conduct the research projects that would be out of the public eye. Dr Morrall's project was not the only one she had to keep under wraps. She needed several isolated locations, but the facilities had to be already in place. She opened her mail window and typed a question to her research team. "Are there any BRAC locations that could be reactivated to study solutions to the Virus-C pandemic?" She slid the mouse towards the send button and then paused as another idea popped into her head. She began to type again, "Also check to see if any federal prisons have closed recently. High security would be a nice touch." She clicked send.

She glanced in her inbox before logging out. It was mostly low priority issues that her staff could handle without her. Then she noticed the encrypted message. She frowned when she recognized the address that had sent the message. Why had Boboden contacted her directly? It was out of character for him. She tapped on the message and placed her index finger on the security pad. She tapped her fingers impatiently as the letters on the screen rearranged themselves into something readable. The message was short.

*AC*

*Processing of new applicants way ahead of schedule. Concerned about the results. Request priority transport of AM from Cambridge. Meeting with Jacob and Herrera to see if they have any suggestions. Note: suggest you review applicant screening criteria.*

Anita frowned as she stared at the message. Something had spooked her project lead badly. Maybe the President wasn't the only leadership change she needed to consider. It wasn't just that he was spooked. She did not like the fact that he was getting so personal with the test subjects. Dr Morrall's patient IDs were rather simplistic, but they were effective. She did not have to worry about Alfred getting sentimental about his lab rats. John was becoming too familiar with what she deemed to be disposable assets. The last thing she needed was for John to become friends with them. If she wasn't careful, her project lead might actually grow a conscience.

She considered her options if she were to remove Boboden from the project. At the moment, there was only one. Could she let Dr Morrall run the project himself? The answer was definitely not. The problem was that Morrall wasn't trustworthy. She knew he was keeping secrets from her. Morrall would do what was best for himself and not for her. That was unacceptable. So, John Boboden's position was safe for now. Boboden would stay for now, but she would need to keep a closer eye on him. And, she would need to groom the new head of the Cambridge facility to take John's place when he became unreliable. For now, though, she must trust John's judgement that there was a problem.

Anita deleted the message and reached for her phone. She would need to personally arrange for a helicopter to pick up Dr Morrall from Cambridge and get him back to the other lab. Then she needed to figure out why John was worried about the subjects she had rounded up. Patients were frequently misplaced all the time in the pandemic. What difference did one girl or even ten college students make?

John stared in frustration at the five pieces of paper spread across his desk. There was one page for each of the new test subjects that had been sent to his lab to be experimented on. Each sheet contained a picture and a bio. The problem was, John was no longer able to ignore the fact that they were people. Jacob had made it clear that the people Anita sent him were more than just lab rats. And some of those people were at risk.

Something had gone wrong with the ongoing trial. It normally took at least four days from the time of injection before the transformations started. The patients had time to stabilize after the Virus-C was purged from their systems. But not this time. All five had begun to change 36 hours after the injection, only twelve hours after Dr Morrall had left for Cambridge.

John's concern wasn't just the early onset of the change. All five kids, or test subjects as he was supposed to refer to them, were changing so fast. Their bodies were transforming at an alarming rate and their vitals were dangerously erratic. He was afraid he was going to lose some of them. They were all so young. He needed his chief virologist here to monitor the situation. And of course, Morrall was a five-hour drive away even if Boston traffic was good. And Boston traffic was never good, even during a pandemic.

John began tapping his touch screen. He entered the security override code that allowed him to open Dr Morrall's personal records. It only took a moment to find the problem. His mad scientist had not stuck with the plan. Instead of using the same serum he had given to Jacob and Herrera, Morrall had used a new variant of the serum. All five college students had been injected with serum D4Y002. Then he left John and the lab team to deal with the results.

John swore softly as he closed the window on his computer. He reached over and picked up the bio sheet for the first of the male subjects in Containment Room 1. Subject 8GU20M was named Danny Markos. The boy was probably the only one of the five students that did not pose a security risk. Had Anita's sweeper team even bothered to do a background check before they selected these kids for the trial? John wasn't sure.

All John knew was that in a matter of hours, ten college students with severe Virus-C symptoms had been transferred from Georgetown University Hospital. Five of them had ended up in his facility. The others had been shipped to the Cambridge facility. John couldn't do anything for the kids at Cambridge. But he would do his best to save the ones he had here.

He continued rereading the bio. Danny was a mediocre student who had few friends that might come looking for him. John guessed that the boy avoided his peers because of his extracurricular activities. Apparently, Danny was paying GU's expensive tuition by stripping cars each night. There was an active FBI investigation centered around the boy and his activities. One by one, Danny had exposed those who bought his stolen parts. John could only hope the Feds thought the boy had cut and run before they closed their net.

John touched a camera icon in the bottom left of his screen. Then he activated the cameras in Room 1. At his touch, the camera zoomed in on the diminutive figure lying on a hospital bed. The boy was now even smaller than Herrera was. The notes made by the nursing staff indicated that Danny had lost over three feet in height and at least a hundred pounds. John turned over the page to check his notes. The last measurements placed the boy at a touch under three feet tall and 74.7 pounds. There had been no apparent change in the last six hours. John could only hope the worst was over.

Touching the camera controls again, John zoomed out and panned the camera to the opposite side of the room. There was no hospital bed for this patient. Instead, three mattresses had been placed side by side on the floor. John did not need to zoom in to see the figure that covered all three mattresses.

Geoff Harding, 10GU19M had gained everything Danny had lost and then some. At nearly eight feet and 585 pounds, Geoff no longer fit in a standard hospital bed. They had been forced to move him to the floor soon after his transformation started. Geoff appeared to be changing into what the Cambridge team referred to as an 'ogre.' Geoff was not the first person to grow like this. John just hoped that it would end better this time. He had no desire to kill Geoff or to lose another member of his staff.

Geoff's size and strength was not John's biggest concern. What had Anita been thinking when she let her team grab this boy? The boy was the star of the GU wrestling team. Geoff was ranked third in the nation in the 149-pound weight class. Someone would come looking for this talented young man. John wasn't sure he trusted Anita's people to cover their tracks well enough. Geoff was a security nightmare, but he was far from the biggest risk among the new test cases.

John switched off the camera in Room 1 and activated the camera monitoring the lone person in Room 2. This was the real hot potato of the bunch. Alicia Condemn, aka 6GU20F, was the only daughter of the flamboyant Congresswoman, Alexis Condemn. Alicia was an honor student in GU's pre-law program and a well-known figure around the Capital and in the media. Her disappearance was going to send shock waves through Washington, if not the nation.

John stared at the picture of her on the bio sheet. Pale skin and long dark hair. Those blue eyes that he wasn't sure were natural stared back at him. The girl was beautiful enough to be a model. But Alicia did not just want to be a show piece, she craved power of politics like her mother did.

John studied the figure sleeping on the hospital bed. The facial lines were similar. She was still beautiful in a strange and frightening way. Her skin was now as dark as a moonless night. Her hair was still long and lustrous, but it had lost all of its natural coloring. Its white color stood in stark contrast to her dark skin. Strangest of all were the violet irises that were now hidden below her dark eyelids. There was something strangely disturbing about what Alicia had become. The only good news was that even if someone traced her here, no one would ever connect her with the congresswoman's daughter.

John wondered briefly if the girl's presence here was really an accident. Had the girl been taken to pay Congresswoman Condemn back for some slight? Had Anita used this opportunity to get revenge? He would never know for certain.

John switched to the camera feed from Room 3. This was the room he was the most curious about. His fingers hovered over the two remaining bio sheets. He picked up the one for 7GU17F. The smiling face of a seventeen-year-old girl stared back at him. Ruth was the daughter of Walter Starling and a young woman he had met and married in Puerto Rico. Ruth had the brains that made her father a top investigative reporter and the dark skin color and good looks of her island-born mother. John suspected that Ruth's mother was at least as smart as her father because Ruth was a child prodigy.

Ruth had completed high school at age fifteen. She had been taking college classes on various campuses since she was twelve. Every one of those schools would have given her a free ride, but Ruth had not been interested. The little girl with the big eyes only wanted one thing, to be a stage magician. Apparently, Ruth was already credited with designing several top illusions for some of the biggest names in the magic business. In the end, Ruth's father had put his foot down. No magic career until Ruth had a degree to fall back on. Walter had enrolled her at Georgetown and Ruth had eventually given in.

John had to wonder how long it would take Ruth's parents to track her to his door. He didn't like the thought of being the lead story on every major network news broadcast.

With a sigh, John zoomed a camera in on Ruth's bed. The illusion that appeared to lay there was not one of Ruth's making. The young woman had been just over five feet tall before Dr Morrall had stuck that needle in her arm. Now she was barely three and a half feet tall. Her once dark skin was very different now, it was the brown of natural oak and had the heavy grain-like texture of an unfinished table. Her skin was still flexible to the touch, but it resisted an IV needle just like the wood it resembled.

Other changes were evident in the girl's looks. Ruth's dark hair had also turned white, but not the monotone white of the girl Alicia. Ruth's hair seemed to hold many shades and tones of white. It could mesmerize anyone who stared at it for too long.

John considered Ruth's changed face. Her delicate features were gone now. Her face seemed wider and her features had grown to fill in the extra space. Her eyes had grown even larger. Their once deep brown color had turned sky-blue. He wondered if people would get lost in her gaze the way they did in her hair. John closed his eyes to the strangeness of it all. He wondered what this child might have become if she had not been brought here. What might she have accomplished in this world if they had not changed her?

John rotated the camera to stare at the other occupant of the room. This form was now even smaller than Ruth. She was the reason he had asked Anita to bring Dr Morrall back as soon as possible.

A mound of greyish silver fur lay in the center of the bed. A long tail with seven rings wrapped around the small body hiding the long snout that projected from her face. Subject 9GU21F was, to all appearances, a somewhat large female raccoon. The creature was not doing well on the sedatives they were using to keep her under. John wanted Alfred to check her out before they lost her. Her now thirty-five-pound body did not fit any of their profiles.

Conchia Alimara was an above average student. Her picture showed a somewhat plain looking girl, perhaps a tad overweight. The bio indicated that Conchia had few friends. Well, one actually and that was Ruth. It was why he had ordered the two girls placed in Room 3 together. Conchia had never been exactly popular. There was a strange note that Conchia was officially listed at school as a furry. John had no clue what that meant. Two lines later, John's finger froze as he sucked in a ragged breath. Conchia had a nickname. She liked to be called Coon!

Could there be some validity in Jacob's belief that the change was influenced by the desires of the subject? The idea was at odds with every theory John knew about DNA manipulation. Whatever the truth was, he would not bring up any of Jacob's theories with Dr Caufi. John knew he was already on thin ice with her.

John shut down the camera's and turned off his monitor. He needed to get something to eat before Alfred returned. The man would be angry about being called back before he was done with the other test group. It was going to be a long night.

---

Sweat beaded Dr Alfred Morrall face as he sat in one of the two rear seats of the small military chopper. His body was buckled into what the soldier sitting across from him called a five-point harness. Despite the tightness of the seatbelts, Alfred felt his hands tighten on the two straps at his side. He had never been a fan of flying, but this trip was insane. Nothing was meant to fly this low or this fast.

He did not want to look, but Alfred's eyes were drawn to the small window on the side of the cabin. He swore the trees whizzing by were close enough to touch. Why were they putting him through this? Alfred felt bile rise in his throat. He coughed as a bitter taste began to burn in the back of his mouth. Alfred turned from the window to see the grinning soldier staring at him. The man, no, the boy did not have half of Alfred's intelligence. He should not be laughing at his better.

The soldier wasn't even holding on. It infuriated Alfred. The boy held out a white bag and winked at Alfred. Grudgingly, he released his grip with his right hand so he could take the air sickness bag.

Suddenly the helicopter shot up and tilted hard to the left. Alfred's eyes shot back to the small window. Not far below the chopper was an overpass. Alfred saw cars moving across it, he could almost make out the faces of people staring up at him. Then his ride tilted back to the right and dropped without warning. That was all Alfred's stomach could take. He barely got the white bag to his face before his expensive bistro dinner came back up.

A voice came over the cabin speaker as Alfred tried to catch his breath. "Ten minutes to touchdown, Sir. Your ride to the lab is already waiting for you."

Alfred sealed the air sickness bag and dropped it on the floor in front of the still grinning soldier. Alfred pulled his silk handkerchief out and wiped around his mouth. The handkerchief now smelled as bad as the bag did. Alfred dropped that too. He sat stiff and silent until he felt the helicopter touch down.

Of course, the embarrassment did not end there. The soldier had to help him out of the harness. John Boboden would pay for this indignity. Alfred wasn't sure how, but he would get even with the man for putting him through this.

# Part II
# Containment Breach

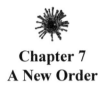

## Chapter 7
## A New Order

***CNN.com***
*Four dead as riots break out in the Capitol*
*Jan 6, 2021— UNITED STATES – Supporters of President Ondald stormed the halls of congress today in an effort to block ...*

>  ***AP News***
> *Despite predictions, no security issues at inauguration*
> *Jan 20, 2021 — President Bendi sworn in as 46th President of the United States at the U.S. Capitol in Washington, while National Guard members walk ...*

***ABC News - Breaking News, Latest News and Videos***
*President Bendi issues 22 executive orders during first week in office*
*Jan 27, 2021 — President Robin Bendi has now signed 22 executive orders and at least fourteen other executive actions addressing climate change and the Virus-C pandemic. White House indicates more ...*

The scroll was old. The papyrus was beginning to yellow with age. The characters drawn on its inner surface had begun to fade. Worst of all, mold had begun to eat at the ancient document. Jacob held the scroll gently as he scanned the symbols that had been drawn so carefully on it. Words in Hebrew written over the corresponding word in Aramaic. Some of the words shown with a glow that was almost magical. More of the words glowed that way each night.

Jacob was dreaming again. He knew that. It happened every night. Sometimes he was in a library. Sometimes in a temple. And sometimes, like tonight, he was in a cave lit by the light of one of the glowing words. He knew this was a dream because there were no ancient scrolls in the medical facility where he was being held. The lab was worse than a prison. He wasn't even allowed to read books here. Jacob stared at the runes, memorizing the subtle differences between the two ancient languages. And, allowing the glowing words to burn themselves into his mind.

The words were important and they held power. If he spoke them in the dream, wonderful things happened all around him. But if he spoke those glowing words when he was awake, the wonder of what he did was overshadowed by alarms and the failure of the equipment in the labs. The failure of their machines made his captors angry and confused. His excitement at what the words could do was seldom worth the chaos that ensued.

Jacob felt a slight tug at his left hand. He released that side of the scroll and watched as the scroll rolled itself closed. The dream was telling him that it was time to end. Jacob set the scroll down and waited for his return to consciousness. The light in the cave faded. But instead of waking, another source of light began to grow. Dawn came outside the cave.

Jacob rose and walked to the entrance. The rising sun revealed an arid land. The outside world was much drier than the dampness of the cave. Jacob did not recognize any of the small trees that grew nearby. He stepped out of the cave. The air was fresh and good. A gentle breeze began to blow. The breeze carried a single sound that came softly to his ears.

"Jacob."

Jacob stared all around him. But there was no one there. Perhaps it was Herrera or one of his captors. Jacob tried to wake. But he could not. The landscape remained unchanged.

The breeze blew again and again he heard, "Jacob."

Unable to wake, Jacob called out. "Hello. Where are you?"

The breeze blew again, longer this time. More words came.

"Jacob Dror. Know ye that even the captives of the most mighty and most terrible shall all be freed; I will be beside you as you contend with those who persecute you. Go and save the children."

Jacob was confused. He had no idea what the voice was talking about. He replied to the voice, "I don't understand. What children?"

The breeze blew its response to him, "All of them, Jacob Freedom, all of them."

Jacob woke in the lab room where he was being held. The only sound other than the beeping of the monitors was the deep rumble of Herrera snoring.

———————————

John stared down at the shipping document and grimaced. Two pallets of shielded network cable, a pallet of shielded routers and hubs, three hardened servers and a half dozen hardened computers. This one order had exceeded his IT budget for the next three years. How had the purchase request gotten approved without his knowledge? And why did they need shielded equipment? It made no sense.

He leaned over the keypad and began typing. First, John established a remote session with Corporate's secure server. He slid his badge into the reader and was granted access to the purchasing sub-system. John pulled the shipping document closer and began to type in the requisition number, ND4Z352021DP979IT. The requisition came up almost immediately. The order had been placed four days ago while he was in DC meeting with Dr Caufi. The expedite charges alone were outrageous. John scrolled down to the end of the third page to see who had approved the order. John cursed softly when he read what was typed below the digital signature: A. Morrall.

John picked up the shipping document and headed for the elevator. It was time to visit his chief medical officer. Morrall had been a pain in John's backside since the man had returned from Cambridge. The man's attitude had gotten worse after the meeting with Jacob. It was past time they had this out. John was still the program head and the good doctor needed to learn to play by the rules. John's discretionary budget could not handle a $113,000 shopping spree. Morrall was going to have to cover this out of his own funding line.

John used the elevator ride to get his anger under control. Blowing up on Alfred wouldn't make working with the man any easier. The elevator slid open on the medical level and John approached the closed door to Dr Morrall's office. John gave the door three sharp raps. An impatient voice came from the room beyond the door. "Go away. I'm busy."

John ignored Morrall and opened the door. Alfred spun his chair around with a growl. "What part of I'm busy don't you…"

John noted Morrall's disheveled appearance as the man realized who had opened his door. Alfred sighed as he spoke, "What do you need, John? I have too much to do and no time for one of your little lectures. If you are lonely, have another chat with 4NY62M."

John closed the door and pulled over one of Morrall's spare chairs. John lifted a large stack of computer printouts and dropped them on the floor before sitting down. "What are you so busy with, Alfred? You have been back from Cambridge for a week now. All of the new test cases are stable now. What's gotten you so worked up?"

Alfred ran his hand through his hair making it look worse than it had before. He pointed to the printouts now sitting on the floor and to his own computer screen. "I am comparing the DNA sequences of seven different specimens. I am searching for a common amino acid sequence. I am trying very hard to identify what they have become. I am cross-referencing the results with every known genome and variant. There is no logic to any of the deviations between these specimens or the ones in Cambridge. Hell, John, even the racoon really isn't a raccoon."

John dropped the shipping documents on Morrall's desk. "But you had time to work with IT to put together this equipment order that I don't have the budget to cover. An order that you approved behind my back, I might add. How does any of this help you with your analysis?"

John watched as Alfred ignored the papers. The man didn't even bother to look guilty about what he had done. Instead, he glared at John. "I need every piece of that equipment."

John remained calm as he asked, "For what, Dr Morrall?"

A frantic look came into the doctor's eyes as he responded. "To prevent more failures. It's them! The specimens! I don't know how they do it, but it's them."

The seriousness in Morrall's tone took John by surprise. "Come on, Alfred. How can it be them? They have no access to the equipment. They literally have nothing except the clothes that we gave them. How could they be responsible for the computer failures or anything else that had died recently?"

Alfred shrugged. "I don't know. But think about it. The IV pumps kept failing back in Cambridge. We tested every one of those pumps before we hooked them up to him. And yet, every pump that we connected to that damn ogre failed. What about your security door? How did that fail?"

John shrugged. "We're still looking into it. But I don't see how the Corporal could have been responsible. After he changed, he wasn't smart enough to tamper with any of the systems."

Morrall leaned forward in his chair. "And now the problems are here, too! Remember that strange light after the two New York specimens woke up? The one that destroyed most of the systems on the observation level? And the day of the interview? When all of my test equipment in 4NY62M's room burned out?"

John wanted to scoff at the craziness of the idea, but he paused to think it through. The tech crew had never found a reason for any of the failures. There was no reason for the software errors that had killed Kevin. But blaming the Changed? It made no sense. There had to be a scientific explanation other than Morrall's insinuation that they had brought a gremlin with them from Cambridge. "I am sorry Dr Morrall. There isn't any evidence that your subjects are responsible for what happened. Are you suggesting that they have some strange powers that defy the laws of science?"

The belligerent look that had become common on Morrall's face returned. John picked the shipping document back up. "I can't afford these, Doctor. I am going to refuse to accept the shipment."

John stiffened as Morrall's suddenly smiled. "You can't. I already have approval from Anita. She agreed with the purchase. She thinks we need to improve our security before I let the new specimens wake up."

John raised an eyebrow as he asked, "Are you are in charge of the project now, Dr Morrall?"

John remained tense as he watched the doctor deflate a little. "No, she doesn't trust me either. She is using us to keep each other in check."

John puzzled over that. He knew that Anita considered Alfred to be a bit impulsive. But he wasn't sure when he had lost her trust. He decided to probe a little. "Either?"

Alfred chuckled. "I warned you not to get personal with the specimens. You act like they are your friends. You call them by name. Apparently, I am not the only one that thinks you have lost your objectivity."

John's face remained cold as he rose from his chair and moved to the door. "I do my job, Alfred. Make sure you do yours. And for the record, the funds to cover most of this are coming out of your lab budget since you are the one who approved the purchase."

John closed the door behind him before the doctor could argue the point. His thoughts were a blur as he headed back to his own office. He would have to be very careful for a while. It would be very bad if either doctor realized just how much he questioned the morality of what they were doing. Objectivity? At least he had his humanity still.

**Chapter 8
Dreams**

### Washington Post
*Illegal immigration surges as thousands seek American Dream*
Mar 25, 2021 — Mere weeks after President Bendi revised U.S. border policies, there has been a 28 percent surge in the apprehension of immigrants along the southern border ...

### BBC
*How Virus-C changed our dreams and nightmares ...*
May 25, 2021 — Across the world, people report the pandemic has evoked nocturnal visions. These bizarre and often vivid dreams had a profound effect on ...

### The White House (.gov)
*Statement by President Robin Bendi on ...*
Jul 17, 2021 — I have repeatedly called on Congress to pass the American Dream and Promise Act, and I now renew that call with the greatest urgency. It is ...

John paused just outside the main conference room. He so hated staff meetings. He preferred to meet one on one with his section leads. Staff meetings encouraged people to recite monologues. Inevitably, it became a competition to see who could interrupt the most times. Meetings that should be done in fifteen minutes ended up taking hours. This wasn't the best way to start a Monday, but there were too many hot issues that involved multiple sections. It was time to suck it up and be the boss.

John opened the door and stepped inside. There were three people sitting at the main table. Dr Morrall representing the labs, Chief Barreau from security, and Gretta Haley who was the head of IT.

Gretta looked tired. John knew her team had been in all weekend installing the new shielded network. Gretta would have been here working until every last one of her folks had gone home.

There were six other staffers sitting in the chairs behind their bosses. None of them really needed to be here, but apparently everyone wanted a piece of the action today. John walked to the far end of the table and took his seat.

He looked directly at each person in the room before he spoke. "Good morning, everyone. Let's try to keep this brief. We all have a lot on our plates right now." John turned his gaze to his IT Chief. "Why don't you go first Gretta. I know you had a long weekend. You probably could use some sleep."

The IT head looked much younger than John knew she really was. Gretta thought it helped her connect with all the young 'geniuses' that worked in her section. She slid a single sheet of paper across the table to John. "That's the network security certification for the new installation. It requires your signature as facility manager before we go live."

John scanned the document looking for where to sign. He pulled a pen from his pocket and scribbled his signature at the bottom of the letter. He didn't need to second guess Gretta. She wasn't about to let anything go wrong on her watch. But he was curious, so he asked, "How does it look?"

Gretta shook her head. "It looks ugly as hell, John. The conduits we ran the new cable through are clearly visible in each of the rooms. The shielded servers and laptops are sitting on desks all over the observation room. It looks cluttered, but it all works. If the power stayed up, we could survive an EMP blast." She gave a sour look in Morrall's direction before turning back to John. "My team is exhausted, and I still don't understand what this is going to do to prevent more of the system failures we have experienced lately."

John couldn't answer her question, so he just smiled at her. "Tell your team they have my thanks. Keep the call center manned and one techie on call. Send everybody else home for a couple days. I will take care of their time sheets and authorize the overtime."

Gretta nodded. "You mind if I skip the rest of the dog and pony show? I am going on 30 hours straight right now."

John chuckled and waved a hand towards the door. "Go get some sleep and thanks again."

John waited until she left the room before passing the certification to Chief Barreau. Then he turned to the brooding form at the far end of the table. "You have your secure network now, Dr Morrall. What's next?"

John watched as the doctor prepared to give a speech. He raised his hand. "Briefly, Alfred. We are all busy."

Dr Morrall appeared to deflate like a balloon with a large hole. He frowned at John and began. "We reduce the sedatives the five GU specimens are getting. I want them in a normal sleep cycle by this evening. If there are no equipment failures, I recommend letting them wake when the drugs clear their systems."

Chief Barreau studied the doctor before asking, "And if there are problems with the new systems?"

Dr Morrall's face was a determined mask. "Then I keep them under for the rest of their lives."

John rose so he could stare down at his chief medical officer. "That won't be your call Dr Morrall." When the man started to argue, John smiled. "This time I am the one who called Dr Caufi. She reserves the right to make the final decision."

John wanted the meeting over before anyone could go on a rant, especially Alfred. Chief Barreau looked up from his seat. "Your other two guests have asked if they will be allowed to meet the new group."

Before Morrall could object, John replied, "To be determined, Chief. Let's see what wakes up before we decide."

---

Herrera sat down on the thin pad that had once covered the hospital gurney he had woken up on. Now, the pad lay on the floor in the corner of the room. The gurney might work for someone Jacob's size, but he was far too short now to climb that high without help. Inevitably, he ended up yanking his beard somewhere in the process of climbing up on the chair or going from the chair to the gurney. Pulling his own beard was painful, but he had never considered cutting it off. He had just dragged the pad and blankets off the gurney and thrown them into the corner.

Herrera ran his fingers through the long red curls of his beard. The young Hispanic boy who had trouble growing a descent mustache, now had a two-foot tangle of hair hanging from his chin. His fingers burrowed into the beard's softness. It felt right hanging there even if it was red instead of the black that he had been born with.

The gurney still sat there halfway across the room from Jacob's. Herrera now used it as a display for his creations. He had always been good with his hands, but it had changed when he became whatever he now was. The things he was creating worked beyond anything Herrera had ever believed himself capable of.

It had started with a small bar of soap. He had not even been aware of opening the new bar or of picking at it with his fingernails. When Jacob had eventually asked him about the mess he was making, Herrera had looked down to see an intricate shield. This was a real shield like in the old movies. It was nothing like the shields he made from trash can lids for the Banda. The shield sat on top of the gurney with the other things he had carved from the thin bars of soap he could steal.

Los desconocidos in the white coats had gotten tired of cleaning tiny soap curls off the floor. They had replaced the small soap bars with liquid soap and given him several containers filled with a soft modeling clay. His fingers had been able to make even more complicated creations with the clay. The dreams had begun the day he had started working with the clay.

Herrera took a large handful of clay from the jar and lay back on the pad. His fingers began to work the clay, softening it, as he thought about the dreams. Herrera had never had dreams like these before. He was in the dreams, or his new body was at least. But Herrera was not in his body. In the dreams, he hovered above himself where he could watch his new hands and what they created. In the dreams, his hands did not work with clay, they worked with metal. Those dream hands were skilled in ways that Herrera had wanted to be but never was.

Herrera felt his eyes flutter closed as he lay there working the clay. Once again, he hovered above his small, heavily-muscled body. His new body's red beard was hidden behind a leather apron. Intense flames burned around the room with pots of molten metal resting above the flames. Herrera knew those pots contained silver, gold, platinum, iron, and a shiny metal that he did not have a name for.

He watched himself mix the melted ores in precise quantities before pouring them into each mold. When all the molds were filled, his new body went to a set of molds that had already cooled. He cracked the molds open and drew forth shining metal feathers. As the dream progressed, his hands cleaned and polished each feather. Soon a dozen or so perfect metal feathers sat on the table. Herrera grew excited as he watched himself carry the feathers to the final workstation.

The final table was the assembly area. Herrera's eyes were instantly drawn to the seven ivory perches along the back edge of the table. Three of those perches were occupied by metal owls of exquisite workmanship. Each of the owls was a different breed and each was perfect in every detail. If not for the metal of their plumage, Herrera knew they would have flown around the room.

Herrera felt pride as he stared at them. He had built each of those owls in his dreams. His work was far from done though; four empty perches remained. Herrera turned his attention to his dream body. He watched intently as those stubby fingers lifted the first shining feather with care. With unexpected dexterity, those fingers began to weave the feather into a half-finished wing. This owl was much smaller and required great care. Herrera became absorbed in what his other self was doing, forgetting that this was just a dream.

---

Geoff stood in the shade of a pavilion style tent. Red stripes and whorls ran from the ground up to meet the golden fabric at the top of the tent. It reminded Geoff of the circus tents he had seen in old movies. Well, except for the fact that it was too small. Circus tents were huge, but the side of the tent barely came up to Geoff's nose. Perhaps the tent was for children.

There were many similar tents scattered nearby in the clearing and even among the trees. People in costumes wandered from tent to tent. There were men wearing medieval armor and women in flowing gowns and some in simple tunics. Children milled around the adults, most staring wide-eyed. There were a few people in normal clothing that meandered around, pointing excitedly at those in costume. Geoff had never seen anything like this before.

In a field a few hundred yards from where he stood, a dashing young man in a cape was dueling with three men who were obviously intended to be villains. The hero's sword darted here and there keeping the villains at bay. But despite his flamboyant sword work, he could not defeat the three men. Then the hero turned in Geoff's direction and motioned Geoff forward. His clear voice rang out, "Fezzik, Hero. I need your great strength."

People turned to face Geoff. The crowd began to chant, "Fezzik! Fezzik! Fezzik!"

Geoff was confused. Why were they all staring at him? And who was Fezzik?

The name seemed familiar, but Geoff could not remember where he had heard it before. He tried to take a step backwards. He wanted to run away, but the tent wall was directly behind him. There was no place he could go.

A tiny boy broke from the crowd and ran up to stand before Geoff. The boy was so small. He barely came to Geoff's knee. The boy grabbed one of Geoff's fingers and began to tug. "Hurry, Fezzik, Hurry! Wesley needs your help!"

Geoff allowed himself to be pulled out into the waiting crowd. He paused, confused. Now that he was among them, he realized how small everyone was. Even the tallest men only came to Geoff's shoulder. Geoff knew he wasn't tall. He was the shortest person on the wrestling team. What was going on?

The boy began to tug harder on Geoff's finger. "It's okay, Fezzik. You can do it. You have to save Wesley so he can rescue Princess Buttercup."

This had to be a dream. Nothing else made sense. Geoff began to move again. He had no idea what he would do against men with swords, but everyone seemed to believe he could save this Wesley. If this was a dream, he should wake up before he got himself killed. You always wake up before you die, don't you?

---

Conchia lay on soft grass below a large tree. She was more aware of her surroundings than she had ever been before. She felt each and every blade of grass on the ground beneath her. She could smell… well… everything. She recognized each of the smells: the pungent smell of wet grass, the vinegary smell of the oak tree over her head, the smell of dandelions scattered across the lawn, and the delicious odor of ripe blueberries.

Her stomach began to growl at that last scent. Conchia realized she was starving. She turned her head until she located the blueberry bush. She scurried over to stand beside it. Conchia reached out to take a berry.

Then she noticed her hand and the arm that it was attached to. Her hand had five fingers, but it did not have a thumb. The hand was attached to a furry arm, or was it a leg? She wasn't sure. The fur was a greyish-brown. The fur rippled gently in the breeze. Conchia turned her head and examined the rest of her body. It was a shape she knew well. She had pictures of it all over the walls of her dorm room.

A striped tail curled up and around her. Conchia clutched it with both hands and hugged it. She was a raccoon! It was a dream come true. Conchia knew this was a dream, but it was a really good dream. Being sick wasn't so bad if she could have dreams like this. She let go of her tail and reached out with both hands to pluck the purple berry from the bush. She held it to her sensitive nose and sniffed. Her mouth began to water. Conchia shoved the berry into her mouth with both hands.

When she bit down, the juice exploded in her small mouth. The burst of flavor she expected wasn't there. It was so disappointing. She wondered if this was how things tasted to a raccoon. Or was it because this was only a dream? Conchia tried to remember if she had ever tasted anything in a dream before. She wasn't sure.

Then her ears twitched. The sound of humming came through the trees on the far side of the bush. Conchia found herself halfway up the oak tree before she even realized that she was moving. She forced herself to stop on the first large branch she came to. She settled down to see what was coming.

A small human-like figure was walking through the trees. She thought it was a child, not much bigger than her raccoon body. Its skin was brown and grainy like the wood of a tree. Its hair...no... her hair was a startling array of whites. Conchia had never seen so many shades of white before. Was it her raccoon eyes or was it really the girl's hair? The child that couldn't possibly be human looked up at Conchia. Huge blue eyes, much bigger than those of any person she had ever seen, stared up at her. She chittered in surprise as she felt herself drawn into the sky-blue of those eyes.

---

Danny skipped through the fairgrounds watching all the big people around him. At least he thought it was a fairground. It had tents but there weren't any rides. It did not matter really; this place wasn't real.

He knew it was a dream. It was the only way to explain why he was suddenly so small. Even the kids around him were taller than he was. Danny glanced down. And those feet. They just could not be real. His adult feet weren't that big. And, his own feet did not have a carpet of hair on top of them. At least these feet were well callused. He felt no discomfort despite running around barefoot. He had bigger concerns right now than his lack of shoes, like figuring out where he was.

Wherever he was, this place was filled with bright colorful tents and unsuspecting people. With all the strange costumes people were wearing, no one would notice him. It was a recipe for fun. As dreams went, this one wasn't half bad.

Danny ran through the crowd looking for something worth doing. He watched as two kids about his own size begged their mother for a funnel cake. They were 20 feet away and still he heard her tell them she did not have enough money for funnel cake. That seemed wrong. Danny wanted those kids to enjoy his dream too.

Danny looked around. Next to the funnel cake tent was a tent that sold hand-made leather boots. A fat man was arguing with the boot maker over the price of his boots. Danny ran up behind the fat man, but the man hardly noticed Danny's small form. Danny reached up and….

His sensitive fingers slid into the man's pocket. The large wallet seemed to leap into Danny's hand. Danny moved on without even looking to see if the fat man or the man selling the boots noticed the theft. Danny reached into the wallet without looking. He ignored the credit cards and pulled a dozen bills from the wallet before tossing the wallet in a trash can beside the funnel cake tent. In the dream, Danny could feel the denominations of the bills without looking at them. The fifties and the tens went into one of Danny's many pockets. He ran up to the concession and dropped two twenties on the counter. "Three Funnel cakes, please. Keep the change." The two teenagers inside hurried to fill his order.

Danny handed the first funnel cake to the smaller of the two children standing beside the woman. The child smiled but the woman began to protest. "Oh, we can't accept that, child."

Danny laughed loud and hard. Then he handed the second cake to the other child. He grinned up at the woman. "I won the lottery. No, wait, money grows on trees." Then he grabbed the third cake and disappeared into the crowd before she could protest further.

Danny continued to roam the fair. It was much easier to be nice, to do things for others, in his dream. It was really easy when the rich people who treated others badly paid for all of his generous gifts. As Danny wandered the dream fair, he wondered if this was what it was like to be Robin Hood.

---

The sound of many voices began their assault on Alicia's senses. The voices were so loud that she could feel their vibrations ripple across her skin. Why was it suddenly so noisy in her room? Her mother had demanded that Alicia be placed in a private room despite the overcrowding caused by the pandemic. Being the daughter of a congresswoman had its perks. The voices grew more annoying. Someone was going to be in very big trouble when Mother found out about this.

Alicia opened her eyes to find that she wasn't lying in her hospital bed anymore. She was standing on a stage right behind its closed curtains. The noise came from beyond those curtains. Alicia stepped closer and peeked through to see what all of the excitement was.

The stage sat at the front of an enormous auditorium. Thousands of seats were arrayed in curved rows below the stage. Even more seats were slightly above her in a large balcony. As near as she could tell, every seat had someone sitting in it, standing on it, or standing before it. The auditorium was packed with people. As the details of what she was seeing began to sink in, Alicia began to wonder if anyone out there was a person at all.

Her eyes darted from one group of figures to the next as the crowd milled around in the auditorium. Strangely, she could clearly see even the creatures in the very last row of seats. Without her glasses, they should have been little more than fuzzy shapes. The creatures, for they were obviously not human, were like nothing she had ever seen or even imagined before.

Some of the creatures were taller than the NBA players that Mother sometimes invited to the house. They were powerfully built with broad, almost stupid looking faces. Others were so small that she could only see them because they stood in their seats. Many of those smaller creatures had red, orange, and yellow skin. Still others had skin so black that it seemed to absorb the light. These had white hair braided down their backs. And, were those pointed ears? The largest group were more human looking, but they had flat, round noses that reminded her of a pig's nose. The entire crowd seemed deformed in one way or another. And all of them were yelling or screaming.

A fight broke out near the front of the auditorium. Alicia's keen eyesight focused on one of the really large, stupid-looking creatures. It was arguing with one of the dark-skinned figures with the pointed ears. The large creature raised a massive fist over its head. Alicia's breathing quickened as she waited for the blow to crush the smaller, dark form. The blow never came down. A second dark form, a female Alicia realized, stepped up behind the larger creature. Without hesitation, the female drove a knife into the larger brute's back.

Alicia watched as blood spurted across the hand holding the knife. Alicia felt herself grow excited. The blood called to her. She imagined the pain that strike had caused and she almost swooned at the thought. Her breathing quickened as the large figure slumped to its knees. The knife came out of the kneeling figure's back. The dark female reached around and slit the tall thing's throat. More blood spurted. A feeling akin to ecstasy washed over Alicia.

The voices grew louder. Alicia realized that most of the crowd was chanting now. Their cries called for someone. For her? "Priestess! Priestess! Priestess!"

A soft almost sinister voice cut through the sound of the crowd. "They call for you, Alicia Octavia Condemn."

Alicia looked around but there was no one there. The voice came again. "Go to them, my child."

Alicia did not hesitate. She raised her hands to pull the curtains aside. He arms and hands were as black as those of the woman with the knife. She reached up. Her ears were pointed too. Alicia did not care. What mattered were the cries of the crowd. She grasped the curtains and threw then aside. Alicia stepped out on the stage and the crowd began to cheer. They were cheering for her as was her due.

Once more the voice whispered to her, "This can be more than just a dream, My Lady. All this I will give to you if you bow down and serve me."

---

Ruth leaned back against the trunk of the tree. The sun warmed her skin. It would be so easy to sleep here forever. But that would be wrong. Her parents would miss her. A light breeze blew and Ruth felt wisps of her hair tickle her nose and cheek. Her right hand came up to tuck the strands of hair behind her ear. The sound of paper fluttering in the breeze made her look down. A worn book lay open in her lap, its pages turning with the wind.

Her right hand came back down to clasp the top of the book. She held the pages still once more. Strange markings stared up at her from the open pages. They were words, but not in English. Most of the strange symbols were written with a dark ink that stood out from the page. Others glowed with an internal light that rivaled the brightness of the sun. Ruth knew these characters. The language was ancient Hebrew. She had studied these symbols for a semester at New York University. That had been several years ago, but she still remembered the runes and their meaning. The words for light and darkness, the word for self, and another that meant change.

The glowing words were important. Ruth just did not understand why. She regretted that she could not remember how to pronounce them anymore. She had lost that skill after two years with no one to practice with. She had enjoyed her time in Professor Dror's class. She had been angry when her father had refused to let her take another semester of Ancient Languages. Her father had called it a waste of her talents.

The breeze blew again and Ruth heard a soft voice say, "A teacher shall come to add to your learning."

Ruth smiled and closed the book. She tucked the book under her arm as she rose to her feet. It did not matter where those words had come from or if they were real. They comforted her and that was what mattered. Ruth began to walk through the trees. This was a much nicer place than the hospital room had been. Ruth wondered if she was dead and this was heaven. The breeze blew again and the leaves of the tree rustled. They seem to say, "No, child. It is not yet your time."

Ruth began to hum a Puerto Rican lullaby that Mama had sung to her long ago. That too made her happy. She wandered for a while. A loud chittering noise startled Ruth from her mental wandering. She looked up to see a large raccoon sitting on a branch over her head. Ruth raised a small hand that must be hers now and waved at the raccoon. "Hello there. I have a friend that would absolutely adore you. Her name is Conchia, but she likes to be called Coon."

The raccoon chittered again, but this time is sounded more like a question than a scolding. Was the raccoon speaking to her? It appeared to be. That was strange because raccoons did not speak. Perhaps this was a dream, because Ruth thought she understood what it was asking. It was a nice dream. Since the raccoon was being polite, so Ruth answered. "My name is Ruth. I was a little girl before I came here. Conchia is older than me, but we are still best friends."

The raccoon came part way down the tree. Ruth marveled at how it could walk down the trunk without falling. Its little furry face was pointed directly down at Ruth. Its ears swiveled towards her. It chittered again softly. Ruth grinned as she answered its obvious confusion. "I know I don't look like myself. This is a dream silly. I don't know what I am in my dream."

The raccoon took several more steps down the trunk. Ruth could almost touch it if she stood on her tip toes. This time the animal that was almost as big as Ruth's dream body made a mewling noise. Ruth's eyes opened wide. "Are you really Conchia? She, I mean you, will be so happy when I tell her about this dream. She always wanted to be a raccoon."

The raccoon came the rest of the way down the tree to stand right at Ruth's feet. It rose up on its hind legs and leaned into Ruth. Dream Conchia chittered softly in her ear. Ruth wrapped her arms around the soft furry form of her friend. "Of course, I will still be your friend, Coon. We will always be best friends."

Ruth thought that this was the nicest dream she had ever had.

---

Herrera woke to the sound of Jacob's rhythmic breathing. The room was dim and the window overlooking the room was dark. The dark window did not mean that no one was watching though. Herrera knew that someone was always watching them. Their observers did not want to miss any part of the experiment.

The dim lighting told Herrera that it was sometime during the night. He had no idea how long he had slept or how long he had dreamed.

It had seemed to take days to finish the next owl in his dream. But he doubted he had slept for more than a few hours.

A warm weight was nestled into the palm of Herrera's right hand. He did not squeeze the lump even though he knew the clay would be hard now. Herrera sat up before looking at the owl he had created during the night. Somehow, the city boy knew this was a great gray owl. It was the largest owl in the United States. He had never seen a real owl before, but he knew that the image he had created in his sleep was accurate. It was the same owl his dream self had built.

Herrera rose and crossed the room to his gurney. He placed the gray owl on top between the Horned Owl and the Snowy Owl. The little Elf Owl sat off to the side by itself. Herrera didn't know why that was important, but he knew it was. Then he returned to the pad and lay down again. This time, he knew he would sleep without dreaming.

## Chapter 9
## Harsh Realities

*The New York Times*
Prison Authorities announce closure of 6 facilities in New York
May 19, 2021 — The NY Department of Corrections announced
their decision on Monday. The closures are driven by the large
number of guards who have fallen ill from Virus-C. The
facilities affected include Ogdensburg Correctional Facility,
Moriah Shock Incarceration Correctional Facility, ...

*Forbes*
Chicago Mayor takes first steps to 'Defund the Police' ...
July 20, 2021 — The city's Dem mayor has slashed 120 police
officers from the budget. The reduction will be accomplished
attrition and not hiring new officers, saving $430,000 ...

*ABC News - Breaking News, Latest News and Videos*
Protests against mask and vaccine mandates surge in US and Europe
August 8, 2021, 8:36 PM ET. ... Protests against Virus-C policies in the
United States and many countries in Europe are becoming more
frequent and more violent despite an increase in infection rates ...

*Los Angeles Times*
Another autonomous zone in Portland ...
Aug 25, 2021 — Portland Antifa members attempted to
reestablish an autonomous zone; the new zone stretched
along the Portland's waterfront. ...

Anita spread the analysis reports out across her desk. Why was this so difficult? The Base Realignment and Closure list had been utterly useless. Even the podunk towns in the middle of nowhere wanted to take over facilities that were basically falling apart. And, of course, the military was bending over backwards to dump their building code violations off on any local community stupid enough to take them.

At least no one was rushing to take over any of the old prisons. She could probably take her pick of any of them, or more than one if Morrall's serum panned out. Negotiating with whatever state controlled the facility shouldn't take much effort. Every governor wanted extra vaccine allocations. Thankfully she controlled the most valuable currency in the world these days. Besides, practically all of the prisons had been shut down to cut costs. She would be doing whatever state she chose a favor by reducing facility maintenance budget. The only hard question was, which prison was the best for her needs.

The decision wasn't a complicated one and the analysis reports were thorough. From what she was reading, most prisons were essentially the same. There really were only two factors that she needed to consider: security level vs location. She preferred at least a medium-security facility but, surprisingly, those were frequently not as isolated as some of the minimum-security prisons.

Anita frowned at the twenty-two reports scattered across her desk. She needed to pare down her options to a manageable level. There were twelve BRAC locations. She picked those up and tossed them in a pile on the floor. Six of the remaining facilities were close to large population centers. Those reports were quickly added to the pile on the floor. Anita took the remaining reports and began to read them more carefully.

An hour and a half later, she realized there were really only two good options and both were in New York. Ogdensburg was more secure, but Moriah Shock was located in a remote part of the Adirondack Mountains. Anita liked how isolated the Moriah facility was. The mountains around it should ensure that none of Morrall's oddities would end up on the cover of the National Enquirer. The facility would need a number of security upgrades, but her team believed they could have it ready for its strange new residents by the end of September.

Anita scribbled a quick note at the top of the Moriah packet. "Move on this one ASAP! Option 2 will be Ogdensburg." After placing the report in her outbox, Anita glanced at her watch. It was nearly noon and she was in the mood for lunch and a nice glass of wine. What was left in her inbox could wait.

---

Conchia became aware of the world again. This time she wasn't lying on soft grass beneath a nice safe tree. Instead, she lay on something hard. Her nose twitched as she drew in a breath. Whatever she lay on smelled really bad. Conchia opened her eyes. She wasn't in a hospital hallway anymore. Or at least it didn't look like a hospital. As far as she knew, hospitals did not come with thin, black bars instead of a door. The sight of those bars was not nearly as disturbing as the shiny black nose and long snout that she recognized from her dream of the forest.

Conchia turned her head to study her herself in the dim light. Yep, she was still a raccoon. This time though, her body was thinner and her fur was matted with dirt and grime that smelled as bad as the mat she lay on. If the last time she had woken up had been a dream, this time it was more like a nightmare. What could be worse than being a dirty racoon behind bars? Then again, she could have woken up as herself.

She scanned the rest of her prison cell. Light brown walls of plastic surrounded her. There were small, barred windows in each of the side walls. Recognition came almost instantly and an angry hiss escaped before she could control it. Someone had locked her in a dog crate. It was humiliating! She was not some stupid mutt; she was a raccoon. Her captors couldn't have been more insulting if they had tried.

Over the years, she had been bullied, teased, and picked on. She had endured it all. But being locked in this dog crate was more than even she could tolerate. This time, she would not put up with being tormented. She would free herself. She would be cautious though. Before she escaped from her cell, she wanted to see more of what lay beyond the walls of the crate. The view from the two small windows should tell her if it was safe to make a run for it.

Conchia rose unsteadily to her feet. Her body was weaker than she had realized. She felt like she had not eaten in forever. She pushed her hunger aside and took a tentative step towards the window on her right. She stumbled and fell. Something clamped tight around her neck. Fear shot through her body as the pressure increased. She wanted to cry out, but she could not draw a breath to do so. Her front paws reached instinctively to tear at whatever was choking her. Instead of the flesh of an attacker, her tiny fingers found a band of leather pulled taught about her neck.

Conchia regained her footing and backed up. The pressure on the throat eased and she drew in a deep breath of foul-smelling air. This time, her angry hiss was followed by a low growl. There was no doubt about what the leather that circled her neck was. Someone had placed a dog collar on her too. Her hope that this was just another dream was swept away by the reality of the collar. Even her sub-conscious mind wasn't this twisted. She was actually a raccoon and all of this was really happening to her.

Conchia allowed her hindquarters to settle back on the mat. As her mind struggled to comprehend her transformation, her hands continued to explore the collar. Her small fingers moved until they found the plastic clasp on the side of her neck. She traced the lines of the clasp as a part of her brain analyzed how to open it.

She felt another spark of anger. She wasn't a pet that someone could own. She was a person, or she had been before... Well, before whatever had happened to her. She didn't need a collar just because she had wanted to be a raccoon. And her desire to be furry did not mean she wanted to be owned by someone. Besides, it wasn't even a nice collar. It had probably come from the local dollar store. Her fingers moved past the clasp and continued to the back of her neck. She needed to know what had caused the collar to tighten when she stumbled.

Then she found the answer to her question. A large metal ring pierced the leather on the back of the collar. A chain was padlocked to the ring. The padlock and ring were both sturdy. She couldn't understand why someone would go to so much effort to secure the chain to a collar that any three-year-old could open. What part of raccoon did her captors not understand?

The part of her that was trying to understand how she had become a raccoon was stumped. Even if her human brain fit in the raccoon's skull, no one knew how to do brain transplants yet. The only other answer she came up with was magic. Even Ruth with her illusions knew that magic wasn't real. Conchia gave up on that problem and focused on removing the collar.

Her front paws returned to the plastic clasp. Conceptually, it was easy. Squeeze the two tabs together and the clasp should release. It was a simple maneuver if you had a thumb. Raccoons might be able to disappear into the woods to escape from a group of bullies, but they weren't great at squeezing tabs together. It took several agonizing moments to get her hands in just the right positions to squeeze. Then, there was a click and she was free. If anyone opened the crate, they would have a very frustrated raccoon to deal with.

Now that she could move without choking, Conchia wanted to check out both of the crate's windows. The right window didn't reveal much. Ten feet away was a shiny metal wall with several equipment carts lined up against it. She did not know what the equipment was, but she had seen similar devices when they had admitted her to the GU Hospital. Whatever their intended function, the screens and panels were dark and lifeless.

The view from the left window showed her more of the room. This time, the shiny wall was at least thirty feet away. Between her and the wall was a hospital bed. Beyond the bed, more carts and monitors lined the wall. But the equipment on this side of the room wasn't off. Flashing lights danced across the surfaces facing her. Conchia turned her attention to the hospital bed. A small arm was just visible strapped to the edge of the bed. Was her roommate a child?

Conchia stepped away from the small window. Whoever the occupant of that bed was, they appeared to be as much a prisoner as she was. There appeared to be no one else in the room, but she had no way to see what lay behind the crate. That only left the front of her little prison to check out. Would anyone be watching for movement behind those thin black bars? And if so, how would they react to her taking off the collar?

Conchia moved slowly forward, trying not to call attention to herself. Another metal wall lay beyond the bars. A wooden table sat against the wall directly across from the crate door. A single rolling chair sat in from of the table. What looked like a pile of papers sat on the left corner of the table. It was what lay to the right of that table that interested Conchia the most.

To her relief, there was a door in the right corner of the room. A door meant a possible escape from this place. She just wasn't sure that she could even reach the doorknob. A black box with shiny silver buttons was mounted on the wall beside the door. There appeared to be a slot below the buttons and several lights above it. Conchia suspected that box would be an even bigger obstacle to opening the door than reaching the doorknob was.

A whirring noise came from somewhere over her head. Conchia crouched to look up. High on the wall near the center of the room was a large window. The window's glass was dark and Conchia wondered if it was nighttime. The whirring sounded again, Conchia noticed that there were cameras on both sides of the window. The two cameras were pointed towards the hospital bed where the child was being held. Good, she thought. Whoever was on the other side of that window was not watching the crate door right now.

Since there was little more she could learn with her eyes, Conchia stuck her nose through the bars and sniffed. The air was sterile or maybe dead was a better description. The harsh bite of bleach burned as she drew a deep breath. She learned nothing from that breath except that the stink of bleach was painful to raccoons. At the same time, she was searching for scents, her racoon ears twitched and rotated, searching for sounds. Sadly, the room was silent except for the low hum of the monitors and a steady beeping that sounded like a heart monitor.

Conchia pulled her nose back through the bars and examined the latch that held the door closed. Like the dog collar, the crate was never designed to hold a creature as smart or as intelligent as a raccoon. Why did humans always underestimate the capabilities of animals? Many animals, like raccoons, were really smart. It was silly to assume animals were dumb. Then again, she thought, most of the people she knew weren't much better at seeing the potential in the people around them. Looks were all that mattered. Supposedly smart people just assumed that being different meant that there was something wrong with you. Different meant you were somehow inferior or maybe that you didn't have feelings that could be hurt. And overweight meant you were stupid. Conchia had learned that harsh lesson a long time ago.

Her tiny hand slid through the bars where her nose had been. She lifted the knob out of its slot and slid the small bar to the open position. It would have been simple for even a normal raccoon. The lock was a joke for a someone like her. She pulled her hand back through the bars and waited to see if anyone came to prevent her escape.

She counted to twenty and nothing happened. Conchia focused on the table. If she could get there without falling, it would hide her from the window and the cameras. She pushed the bars open and stepped out. Conchia paused to close the door, but did not bother with the latch. Then she scurried carefully to the table and darted under it.

Again, she waited for an alarm or the sound of running feet. To her relief, the room remained silent except for the beeping. Conchia studied the other side of the room, the only direction she had been unable to see from the crate. On the far wall, between the distorted reflections of the bed and the crate, was another door. This door didn't have a black box on the wall beside it.

What should she do next? Conchia considered her options. The far door would put her in clear view of the window and the cameras. She dismissed it for now. The nearest door or the bed? The desire for freedom won out and she turned towards the door.

Conchia left the shelter of the table, her left side pressed against the cold metal of the wall. She told herself that staying close to the wall meant the no one could see her through the windows or on the camera. But her weakened body also needed the extra support as she walked.

The door was made from the same shiny metal that the walls were. The door was probably heavy, possibly heavier than her raccoon body could open. The doorknob seemed impossibly far over her head. Conchia stood on her hind legs and reached for the knob. It felt strange the way her new body seemed to lengthen and stretch as she reached upwards. The extra length did not help. The doorknob remained stubbornly out of reach. The black box with its buttons was even higher than the knob. Even if she knew whatever code was needed to unlock the door, her raccoon body would need help to open the door. Her freedom would not come easy. The help she needed would have to come from the captive on the bed.

Conchia turned, retracing her steps to the table. She passed under it and back out the other side, following the wall until she reached the foot of the bed. Then she sat and studied the bed and the bare toes that peeked out from beneath a white hospital blanket.

The toes confirmed that bed was occupied. But by who? The toes were small and that arm had not been very big either. Were her captors keeping a child prisoner here too? She needed an ally that could do things she could not. A child would not be much help. Conchia badly needed the help of someone she trusted. The list of people she trusted was pretty small. She shook her head as she realized the list actually only included one individual and that person was Ruth.

Where was Ruth? The last thing Conchia remembered was the hallway in the GU hospital. Every room in the hospital had been full, so they had both been left in a hallway near the emergency room. The nurse had placed their beds across the hall from each other so they would have someone to talk to. Sadly, both girls had been too sick to care.

She had not seen Ruth after that, except in that strange dream. In that dream, Ruth had not been the skinny young girl Conchia remembered. Ruth had been smaller then, about the size of a child. About the size of the figure strapped to that bed. Was it possible that Ruth lay up there waiting for her? Was that thought any crazier than the idea that Conchia was now a raccoon? The urge to see who was up there was more than Conchia could resist.

Conchia moved across the open space between the wall and the bed. She forgot her weakness in her need to see who or what lay on top of that bed. Her tiny hands reached for the bars on the underside of the bed. Her raccoon body instinctively found handholds and she easily pulled herself up onto the bed. Conchia stared down at a form she had only seen in her dream.

The small figure was no more human that Conchia was. Despite its size, the tiny body was not that of a child. Her shape under the thin hospital gown made it clear that the figure was female and fully grown. Skin, the golden brown of grandmother's dining room table, beckoned for her touch. Conchia ran her small fingers along the arm strapped to the bed. The faint lines she saw on the woman's skin were like the deep grain of that oak table where she had eaten so many of Grandma's cookies.

Conchia's eyes followed the form down to the two small feet sticking out from the blanket. White straps held both feet firmly in place. Conchia turned her gaze to the woman's face. Despite waking up as a raccoon, there was still a touch of shock when she saw the familiar face from her dream.

Dream Ruth's face, surrounded by that mesmerizing halo of white hair, rested on a thin pillow. The mass of curly white strands was like a painter's masterpiece. So many shades and tons of white that Conchia never knew existed before seeing Ruth this way. Conchia found it hard to stop staring at the patterns she saw in those curls.

Then the head turned her way and the patterns shifted. Conchia started and looked from the hair to the small face it framed. The woman opened her impossibly large eyes and Conchia felt herself soar into the pale blueness of a perfect spring sky. In that gaze, Conchia felt love and acceptance. Those eyes would not, had not, ever judged her. This creature was truly her friend.

A soft voice, scratchy with disuse, called Conchia back to herself. The voice sounded uncertain as it asked, "Is it really you, Coon? I thought that was just a dream, but somehow you got your wish."

Conchia, or Coon as she could finally be, reached out and patted the small woman's cheek. Ruth smiled at her. "I would hug you, but it appears that I am a bit tied up at the moment."

Coon spun around and reached for the white straps that bound Ruth's legs to the bed. The restraints were made of Velcro. She tugged on the first strap and it emitted a satisfying ripping noise as it released Ruth's leg. Another quick tug and both legs were free. One after the other, Coon freed Ruth's hands too.

Ruth sat up slowly. Again. Coon felt herself soar up into the blue of those shining eyes. Far away, she heard Ruth ask, "May I hug you now? Can we still BFFs now that you have become what you always wanted to be?"

Coon threw herself into Ruth's open arms. She began to cry as those arms tightened around her tired and very dirty body.

———————————

The fairground, or whatever it was he had been dreaming about, faded away. The soft grass beneath Danny's feet was replaced by a hard surface beneath his back. His body was stiff and sore like he hadn't moved in a long, long time. How many days had he spent in this hospital anyway? His mind said it had only been a day or two since his roommate had driven him to the emergency room. The stiffness in his limbs said it was much longer.

 Danny lay still on the hospital bed. He was still tired, so he kept his eyes closed. Maybe the nurses would just let him go back to sleep. If he was lucky, he could go back to that wonderful dream world where everything seemed possible. But sleep wouldn't come and Danny lay there listening to the sounds around him.

As he listened, curiosity chased away the last remnants of sleep. This couldn't be the hospital he remembered. He, like most of the sick kids from GU, hadn't even rated a hospital room. Those rooms had been filled long before the outbreak at GU. The GU students had gotten whatever residual space could be found. Offices, the cafeteria, and hallways, like the one where he had been left, became the storage space for those not sick enough to be placed on ventilators. Danny grinned. At least there had been someone to empty the urinal when it got full. Without that small luxury, things would have been much worse.

He knew something had changed because the moans and coughs that he had fallen asleep to were gone now. Wherever here was, it seemed almost silent in comparison. Other than the regular beep of a single monitor, the only sound was the deep rumble of someone snoring. He at least knew he wasn't alone.

Danny's attention shifted from his surroundings to himself. It no longer hurt to breathe. His fever and cough were gone. He felt really good for the first time since he had returned from Florida. The flight to Ronald Reagan Airport had been miserable. What he thought was just a nasty hangover had turned out to be that new virus. Danny hadn't been worried at first. He was young and invulnerable. The fear had begun the first time he took a breath that felt like there was broken glass in his lungs. His fear had grown to terror at the sight of so many bodies lining the hallways at the hospital. Danny could only hope that he was done with hospitals and being sick. He just wanted to go back to his old life.

Danny opened his eyes and looked around. He lay in a fairly large room. It was hard to see much of the room while flat on his back, so he tried to sit up. Sitting up didn't work. Not because he was weak, but because his wrists were pinned to the bed. Danny tried to move his feet, but his ankles were also locked in place. Fear began to eat at him again.

Danny turned his head from side to side. But the only thing he could see was the dark window high on the steel wall at the foot of his bed. Was someone up there watching? Danny tried yelling for help. Surely a nurse would hear him. "Hello, is there anyone there? I feel better now. Can you let me up?" On a whim, he cried out, "I really need to pee."

The nurse that he was hoping for never came. The room remained silent and dim. The snoring and the beeping continued, unconcerned about his desire to be free.

An eternity seemed to pass as Danny waited for someone to come. The snoring continued unabated as did the beeping of the monitor. Danny wondered if maybe he could free himself. His hands were free to move, only his wrists were pinned to the bed.

Danny slid his fingers towards to edge of the bed. The sensation of his fingers moving over the sheet felt strange. He swore his fingertips detected each individual thread woven into the bedding. He plucked at the sheet and rubbed it between his thumb and index finger. The material was painfully rough and scratchy. He should not have been able to tell soft from rough. The calluses on his hands were thick from years of working on car engines. The feel of the sheet made no sense.

Danny didn't like being confused. He wondered how long he had been unconscious. Could he have been here so long that his calluses were gone? Danny suddenly wanted a mirror so he could see himself, but all he had was a distorted view from the steel wall across the room.

He wanted answers and that meant getting out of his restraints. Danny wiggled and flexed his right wrist. As he worked, he heard tiny pops and an occasional rippling sound as the restraint slowly loosened. He kept at it until he had enough space to turn his arm over. His fingers explored the strap that held his wrist to the bar at the edge of the mattress.

He felt a tiny gap between the upper and lower surfaces of the strap. Danny probed that gap with his index finger. The upper surface scratched across his fingernail while the lower surface was soft. "Velcro," he whispered. Danny knew that, with a little patience, he could free himself.

His finger continued to push its way into that small gap. There were many beeps of the monitor before he was able to work a second finger into that loosening seam. With two fingers in the gap, he could push in opposite directions at the same time. The Velcro separated with a tearing noise. The small gap became a large opening and his hand slipped free. Danny didn't wait to see if anyone would come to protest his accomplishment. He reached across and gave two quick tugs on the strap holding his left wrist. There was a tearing sound and he was free.

Danny used both arms to push himself into a sitting position. The room spun for a moment before Danny could find the straps that held his feet. He reached for the first of those straps, but his fingers faltered as he saw what lay just past the ankle restraints. The feet sticking up at the end of the bed could not be his. They were… well…wrong in so many ways.

The two feet strapped to the bed were almost as wide as they were long. They were nothing like Danny's 10Ds. Did feet even come in a 6Z? Thick slabs of callus showed on the stubby toes. But the most striking feature was the carper of thick, dark curls that covered the upper surface of those strange feet. Even the toes had curly hair all the way down to the toenails. Those feet could not be real. It had to be some kind of a joke.

Danny pinched several of the hairs between his fingers and yanked. There was pain as three long, dark hairs pulled free of that foot. He opened his fingers and watched the hairs fall to the blanket. How could those things be a part of him? But apparently, they were.

Danny wondered what else had changed while he slept. He lifted the blanket that covered his legs and tossed it to the floor. Two short, powerful legs connected those hairy feet to his body. Those legs were more muscular than any part of Danny's body had ever been. Danny stared at his arms, finally realizing that they were also short and heavily muscled. Strong hands began to move up a body that Danny didn't recognize. They came to a stop when they found the tangle of thick curls on the top of his head. Even his short, straight hair was gone.

Danny wondered briefly if the hospital had him on something that caused hallucinations. But did hallucinations include his sense of touch? He wasn't sure, but he doubted hallucinations included touch and pain. What he wanted and needed was to see his own reflection. Then he might be able to believe.

He craned his neck to scan the entire room. There weren't any mirrors that he could use to study his reflection. He would have to make do with the vague shapes visible in the surface of the steel wall. Danny reached out and pulled apart the Velcro holding those strange feet in place. Those legs and feet twitched and it felt really good to move them closer to his body.

Danny peered over the edge of the bed. The floor seemed a long way down now that he was so short. Danny rolled and slid his feet over the side of the bed. Instead of being clumsy, those wide feed and pudgy toes found purchase on each crossbar and projection from the side of the bed. Climbing down was almost too easy. The only problem was the cool flow of air through the opening at the back of the johnny he was wearing. As his feet settled to the floor, Danny reached behind his back to tie the johnny closed.

Glancing up at the dark window, Danny wondered if whoever was up there had gotten a great view as he climbed down. Then he shrugged. It wasn't like there was anything he could do about it. Danny walked slowly toward the closest wall. He watched the child-like reflection that matched him step for step.

The image in the steel wasn't as clear as Danny would have liked. But there was little doubt that the small form was really him. It stepped when he stepped and its arms moved when his did. Danny didn't stop until he was close enough to touch the wall. His hand came up instinctively, reaching for the gown-clad figure standing in front of him. Danny felt his fingers twitch as if they were confused. Danny realized with a start that the stained white gown with the blue diamond pattern had no pockets for his fingers to dip into. There was nothing for those twitching fingers to explore. Danny gaped at his hand as memories of that dream park rushed back. The hand was suddenly familiar. He raised both hands up before his face. These hands had seemed magical as they emptied pockets and purses without fail. But how could they be here in the real world? Or had he somehow been transported to the land of his dreams?

The change was more than Danny could process. He needed to focus on something else before this new reality could make him crazy. The rumbling snore repeated again. Danny turned away from his reflection. Finding the source of that reassuring sound had to be easier than understanding what had happened to him.

Danny walked around the bed where he had been held captive. Where the side of his room to the left of his bed had been empty, this side of the room was more than a bit cluttered. Carts lined most of the far wall. Several held drawers that begged to be explored while several more had monitors that were dark and lifeless.

A single monitor was lit up. A green light on its front face flashed in time with the beeps. Two large IV bags hung above the flashing light on long poles. A clear fluid filled one bag and a brownish fluid filled the other. Tubes carried both fluids into the backside of the beeping device. Another tube carried the mixture down towards an immense tangle lying on the floor.

The snoring that had been his companion since he awoke came from a pile of hospital mattresses that lay at the end of the IV tube. Danny paused as his mind struggled to take in the figure lying on those mattresses. The sanity Danny had sought when he turned from his own reflection was not going to be found on this side of the room either.

A man, or was he some kind of giant, lay sprawled across those mattresses. Danny had never seen anyone that tall before, not on the Wizards or any other NBA team. It wasn't just that the giant was tall, the dude was at least twice the size of any NFL linebacker. Danny wasn't sure that even the Hulk had muscles that big. This thing could not be real and yet it lay before him covered by an oversized blanket.

Danny edged closer to study his new roommate. It was like staring at a fairy tale come to life. An overly broad face stuck out from under the blanket. Two large eyes sat below the giant's thick brow. The comically huge nose should have been its most prominent feature. Instead, it was the giant's mouth that captured Danny's attention. Thick lips fluttered in the breeze of its every breath. Each time it exhaled, Danny could see the two large incisors rising out of the giant's lower jaw. They were more like tusks with flat tops than teeth.

Danny started to back away. Better to let sleeping giants lie. Then the figure shifted in its sleep and Danny froze. The giant's snoring was replaced by the rattling of metal on metal. Danny didn't relax until the giant began to snore once more.

The desire to back away was still there. The giant was so much bigger than Danny felt at that moment. But that noise had been unexpected. Why would the giant rattle when it moved? Danny silently cursed his own curiosity as his fingers reached for the frayed edge of the blanket.

It only took a gentle tug to pull the blanket from the giant's sleeping form. The giant never noticed the loss of his covering, but to Danny's dismay, he himself did. Apparently, giant-sized johnnies were in short supply. Danny picked up the blanket and tossed it over the parts of the giant's body that he really did not want exposed.

With decency restored, Danny examined the giant. The source of the rattling noise was as obvious as the giant's nakedness had been. Heavy steel manacles were locked around the big man's wrists and ankles. There was also a chain wrapped several times around the giant's knees. The chain was secured with the largest lock that Danny had ever seen.

Someone had gone to a lot of trouble to make sure his roommate could not move.

Seeing the giant trussed up this way triggered a protective response in Danny's small body. Kind of stupid, he thought, me protecting him. But the sight of the IV needle jammed into the giant's arm just intensified the feeling that the giant needed someone to look after him. Danny wasn't sure he was the right person to look after anybody, but someone had to do it.

Danny scowled as he considered the giant's plight. His own Velcro straps had been bad enough, but manacles and chains were just plain harsh. What had either of them done to deserve any of this? He wondered if the giant had any idea what was going on? Or if it knew why Danny wasn't himself anymore? Danny wasn't sure what the giant knew, but he was going to find out.

Danny reached out and rolled the lock over. It was a standard Master Lock with a four number combination. A thousand possible choices could take quite a while to check. Even if he opened the lock, there were still the manacles to deal with. Danny began spinning the first dial as he considered his options. The numbers rotated easily. There was a soft click as each number settled into place. But when the dial reached the number 3, Danny's wondrous new fingers felt the dial sink a fraction of an inch lower.

Danny spun the dial in both directions, coming back each time to 3. Yes, he was sure of it. There was definitely a difference in that position. Danny began to spin each of the remaining dials until he felt each settle the same way. Danny looked down at the lock. The face showed 3773. Danny grinned and squeezed the two parts of the lock together. When he let go, the lock popped open.

Danny removed the lock from the chain before standing up. The confidence that he had felt in the dream world came rushing back. Danny stared down at the keyholes on the manacles. He knew he could open them as well. He just needed some tools. Danny reached across the giant's body and turned off the IV. The beeping sound came to a stop as the lights on the front of the box went dark.

Danny grinned as he faced the drawers waiting to be explored.

His mind was filled with soft white clouds. The cloud had a name, but he could not remember it. He had a name too, but it was lost in the white clouds. Feelings chased each other around in the recesses of his mind. Anger, fear, and loneliness. He knew there should be more, but that was lost in the cloud too.

In time, he began to see things in the cloud. Small random thoughts escaped the cloud. Some of those thoughts flew away beyond his reach. Some came close enough to grab. Those thoughts became words. Small words but he held them tightly so they could not get away again. The first word that he captured was 'fog.' He understood that this was the name of the white clouds that filled his head.

He caught another thought and he remembered that his name was Geoff. Other thoughts came at him and he became confused. There were too many to hold at once. Was he really Geoff? The next thought showed him an image of a child. The child had called him something else, a name that started with an F. But it was a big word and big words were hard to hold onto.

The fog continued to disappear. Memories began to bubble up from somewhere to mix with the thoughts he had captured. Big words hadn't always been hard. Once upon a time he had gone to a place called school. No, it was called a… It took time to dig that big word from those memories. That place was called university.

Geoff became aware that he lay on something hard. He tried to shift positions, but his hands and feet didn't move properly. They hardly moved at all. Geoff lay still trying to remember more. Something had been wrong with him. He had been sick. Did sick make your parts stop working? He wasn't sure.

He remembered that sick felt very bad. It hurt. He did not feel bad now. Everything felt good except thinking and moving his arms and legs. Maybe it was the fog's fault that he could not move. But Geoff didn't think so.

Maybe, Geoff thought, he should open his eyes and see where he was. Maybe then he could remember something that would help him to move. Geoff cracked open one eyelid. The place he was in was kind of dark. Geoff was glad. Even that much light was painful.

Geoff closed his eyes and waited for a memory. It took a while, but he remembered a beeping noise. That noise was gone now. The beeping had been replaced by a much nicer sound. Geoff kept his eyes closed as he thought about the new sound. Whistling. Someone was whistling and it sounded nice.

Geoff opened both eyes to see who was making the wonderful… music. A small boy stood right in front of him. For a moment, Geoff that it was the same child that had called him Fez something. But no, Geoff thought. That had been a dream. This boy was different. This boy did not have any shoes and his feet were very hairy. This new boy was holding a piece of shiny metal in his hand. It took a minute for Geoff to remember its name. It was a lock.

The boy stared at Geoff for a long time, tapping his foot and twirling the lock on his finger like he was waiting for something. Geoff wasn't sure what the boy wanted. Was Geoff supposed to do something? Finally, the boy shook his head and asked, "Do you speak? Can you understand me?"

Geoff thought the questions were silly. He wasn't dumb or anything like that. But his mouth felt funny, so Geoff just nodded his head.

The boy's hand that wasn't spinning the lock pointed at the room around them. The boy's voice sounded hopeful as he asked, "Any idea where we are or what is going on?"

Geoff took a quick look around him. Shiny walls were on every side. They were familiar, but Geoff could not find a clear memory of them. He looked back at the boy and shook his head. The boy did not get angry when Geoff couldn't answer his question. Geoff was glad.

The boy stared at Geoff for a while. "I thought you said you could talk?"

Geoff tried to reach up to touch his mouth to see why it wasn't working right. But again, he could not move his arms. Geoff concentrated really hard and forced his mouth to open. A deep rumble that sounded like someone else's voice rasped out, "Can no move. Not like it. Help?"

The boy dropped to one knee and stared into Geoff's eyes. "Before I help you, I need to be sure I can trust you. You are very big. You might hurt me."

Geoff shook his head but the boy didn't move to help him. The boy asked another hard question. "Why are you chained up like this?"

It took Geoff a long time to think of an answer. "No know. Wake up dis way. Neber hurts you."

The boy did not seem to believe Geoff. He just asked more hard questions. "I was a student at Georgetown University. The last thing I remember was getting sick and going to the hospital. Have you ever heard of Georgetown?"

Geoff felt his mouth open and close as words slipped from his mind before he could get them out. It took all of his concentration but he finally managed to get some words out. "Me go dat place too. Birus make sick."

The boy seemed surprised. "You from GU too? Do I know you?"

This time Geoff's words came a little easier. "Yes, dat place. Me be Geoff. Wrestle."

Recognition flashed on the boy's face and then confusion. "You are the Olympic wrestler that joined the team? Everybody has heard of you. But I didn't think you were a heavyweight."

Geoff did not know what to say to the boy.

The boy began to walk back and forth taking occasional looks in Geoff's direction. Finally, he stopped and knelt once more. "Maybe you changed too. I wasn't always this small. I will get you out of your manacles, but you have to promise to protect me. You are big and I am very small. Is it a deal?"

Geoff smiled happily. That was an easy deal. He really wanted a friend right now and he liked this boy. "Me promise. Not know you name."

The boy winked at him and said, "My name is Danny."

91

"Hello Dan-ny." Geoff worked very hard to remember that name as he watched the boy pick up several strange looking things from a pile on the floor. The boy named Dan-ny moved down to Geoff's feet and began to poke things at the metal wrapped around Geoff's ankles. Geoff felt the metal release one leg and then the other. Geoff sighed in relief. "Tank you," he whispered.

Little Dan-ny moved closer to Geoff's hands. He gave Geoff a hard look and said, "Don't forget your promise." Then Dan-ny began working on the bands that circled Geoff's wrists. The boy was even quicker this time. Geoff began to laugh as the strange metal bands fell away. Geoff's arms were stiff and sore, but they were free.

Geoff lay still until the boy moved back and then he stood up. His blanket fell to the ground fallowed by chains that pooled at Geoff's feet. Geoff stared down at himself. Something was not as he remembered. Then he realized he had no clothes. Geoff knew that wearing clothes was a rule, so he reached down and grabbed the blanket. His big hands were stiff, but he managed to tie the blanket around his waist.

The boy Dan-ny backed up as Geoff came to his feet. Geoff gave him a crooked smile. "Dan-ny be a good boy."

Geoff's legs and arms and even his back hurt. Rubbing them helped, but it was not enough. Geoff knew there was something he was supposed to do when he hurt this way. Images flowed into Geoff's mind. He began to move, slowly at first and then with increasing confidence. He could not keep the pictures in his head in the right order. It was just too hard. But his body remembered for him. At first, the moves hurt. But as his body warmed up, the pain turned into pleasure.

The boy just stood and watched him. Geoff soon forgot his new friend as his mind sank into the dance.

---

The screams in the crowd slowly faded away to be replaced by a slow, steady beeping noise from somewhere behind her head. Alicia felt a thin, hard mattress beneath her body. Memories of the hospital and being sick flowed through her mind. She was finally awake again. Awake wasn't so great if she had to suffer in an uncomfortable hospital bed. But why was her bed so uncomfortable? She had fallen asleep in a really soft bed in the private room her mother had demanded for her. Who would dare to defy Mother by moving her?

Alicia's eyes snapped open. The soft blue walls and the large window of her private room were gone. They had been replaced with steel walls that felt more like a prison cell than a place to heal. Anger flooded her system as reality replaced the joy of her dream. She wanted to go back to the world of that dream. She wanted the violence and the crowd calling for her. She desperately needed to find a way back to that place. Alicia knew that she belonged there.

A familiar voice whispered in the back of her mind, "Patience, daughter."

Her jaw opened wide as the urge to yawn overwhelmed her. The deep breath she drew in was immensely satisfying. She noted with satisfaction that there was no pain when her lungs expanded. In fact, nothing hurt anymore. She obviously wasn't sick so there was no reason to lie here in this substandard room. She reached for the bedrail to pull herself up, but her arm was pinned to the mattress. Alicia tried her other arm, but it was pinned too.

Alicia jerked her arms in irritation, but whatever held her arms in place did not give at all. Turning her head to the side, she glared down at her arm, cursing it for not responding. Alicia blinked in surprise at what lay beside her on the bed. Gone was the tan she had spent weeks in a tanning bed to perfect for her vacation in Florida. Her tan had been replaced by the night-black skin from her dream. That slender arm stretched from the sleeve of a tasteless hospital gown to the side of the bed. A thick white strap stood in sharp contrast to the black wrist it pinned to the bed frame.

Alicia turned her head to check her other arm. Her left arm had the same perfect black skin. That wrist was also bound by a white strap. Anger blossomed as she began to understand her helplessness. She was being held prisoner.

At the same time, there was a sense of excitement. Those were the arms that had opened the curtains on the stage. Was it possible that she could be all that she had been in that dream? Could all that power be hers? The dream voice had promised it to her, but Alicia hadn't really believed.

That dream, if it was even possible, was in her future. For the time being, she had enough power to make them let her go. She was the daughter of Congresswoman Condemn from the State of New York. They wouldn't dare keep her here against her will. Allica raised her voice, "I am awake now. Take these stupid straps off my arms so I can get up." The lights remained low. The only response to her demands was the annoying beeping.

Alicia tried to look around the room. There was little she could see from flat on her back. Her private nurse hadn't even given her a pillow. The woman was so going to be fired. Mother's reference would end her career.

Still, no one came to her. The room appeared empty except for the metal walls that glowed in the low lighting and a dark window high on the wall in front of her. She stared up at that glass hoping for a sign that someone was up there. Someone behind that glass had to have heard her. And yet, no light showed through the glass. The only lights were small red dots to either side of that dark glass.

She focused on those tiny lights, hoping without any real hope that she could see something without the thick glasses she had been forced to wear since early childhood. Her eyes were so bad that even contacts had not been an option. But somehow, here in the dim light, she could make out two small black cameras. Their lenses were focused on her. Her temper began to flare once more. Those red lights had to mean that someone was watching her, possibly even recording her. That someone needed to get down here and release her from this damn bed.

Both of her hands clenched into fists as she yelled, "Get down here and let me out of this bed! Now! Or I will make sure you are fired from this hospital!" Alicia expected an immediate response. They had to know who she was. But the window remained dark and the room remained silent except for that annoying beep. Her anger blazed as she yelled once again. "When Congresswoman Condemn finds out you had her daughter tied up like a criminal, this hospital is so getting sued!"

No doors opened. No feet came running. The window remained dark and the cameras continued to watch her. Her anger turned to rage. The rage felt good. It warmed her inside. There was power in that rage, if only she could learn to harness it. Her yelling became a shriek as she threatened lawsuits and legal action.

As she continued to rant at her captors, thoughts of the things she had seen and done in the dream came back to her. Threats of legal action became promises of personal vengeance. And then her words promised violence, torture, and even death. Her voice grew hoarse and still there was no response. Was it possible that she had been left here to die? Or didn't her captors realize what she was capable of? The voice from her dreams began to speak to her once more, "We will teach them when it is time."

Her anger brought exhaustion and eventually sleep. There was also anger in her sleep because the dream did not return.

---

The dream came to an end, but it didn't really. The words from the book sill pulsed in her mind, she just did not know how to pronounce them anymore. The small body that had felt so right was still hers. Ruth didn't have to look to know it was true. How could it not be? A racoon that she just knew was Coon was freeing her from the straps that held her to the hospital bed. She wasn't sick anymore and nothing hurt. And then the soft form of Coon was in her arms. Everything was good except maybe that Coon needed a bath really bad.

# Chapter 10
# Discord

*National Institutes of Health (.gov)*
*Scientific Breakthrough of the Century*
*Jun 2, 2021 — One of the most promising areas of*
*research in recent years has been gene editing, including*
*CRISPR/Cas9, for fixing misspellings in genes to ...*

*Washington Times*
*Scandal over emails grows as White Hose denies ...*
*Jun 25, 2021 — White House press secretary insisted today*
*that the laptop and emails are Russian disinformation*
*being spread to discredit President Bendi and his son ...*

*New York Post*
*Was Caufi untruthful about gain-of-function research?*
*Jul 7, 2021 6:35 a.m. ET. --- Newly released documents appear*
*to contradict Dr Anita Caufi's statements to Congress*
*about research conducted at Wuhan ...*

John paused in the doorway of the outer office to take a careful sip from the cup of hot coffee in his right hand. He groaned as the sensation of the dark liquid bathed his taste buds. As he intended, the 30-something (John knew better than to ask what that something was) brunette sitting at the desk outside his office door looked up and glared at him.

The woman began to tap her long nails on the surface of her desk. John just grinned at her. She shook her head and pushed herself back from the desk. "It's been a long morning already. I think I need about a four-hour lunch break to make it through the rest of the day."

John began to laugh as he walked through the door. He pulled his left hand out from behind his back revealing a second large cup. "And a fine morning to you too, Trish." He stopped in front of her desk. Placing the cup in the center of the desk, he bowed deeply. "For you, your Majesty. Mountain blend with two sugar and light cream. The pot was fresh this morning."

Trish's bubbly laughter joined his as she wrapped her hands around the white Styrofoam cup. Her thumb quickly pried the black plastic lid from the cup. She stared at the cup as steam rose into the air. John watched her sniff appreciatively before taking a drink. Then she grinned up at him. "If you don't like answering your own phone, I suggest you remember that your Majesty line. I think I like it almost as much as the coffee."

John chuckled. "I will do my best to keep that in mind, Milady." John took a seat in the chair to the left of her desk, leaning back as he took another drink from his own cup. "Anything I need to worry about this morning?"

She put her cup down, frowning. "Chief Barreau was here about half an hour ago. He requests that you join him in the observation room when you have a spare moment. Sooner if you can manage it."

John sighed as he stood up. "So much for catching up on paperwork. You know where to find me, Trish." John turned and headed back to the elevator.

He pressed the button and the door opened immediately. Even the ride down to face whatever problem had arisen was far too short. The doors reopened before John could take more than another sip of coffee. He wasn't going to get much caffeine into his system this way.

He did manage to swipe his badge and open the door without spilling his coffee. Maybe he would get lucky and this wouldn't be so bad. That hope died as soon as John got a glimpse through the door. The large room was full of people. John scanned the crowd. The entire security team appeared to be in the room including Michel's containment team. Their conversations were loud as people peered through three of the four windows. Other members of security were leaning over computer screens staring intently at whatever the camera feeds had picked up. There was a tension in the room that John had not felt since Cambridge.

John tried to slip into the room unnoticed. But every head turned in his direction as soon as the door closed. With one exception, their attention shifted right back to what they had been studying when John opened the door. That exception was Chief Barreau. The Chief broke off his discussion with the containment team and came to meet John.

John indicated the people scattered around the room with his half-full cup. "What's going on? Or am I better off not knowing?"

John could not read the Chief's expression as the man replied, "All of our guests woke up last night, Mr Boboden."

John took another sip from the cup as he considered what to do next. "Has medical examined them yet? If they aren't dangerous, we can consider releasing them from their restraints."

John was about to take another sip of his coffee when the Chief replied, "None of them has been examined yet, sir. The medical staff refuses to enter any of the rooms."

John coughed as the coffee seemed to stick in his throat. "Why?" John asked.

Chief Barreau motioned towards the three windows that his staff were taking turns staring through. "Because four of the five are already out of their restraints and the fifth appears homicidal at best."

John took a deep breath before asking, "What was Dr Morrall's recommendation?"

A look of exasperation flashed across the security chief's face. "And I quote, sir, 'Just shoot them all and be done with it. But do not damage any tissues that we need to analyze.'"

John dropped his cup in the trash can near the door. He had lost his taste for coffee. "Show me what you have, Chief. Someone other than the good doctor needs to make a rational decision."

Chief Barreau turned and walked to the second window. John followed along, wondering how things could had gotten so screwed up overnight. The security personnel in front of the window scattered, giving their boss some privacy to speak with management.

John looked down at the young woman who was now no taller than a four-year-old. Ruth sat on her hospital bed rocking a raccoon in her arms. She looked like a child cuddling a beloved pet. John sounded curious as he asked Barreau, "How did Ruth get out of her restraints? And how did she get the collar off the raccoon?"

Chief Barreau began to laugh. "Wrong on both counts, sir. Don't feel bad though. That was my assumption too."

The Chief stepped to the monitor beside the window and began clicking with the mouse. He motioned for John to join him. As they stared down at the screen, a video began to play.

John watched as a small black nose poked from between the bars on the front of the crate they had used to confine the raccoon. The nose was quickly replaced by a furred arm. The tiny hand at the end of that arm easily opened the crate door. The raccoon darted towards the camera and disappeared.

Barreau began to speak as the room appeared empty for a long segment. "It appears to understand the camera's field of view. It's staying where it can't be detected. Or it did until it went to help the girl." Michel jabbed a finger at the screen as the raccoon rushed to the bed and scampered up the side.

John watched in amazement as the raccoon released the girl. The chief paused the video as the girl wrapped the racoon in her arms. Barreau appeared unconcerned as he continued, "They haven't moved from that spot since the girl was freed. We enhanced the audio, but there isn't anything useful in the girl's rambling. Just some idle chatter about meeting in a forest somewhere."

"Analysis?" John asked his security chief.

Barreau stepped back to the window and stared down at the two figures on the hospital bed. "Raccoons are clever. It is conceivable that an animal could have escaped from that crate."

"But you don't think so," John prompted.

"No, sir." Barreau moved up to rest on the glass. "I think her human mind is in that furry body. Hiding from the cameras isn't something a raccoon would do."

John considered Barreau's words. "I assume your team will keep a close eye on the raccoon. I want reports on any other unusual behavior."

The Chief nodded. Then he turned and motioned his staff away from the next window. "If you think the raccoon was a bit odd, wait until you see what is happening behind door number three." Barreau walked to the next window and stared through it.

John moved to stand beside Chief Barreau. He stared through the tinted glass looking for the two young men imprisoned below. The activity in the room below should not have been possible. Danny's small form should still be strapped into the hospital bed on the right side of the room. Only, he wasn't. Geoff's larger form should have been comatose on the pile of mattresses on the left side of the room. John had agreed with Dr Morrall that waking the large man was too risky at this stage. But Geoff was obviously not sedated anymore and his military grade restraints were missing from his ankles and wrists. John didn't understand how either of them could have gotten free.

Now, the childlike form of the thief, Danny, sat on a pile of mattresses that had been Geoff's bed. Danny was methodically dismantling something that might once have been Geoff's IV pump. Danny carefully examined each piece he removed from the guts of the pump. Occasionally, he added a piece to a small pile of medical instruments by his right knee. The rest were tossed behind him to bounce off the wall. What possible use could Danny have for a stethoscope or any of the random pieces of electronics in Danny's pile? But if Danny's actions were incomprehensible, an even bigger mystery pranced around in the back of the room.

John could hardly believe his eyes. In the open area near the bathroom door, Geoff was dancing without a partner. John watched as Geoff moved in circles, sometimes reversing direction for no apparent reason. Geoff's arms and legs, feet and hands, moved in complicated patterns as he danced. Each of the big man's moves seemed carefully choreographed.

As John watched Geoff's strange performance, he thought about the first 'ogre' that they had created in the lab at Cambridge. Geoff was larger than the 'ogre' that had killed Kevin. John wasn't sure Geoff was any more sane than his predecessor, but at least Geoff wasn't smashing equipment or breaking down doors. Or, John added mentally, killing little Danny.

John gestured as Geoff spun in a tight circle with his arms extended, "How long has he been dancing like this?"

Chief Barreau stared intently as Geoff came to a stop and bowed towards the window. "He isn't dancing, Mr Boboden. What you are seeing is called Kata. He is actually quite talented."

John was confused. "I am sorry, Chief. I have never heard that term before. What is Kata?"

Barreau turned from the window to stare into John's eyes. "It is a martial arts term, Mr Boboden. Kata is a series of training exercises used by many different disciplines to train without a partner." The Chief gestured towards the window. "What you just watched was a fairly advanced series of Judo moves. Your test subject has been well trained in martial arts."

"How dangerous does that make him?" John blurted out as memories of the Marine Corporal flooded back.

Barreau turned back to the window. "Very and not at all."

"What the hell does that mean?" John asked.

The Chief pointed at the window as Geoff began to move once more. "Watch the precision as he moves his hands and feet. Each motion flows into the next. I was pretty good at hand-to-hand when I was a Marine. I am a brown belt in Judo. Your test subject is way, way beyond my skill level."

Concern bordering on fear was in John's voice as he spoke, "Then he is dangerous."

The Chief shook his head. "If you want to know if he could be dangerous, then the answer is yes. If you want to know if I think he is dangerous, then the answer is no. The forms he is practicing require an incredible amount of self-discipline. I think it would take a lot to provoke him. Something on the order of hurting his little friend down there. I, for one, have no intention of trying to set him off."

John listened to the Chief's calm assessment and his fear began to slip away. Finally, John nodded. Barreau knew his business. But there was still something that bothered him about the scene below. "How did they get free?"

The Chief led him to another monitor. Several members of Barreau's team moved reluctantly away from the video they were watching. The Chief paused the video and then set the video playback for 3:47 that morning. He changed the playback speed to 2x and pressed play.

John watched the high-speed playback that showed Danny working his way free from the straps holding him to the bed. Danny made his escape look so simple. The video continued and John watched Danny approaching Geoff's sleeping form. John winced as Danny turned off the IV that kept Geoff sedated. Then the small thief proceeded to removed Geoff's restraints. Danny easily picked the locks on the chain and both sets of manacles. Barreau paused the playback as Geoff began to rise.

John whispered, "How?"

The Chief just shrugged, "I haven't a clue, sir. We knew he was good with stealing car parts, but nothing in his profile suggested this level of skill. We will be adjusting some of our protocols to make sure he can't escape."

John turned from the monitor. "Good. I don't want to find him sitting at my desk one morning."

The Chief grinned at the thought. "Understood. But neither of those boys are your real concern."

"Then who is?" John asked.

Barreau led John to the next window.

A lone figure appeared to be sleeping in the hospital bed below. John studied that motionless form carefully. Her arms were still strapped to the bed. John felt an immense sense of relief at the sight of the restraints on her wrists. Of all the changed that Morrall's serum had created so far, this woman disturbed him the most and he had no idea why.

John's gaze moved to that dark face, almost human looking and yet so alien. It wasn't that her skin was blacker than any black that John had ever seen. Or that her white hair appeared to take on a life of its own as it caressed that dark skin. It wasn't even the ears that were even more pointed than Jacob's. All of those were things he could accept. Given time, he might even have been able to accept those too perfect features that made her seem other than human. In the end, it was her lavender eyes that glowed with hatred as she stared up at him.

John felt a moment of panic as he realized she wasn't asleep like he had thought. Her hate-filled eyes glared up at the window that now seemed an inadequate barrier. Those lavender orbs were locked on him. John knew there was no way she could see him through that tinted glass, but a part of him still felt exposed to those predatory eyes.

With an effort of will, John pushed aside the fear growing in his subconscious. The Chief had warned him that this woman was a problem, but why? She wasn't doing anything but lying in her bed. There had to be something that he was missing. John finally asked, "Why is she a problem?" John added mentally, "Other than she scares me."

At John's questioning look, Barreau turned to another monitor and selected a video sequence to play back. This time he did not speed the video up. Instead, he turned the volume up to maximum. The room went silent as the dark figure on the screen began to yell. John stepped away from the window when her threats of legal action turned to promises of physical violence. The vivid descriptions of what she intended to do to her captors made the horror movies of John's youth seem childish. The menace in her voice made it hard to dismiss her words. Looking at the faces of the security team, John realized that every one of them took the threats as seriously as he did.

The playback ended, but the silence in the room continued. Barreau waited patiently as John considered everything he had seen. The Chief looked surprised as John finally spoke. "I want to speak with each of them. Now. Or as soon as you can have your team ready."

A slight hesitation preceded Barreau's response. "All of them, Mr Boboden?"

John sighed. "Yes, Chief." John motioned to the nearby window. "But I will let you assess the crazy one first. Feel free to override me."

Chief Barreau was a soldier, he didn't waste time arguing with orders. He started to turn away when John asked, "Do we have clothing for them?"

Barreau nodded. "For the most part. Shoes were a challenge. Slippers were the best we could do for several of them. The giant is lucky we found sweatpants and a t-shirt. Goodwill didn't have much his size."

John stared at the windows knowing what he needed to do. "Do what you can for food and bottled water. They need to eat. I would like everything ready as soon as possible."

The Chief turned and began issuing orders. "Containment team get your gear. You will be right outside each door when Mr Boboden goes in. Triple tap on the tactical frequency and you will neutralize the threat. Everyone else, I want food, clothing, and water stationed outside each door. Understood?"

There was a chorus of ayes and yesses Chief as the room began to empty. Barreau followed them out. He paused at the door long enough to say, "I really don't think this is a good idea." And then he was gone and John was alone with his thoughts.

An hour later, John stood outside containment room 4. Chief Barreau stood before the door in body armor with a tactical headset on and a military-grade taser on his belt. The ex-Marine looked like he was about to step onto the battlefield. John swallowed hard, wondering what he had gotten himself into. He waited until the Chief looked his way before he asked, "Any particular reason you want to start with her? The other rooms seem less… intense."

Chief Barreau winked at him. "Maybe she will be scary enough that you stop taking risks and let my team handle the other rooms. You can always watch from the observation room."

John had to admit that the idea was tempting, but he just shook his head. "No, Chief. This is my responsibility. I want to be able to look at myself in the mirror when this is done. Especially if anything goes wrong."

Barreau sighed. "Fine, but if this does go bad then you will be removed from the room."

---

Michel tapped his headset and spoke softly, "Bring up the lights. Fast. I want her blinded." Then he took two breaths and closed his own eyes before opening the door.

Michel stepped from a well-lit hallway into what felt like blazing sunshine. He entered the lioness's den with only a bottle of water in his left hand. He slowly opened his eyes to study the hospital bed sitting in the middle of the room. A dark figure lay on that bed clad only in a thin hospital johnny, a white blanket covering her lower body. Michel watched as the woman blinked rapidly in the bright light. He wasn't happy about how quickly she recovered her sight.

He had only taken a few steps towards the bed when her eyes focused on him. She growled at him in an obvious effort to intimidate him. Michel ignored it. He had known mess sergeants who did scary better than she did.

Her first two words were raspy from all the yelling she had done that morning. "You dare?!"

Michel ignored both the words and the woman's tone. He tossed the water bottle on the bed between her legs and stepped back. The woman's fingers twitched as she eyed the bottle with obvious longing. A swollen black tongue came out and licked at her dark lips. She turned her lavender eyes on him and glared. "Bastard!"

"Yes, I am," Michel replied. Then he motioned towards the water. "If we can agree on a few ground rules then you can have it. Decide to play nice and you get something to drink. Or, I can come back tomorrow and try again."

Michel watched as she fought to keep the intensity of her anger from showing on her face. Her efforts were useless. Enough of what she felt slipped out that he would never trust her. Finally, she calmed herself enough to ask, "And if I don't play nice?"

Michel reached down to his belt and pulled the taser from its holster. "This is a military-grade taser. If I expend the full charge, I could probably take down a rhino. In someone your size, it just might stop your heart."

She stared at the taser. Instead of fear, he saw anticipation. In that instant, Michel thought she was eager to take him on. But a heartbeat later, her face went flat and emotionless. Well, almost flat. There was a slight smile on her lips that only promised more trouble to come. The smile grew as she taunted him, "Do you truly believe I fear you or your toy? You would not dare use that thing if you had any idea who I am."

Michel shook his head. "Lady, I don't care who you are or what you fear. I have a job to do. I protect the people in this facility. The moment I think you are a risk to anyone under my protection, I will take you down. Do you understand that?"

She stared at him thoughtfully. "Hmm. Knight in shining armor or paid mercenary? Is it honor that drives you or does your loyalty have a price? How much would it cost to shift that loyalty to me?"

Barreau's eyes became hard and he raised the taser in her direction.

She sighed dramatically. "An honorable fool then. I could have offered much and not just money. So be it, it is your loss. What are these rules of yours?"

Michel kept the taser where she could see it clearly. He didn't like her. Not at all. Thankfully, liking her wasn't part of his duties. "I free one arm so you can drink. You do not try to free your other arm. If you do, I use this." Michel wiggled the taser in his hand.

She nodded. "And that is all?"

Michel replied, "My boss is about to come in here to talk with you. No problems and no more threats. I don't like threats."

She glanced down at the water bottle again. Then she answered. "I agree, Sir Knight."

Michel stepped forward and yanked the strap on her right arm. He watched as her hand unclenched. Long dark nails stuck out from each of her slender fingers. Michel was willing to bet those nails were sharp enough to cut him. She lifted the bottle to her mouth. She bit down on the cap and twisted the bottle open. The incisor she revealed was longer and more pointed than any humans should be. She was a predator now. Had she always been one or was this a result of her change?

The woman spat the bottle top across the room and raised the bottle to her lips. She drained the bottle in seconds, crushing the thin plastic as she drank. When she finished, she dropped the bottle on the floor in front of him. "So, who is your boss? Does she have the power to release me? My mother will be quite generous."

Michel shook his head and keyed his radio. "Send him in, but be ready."

The door opened behind Michel. He wanted to turn and watch John Boboden's reaction to this woman, but only a fool would turn his back on her. To Michel's surprise, John's voice had the same bored tone it often did in staff meetings. "Good afternoon, Ms Condemn. My name is John Boboden. I am the director of this facility."

At John's greeting, the calculating expression on the woman's face became one of distain. Michel wasn't sure what triggered her sneer or the sudden demeaning tone in her voice. "Then you do know who I am. Are you really such a fool? When my mother finds out what you have done, your cell will be much worse than this one."

John's voice did not falter. "Ms Condemn, Alicia, all we have done is save your life. You were in critical condition. The Virus C in your system was slowly killing you. Since your life was in danger, my staff was forced to try an experimental drug treatment. Luckily, the treatment not only cured you, it also made you immune to the virus."

The woman lifted her free arm up where she could examine it. The smooth, darkness of her skin seemed to fascinate her. Finally, she turned to look at John. "And how will you explain the changes to my appearance, Director? Mother is unlikely to be pleased."

John's voice became soft and patronizing, like a parent explaining the obvious to a spoiled child. "That is an unfortunate side effect of the serum we used to save your life."

Michel tensed as the woman clenched her jaw in anger. Then her hand moved towards the strap holding her left arm to the bed. Michel gripped the taser tighter as he prepared to step between her and Boboden. But the hand stopped short of the strap. Her index finger pointed at the restraint and she whispered accusingly, "And those? You needed to tie me to the bed to save my life? How will you convince Mother of that?"

John stepped past Michel, almost within the woman's reach. The man's face was so calm that Michel could have sworn it was a mask. "We were, in fact, quite worried that you might harm yourself. Now, it also appears that there was reason to believe you might harm members of my staff. The straps were purely a safety precaution. I am sure your mother and any judge would agree once we show some excerpts from your outburst earlier this morning."

The woman bared her teeth in a snarl of rage; those sharp incisors shone in the bright overhead lights. The anger faded quickly from her face, but not from those lavender eyes. Her voice was calmer as she continued, "I see. Well then, since you say that I am cured, I assume that you will release me and allow me to return home."

John shook his head. "I am very sorry, Alicia. But until we fully understand the side effects of the serum, we must keep you here under careful observation."

She turned her head to face the far wall. She gave a dismissive wave of her hand. "I am tired now. You may leave so I can rest." Her voice dropped several octaves as she continued. "I will find a way to contact my mother and, you will pay for this insult."

John smiled, "There are a few things you should know before I leave, Ms Condemn. First, your mother would not recognize you right now. You do not resemble her daughter in any way. Second, the changes you have noted are at a genetic level. Not even a DNA test will support your claim to be the congresswoman's daughter. I have a great many more pressing concerns than the reactions of your mother. Goodbye for now, Alicia."

Michel sucked in his breath as John turned his back on the woman and began to walk towards the door. Michel watched her closely, but she did not move. He heard John's footsteps pause just before he began speaking again. "There are clothes in the box beside the door as well as food and more water. You are free to make use of them after we leave the room. But if you try to harm my staff, I will let the Chief deal with you as he sees fit."

Michel heard John turn the doorknob. Michel whispered a single word into the radio, "Exit."

The heavy door opened and Michel heard his boss's calm voice call for him, "Come along, Chief Barreau. She needs privacy while she changes."

Michel held the taser where it was visible as he backed out of the door that was being held open for him. Michel watched the woman reach for the strap holding her left hand to the bed. The sound of the Velcro was cut off as the door closed. The tension did not leave his body until he heard the lock engage.

Michel turned to see John Boboden leaning his forehead against the wall. The tension that had not shown in the room was now evident in the rigid set of his boss's back and shoulders. Michel's chuckle held little humor as he muttered, "Remind me not to play poker with you. Where did you learn to play hardball like that?"

John turned around slowly, leaning back against the wall. "Have you ever had to face a funding board that was looking to eliminate your project so they can reallocate your budget? Instead of one scared young woman, you have to face a room full of hungry accountants. You learn really quick not to show fear when the sharks are circling."

Michel watched as his boss stood up straight and gestured down the hall. "Let's move on. I want to get this over with before I lose my nerve."

Michel nodded and stepped past his team. "Yes, sir."

Michel led the way to the next door. Sitting beside it was a medical cart. Instead of monitors, the top shelf of the cart was loaded with food and water. Quite a bit of food, Michel thought. Then again, how much did an 'ogre' eat? The middle shelf had a set of children's clothing, a large pair of sweatpants and a lime-green t-shirt, the only 6x shirt they had been able to find. Michel hoped it would fit. Two pairs of slippers sat on the bottom shelf. Shoes weren't an option for either of the men on the other side of the door.

Michel hesitated as he raised his hand to swipe his badge. He carefully considered his next order. He really did not believe that the big man was dangerous. But would he risk his team on a gut feeling? No one was going to die this time. He would make sure of it.

He used his best drill sergeant voice to make sure everyone paid attention. "The ogre and the thief are not to be taken lightly. Neither of them. If there is a problem, use the full charge on the big man. It may take several of you to knock him down. "The thief is a different kind of risk. Do NOT let him get close enough to touch you. I don't want any badges or weapons getting lost in this room."

Five single clicks came in response to his orders. As he swiped his badge, the cart shifted away from the wall. Michel glanced right to see John standing behind the cart. The calm tone came back in Boboden's voice, "Together this time."

Michel nodded and pushed the door open. Stepping inside, he held the door open with the toe of his boot. His attention never wavered from the two figures across the room. At a whispered "In," Michel slid his foot out of the way and let the door swing closed.

The big man paused his kata and stared at the two men entering the room. His emotions were as easy to read as those of a small child. Confusion, curiosity, and even fear. Michel lowered his hand from the taser on his belt. There was no sign of anger or aggression in the man's face or posture. As Michel watched, the big man edged closer to the Thief. Whether the move was to protect or to be protected by the tiny man wasn't clear.

Michel almost smiled when the Thief stood and moved protectively in front of his larger companion. Seeing the two of them side by side was like a recreation of an old "Mutt and Jeff" comic strip. Michel just hoped that it remained as harmless.

John again stepped past Michel to confront their guests. The confident mask he had worn for the congresswoman's daughter was firmly in place. "Hello, Danny and Geoff. I apologize for making you wait this morning."

John gestured towards the cart behind him. "It took me a little while to round up clothing that would fit you. My name is John and I am in charge of this research facility."

The child-like figure took a step closer. "Are you the one that gave the order to lock my friend in chains?"

Michel started to speak, but John raised a hand to silence him. John turned to stare up into the big man's eyes. "I apologize for the way you were locked up, Geoff. You are very big and very strong. We were afraid you might hurt someone."

The giant sounded hurt as he replied, "No hurts nobody. Me promise."

The small figure seemed to relax a little at John's apology, but his questions continued. "What did you do to us? And where are we?"

"The Virus C in your systems was killing both of you. You were brought to this lab to receive an experimental treatment. It saved your lives, but as you can see, there were some side effects that we are still trying to understand."

Danny opened his mouth to ask another question, but Geoff placed a gentle hand on his shoulder. The big man patted his own stomach as he asked, "Eat? Bery hungry."

John began to back towards the door. There is clothing, food, and water on the cart by the door. I am sorry if things don't fit well, Geoff.

Clothing your size is not easy to find around here. Our lab is somewhat isolated. Eat, change, and we will talk again soon."

Danny looked ready to protest. John tried to reassure him. "I know you have more questions. Be patient and let Geoff eat. If you need more food, simply ask. Someone will be listening on the observation level."

Again, Michel backed out the door behind John. He pulled the door closed and turned to check on his boss. Boboden appeared lost in thought. Michel stepped closer and spoke in a low tone. "You ended that rather quickly. Are you okay? I don't think you need to worry about a repeat of what happened at Cambridge."

The faraway look in John's eyes cleared and he smiled. "Actually, I am doing better, Chief. And you are right, that was nothing like Cambridge. I don't think I really believed it until Geoff spoke. The Corporal never spoke. The only sounds we ever heard at Cambridge were his angry bellows. There was pain in Geoff's eyes, not the rage I expected to see. I think Geoff will be fine as long as we don't try to hurt Danny."

With a half grin, Michel replied. "I will make sure to warn everyone not to hurt the little guy."

This time, John led the way to the next door.

———————————

He waited as the Chief gave a few last-minute instructions. The containment team really wasn't necessary in John's opinion. Neither Ruth or the raccoon were any more dangerous than the occupants of the final room at the end of this hall. Jacob and Herrera might be locked in that last room, but that didn't mean either man was dangerous. John trusted them both. The lock simply meant that John had orders he didn't agree with.

John picked up the two small bags on the floor beside the door. One held clothing and the other food for Ruth and her friend. Then he reached for the doorknob. John felt a sense of anticipation as he wrapped his fingers around the knob. It was finally time to meet the young woman whose future had seemed so promising. If her bio was accurate, Ruth could change the world. John wondered if that was still possible now that Ruth had been changed. He hoped so. He needed to talk to her to see if she was still the same person he had read about. If so, John wanted to find a way to help her. But he didn't know if it was even possible to help her anymore.

The Chief moved to stand beside John. Barreau raised his badge and asked, "Ready?"

At John's nod, the badge slid across the surface of the lock. There was a sharp click and the doorknob rotated. John pushed the door open and stepped inside.

Nothing moved in the room. The only sound was a soft humming that came from a blanket pile up in the center of the bed. John slowly took several slow steps towards that bed. As he got closer, he could make out two sets of eyes peering out from beneath the blanket. John smiled as he eased forward and set the two bags on the end of the bed. John stepped back and waited patiently.

The blanket rose and then fell back onto the pillow at the head of the bed. A tiny girl rose to stand on the bed. Even standing on the bed, Ruth was still shorter than he was. A gray and black ball of fur slipped around to hide behind Ruth's legs.

It was like watching a child with her pet. Except that John knew she wasn't really a human girl anymore and the raccoon was far from being a pet. As Ruth stood there with the thin hospital gown hanging to her ankles. Other changes became apparent. Despite her size, Ruth was not a small child. The body of a mature woman was barely hidden by that gown.

John wasn't sure whether to speak or to wait. He did not want to frighten them any more than they already were. Ruth seemed to be studying him as carefully as he was studying her. And then she spoke. Her voice was strange. It was almost like leaves fluttering in the wind. But John understood her. "Why are we here?"

John answered but the words felt wrong as they came out of his mouth. "We brought you here to save you from the virus, Ruth."

The small woman frowned at his answer. She shook her head. "Then why are we different from what we were before?"

John took an unconscious step forward. "An unfortunate side effect," slipped from between his lips. He could taste the lie as he uttered it.

Ruth stepped forward to stand at the end of the bed. John's gaze moved up to study the mass of white hair that surrounded Ruth's face. John was certain there was an image or perhaps a message hidden in those white strands. He would understand so much if only his eyes could just find it. John stared intently as he sought what had to be there. He saw a look of intense concentration distort Ruth's beautiful face. Then she whispered something he could not understand, "laKH ash."

John tried to comprehend that word, but the sounds slid from his mind like mist through his fingers. The word was gone as soon as Ruth uttered it. John was certain that word was important. He looked into Ruth's eyes, seeking her help. He forgot that she had even spoken as he stared into those enormous blue orbs. Her eyes were the palest blue that he had ever seen. They were the color of the sky, but he wasn't sure where or when he had ever seen a sky that perfect. John was lost in her gaze.

He started when a hand fell onto his shoulder. "Mr Boboden? Are you alright? The lights just flickered and you kind of spaced out."

John reached up and patted the Chief's hand. "I'm fine, Chief. Just lost my train of thought for a moment."

John remained focused on Ruth despite the interruption. "Hello, Ruth. My name is John. I am responsible for your care here. We did our best to take care of you and your friend." John hesitated, unsure of where he was going with this speech. He wanted…no needed…to reassure Ruth that she would be kept safe.

Ruth smiled at him and John forgot his worries. Ruth reached behind her to place a comforting hand on the raccoon's head. "Hello, John. I am sure that you have done your best for us. This is my friend from school. Her name is Conchia, but she prefers to be called Coon."

John did not turn his eyes from Ruth's as he greeted the raccoon. "Hello, Coon. I have brought some fruit and other foods. I hope you like something in the bag."

Ruth's smile grew wider. "Thank you, John. We appreciate the food. I have questions, but we would like to eat and clean up first. Is there a place we can bathe and maybe use the restroom?"

John nodded and pointed to the door at the back of the room. "Chief, please open the door for them. I am not sure poor Ruth can reach the knob." John began to back towards the door to the hallway. "Please let me know when you want to talk again. I will make myself available."

John turned then and walked from the room.

---

Michel watched in confusion as the man who had faced down the crazy woman walked from the room with a bemused smile on his face. What was that word the child had whispered just before the lights had flickered? Michel wasn't sure. He didn't understand why Boboden had suddenly begun to babble. He was beginning to suspect that this young woman was dangerous too. But Michel had no idea what that danger was or how to protect anyone from it.

Michel walked to the bathroom and opened the door. He made a quick adjustment to the tension bar to keep the door from closing completely. Then he headed for the hall to check on his boss.

---

Anita stared down at the Congressional Subpoena. What had the snoops from the WHO found in Wuhan and how had that information gotten into the Oversight Committee's hands. Whether Congress had anything incriminating or not, she knew she would be grilled about the origin of Virus C. Damn. She hated this.

Her team would need to pick up the pace at Moriah Shock. She needed all of the specimens under her control as soon as possible. She had to get results from Morrall's research and soon. She was running out of fallback options. The help she had expected from the new President wasn't going to happen as long as he was fending off corruption charges.

With a sigh, she tossed the subpoena into the trash. Maybe she could find a way around answering their questions.

## Chapter 11
## The Peacemaker

***The White House (.gov)***
*Remarks by President Bendi on the end of the war*
*Aug 31, 2021 — THE PRESIDENT: Last night in*
*Kabul, the United States ended 20 years of war in*
*Afghanistan — the longest war in American history. ...*

### *BBC*
*Taliban Return to power. What lies ahead for Afghanistan?*
*16 August 2021. The Taliban has regained control of*
*Afghanistan nearly 20 years after being ousted by the*
*United States. The rapid fall of towns and ...*

***Washington Post***
*Violent Crime rising in many U.S. Cities ...*
*Aug 19, 2023 — Officials in Chicago, New York, D.C.*
*and many other large U.S. cities admit they are struggling*
*with the rise in homicide and other violent crimes. ...*

John stared through the tinted glass in vain. The small form he longed to see wasn't visible. A hospital blanket was stretched between the bed rails and the crate. It reminded John of the pretend tents that young children made. Pretend or not, it was very effective at blocking the camera feeds and the view from the window. He thought about ordering security to take the damn thing down, but Ruth probably wouldn't like that and John didn't want her to be unhappy.

Ruth? There was something strange about his feelings for her. His desire to protect her was so intense and that really didn't make sense. Her bio had been interesting. A child prodigy with great potential. But that didn't explain his need to talk to her or help her. Something, no everything, had changed when he met her. He didn't understand it. The curiosity about his feeling slid away as someone from security brought a box of food and water into the room. Maybe Ruth would step out where he could see her.

John jumped when a voice spoke from right beside him. John had been so focused on the scene below that he missed Chief Barreau's words. John felt the Chief's strong hand grip on his elbow. "Are you alright, Sir?"

John reluctantly turned to face his security chief. "I am fine. How is she?"

Barreau's gaze grew intent as he asked, "She?"

A part of John's mind struggled with his own request. He knew it wasn't the question he should have asked. It wasn't just Ruth he needed to be concerned with. "How are they, Chief? Are they adjusting? Should I visit them all again?"

Barreau's voice was firm, "Sir, I think it would be best if you stayed away from them for a while. Especially that little girl. Just let the rest of us do our jobs. Our job includes keeping you safe, Mr Boboden."

John turned back towards the window. "I think you worry too much Chief. You were right there with me the last time. I was never in danger."

Barreau seemed ready to argue. John couldn't have that. If the Chief thought he was in danger, John would never get to talk to Ruth again. He needed to distract the Chief. "Does your team have any concerns about how this batch is adjusting to the change? Are there any issues other than the congresswoman's daughter?"

Barreau sighed. "They are all a bit unsettled. I think a big part of the problem is boredom. They have nothing to do but sit around and worry about what is going to happen to them next. I am not sure how to help with that."

John turned to face the window overlooking containment room 1. "Jacob and Herrera don't seem to be bored and they have been here a lot longer."

The Chief chuckled. "Jacob was an old man. A college professor. He is happy writing that strange book of his. Wish I had a clue what those symbols he is drawing mean. As for Herrera, he has always been a loner. Give him something to do with his hands and he is content. That was true even before he changed. As long as he has something to work on, he will spend the next hundred years in that room. The new subjects are different."

"Different how?" John asked. "How do you get bored in less than a day. They just woke up."

"They are college students," Chief Barreau replied. "They are used to sleeping in as late as possible and then being on the go for the rest of the day. They spend hours each day interacting with friends and classmates. Here, they are isolated."

John snapped his fingers. "That's it. You are brilliant, Chief. We need to let them interact with each other. Jacob and Herrera can help them adjust. Jacob understands college students. He was a professor. We can use him as an ambassador of sorts."

Barreau's didn't seem convinced. "Are you suggesting that we let them come and go as they please? Move freely between rooms?"

John grew excited as he considered the possibilities. "Could you do that? Secure the elevator somehow and let them interact with each other?" At Barreau's look of disapproval, John added. "Think of what we could learn as we watch them. Can you imagine Dr Caufi's reaction to our reports?"

"What about Morrall's reaction?" the Chief objected.

John shrugged. "The Doctor is already on his way to Cambridge. This will give him a good reason to extend his stay there. Can you maintain security if they are free to move between rooms, Chief?"

Barreau nodded but looked unsure as he voiced one final objection, "All of them, Sir?"

That question brought John up short. But he would not let her derail his plan. "We can start with the other three rooms and leave her for later."

Barreau gestured towards the door that led to the elevator. "I will see what I can do, but only if you promise to stay away from the subjects for a few days. No visits, not even to this room. Agreed?"

John smiled and turned from the window. "Of course, Chief. I might even take a few days off." John headed to the elevator happy that he had found a way to make Ruth's existence less dreary.

---

Herrera cut another two-inch segment of heavy gauge wire from the spool in his lap. He used his new needle nose pliers to wind the piece of wire around a drumstick. Once the loops were nice and tight, he slid it off the end of the stick. It took only a second to weave the new loop into the chainmail shirt he was making.

The new weave pattern he was using for this shirt had come to him in one of his nightly dreams. He could already tell that it was a more durable design than anything he had ever made for the Banda. This design might have kept his friends safe as they fought to defend their small slice of the borough. Instead of saving lives, this shirt would be given as a Christmas present to a ten-year-old boy, the son of Colin from security.

Deep down, Herrera was saddened that he could not use his new skills to help the people who had offered him the chance to be a part of something, even if that something was just a street gang. But that small sadness could not compete with the excitement of the new tools that Colin had bought for him or the contentment that keeping his hands busy brought as hours passed unnoticed.

Herrera glanced up from his work as the door opened. Jacob walked in with a strange look on his face. As he cut another segment of wire, Herrera asked, "What did the warden want this time, Jacob? You look troubled."

Jacob came and sat beside him on the floor. "I didn't meet with John today. They took me to see Chief Barreau. The Chief has a job for us."

Herrera snorted as he pulled the wire tight around the drumstick. "I don't come cheap. Besides, I promised Colin I would finish this." Herrera wove the next link in before asking, "What kind of job?"

"He asked us to help another group of changelings. Apparently, they are not adjusting well to whatever it is we have become," was Jacob's troubled reply.

Herrera's fingers whitened as he clenched the wire cutters. Herrera avoided Jacob's troubled gaze as he asked, "What others? I know you thought they were still experimenting on people. I take it you know for certain now. How many more of us are there? Are they like either of us?"

Jacob's hands made a vague gesture. "What I know for certain is that they injected five kids from Georgetown University with the Doctor's serum. They all survived, but the Chief didn't tell me anything about what they became. All he would tell me is that they are bored and need help adjusting."

Herrera cut another piece of wire. "What the hell do we know about helping them adjust? Are we supposed to run some kind of victim support group?"

Jacob shrugged. "We keep ourselves busy and don't make trouble. Apparently, someone thinks that makes us role models. Maybe you need to bite more security people instead of making presents for their kids."

Herrera chuckled. "The man sold you a bridge, Jacob. We don't make trouble means one or more of the college kids is trouble. When do we get to find which of the college kids scares them?"

Jacob sighed as he considered Herrera's words. "Two of the rooms will be opened for us tomorrow. Barreau wants to see how that goes before they add the last student into the mix."

Herrera gave Jacob a knowing smile. "Want to bet on how that last room goes?"

Jacob shook his head and rose from the floor. "No bets. Now play with your toys quietly so I can work on my book for a while. By the way, the mail shirt looks nice."

Herrera grinned as he continued working. The rest of the day and most of the night passed as both men focused on their own projects. Neither woke when their breakfast was dropped just inside their door.

About an hour after their lunch was delivered, the lock on their door gave a strange click. The lights on the card reader beside the door went out. Jacob closed his notebook and rose from his chair. "I'm guessing that is our cue."

Herrera set aside the half-finished shirt, placing his tools safely beside his many creations. "You in a hurry to enter the lion's den?"

Jacob headed to the door. "No, Daniel at least had angels to keep him safe. All I have is you, Herrera. Are you up to the challenge of keeping me safe?"

Herrera ran thoughtful fingers through his long beard. He had a broad grin on his face as he reached out and opened the door. "You'll be fine as long as you can run faster me."

Jacob groaned as he walked through the doorway.

The hallway was silent and empty. Three more doors like their own were spaced out along the left wall. An alcove in the center of the right wall held the large elevator.

Jacob looked down at Herrera. "I feel like Bob Barker. Do you want door number one, two, or three?"

"Who is Bob what's his name?" Herrera asked.

Jacob shook his head at the question. "You led a deprived childhood, my young friend. Didn't you watch any game shows?"

Herrera shook his head. "My mother couldn't afford cable and reception sucks in the city. But if it's my choice, I say take the middle door. It's a much better door."

Jacob chuckled as he headed for the second door. "They are all the same, Herrera."

Disagreement was clear on Herrera's face as he ran his hand over the lower part of the door. "Nope. This one has less flaws. Much better craftsmanship." With that, Herrera turned the knob and opened the door.

Jacob patted Herrera on the shoulder as he walked past him. "I'll have to take your word for it." Herrera followed Jacob into the room.

Herrera stopped just inside the door. Adrenalin shot through his system as he caught sight of the two figures standing at the far end of the room. His instincts told him to run, but his brain couldn't accept what his eyes reported to him. Nobody could be that big. The larger of the two men was a brute, ten feet tall if he was an inch. Whoever he was, the large man looked like he could bench press a Camaro. Herrera wanted an AR-15 and several extra clips if he was going to have to fight this guy. Jacob was going to have to save himself.

With difficulty, Herrera turned his attention to the second figure. The second man was even smaller than Herrera was now. Despite his size, something about the tiny man caused the tip of Herrera's beard to curl up in warning. He would not allow this one to get behind him in a fight. That was for sure.

Jacob had also come to a stop several steps ahead of Hererra. Jacob appeared to be studying the two men as well. Before Jacob could speak, the shorter of the two men leaned casually against the tree trunk leg of the larger man and asked, "If you guys are the welcome to the neighborhood delegation, where are our fresh baked cookies?"

Jacob's response was unruffled by the small man's sarcasm. "I doubt you would enjoy anything I baked. My wife was the talented one in the kitchen. As for being the welcoming committee, we are captives here just like you." Jacob pushed his hair aside revealing a pointed ear. "Like you, we have been experimented on by those who hold us captive."

"Why should we trust you any more than the other two guys that visited us?" The small nan asked, "Having pointy ears or a dust mop for a beard doesn't make you like us. Why did they send you in here?"

The tall man leaned down and spoke in a loud whisper, "Danny should be nice. No picking fights."

Jacob smiled up at the big man before continuing. "We aren't your enemy, Danny. And we aren't working for the people that changed you. We have been trapped here a bit longer than you have. Our captors thought having someone to talk to might help."

"Who?" the big man asked.

Jacob paused as he considered the question. "If you mean who are our captors, I don't really know. If you mean, who am I, my name is Jacob Dror. I was a professor in New York City. My friend here is called Herrera. He is also from New York City. May I ask your name?"

The big man gave Jacob a happy grin. "Geoff. My name be Geoff."

Herrera watched the one named Danny's face. It was clear he did not trust Jacob. Herrera decided to try a different approach. "I was in a gang in the Boroughs before I got sick with that new virus. I made armor and weapons for my gang. Now I make things to keep myself busy. The old professor is more boring. He just writes in his book. What about the two of you?"

Herrera felt a spark of triumph at the look of curiosity that the small man gave him.

"Gang, eh? That sounds kind of cool," Danny replied. After a second's hesitation, he continued. "We were students at Georgetown. Geoff was the star of our wrestling team. He does Judo too. I was a business major. My thing is cars. I am really good at taking them apart and putting them back together."

Herrera sensed that Jacob was about to start another of his talks. Jacob meant well, but this was not the time for one of the old man's meandering lectures. Herrera stepped up beside him and nudged him with his elbow. Somehow the nudge seemed more effective when the elbow caught Jacob on the side of his knee. Jacob staggered slightly and glared down at him. Herrera tried to look apologetic as he said, "Maybe you should go check on the next room. Let us young guys hang out for a bit and get to know one another."

The argument that Herrera was expecting didn't come. What he saw instead was trust in the old man's eyes. It was unexpected and it felt really good. Jacob nodded and looked back at the two across the room.

"You are not the only students from Georgetown here. I really look forward to talking with each of you again."

Herrera watched as Jacob walked out the door. As it closed behind him, Herrera looked up at the big man. "Geoff. Are you any good at that judo stuff?" At Geoff's vigorous nod, Herrera asked, "Can you teach me? I might have been in a gang, but I was never any good at fighting. The body that I was born with was kind of wimpy."

Herrera flexed his right arm. "This body is different. It's not weak. In this body, I don't have to hide behind everyone else. I really would like to find out what I am capable of now. What do you say, Geoff?"

"I can do dat. Likes to teach." Geoff answered.

There was suspicion in Danny's voice as he asked, "Is this some scheme to buddy up to my friend?"

Herrera stooped to unlace his shoes. "You have been awake for a couple hours now. How bored are you? I have been trapped in this place for months. I have been locked in a room with nothing to do but build stuff with the handouts the staff gives me. Now I have a chance to do something I always wanted to do. Call it whatever you want. I intend to learn everything I can, especially if the lessons are free."

Danny sputtered, "This is stupid. We need to find a way to escape."

Herrera dropped his shoes and walked across the floor in his sock feet. "Good luck with that. The security chief is damn good at his job. Watch or learn, little man. It's your choice."

Herrera stepped in front of Geoff. Craning his head to look up into the large man's face, Herrera wondered if he was going to regret this. "What do I do first, Geoff?"

Geoff smiled. "No be Geoff now. Am Sensei. First bow then stretch."

The large man demonstrated a bow that Herrera did his best to imitate. Then the pain began as muscles Herrera didn't even know he had began to crumble and protest.

---

Jacob closed the door behind him. The thick metal door cut off the voices in the room. He would have to trust that Herrera's plan was a good one. That wasn't hard, Jacob mused. There was more to that boy than even the boy suspected.

Jacob walked back towards his own room, stopping at the next door in line. The Chief had indicated this was occupied by two young women. Just walking in wouldn't be appropriate. Jacob turned the knob and pushed the door inward about an inch. Raising his left hand, Jacob knocked. "Ladies, may I come in?"

There was no reply. The room remained silent. Jacob opened the door a little further and knocked a second time. "Hello? Are you okay?"

The fine hairs along Jacob's arms stood up. A power he recognized began to gather within the room. If that power was released, equipment would fail and alarms would begin to blare. He could not allow that to happen or what little freedom they were being given would be ripped away forever.

Jacob thrust the door open and stepped across the threshold. He still couldn't see anyone in the room. There was nothing visible except a hospital bed like his own and a dog crate. A blanket was stretched between the bed and crate like some kind of tent or pavilion. The power continued to intensify even though he could not see the person summoning it. He had to stop what was about to happen.

Jacob remembered the tone of reprimand the old Rabbi used to use when Jacob badly mispronounced a key word. He used that same tone as he barked out, "Do NOT speak that here. Not in this place."

A small childlike figure appeared as if by magic below the blanket. It took Jacob a moment to realize she had been hiding in the pile of bedding lying on the floor. Defiance marred the simple beauty of the woman's face as she scowled up at him. "Why? I have no reason to do what you tell me to."

Jacob dropped to one knee so he did not tower over her. "Because the power you gather will draw attention we don't want right now."

Jacob could feel her anger, but there was also fear in her voice. "So what? They changed us. We are prisoners here. How much worse can it get if I use what I know?"

Jacob's voice softened in sympathy. He had been a lonely old man with little to go back to. This must be much harder on her. But what the people here had done to her did not justify what she was about to. "Step not onto the path of the wicked, and go not in the way of evil men." It was not what Jacob had meant to say to her, but those were the words that came from his heart.

The power that he had felt in her began to slip away. A tear ran down the woman's cheek. "I didn't hurt him. Not really. I just made him want to like me. I thought if I made them all like me, maybe they would let us go."

Jacob shuddered at what she had been prepared to do. Could she really bend someone's will that way? Jacob considered the words he knew and realized what she wanted to do. It was wrong. "That would make you no better than those who hold us here. May I ask who you used your power on?"

The small form seemed to deflate as the power dissipated. "It was the man who called himself the director of this place. I didn't think it would hurt him when I made him like me. But maybe it did. He hasn't come back since I …" her voice trailed off as another tear ran down her face.

Jacob winced. Boboden had his flaws, but if the woman-child before him had used that word on John, then John's judgment could be seriously impaired. Jacob shook his head.

One step at a time. First, he needed to establish a bond with this woman. "The word that you spoke. It is very old. Where did you learn it?"

The woman stared at Jacob, but he did not think she was seeing him at that moment. "I took a class a few years ago. Daddy let me take a class at NYU. He let me pick anything I wanted. I really liked studying Hebrew and Aramaic. But my father wouldn't let me take the next class. He wanted me to study something practical."

Jacob went still inside. That was his class and had been for over twenty years. She was one of his students. But which one? The clues were there, he just had to figure it out. His classes were made up of two kinds of students: young men studying to be rabbis and archelogy students. Women, especially young ones, had been a rarity even in recent years.

Jacob searched his memory for a clue to who she was. And then it came to him. He had had only one female student that would have needed her father's permission to take a class. The young woman had only been fifteen when she had taken his class, but Ruth had been brilliant. Her mind had been a sponge that absorbed everything he had taught her. He had regretted that she had not returned for a second semester. Now, Ruth was here in what amounted to a prison with him. What twist of fate had brought them together again?

Ruth still seemed lost in her own guilt. Jacob smiled warmly and tried to get her attention again, "Hello, Ruth. Please forgive me for not recognizing you. You and I have both changed a bit since you attended my class."

The young woman shook her head. "I don't understand. How do you know my name?"

"Your hair was dark brown in my class, Ruth. Not white like it is now," he replied. "I was an old man and you were a young woman."

Jacob watched as she stared at him looking for some clue as to his identity. He couldn't make her wait any longer. "My name is Jacob Dror." He could see the disbelief in her sky-blue eyes. "You were the only student to finish the whole book that class. The only one that could converse with me in Hebrew. Hello, Ruth."

The young woman stepped out from beneath the blanket. As she did so, there was an angry chittering from the pile of blankets and a large raccoon emerged to stand at Ruth's side. Ruth looked down at it. "It's okay, Coon. I know him. The Professor was nice to me."

Jacob remained where he knelt on one knee, watching the two communicate. The Chief had left a number of important details out when he had asked for Jacob's help. Herrera had been wrong; Jacob had been sold more than one bridge. It would have been helpful to know about the giant and the raccoon before he opened either door.

Ruth leaned down and whispered something to the raccoon. It hissed angrily but did not protest as Ruth turned to face him. Jacob could see the uncertainty in her eyes as she asked, "Will you help me, Professor? I see the words you taught me in my dreams. I remember what they mean, but it's been too long since I spoke them out loud. Can you teach me to pronounce Hebrew again? I am afraid of what might happen if I say one wrong."

The mention of her dreams caused Jacob's pulse to race. "Do you see the scroll too, Ruth?"

Ruth shook her head. "Scroll? No, I dream about that old textbook you used in class. All of the words I want to know are in it. I know what they mean, but I can't remember how to pronounce them anymore."

Jacob considered her request. He wanted to teach again. He wanted to teach Ruth, but there would have to be rules. "I am willing to teach you, Ruth. But I have two conditions."

Ruth smiled hopefully. "What are they, Professor?"

He rose to his feet. She would need to accept his authority if she was to be his student. "First, you will only speak what and when I allow it. There are dangers that you do not understand yet. I meant what I said about getting the wrong kind of attention."

Ruth nodded. "Okay. I don't really understand, but I agree. And the second condition?"

Jacob's face grew stern. "You must release Mr Boboden from the word that you used."

Ruth's face fell. "I don't know how, Professor."

Jacob smiled encouragingly. "Concentrate on the word that you spoke, Ruth. See the symbols in your mind, but do not speak them."

Ruth closed her eyes and her face relaxed. "I see the runes. What is that line coming out of the last rune and where does it go? I never noticed it before."

Gently, Jacob explained, "That is the chain that binds John Boboden to you. I want you to break that line, Ruth. Reach out with your mind and break that connection."

Ruth smiled slowly. "I did it. Professor. I did it."

Jacob grinned at her and turned to face the table at the front of the room. He pulled the chair out and sat down. "I am not old anymore, but my mind still has trouble accepting that fact. Ruth, please introduce me to your friend and tell me how you both came to be here. Please. I suspect we will spend a lot of time together so let's get acquainted again, shall we?"

---

John turned off the television. The news never changed. Another new variant of the virus, more economic problems, or more political infighting and scandals. He wasn't sure why he had even bothered to turn the news on to begin with.

He was so bored. What did people do with themselves when they took time off from work? He didn't have a clue. Three days into his week off and John was ready to call it quits.

The movies on the local station had gotten old on the first day. He had tried reading on the second day, but his worries about Ruth had made it impossible to concentrate. He quickly tired of reading the same paragraph. Even his morning run hadn't eased any of the tension he felt. John dropped the remote on the arm of the chair and headed for the shower. Maybe he could grab a bite to eat after he cleaned up. Could he get away with a casual stop at the office after lunch? If he stayed off the observation level, he really wouldn't be breaking his promise to Chief Barreau.

Somewhere during that a long, hot shower that left moisture on all of the bathroom walls, the urgent need to go back to work faded from John's mind. He began to consider other things to do with his week off. It was his first vacation in years, after all.

John got out of the shower and wiped off the mirror above the sink. He spread shaving cream on the three-day growth that was now much more than stubble. As he shaved, he considered his options. He was only a couple hours from Bennington, Vermont. He could visit the revolutionary war memorial there. And if he went that far, why not head north from there to visit Fort Ticonderoga and maybe even that Star Trek museum that was supposed to be nearby. He had four days left, he probably had time to see the Saratoga battlefield as well.

John began to whistle as he splashed on some aftershave to ease the burn of the shave. Maybe vacations weren't so bad after all.

---

Michel dropped his kit behind his desk and headed back to the elevator. John Boboden had come back from vacation and headed straight down to the observation room. Michel wasn't sure what the short woman had done to Boboden, but the recording of her discussion with Jacob made it clear something had happened. What the hell did "make him like her" mean anyway.

Michel burst into the observation room and stopped. Boboden wasn't staring into the woman's room like Michel expected. Instead, Boboden was watching the activity in the room Michel's team had dubbed the family room. Michel walked calmly over to stand by his boss.

Boboden glanced at him briefly. The intensity that had been in his eyes a week ago was gone now. Boboden pointed down into the room. "They've been busy. What have I missed?"

Michel looked down into the room that seemed even more crowded than it had yesterday. The front part of the room now had three tables and half a dozen chairs. Jacob and the woman, Ruth, sat together at the table farthest from the door. They were speaking the same gibberish that they had been repeating for two days now. None of the linguistics programs he had used had been able to decipher it so far.

In the back half of the room, the giant was teaching another judo class. The thief was participating marginally, but Herrera was fully engaged in learning everything the big guy would teach him. Michel watched in amusement as the big man tried to teach people that barely came up to his kneecap how to block. Was this what it was like to teach martial arts to little kids? The big man never seemed to get frustrated when things didn't work. He just tried a different approach. It made Michel wish he could be down there learning, too. The big man was very, very good.

Michel shook his head when he realized how absorbed he had gotten in the lesson. He looked over to see Boboden waiting patiently for an explanation. "Sorry. The four men decided to move into the same room. Room 1 is now a sleeping area. Room 3 is now where they hang out during the day. It's a classroom and a place to hang out. The woman, Ruth, and the raccoon are still sleeping under their tent in Room 2. She is still locked in Room 4."

Boboden watched with interest as Danny attempted a leg sweep on Herrera. The move was an utter failure. Geoff knelt beside the two smaller men. Boboden turned from the window. "Any problems while I was gone?"

"Not with this group," Michel replied. "Once they got the furniture arranged the way they wanted it, their days settled into a routine. Each morning, they meet and talk while they eat. Then everyone stretches and works out. The rest of the morning is spent in classes. Jacob teaches Ruth that strange language of his. The thief and the raccoon practice opening locks together. The big man teaches Herrera judo. By lunchtime, the raccoon goes back to her room to sleep. After lunch, it's more of the same. The Thief joins the judo lessons most days but he doesn't seem that interested in it."

Michel followed as Boboden moved down to the window overlooking Room 4. As they stared down at her, the dark woman looked up at the window and frowned. Michel always wondered how she knew when she was being watched.

"And this one?" John asked.

"Nothing but attitude still," Michel said with a sigh. "The outbursts have slowed since we started picking up newspapers and magazines for her to read. She seems very interested in politics and anything violent. She gets absorbed in articles about riots or shootings. She devores them like a best-selling novel. In my opinion, she isn't sane."

Michel watched Boboden's face as the man seemed to lock gazes with the congresswoman's daughter. "Warn Jacob, but I want her in the mix tomorrow. We need to find out if they can all get along or not."

Michel stiffened at the thought of letting the crazy woman out of her cell. He understood Boboden's reasoning, but he did not have to like it. "May I remind her of the consequences of hurting anyone, Sir?"

Boboden turned from the window with a grim expression on his face. "Yes. And please have the containment team ready to move if she loses it."

Michel nodded, "Yes, Sir." Then he watched as Boboden walked from the room without looking back. Michel wasn't sure what had changed again. Boboden's obsession with Ruth appeared to have ended. Michel could mark one worry off his list. But that one problem was about to be replaced by at least a dozen new ones as Michel considered how to implement his latest orders.

---

There was a loud click as the lock on her door disengaged. Alicia resumed reading the day-old copy of the New York Times she had been reading. Mother was causing another uproar at the capital. She wasn't really surprised, that was what Mother's financial backers paid her so well to do… Keep the public distracted from what was really happening in the halls of Congress. Alicia thought it was a lot like being a high-priced hooker. The main problem with that analogy was that Mother enjoyed her work a bit too much.

Alicia considered whether to go meet the other inmates or not. Playing nice wasn't really her thing and she hated letting the security chief get away with dictating what she did or how she acted. She was tempted to just stay in her room and reread the paper. The problem was that she was curious about who and what was trapped in this place with her. Would they be potential allies or just obstacles when it came time to escape?

Mother's face stared up at her from the front page. She could hear Mother lecturing her, "Always make sure you know who the players are and who is just a tool." It really wasn't bad advice.

Alicia folded the newspaper and dropped it on the growing pile beside her chair. The world was preparing itself for her rule. Each day, there was a little more chaos. Maybe the fools she was locked up with could be put to use. Alicia rose and walked to the door. She paused to check her appearance. She grimaced as she stared down at the ill-fitting clothes that she wore. There was only so much you could do with commoner clothing. With a grunt of disgust, she opened the door and stepped out into the hall.

The door next to hers was open. Voices drifted from within, but they made little sense. "Kho… Block!... kho… No hard nuf…No, more emphasis on the hard sound…"

Alicia placed her feet carefully, moving with soundless grace to the opening. Through the open door, she could see three men engaged in mock combat. The one that caught her eye was huge. Ten feet of muscle glistening with sweat. A warrior. He would be an interesting plaything. At least until she grew tired of him. He moved with confidence, blocking the attacks by the two midgets arrayed against him.

Alicia liked what she saw. But the voice that was now her constant companion whispered to her. "No, Daughter. You cannot sway that one. He will not see your beauty or believe your lies."

The second figure barely reached the waist of the larger warrior. Nothing about the short man with the bushy red beard stirred her. She had no doubt he was strong, he did not even stumble when the big man struck him. But something about his squat form and thick muscles repelled her. She dismissed him and the voice did not argue.

The third man was the smallest of the three. His moves were the most graceful of the three. The tiny form managed to avoid blow after blow. But the little man's return strikes were no more effective against the big man than the bite of a mosquito. At least the tiny bug had a chance to draw blood. Utterly useless, Alicia thought. The voice whispered to her again, "His kind have their uses. And their loyalty can often be purchased cheaply. Do not dismiss him so quickly, Daughter."

Alicia watched the three men battle, but without pain or blood, she grew bored. The other voices in the room now drew her attention.

Neither speaker was visible, but their voices were clear. They spoke a mixture of English and a language that both drew and repelled her. There was power in those strange sounds, but it was a power she did not trust. Could she control it, or would it control her? But like a moth drawn to the flame, she had to learn more.

Alicia understood how to make an entrance. She had watched Mother take control of so many interviews over the years. With the confidence of one born to rule, Alicia stood tall and stepped into the room. The battle at the back of the room stopped as she entered. All three men stared at her. Alicia ignored them, but she was thrilled to be the focus of all their attention.

That pleasure quickly faded as the two voices continued speaking, oblivious to her grand entrance. Alicia turned to stare at the two people sitting at a table in the corner of the room.

A small child with strange white hair that seemed to have a life of its own, sat with her back to Alicia. An extremely beautiful man with ears as pointed as her own, leaned over the table. The man glanced up at her and then went back to instructing the child. Anger rose in her. How dare he ignore her like that? And for a child?

She marched over and stood behind the child glaring over her shoulder at the insolent male. She glanced down at the strange marks written in the notebook the child was studying. Then the man had the audacity to raise his index finger to indicate that she should wait, "One more time, please." Her temper began to flare at the insult.

"Kho," the girl-child said.

The man lowered his hand as he praised the child. "Excellent, Ruth. Exactly like that."

Alicia had enough of being ignored. Wounded pride fueled her indignation as she demanded, "What kind of nonsense was that?"

Without turning, the child replied, "That was Hebrew. It is one of the runes I must learn to pronounce properly."

Alicia froze. Her anger became something darker and colder. "Hebrew? As in Jewish?"

The man who no longer seemed quite so beautiful met her gaze. "It is one of the ancient languages used by the people of Israel. Aramaic was the other. I am fluent in both."

All the things Mother had taught her about Jews and all the words that Mother used at home that were not supposed to be used in public to describe Jews flooded into Alicia's thoughts. That bastard of a security chief had betrayed her. He had sent her in here to be defiled. She wanted to lash out, but the threat of the taser kept her from striking out. Alicia began to back away. The child spun around on her chair and Alicia managed to spit out, "Are you an accursed Jew as well, child?"

The small form stood on the chair and smiled mischievously. "No, I am not Jewish. But there are many who would say I am something much worse."

Alicia looked into the small girl's blue eyes. Something within that gaze disturbed her more than the Jew did. The child was an abomination. Alicia continued to back away. Her hands reached back, feeling for the door frame. She would not turn her back on either of them. Her voiced trembled as she asked. "What are you?"

The girl smiled up at her. "Mama is from the islands. I am a Catholic."

Alicia found the door frame and backed out of the room. "No, you are something much more than that, child."

The girl nodded. "I am Jacob's friend. I won't let you hurt him."

Alicia refused to run as she returned to her room. Fools! She knew now that she was truly alone. There would be no one to help her regain her freedom. Those others could not be trusted. She would escape and leave them to rot in this place. She would be free again, but it would not be easy. She just had to be smarter and more devious that her foes. Neither of those thoughts worried her. Smarter was what she was and she had been taught devious practically from the day her birth. Alicia smiled at the thought of the chao to come.

———————————

John turned from his screen to stare across the desk at Chief Barreau. "That couldn't have gone much worse. Is there any good news in this?"

Barreau shrugged. "She didn't kill anyone and she hasn't set foot out of her room since. The others are even closer now than they were."

John nodded. "It was a mistake to allow her to mix with the others. I should have anticipated this."

Barreau looked puzzled. "How could you have anticipated her reaction to Jacob?"

John gestured towards his computer. "There is more than enough information out on the internet. The congresswoman's biases are a matter of public record. How she stays in office is beyond my comprehension. Her political allies and the bills she supports should have warned me. Even if wasn't indoctrinated as a child, only a fool wouldn't expect years of prejudice to take root."

John saw sympathy in the Chief's eyes, but it did not change things. "We have work to do, Chief. Thank you."

Chief Barreau rose and backed towards the door. "Do you want her locked in her room again?"

John considered the question carefully. "No, Chief. I don't see any chance that we can put the cat back in the bag now. Please have your team keep a close watch on her any time she comes out of her room. No one gets hurt this time."

Barreau gave him a tight-lipped smile. "On it, Sir."

John watched the door to his office close as he wondered what kind of war he had started in his ignorance.

———————————

Michel dropped his cell phone down on his desk, raised his fingers up to his eyes, and squeezed. This was no time for tears. His daughter, Emma needed him. He had to be strong for her. She was alone and afraid. How was a twelve-year old girl supposed to take care of her mother when the nearest hospital was 36 miles away. It wasn't like there were that many people in Frenchboro, Maine that Emma could even ask for help.

His wife… no, Michel corrected himself. His ex-wife. Esther had ended their marriage when he had accepted the deployment to Afghanistan. She had never really understood the whole 'go where you are ordered' concept. She had taken their three-year-old daughter and headed home to the kelp farms of Frenchboro. He had come home from the sandbox eighteen months later to an empty house.

Michel had left the Marines, but Esther had never forgiven him. He had taken a number of security positions in New England just to be close to them. She had refused to even talk to him. He had no idea how or if he could ever make things right with her. He did not know if Esther would ever forgive him.

Now the woman he still loved had Virus-C. Based on Emma's description, Esther might be dying. He suspected that Emma was sick too, but his daughter was more worried about her mother than she was herself. They needed him now, but Michel was eight hours away by truck, six if he ignored the speed limit and any police cars he met along the way.

Michel sat down at his computer and began to type a simple letter of resignation. He apologized to John, explaining why he had to leave. He hit print and waited as the laser printer began to hum.

Michel's thoughts were already in Frenchboro when the single page fell into the tray. What could he do if Esther really was that bad? The little hospital in Rockport wasn't going to be able to save her. They probably didn't even have a ventilator. From what he was seeing on the news, any place with the resources to keep Esther alive was probably already full. There might not be any place that could save Esther. Or Emma if she got worse. As far as Michel knew, there was only one thing that could save them.

The question was, would they survive the cure? And if they did, what might they become? Michel wasn't sure. If Jacob was right, it was all about a desire to be more than you were before. Did Esther have a dream other than to farm kelp? Or would Esther's love for Emma be enough? He did not know and that scared him. In the end, Dr Morrell's experiments might be all he had.

He checked his watch. Derek should be on rounds at the moment. Michel left his office and headed for security. He badged in and slid into Derek's chair. This had to be done carefully. Michel didn't want the Corporation coming to Frenchboro to collect his family for its experiments. Michel considered how to best conceal what he was about to do. There were things he could and could not get away with doing.

He eliminated the obvious choices. If he attempted to alter any of the monitoring systems, Derek would notice right away. He needed something less obvious. John scanned the processes running on the security server. The answer he sought was on the sixth line down. The monitoring systems tracked each time a badge was used to enter a room. The application verified that the badge holder was authorized to enter that space. As Chief of Security, Michel could access any room in the complex.

The monitoring system sent a record of each entry attempt to the journal application which prepared the nightly reports. Michel selected the journal application and then shut it down. When they finally noticed the serum vial was missing, there would be no record of who had entered the room. The system would get turned back on in the morning when the nightly reports didn't print. By that time, he should be in Maine.

Michel slipped out of security and headed for the lab level. Michel checked the numbers over the elevator. Derek was on the observation level. He was probably chatting up one of the nurses to pass the time. Michel hit the down button and waited. If all went well, he would remain unseen until he headed out to his truck.

The elevator doors opened to an empty hallway. The only sound was the soft scuff of Michel's combat boots as he moved down the hall. He reached Morrall's private domain and tapped his badge against the reader. The door clicked and Michel stepped inside. He closed the door and turned to study the meticulously clean room. Two empty lab tables sat in the center of the room. The back wall was lined with cabinets and drawers, each carefully labeled. In one corner sat a specialized refrigeration unit used to keep the serum cold enough.

Several vaccine canisters sat on top of the fancy refrigerator. Michel opened the freezer compartment and loaded the outer chamber of the carrier with dry ice. He had to hope it kept things cold until he got home.

The next step was to find the serum he was looking for. Michel slid on a glove and opened the cold box. The shelves were lined with more vials than Michel had expected. He lifted several and scanned their labels. Morrall had apparently developed several new variants since injecting the five college kids. Michel returned each to its slot in the box and kept looking.

Finally, at the back of the unit, he found what he was looking for. A single vial labeled D3Y01s, the serum that had been used to change Jacob and Herrera. It was the only one he would even consider using on his family, and even it might prove fatal to those Michel loved. He slid the vial into the vaccine chamber and sealed the carrier. There was one more thing Michel needed.

The second drawer down was labeled syringes. Michel opened it and took two. Then he paused before taking a third. He would not send his wife and daughter into a changed world without him. He needed to be sure he was infected before he gave himself the serum. He grabbed two test kits from the cabinet beside the drawers and headed for the door.

His retreat from the complex was quick from that point. A short stop at his office to collect his go bag. He put the vaccine carrier in it along with the needles, his phone and a couple of family pictures. Then he grabbed his resignation and took everything to John's office. There he left his letter along with his badge and keys.

Michel was across the dark parking lot and in his truck five minutes later. He didn't bother returning to his apartment. There was nothing there that he needed anymore. He headed north to New Hampshire. Interstate 89 would take him most of the way to Maine. He knew the back roads from there.

Michel glanced at his watch. It was almost 9 p.m. He had 11 hours to catch the ferry. He considered the risk and then pressed his foot down hard on the accelerator. His night run wasn't likely to be noticed. The state troopers were short on staff too. Law enforcement wasn't immune to Virus-C either. Unless there was an accident they would not be out tonight. Michel hit his high beams as the truck roared up the on-ramp.

## Chapter 12
## Freedom isn't Free

***National Review***
*Mask Mandates: An encroachment on civil rights? ...*
*Aug 10, 2021 — ... In an interview earlier today, Dr Anita Caufi stated that it was inexplicable to her how Americans could consider mask mandates a violation of their freedom. "It is our civic duty ..."*

***AP News***
*The desperate plight of Americans trying to escape Afghanistan...*
*Aug 16, 2021 — KABUL, Afghanistan (AP) — The failure of President Bendi's evacuation plan and the unprecedented collapse of the Afghan government has trapped thousands of Americans...*

***Military Times***
*Pentagon announces mandatory Virus-C Vaccines*
*Aug 25, 2021 — All active-duty, reserve, and National Guard personnel will be required to get vaccinated against Virus-C or they will be discharged. A surge of senior combat-ready personnel are already separating ...*

John sat at his desk idly flicking the fifty-cent piece the clerk at the Quick Mart had given him as change from his morning coffee. It had been years since he had seen one of the oversized coins. Hell, was it even legal tender anymore? John flicked it again with his middle finger and watched it spin in the center of his desk. The coin really wasn't what was eating at him. It was that damn email from Anita.

His team had barely had time to get settled into this location. The new test subjects were finally stable. Or, at least, all of them except the congresswoman's daughter were. John wasn't sure she had been stable to begin with. Now, Anita wanted him to move the entire operation, his staff, and all of the test subjects, to another new facility. He didn't even have a security chief to oversee the transfer. John sighed. None of that was really what was bothering him either.

The issue was that Anita was going to continue to fund the work Morrall had begun at Cambridge. Morrall would be given more innocent people to experiment on, more lives to destroy. John would be expected to make it all work. He would be given new staff that he didn't know, and frankly couldn't trust. It was a recipe for disaster. Anita assured him it would all work out. Her solution to all of the potential problems was to move the entire operation into a prison. She was going to lock the test subjects up in cells.

No, John thought, these people weren't just test subjects anymore. He was being told to lock his friends up in those cells. And for what? Jacob, Hererra, Coon, Geoff, and especially little Ruth had never done anything wrong. Danny probably deserved a little time in prison for the cars he had stripped in D.C. Maybe, the world would probably be a better place if Alicia Octavia Condemn never saw the light of day again. None of the people he held captive here or the future test subjects deserved what Anita had planned. And, if he was a betting man, John would put good money on it that Anita never intended any of the test subjects to leave her little mountain hideaway.

John flicked the coin again and set it spinning again. Even the prison wasn't John's real issue. The problem was that John didn't believe in what he was doing anymore. He was helping Morrall experiment on good people to satisfy his own and Anita's curiosity. Both doctors were as dangerous as hell and John was making it possible for them to do things that were obviously wrong. John couldn't stomach it anymore. The question that John had to answer for himself was... What was John Boboden going to do about it?

In a moment of frustration, John slammed his palm down on the spinning coin. He could let the coin decide. Heads he tried to save his friends, tails he submitted his resignation and disappeared like Michel had done. Except that Michel had left to save his family. Who would John be saving if he left? Himself? But John wouldn't be able to blame the coin if he didn't like the result. The coin had less choice than John did. John lifted his hand anyway. Tails. He frowned at the coin and muttered, "Wrong answer!"

The knock John had been waiting for finally came. John raised his voice, "Come in."

The door opened and Derek from security stood outside. "I have him here with me, sir."

John's face remained expressionless as he replied, "Bring him in, please."

Derek stepped aside and pushed Jacob into the room. Derek started to come in as well, but John raised his hand. "Just him, Derek. Please wait outside. I have things to discuss with this subject."

Derek stared at him with concern. "Are you sure, Mr Boboden? He might try something. Dr Morrall says they are all dangerous."

John smiled and motioned for Derek to close the door. "There are no windows and we are below ground level. There is nowhere he can go. It will be fine, Derek."

John waited till the door was closed before he turned his attention to Jacob. The man's hands were zip tied together. Jacob's body was tense and his face was set in a controlled mask. He motioned with his chin at the office around him and said, "Nice office. You've never invited me here before." Jacob raised his bound hands up where John had a clear view of them. "I take it you are worried I might steal something?"

John looked down, suddenly ashamed. Jacob waited until John met his gaze once more before asking, "Why am I here, John? We could have had one of our 'little chats' in my room where I didn't have to be trussed up like an animal."

The hurt in Jacob's voice bolstered John's resolve. He could not live with himself if this man just disappeared into that damn prison. John rose and motioned to a chair. "Please sit down, Jacob."

Jacob stared at John for a moment before he dropped stiffly into one of the two chairs in front of John's desk. Again, he asked, "Why?"

John sat back down. "Because, Jacob, this is the only place in the entire facility that I can be sure we can't be overheard. It is the only place I can say what I need to say without getting us both in more trouble than we already are."

Jacob's next question wasn't the one John expected. "Why, John?"

John wanted to shake his friend. They didn't have time for this. But maybe John needed to make the time. Jacob deserved an answer after everything the old man had been through. "Because I have been a fool, Jacob. Because, despite my desire to do the right thing, I've made a mess of everything. I have allowed people to be hurt for no good reason. I allowed everything to spiral out of control. I can't change the past, but I can prevent things from getting any worse."

Jacob nodded and some of the coldness left his eyes. But his voice was filled with accusation as he spoke, "Worse how? What else could you or they or whoever the hell is in charge do to us? You already changed our bodies without asking. You keep us like prisoners wherever here is. What could possibly be worse? I guess you could let Dr Frankenstein dissect us so he can do a better job on the next bunch of innocents you kidnap."

John shuddered at the thought of Morrall cutting up people John had come to respect. "Jacob, they are coming to take you all away. The powers that control me and Morrall and this lab are planning to move you all into a prison. They plan to put you into cells. You will be treated like animals."

Jacob didn't even blink as he replied, "Aren't we basically in cages already, John?"

John had no answer to that accusation. Jacob was right. But maybe, just maybe, John could change that. "I think I can get you out, Jacob. Out of here with a decent chance at freedom."

Jacob's eyes grew hard again. "I won't leave without the others, John." Jacob hesitated for a moment before adding, "Not even without Alicia."

John nodded. "I meant all of you, Jacob. Even her."

Jacob no longer glared at John. John swore there was forgiveness in that gaze. "When and how?"

John's fingers began to tap on the desk. "I need a couple of days to set things up. Its Thursday. I think Sunday night is the best time. There will only be a skeleton staff on duty."

Jacob leaned forward. "Can we afford a couple of days?"

John shrugged. "I honestly don't know. But it's all I have to offer, Jacob."

Jacob looked thoughtful. "Where can we go?"

John shook his head. "I don't know and I can't know. Find a way to plan things yourselves. When they catch me and they will catch me, I don't want to be able to betray you."

Jacob finally smiled. He rose and stared down at John without anger. "The wicked have changed their ways. There is hope for you, John. And through you for us. Thank you."

John just watched as Jacob walked back to the office door. Jacob raised his voice as he called, "Derek! I am ready to go back to my cage. I don't need to be humiliated like this any longer. And I want these things off my wrists."

The door opened. Derek looked past Jacob seeking John's approval. John nodded. "Get him out of here, Derek."

Derek pulled Jacob's arm, guiding him out of the office. The door closed and John relaxed. But he could not relax for long. He had a great deal to accomplish in just three days.

---

Jacob paced from one shiny steel corner of the room to the next. Two days had passed and he had yet to find a way to talk to anyone, even to Herrera. He reached the back wall of the room and spun around. High on the far wall was the observation window. To the right and left of the dark glass, digital cameras recorded everything that happened in this steel cage. The people being held prisoner here didn't even have privacy in the bathrooms. Even those small rooms had a camera above the doors. How was he supposed to plan an escape if someone was always watching? As if in response to his thoughts, runes began to glow in his mind. Jacob whispered to himself, "Not yet."

Even with the power of those words, talking to his fellow prisoners would have been hard enough under normal circumstances. But the days since he had met with John had been anything but normal. Between the loss of the security chief and the preparations for the impending move, the entire complex had been in chaos. Lab techs had been taking blood and tissue samples while security had been watching everyone and everything. Now it was Saturday night and Jacob didn't have a clue what they would do or where they would go if John managed to get them out of here. Would any of them even want to stay together? Well, anyone beyond Ruth and Coon? John was certain they would stay with him.

The facility had finally settled down just before their evening bag meals had been delivered. Most of the medical staff had gone back to wherever they lived to pack for the move. Security, missing their leader, was exhausted from working extra shifts. Jacob assumed they would need to pack up their belongings as well. If the seven of them were to have any chance of getting away, Jacob would have to risk everything tonight. There would be no second chance once he fried the cameras in his room.

Jacob nodded to Herrera as he walked past the pad where the boy was working to soften a ball of clay. The young man from Queens rose and walked slowly out the door to 'invite' the other prisoners to their room. Jacob came to a stop in the center of the room as his brain tried to plan what to say in the short time no one would be able to watch them or listen in. The words he needed would not come. His mind just was a blank. Apparently, jail breaks were not really his specialty.

Ruth was the first to arrive. The girl was so much smaller than when she had taken his class several years ago. But she was obviously not a child anymore. She had grown in ways the change could not diminish. Her friend, Coon, came in right on Ruth's heels. The raccoon's masked face studied everything in Jacob's room for danger. Turning into whatever Jacob now was had been hard enough. How much worse had it been for the girl named Conchia to wake up in the body of an animal?

The next two to enter the room looked like a comedy routine from an old-fashioned circus. The first one through the door was Danny. Danny's changed body fell just shy of three feet in height. Geoff followed behind Danny like a little puppy dog, only this puppy was nearly ten-feet tall. Neither of them seemed aware of the difference in their sizes. Jacob couldn't keep a grin off his face. Herrera's three-and-a-half-foot form wandered into the room moments later completing the cast for the show.

The grin slid from Jacob's face when he noticed who was missing. "Is she coming?"

A rather sarcastic answer came from the hall outside the door. "Coming, yes. Staying? That depends on whether this is another of your boring lectures on morality." Alicia strode into the room like she owned it. She walked to the room's only chair and sat in it like a queen assuming the throne. Jacob felt a moment of concern at the thought of loosing this creature on an unsuspecting world. It wasn't her coal black skin or white hair that frightened him. It was the hatred that seemed to burn in the woman's lavender eyes. Was this creature even sane?

Jacob waited until the others had all settled on the floor. Alicia started tapping her long fingernails impatiently on the arm of the chair before everyone had taken a seat.

Jacob knew the time was now or never. If he waited any longer, he would lose them. Glowing words from that ancient scroll in his dreams fought for dominance into his mind. Jacob chose one and the others faded back. The pressure to release that word was intense, but he held it back as he focused his will behind the dark glass of the window. The ancient runes flashed in his mind as his intent to use the word became reality. "tAR-dAY-maw."

Jacob felt power leave his body. That rush of energy did not make him weak though. Manipulating that power both excited and invigorated him.

There was a loud pop on each side of the observation window. Tendrils of smoke rose from both of the cameras. Jacob started to speak, but the dark figure sitting in the chair surged to her feet. "What the hell did you just do, old man?"

Jacob waved his hand for her to sit back down. "We don't have time for that discussion right now. There are things I need to say before our captors wake back up. We are getting out of here tomorrow. Not the transfer Morrall has told us about. We are escaping. Everyone needs to be ready to leave at a moment's notice."

There was a snort of disbelief from the chair, but it was the small form of Danny that began to ask questions. "How? I can't crack these electronic locks. I've tried. What, or maybe the question is, who have you cut a deal with, Jacob?"

Jacob shook his head. "I can't answer that right now, Danny. We only have about ten minutes till whoever is up there wakes up. We need to decide where we are going when we get free. Our help just gets us out of this facility. Then we are on our own."

The sarcasm returned to Alicia's voice. "Who says we even want to stick together?"

Herrera's voice was firm. "Alone we are vulnerable. We stand a better chance if we cover for each other. Besides, Jacob is the only one who still looks normal among us."

"Where can we go looking the way we do?" Ruth asked.

Herrera got a hopeful expression on his face. "Mexico?"

Jacob frowned. "I think that's a long way to go and not get caught. Someplace closer, I think."

Danny grinned. "I can get us wheels. They haven't made a vehicle that I can't start." The small figure held up his hands. "Especially with these fingers. But you will have to drive Jacob. Most of us can't reach the pedals anymore. And whatever we steal has to be big enough for Geoff to fit in."

Coon pulled herself from Ruth's arms and turned so he faced Jacob. Ruth knelt beside Coon and asked, "What is it, Coon?"

The raccoon began to pantomime drawing letters on the floor. Ruth stared down as her friend began to move her hand faster. "Canada? Not a city?"

The raccoon nodded and Jacob looked thoughtful. "Most of Canada is rural. Outside of a few cities, there are a lot of places we can hide. It might work. Anyone have a better idea?"

Silence was the only response. Jacob looked nervously up at the dark glass. "Then we all agree to stick together and head for Canada?"

Jacob relaxed as everyone nodded their agreement. Everyone but Alicia. Jacob silently hoped she would go off on her own.

Herrera stood and motioned for the door. "Back to your own rooms before someone comes to investigate the cameras. Better that Jacob and I get blamed for breaking things again."

As the room emptied, Herrera stepped closer and whispered, "I hope your plan works out, old man. She scares me. I don't want to see how she gets especially if this goes bad."

Jacob nodded. "You aren't alone, Herrera. Alicia scares me too."

---

It was just after 2 p.m. on Sunday when John stepped into his office. Weekend work wasn't unusual for him so his presence shouldn't raise any flags in security. John sat down in his chair and opened the top right drawer of his desk. The two most important pieces in his plan lay there. He lifted out the keys that Michel had left on his desk the day the security chief had resigned. John fingered the two keys that he was most concerned with.

The first was the key to the Escalade parked near the front door. The SUV had heavily tinted glass. No one would know who was inside. Or, more importantly, who was not inside the vehicle. It wasn't armored or anything insane like that, but it would take John a long way before Anita's goons caught up with him.

The second key fit the alarm panel near the front entrance. Using that key placed the entire facility in lock down. Once that key was inserted and turned a quarter turn, no door would open, no elevator would move, no one would be able to go anywhere. No one except the Chief of Security. His badge alone would continue to function. Chief Barreau had intended to lead his response team against any and all internal problems. Michel had made sure there would be no mistakes, no loss of containment, and no unnecessary deaths on his watch.

John reached back into the drawer and pulled out Michel's badge. Security had not deactivated it because John had kept possession of it until Michel's replacement was selected. This badge would allow him to reach his friends and get them out of the facility before Anita's team arrived.

John closed the door and headed for the security panel. It was time to set the people he had imprisoned free.

---

Her fingers traced the smooth lines of her face. The changes went far deeper than the black of her skin and her pointed ears. Her face was thinner, the bone structure sharper than before. Mother would have called the new look aristocratic. Alicia decided she liked the looks of her new body. And not just the looks, she was stronger and faster than she had ever been. Her hearing and eyesight were better too. She did not miss those thick glasses she had worn since childhood.

There was a faint whirring noise from behind her. Alicia turned from the mirror to glare at the small camera mounted over the bathroom door. Her voice came out as a growl as she muttered, "Men! Always trying to get a cheap thrill at a woman's expense."

Alicia turned back to the mirror and stared at her image. A voice she recognized from her dreams whispered softly into her ear. "You don't have to let them watch. Just make them stop."

Alicia was intrigued. She stared at her image and mouthed, "How?"

To her surprise, the image in the mirror raised one hand up between them. Her image stared down at the hand and Alicia did too. A small ball of darkness formed on her image's fingertips. The hand lowered and the darkness hung there between them. Alicia's keen eyesight couldn't pierce that darkness. The voice whispered again, "Now, you do it."

Alicia turned back to face the camera. She focused her anger at being held captive on that small device. She poured her hatred for the men who currently controlled her life into her desire. A globe of darkness formed around the camera. It was not as thick as the one her counterpart had made, but it was a start. She knew she could do better with practice.

Alicia smiled as she turned back to the mirror. Perhaps in time she would show that self-righteous Jew a thing or two.

Alicia looked once more into the lavender eyes of her image. It began to speak. "Don't go with him, Sister. You must follow your own path, find your own destiny."

Alicia nodded. She didn't want to be under the Jew's thumb. She wanted to be free of him. But where should she go?

Her image appeared to read her mind. "To Mother, of course."

Alicia considered the idea. Mother had power and resources right now. Alicia would need Mother's help until she could build her own base of power.

The image smiled. "Yes, but only until it is time to take her place and her power."

Her image smiled as Alicia considered that ultimate betrayal. That betrayal would not come for some time though. Alicia looked at her image and asked, "How do I get there without being caught? The authorities will be searching for me."

Her image began to laugh. "Betray the Jew and his friends. Use them as bait to draw your pursuers away from you."

Alicia began to laugh along with her image. Then she reached into the shower for the small bar of white soap. She faced the image once more and began to write on the mirror in large letters. C A N A D A. She dropped the soap into the sink and smiled with contentment. She was about to teach her enemies a harsh lesson and guarantee her own freedom in the process. This was going to be a very, very good day.

---

John removed the key from its keyhole. The glossy panel now reflected the flashing red light from the hallway behind him. The facility was locked down. Every door was sealed, all external communication was blocked, and both elevators were disabled on the ground floor. Everyone except the containment team was now trapped in whatever room they had been in when John turned Michel's key. Even internal communication was limited to the tactical radio carried by Michel and his team. But there was no Michel anymore and his team had been sent home to pack for the move. There was no one left to prevent John from causing a containment breach.

John turned and began to walk. The path to the elevator went dark every other heartbeat as the security lights went off and on. The doors to the elevator stood open, locked in place until Michel's badge overrode the security protocols. John entered the elevator and faced the dark control panel. He slid Michel's badge into the slot below the nine buttons. The panel lit up and John pressed the '7' for the containment level. The elevator doors closed leaving John in near darkness.

Fifteen minutes later, eight people were squeezing into the elevator. John noted with surprise that even people who owned little more than the clothes on their backs had treasured possessions. Herrera had his tools that security had given him, Danny had his stethoscope and collection of random parts, and little Ruth clutched Jacob's notebook to her chest like it was the most valuable thing in the whole world. It was tight, but they fit.

Geoff was on his knees in the corner behind John. Most of the others were huddled together near the back of the car. All except the congresswoman's daughter who stood by the door in preparation for her grand entrance into the world above. John shook his head as he slid the badge back into its slot. As soon as the panel activated, John selected the ground floor. The car began to rise.

When the elevator doors finally opened, Alicia strode down the hall towards the main entrance. John shivered as he watched her go. The flashing red of the security lights looked like blood on her dark skin. He wondered briefly if he was really doing the right thing. Then the others followed after her with Geoff crawling from the car last. Their whispered words died away as they were drawn into the sunlight shining in through the glass doors. John pulled the badge out of its slot, locking the elevator once more, before he walked after the changed people he was about to turn loose in a world that did not suspect that they even existed.

Alicia reached the outer doors first. John heard her growl in frustration when the door refused to open. John hurried to the main panel and slid Michel's security card into it. There was a loud thunk as the magnetic lock disengaged. Two dark hands shoved again and the door swung open.

All seven of his prisoners rushed out into the sunshine, free at last. John left Michel's badge where it was. It would be needed to free those still trapped below. Then John stepped out into the fresh, mountain air. Was this what freedom smelled like?

The seven, now free, moved slowly away from the door. Little Ruth and Coon stared longingly at the trees across the parking lot. Herrera and Danny were carefully studying the half dozen cars in the parking lot. Danny raised an excited finger to point at John's old '65 Mustang. Geoff and Jacob just stared up into the sky. Only Alicia had a frown on her face.

John stepped around the group to approach the black Escalade parked by the sign that read Security. It was an older model that Michel had picked up at an auction. For its age, the SUV was in good shape. John would have preferred to drive his own car, but the Escalade had one vital piece of equipment that the Mustang did not have. It had a tracker that Anita's team would be able to follow. If John's plan worked, all eyes would be on him as he sped west on I-90. John could only hope that no one would notice the old produce truck as it took Jacob and the others away.

Danny's small form came up to stand beside him. "Nice wheels. Is that an '01? You going to be our getaway driver instead of Jacob?"

John was momentarily confused by the unexpected questions. John regained his focus and replied, "I have no idea what year it is and no, you will not be coming with me."

Jacob moved up to stand behind Danny. "Why aren't we coming with you, John? I assume you aren't just leaving us here in the parking lot."

John pointed at the engine of the Escalade. "This has a tracker. If you come with me, you will be captured when they catch up with me."

Danny moved around to the hood. "Pop it open, I can disable the tracker, piece of cake."

"No!" John blurted out. "They need to follow me so you have time to get away."

Danny raised his hands and stepped back from the Escalade. Jacob's calm voice asked, "Then how do we stay out of sight, John. We are really going to stand out if we are on foot."

John pointed to the left towards a cluster of spruce trees. "About a hundred yards past those trees you will find an old trail. Some of the staff walk it for exercise. Head downhill. In about two miles, the trail opens out into an apple orchard. The man that owns the orchard has a covered truck that he uses to haul his apples to market. I assume Danny can get it started."

Danny grinned up at John. Jacob started to say something, but John just shook his head. "No Jacob. No more words. Don't waste any more time on words. Take them and go. I have no idea how much time you have."

Jacob nodded and John watched as the six people and the raccoon began to run. Geoff paused long enough to pick Ruth up in one arm. Little Coon scampered up the leg of Geoff's sweatpants and perched on the big man's shoulder. The group disappeared into the trees leaving John alone with his guilt.

Moving to the driver's door, John used Michel's keys to unlock the Escalade. The seat was too far back and the mirrors were all wrong. John adjusted everything before putting the key into the ignition. John pumped the gas twice and turned the key. The Escalade roared to life.

There was also a bust of static as the vehicle came to life. John reached for the off switch on the tactical radio when a voice came over its speaker.

"TR21 to Transfer Team Leader. We are at the road leading to the lab. Any idea why the gate is closed and locked?" John heard mumbled voices in the background and then the voice continued. "Transfer Leader, the security lights are flashing on the gate controls."

Damn, John thought as he put the Escalade in gear. He had not expected the transfer to happen today. It was Sunday, after all. John knew he had to get past the vehicles at the gate or everything he had done this afternoon would be for nothing. The Escalade began to creep across the parking lot as John searched for a solution to this unexpected problem.

The tree-lined road up to the lab was just over a mile and a quarter long. The vehicles at the gate would not see him until he came around that final curve near the bottom. John would have to accelerate as he approached the gate and hope the road wasn't blocked. John sped up as he followed the road down the mountain.

The chatter on the radio continued as John followed the curve of the road.

"TR21, use the following code to override gate security. Charlie Echo seven three Bravo one."

John had not known that there even was an override code. John began to speed up.

"Gate is opening, Transfer leader. Do we proceed?"

"Negative, TR21. We are five minutes away. Hold your position."

John gripped the steering wheel tighter. He had a very bad feeling about this. The final curve was just ahead.

A new voice came over the circuit. "Mountain lab. Mountain lab. This is Transit Team 2. What is your situation? We have orders to pick up passengers at your location."

John looked at the hand mic, but kept both hands on the wheel. What could he say that they would believe anyway? John came around the final curve. Three vehicles were parked on the left side of the road. The gate was wide open. At least a dozen men in green camo uniforms milled around just outside the gate. John pressed the gas accelerator to the floor. The engine roared and the big SUV surged forward. John thought he had a chance.

The radio filled with static and partial words as multiple people began to report that a black SUV was accelerating towards the road. John grimaced as the gate suddenly began to close. John said a quick prayer as he continued on. The movement of the gate seemed slow compared to that of the SUV. The vehicle bucked as a loud thump and scrapping noise came from somewhere behind John. John watched in horror as soldiers leapt from the path of his speeding vehicle. Then John was at the road and past them.

John cranked the wheel right, heading south towards I-90. The back of the SUV fishtailed and John frantically cranked the wheels back to the left to keep the Escalade on the road. Through it all, John never let up on the gas.

John saw two more green transports pulled to the side of the road as he sped south. A voice cut across the chatter. "Whoever you are, stop! I am under orders that no one is allowed to leave that facility. I am authorized to use lethal force."

John reached down and switched off the radio. He wasn't interested in anything they had to say. For the first time in a long, long time; John was doing something that felt right. John smiled as he flew past the two transports. From the corner of his eye, John saw a man with a long green tube jump from the second truck. It didn't matter, John was past them now.

John whooped in triumph. The Escalade passed 90 MPH. No one could stop him now. Then there was a strange noise and John glanced in the rear-view mirror. A flash of light reflected off the mirror into John's eyes. John did not care, he had won.

---

Seven bodies crashed through the brush at the end of the trail. They were all out of breath except Geoff and his two passengers. The evergreen forest that they had been moving through came to an abrupt end. Stretching before them were row after neat row of apple trees. Stacks of empty bushel basket sat beneath trees filled with red fruit. Other trees, now bare, had a scattering of rotting fruit lay scattered beneath their empty branches. The smell of apple filled the air.

Danny gave a soft whoop of excitement and pointed towards an old Chevy farm truck with a blue canvas tarp covering the back end. The front end of the truck seemed a mix of rust and faded blue paint. They were running towards the truck when the sounds of an explosion echoed through the trees. Their sprint came to an end as the turned to look around. Herrera muttered, "That can't be good news."

Ruth pointed to a gap in the trees. A large cloud of black smoke was rising into the sky several miles away. Her voice was filled with concern as she asked, "What is that?"

A gleeful laugh came from behind them. They all turned to stare at their dark companion. "What do you know?" Jacob asked.

Alicia laughed again. "Know? Nothing. But I suspect that was your friend who thought he could lead our pursuers away from us. I would say he died in the attempt. I wouldn't be surprised if the rest of you will share a similar fate soon enough."

Jacob frowned at her. "Then you will share our fate."

Alicia began to giggle then. "Me? I never intended to stay with any of you. I will not be ruled by any man, Jew."

Alicia began to back away. Jacob moved to follower her. Glowing words began to flow in his mind. Jacob was trying to decide which one to use when a globe of darkness filled the air between him and his target of his anger. From the far side of that pool of darkness a voice taunted, "Good luck at the border. They know you are headed for Canada. Maybe they will just take you prisoner again, or maybe you will die for nothing like your friend."

Those words stopped Jacob. He spun back towards the truck. "Danny, get that truck started, now. We have to get out of here fast."

"Where can we go?" Ruth asked.

Herrera pointed at the cloud of dark smoke drifting in the light mountain breeze. "Away from that to start with."

Danny ran towards the truck. "Then we change vehicles. Many times. And then we find another place to hide."

Jacob nodded and motioned towards the truck. "In the back. Everyone except Danny. Make sure you can't be seen."

Jacob watched as Geoff helped Danny into the truck's cab. The small thief knelt under the steering column. Jacob couldn't tell what Danny did, but the engine coughed to life as a puff of grey smoke shot from the tail pipe.

Geoff was lifting Herrera into the back end as Jacob walked over to examine their ride.

Freedom had come to the six fugitives, but so had the realization that their pursuers would have no mercy.

# Part III
# Outbreak

## Chapter 13
## Exodus

*BBC News*
Six Palestinians escape from Israeli high-security prison ...
6 September 2021 — A massive manhunt is underway as Israeli police search for six Palestinians who managed to tunnel their way out of Gilboa prison ...

*WWLP*
Berkshire Sherriff's Office searching for driver involved in ...
Sep 19, 2021 — The search for the driver in a deadly hit and run accident has expanded to include Vermont, and New Hampshire ...

*Spectrum Local News*
U.S.-Canada border closure extended until October 21
Sep 20, 2021 — The U.S. Customs and Border Patrol announced today that opening of the Canadian a border has been delayed by 30 days ...

The engine of the old truck settled into a steady rumble. Jacob thought it ran well for a truck that looked older than his own 62 years. The markings on the side of the truck read "Chevrolet C-50." There looked to be more rust than metal around the wheel wells. If they were lucky, the old Chevy would hold together long enough to get them somewhere where they could hide. Not that Jacob had any idea where safe might be anymore.

Geoff climbed up into the bed of the truck and pulled the heavy tailgate closed behind him. Jacob helped Geoff tie the tarp closed so that no one could see what or who was hidden in the back of the truck. When he was sure that his friends were well hidden, Jacob walked around to the open driver's door. Jacob climbed up into the cab with more agility than he had felt in decades. He felt strong and healthy. It wasn't just that his new body was younger, Jacob actually wanted to live his life again for the first time since his wife had died.

As he settled his weight on the bench seat, Jacob almost wished that he hadn't. The driver's side of the seat was lumpy and Jacob could feel several of the springs poking through the worn covering. He was tempted to grumble about the seat until he saw the proud grin on Danny's face.

Danny was practically dancing on his side of the bench seat. The small man ran a loving hand along the dashboard as he boasted, "She cranked on the first try, Jacob. She's a real beaut. I'd say she was a keeper if she wasn't so easy to spot on the roads."

Jacob grinned despite pain in his posterior. Danny's enthusiasm was catching. Jacob looked down to see what Danny had been up to. There was no key in the ignition, just a tangle of wires below the steering column. Some of those wires didn't appear to be a part of the original design. In fact, they looked suspiciously like wiring out of the IV pump. Jacob looked at Danny and winked. "I assume that I shouldn't touch any of that?"

Danny chuckled. "Be my guest. I hope you don't mind the tingle of electricity."

Jacob ignored the sarcasm as he studied the knob at the top of the long gear shift. The old truck had a manual four-speed. Jacob raised his left foot and stepped on the clutch. It was a bit stiff as Jacob pressed the pedal to the floor. Jacob moved the long stick into each of the gears, feeling the exact place where the stick settled into position. Danny sounded a bit nervous as he asked, "You do know how to drive a truck like this, right?"

Jacob returned the old truck to neutral before answering, "I spent three years in the army, Danny. This old girl isn't much different from the deuce and a half I drove back then. Each truck has her own little quirks so it's best to get a feel for the gears before you hit the road."

The look of relief on Danny's face was almost comical. Jacob rapped twice on the rear window and yelled, "Time to roll. Sit down and hang on. It's about to get bumpy back there."

Jacob slid the truck into first gear and released the brake. The C-50 rolled forward without a lurch until it hit the first rut in the dirt road leading out of the orchard. It felt good to be driving again, Jacob thought. Good, except for the springs that stabbed him each time they hit another rut.

Jacob glanced over to see how Danny was doing. The small man was still balanced on the balls of his feet. He wasn't even holding on as he stared out the front window. Based on the grunts and groans coming from the rear of the truck, Danny was the only one unaffected by the truck's bouncing progress.

The truck's oversized tires carried them past row after row of apple trees. Some rows were beginning to turn red and others remained stubbornly green. Passing the last row of trees, the truck rolled onto a small open field. An old wooden fence with an open gate marked the edge of the property. Beyond the fence lay a paved two-lane road. It was at that point that Jacob realized he had no idea where they were headed or which way to go. There was no hesitation on Danny's part though. His stubby finger rose up in front of Jacob's face. "Left," he directed.

Jacob brought the truck to a stop on the edge of the road and turned to give his copilot a curious look. Danny continued to point to the left. "Away from the smoke. We don't want to go anywhere near whatever happened back there."

Jacob nodded and pulled onto the road. The groans of pain from the bed of the truck quickly faded until the only sounds were the rumble of the engine and the hum of tires on the pavement. Jacob was simply happy that the seat springs no longer dug into his backside. He brought the Chevy up to 45 and began to look for clues as to where they were.

The tension in the cab didn't ease as they cruised down the road. Both men kept an eye on the side mirrors, looking for any sign that they were being followed. But the pursuit they feared never came. There wasn't even another vehicle on the road with them. In his paranoia,

Jacob wished for at least a few cars that they could blend in with. But the tiny country road remained empty except for their own big blue truck.

Exactly 6.8 miles later, the road ended in a T-intersection. A small white sign stood across the intersection from them. Below the large black '7' were arrows pointing in both directions. Cars, SUVs, and a few larger trucks passed them on both sides of the new road. Danny again pointed left. This time, Jacob didn't hesitate any longer than it took to find an opening in traffic.

Moments later they passed another white sign that told them they were headed north. Danny whispered excitedly, "Just try to go with the flow. Don't make people pass you and they will ignore us."

Jacob began to laugh at the absurdity of Danny's whispering. The humor of it all allowed some of the tension he felt to evaporate. "Why are you whispering? It's just the two of us in this rather noisy truck."

Danny didn't respond, but the seat suddenly began to move rhythmically up and down again. The springs once more poked Jacob in places that were already sore from previous assaults. Glancing over, he saw Danny bouncing nervously on the far end of the seat. Jacob grinned and whispered back, "If you really don't want people to notice us, it might be better if I didn't look like I had a five-year-old dancing around in the front seat."

Danny looked sheepish as he sat down. "Good point." They both relaxed as the miles passed.

Jacob wasn't sure which of them noticed the soft whump-whump-whump sound that seemed to be growing louder. Jacob found himself fighting the urge to stomp on the gas as he recognized the sound of an approaching helicopter. Danny had rolled onto his knees so he could stare out the passenger window. Danny's finger stabbed the glass as an army helicopter floated past them following the road north.

Jacob winced at the hysterical note in Danny's voice as the small man yelled, "We need someplace to hide! We're too exposed out here on this road."

The fear in Danny's voice made Jacob's grip tighten on the steering wheel. But the green bird flew past them without altering its course. Soon it began to shrink as it sped north. They were safe for the moment, Jacob thought, but only because they hadn't panic during the fly-by. Now he needed to settle his young friend down. He needed Danny's brains, not his fear. "Take a breath, Danny. Think. They were just trying to spook us. We didn't give ourselves away and now they are gone. Getting off the road is a good idea. What do you suggest?"

"Next town, we need to get off and hide this truck," was Danny's nervous reply.

Jacob wasn't sure how much longer they drove north. It might have been a minute or five, or even a half hour. But a much larger sign announced a place to go to ground.

*Williamstown, Ma*
*Population 4565*

"Does it matter where I get off?" Jacob asked.

Danny nodded, "Somewhere with bigger buildings. I'll tell you when to turn."

They slowed down as the small town's traffic grew heavier. Jacob had to focus on not stalling the truck as they were reduced to a crawl at times. Jacob jumped when Danny yelled, "Turn here, Jacob! Main Street is as good as it's going to get."

The engine of the big truck whined as Jacob was forced to drive in first gear down the busy street. After only a block, Danny pointed at a store. "In there, park around back."

"Wild Oats Market?" Jacob muttered, "Why there?"

Danny just gave him a smug grin. "Who is going to think twice about a farm truck parked behind an organic food store. It's perfect."

Jacob didn't bother to argue with Danny's logic. He turned into the parking lot and maneuvered the big Chevy around to the back of the store. He parked it as far from the delivery entrance as he could get it. Jacob had barely set the parking brake when Danny's hand darted between his legs to rip a small blue wire from the tangle below the steering column. The Chevy's engine sputtered and died.

Jacob took a deep breath before he turned to face Danny. "I've trusted your instincts so far, but I'd feel a lot better if I had some idea what your plan is."

Danny sat tapping gently on the arm rest. Jacob waited patiently giving the small man time to organize his thoughts. Finally, Danny swiveled on the seat to face Jacob. We need to figure out where we are going. Is Canada still an option? That is your job. Talk to the others and come up with a plan."

"And your job?" Jacob inquired.

"We need another ride. One that doesn't scream 'Here we are, catch us if you can!' to the whole world." Danny patted the dashboard with his right hand. "As soon as that farmer reports this truck was stolen, those army dudes will know we took it. We need to be far away when that happens."

"Wonderful," Jacob groused. "You planning to turn this into that auto theft video game?"

An excited grin spread across Danny's face. "It's 'Grand Theft Auto', old timer. And no, Geoff won't fit in most of the good cars. Besides, I doubt you could handle a real muscle car."

Jacob's grin matched Danny's own. "I wouldn't want to try. Anything else we need?"

Danny nodded, "We need supplies. Food, clothing, tools. I got a list in my head. I'm sure other things will come to me. The shopping trip is my job too."

Jacob didn't care for the cavalier tone in Danny's voice. The young man had a rather flexible view of right and wrong. Jacob tried for a stern look, but Danny was oblivious to it. Jacob sighed and said, "All of those things cost money, Danny. We don't have money or a way to get any."

Danny snapped his fingers and grinned. "That's right. I forgot to see how much cash we have."

Jacob watched as Danny reached behind his back and pulled a light brown leather tri-fold wallet from out of thin air. Tooled into the leather were the initials 'JB.' Jacob felt a stab of regret as he watched Danny open the wallet and pull out the few bills tucked inside. One glance at his haul set Danny to complaining. "The man is the director of a fancy facility and he only has thirty-seven bucks in his wallet? What the flip, man!"

There was no regret on Danny's face as he stared at the money he held in his hand. Jacob wanted to tell Danny that what he did was wrong. John Boboden had risked so much to set them free. But Jacob wasn't sure he had the right to criticize Danny's actions. In the end, Jacob simply stated the obvious. "You lifted John's wallet while he was helping us escape?"

Danny shrugged. "He wanted us to get away, didn't he? Besides, I figure he kind of owed us." Danny stuffed the bills into his pocket and tossed the wallet to Jacob. "Hang on to that till we find a good place to get rid of it."

Jacob's mouth moved but nothing came out. Danny popped open the passenger door and climbed out. Jacob finally managed to ask, "What do we do while you are gone?"

Danny shrugged. "Decide where we go next. Get some rest. It could be a long night for you, boss. If I find some wheels, you have a lot of driving to do.

The passenger door closed and Jacob watched in the side mirror as Danny disappeared around the corner of the store. After a moment's thought, Jacob climbed out of the cab and walked around to the back of the truck. He unlaced only enough of the tarp to get inside before whispering, "Coming in."

The bed of the truck was dim; the only source of light being the back window of the cab. Four sets of anxious eyes stared at him as Jacob sat cross-legged on the wooden deck of the truck.

Geoff was the first to speak, his overly loud whisper sounding loud in the silence. "Where is Danny?"

"He has gone out scouting. We need a different vehicle. Danny is looking at our options." Jacob replied.

Geoff seemed satisfied with that answer but Jacob sensed that Geoff was the only one willing to let it go at that. Ruth broke the silence next. "Is that wise?"

Jacob shrugged. "I honestly don't know, Ruth. Danny has a unique sense of what is possible and what isn't. If any of us can mingle out there and not be noticed, it's him. We are in a bind and, as much as I hate to say it, Danny is our only solution."

Ruth started to protest, but Herrera laid a gentle hand on her shoulder. "Peace, Ruth. We don't know what's been going on out there." Herrera locked gazes with Jacob. "Tell us what's happened so far, Jacob. Where are we and why did you stop so soon? I thought we were heading for the Canadian border."

Jacob pushed aside his own fears. He wasn't the one who had been trapped in the back of the truck for the last hour. "We are somewhere in Massachusetts. A small town named Williamstown. It's very rural here. I don't think we are anywhere near Boston. This truck is really obvious out there on the highway."

"Obvious to who?" Herrera asked.

Jacob gestured up towards the sky. "An army helicopter flew by us just before we got to this town. I think whoever sent it was hoping someone would do something foolish. We didn't panic, so they kept following the road. We didn't get caught then, but Danny doesn't think it will take them long to start looking for this truck."

There was a long silence as each of them considered what Jacob had said. The raccoon started chittering and Ruth sat nodding her head. Ruth looked up and asked, "Are we still going to Canada?"

Jacob looked uncertain. "If Alicia really betrayed us…"

"Then they will be waiting for us," Herrera finished for him. "Anyone have any idea where we can hide? Massachusetts has mountains, but they will get mighty cold in the wintertime."

"You are assuming she actually betrayed us," Ruth argued, "what if she only said that to scare us?"

"Does it matter?" Herrera replied. "The question is whether we should risk it."

Jacob looked around at his young friends who had been through so much. "Canada is the right answer in the long run, but we need to lay low for a bit first. Anyone have any idea where we can hide out for a month or two?"

Silence descended as each tried to come up with an idea. Jacob was about to give up when Ruth began to grin. Excitement tinged her voice when she explained. "It's like any good illusion. With the right props, we can hide in plain sight and no one will notice us."

Geoff looked confused. "How is it hiding if ebrybody can see us?"

In her enthusiasm. Ruth stood and began to gesture wildly. "It's a simple magician's ploy. Distract the audience by giving them too many things to watch. In an environment full of oddities, the audience can't keep track of what they are supposed to be watching."

"Not understand," Geoff said.

Ruth grinned and walked over to give the big man a hug. "Sorry, Geoff. That means we need to find a place where everyone looks just as strange as we do. Then, no one will notice us. We need to go someplace where no one looks normal."

Geoff smiled as Ruth's small arms unwrapped from around his neck. Then he asked, "Like a circus?"

Ruth grinned at him. "Better than a circus, Geoff." Then she turned to face the others. "We need a ren faire."

Jacob stared at Ruth's smiling face. "A ren faire?"

Ruth beamed as none of them seemed to understand. "Yes, a renaissance faire where everyone dresses up as knights and wizards and ladies in waiting. Some people even dress up as fantasy creatures from movies."

Jacob was about to ask a question when Ruth took off again. "And not just any ren faire. We need to go to THE Ren Faire, King Richard's Faire. We could get jobs there and hide for at least a month."

"Slow down, Ruth." Jacob interrupted as he motioned for her to sit down. "Where and when is this King Richard's? Assuming it's not over? How do we fit in?"

Ruth sat but her hands and arms moved constantly as she explained. "Daddy used to take me to the Faire every year. It's always the whole month of September and most of October. I'm sure it isn't over yet. Remember the orchard? The apples were just starting to turn."

As she paused for a breath, Jacob asked, "Where is it, Ruth? Can we get there?"

She grinned happily. "That's the thing, Jacob. It's right here in Massachusetts. Right outside of Boston in the town of Carver."

Herrera picked at the worn clothing he had been given by security and then gestured at the lime green shirt that Geoff was wearing. "I think we'll still stand out. How many people go there looking like refugees."

Ruth shook her head. "They sell lots of period clothing at the Ren, Herrera. We can get everything we need…." Ruth's excitement faded quickly. "But we don't have money."

Jacob smiled at her. "One problem at a time, Herrera. It's an idea and the only one we have at the moment. If we can hold out there for a month or so, Canada might be feasible. First, Danny has to find us something to replace this truck. Then, as much as I hate to turn him loose on an innocent town, we are going to need his skills to get some cash."

Herrera's fingers ran gently though his beard. "What do we do till the little thief gets back?"

Jacob stretched out on the bed of the truck. "Sleep if you can. We may be driving through the night."

Herrera nodded and lay back and crossed his hands behind his head. Ruth cuddled up with Coon in the corner near the cab. Geoff sat and watched them all drift off to sleep. He would stay on guard. He would keep them safe.

## Chapter 14
## Robbing the Hoods

**NPR**
*L.A. retailers rocked by string of flash-robs ...*
*Sep 27, 2021 — Youth mobs descended on two of L.A.'s high-end electronics stores just days after the 'Smash and Rob' at The Grove's Nordstrom store ...*

### Fox Business
*Marshalls robbed as shoppers and employees watch ...*
*September 28, 2021, 9:38 am EDT. — California. – Business losses to theft are reaching critical levels as more and more stores tell staff not to engage shoplifters and in some cases, to not even report the crimes. Customers watched in amazement as shoplifters casually robbed a California Marshalls while employees did nothing ...*

**News4JAX**
*Four charged with murder in Labor Day home invasion ...*
*Oct 12, 2021 — Jacksonville Police announced the arrest of four teens ranging in age from 14 to 16. All four have been charged with armed robbery and second-degree murder in the death of a 28-year-old man ...*

Danny walked back through the parking lot until he reached the curb on the edge of Main Street. He waited for a break in traffic and then darted across the street to stand on the sidewalk. Which way first, he wondered? Danny gave a mental shrug. Did it really matter? Probably not, he decided, as he walked away from the road that had brought them into town.

As he had hoped, stores, restaurants, and other places to explore were scattered along or near Main Street. Danny began building a mental map of the places where he might find all of the things he wanted to "acquire." After about four blocks, Danny had seen enough. The sun was sinking low in the sky and some of the places he had seen might not be open much longer. Those stops were more important at the moment than exploring any further. After all, shoplifting was a piece of cake… breaking and entering was another thing altogether.

Danny stopped just short of the next intersection. He was trying to decide what to do first when a woman knelt beside him. Based on the grey roots of her hair, Danny guessed that she was old. But he couldn't be sure how old because she was wearing a mask like some kind of wild west bank robber. Only, what kind of bank robber wore a green mask with yellow daisies printed on it? Danny groaned inside as her muffled voice came from under the cloth mask, "Are you lost, little man?"

Several sarcastic answers came to mind. But for a change, Danny managed to control his mouth. The woman obviously thought he was just a little kid. Danny decided it would be best if she didn't know the truth. Not that she was likely to believe the truth if she heard it. Danny hardly believed it himself. Danny drew himself up to his almost three-foot height and answered with all the confidence he could muster, "No, ma'am. I know right where I am. That," Danny pointed at the street corner just ahead, "is as far as I am allowed to go by myself. Now I need to go back."

The mask really bothered Danny. Why was she wearing it? He didn't like that he couldn't see her whole face. It was hard to read her reaction when all he could see were her eyes. Danny glanced around and noticed that everyone else walking up and down the street had a mask on. What was going on? Was there a petty larceny convention in town? Danny turned to go. He needed to figure out what was going on before he called any more attention to himself.

"Wait," the woman called out as Danny backed away. Danny watched as she began digging in her purse. Was she about to offer him a lollipop to go somewhere with her? Instead of candy, she pulled out a blue piece of cloth with tiny racing cars printed all over it. She held it out to him. Danny reached for it tentatively, expecting her to try and grab him when he wasn't looking. But she didn't do anything as he snatched the strange cloth from her hand.

Danny unfolded it to find it had a stretchy loop of string on each end of the cloth. He could feel something that was both stiff and flexible running under one of the long seams of the strange blue cloth. Danny looked up at the masked woman in puzzlement.

Her eyes lit up as the mask over her mouth began to move. "Everyone is supposed to wear a mask these days. Especially little boys. You don't want to catch the virus and get really sick, do you?" She gestured towards the cloth that dangled from Danny's hand. "I made a bunch of these for my grandson. Take it, please."

Danny considered her gift. Why was she being so nice to him? Most people just ignored him. His family wasn't rich or well-connected. He was basically a misfit back at GU. There was no possible benefit to being nice to him, so most of his classmates weren't. It felt really strange getting help from a total stranger. Should he accept the gift or not? It was a rather childish thought, but he did like the little race cars. But wear a mask? Even if everyone else was wearing one, it felt like he was advertising that he was a thief.

Before he could decide what to do, the old woman took the mask and looped it over his ears. Danny wasn't sure how, but she tightened the straps to it fit him. Then she pressed gently on each side of his nose and the mask conformed to his face. "There," she said, "that is much better."

Danny mumbled a quick thank you and hurried towards the market. When he reached the next intersection, Danny turned back to see if old woman was still there. She was and she was watching him. He waved goodbye to the grandmother in the daisy mask and stepped around the corner. Danny leaned against the side of the building. He wasn't sure why the encounter with the old woman had unnerved him, but it had. He needed to get his game face back on. Then again, who would notice with the race car mask on his face.

As he considered his next step, Danny reached up under the mask. His face was hot and the mask felt rough against his lips. Danny decided he really didn't like masks. Hot, scratchy, and they made it hard to breathe. He would have taken it off, but everyone he saw was wearing one. It didn't make sense. Danny decided he would just have to suffer like everyone else. With a sigh, he headed to the first stop on his shopping adventure.

The Dollar General store wasn't far from the Wild Oat Market. He needed something to carry his acquisitions in. A backpack would be best as it would leave his hands free to do what they did best, steal. Sadly, he would have to pay for the backpack. It would be too big to hide in his clothing. Danny hurried across the small parking lot and came to a stop just outside the door. There in large black letters was the explanation Danny had been searching for.

> *By Order of the President of*
> *the United States of America,*
> *masks are required in all*
> *public venues.*

Danny was stunned. There had been discussions about the pros and cons of masks before he had gone to Florida, but no one had even considered the possibility of a mask mandate. What had happened to personal freedom? Did the President really have the power to do that kind of thing? Besides, getting sick was part of life. He'd survived the Virus. Apparently, things had gotten very strange during his time as a lab experiment.

Danny pushed he glass door open. A chime announced that someone had entered the store. The woman at the register stared at him as he entered. The brown eyes above her Dollar General mask warmed as he turned his masked face towards her. "Nice mask, young man, and welcome to Dollar General." Danny smiled back at her but then realized that she could not see his smile under the mask. He gave a quick wave and hurried past.

Danny began to wander the aisles. There wasn't much of a selection. And nothing cost only a dollar. In fact, prices seemed rather high for a discount store. Danny found the backpacks on aisle three. There were only two. Weren't there school kids in this town? How could they only have two backpacks? And the colors, sheesh. The first was a bright yellow that would be visible no matter how dark it was. Danny ignored it. The second was a dark green with blue piping. It wasn't much of a fashion statement, but Danny grabbed it and moved on.

Two rows later, Danny found the hoodies. He hesitated to call it a collection, three hoodies hanging on the back wall. Of course, there were no children's sizes. Nothing that would fit him or Ruth. And there was definitely nothing big enough for Geoff either. Danny took a light grey hoodie off its hanger. It would be a bit big on Jacob, but the hood would at least cover those pointed ears of his.

Danny realized he had already exceeded his budget for this stop, so he headed back to the register. His lone twenty-dollar bill and both ones were soon replaced by a handful of change. The woman didn't even offer him a bag for his purchases. She simply stuffed the hoodie into the larger pocket of the backpack along with his receipt. Danny accepted the backpack, clutching it to his chest. Then he turned to face the door.

On a small shelf beside the door was something Danny had missed when he came in. A box of disposable masks sat beside a sign that said, "In case you forgot your mask." Danny grinned at the sudden opportunity. He crossed to the door and paused. His small arms were both wrapped around the backpack. Danny muttered, "Silly," in his best childish voice before turning the pack around.

Danny stuck his right arm through the correct strap. Spinning in place, he feigned a struggle to get his left arm through the other strap. As his right hand swung past the box of masks, half its contents disappeared. There was a chuckle from behind him as the woman at the register asked, "Do you need help getting that one?"

Danny shook his head as he slipped his left arm in. "No, ma'am. I got it now." Danny pulled the straps tight and opened the door. The woman called, "Have a nice day!" as the door swung shut behind him.

Outside, Danny slid the mask down under his chin. He stood there letting the fresh air caress his face. It felt good to be maskless, even if only for a few minutes. How did people stand these things all day long? Danny wasn't sure. He stared down the street and spotted the sign for his next and most important stop. Aubuchon Hardware and its collection of tools were calling to him. Danny's smile faded away as he pulled the racecar mask back up over his face.

Danny actually began to skip as he hurried towards Aubuchon. His persona of a young boy was actually fun. The parking lot of the hardware store was almost empty. A single, silver SUV sat near the front door. It was in the handicapped slot, but Danny didn't see a handicap placard hanging from the rearview mirror. Another jerk, Danny decided as he crossed the lot. The SUV was a Yukon SLE. At least the jerk had good taste, Danny decided. But why, he wondered, did all the nice rides have to belong to people he didn't feel guilty about stealing from?

Danny ran his fingers softly across the side of the Yukon as he approached the door to Aubuchon. He would never drive a car like this now. Playing little kid might be fun, but it had real drawbacks. But maybe being short would help him get the tools he needed cheap. Or, better yet, free.

Danny reached for the door. Another of the ridiculous mask mandate signs was taped to the inside of the glass door. Danny shook his head as he pushed his way inside.

The store was deathly still. At first Danny thought maybe someone was robbing the place. But the clerk was alone at the front register. The young man with an American Flag on his mask was staring nervously towards the back of the store. Danny's curiosity immediately got the better of him and he began to walk in the direction the clerk was staring.

A voice whispered to him from behind the register, "Wait up here until they're done."

Danny just waved and continued down the main aisle. This was looking more and more interesting. Voices began to argue in the back. One was a calm older man's voice that was trying to be soothing. The other was a voice that was at best demanding and to Danny's thinking, downright rude. Danny was willing to bet that he had found the Yukon's driver.

Danny tiptoed along one of the large displays until he could see two masked men standing near the customer service desk. The man behind the desk was thin with greying hair. His nametag said 'Mike' and 'Manager.' The man on Danny's side of the counter was much larger. Danny could only see the man's back so he couldn't tell much about him. But there was a large bulge in an unbuttoned back pocket of the big man's pants.

Danny crept closer so he could catch all of the conversation.

The man with his back to Danny raised his voice even though Manager Mike was standing right in front of him. His hand was extended and he pointed his index finger at poor Mike. An electronic car key dangled from that lone finger. The 'customer' continued to shout. "It doesn't work. I want one that does start my car. Do the job right this time!"

Despite the mask, Danny could see the regret on Mike's face. "It was the last one we had for your model car, sir. I told you that the box was water-damaged. I wasn't sure if the key would work or not. I will gladly give you a refund."

The rather unpleasant customer slammed his hand on the counter. "I don't want a refund. What I want is a key that works!"

Entitled, Danny thought. He hated bullies who made life difficult for people just trying to do their job. Especially if those bullies were rich or powerful. There wasn't anything that Danny could do to help poor Mike, but he could exact a little revenge for what the man was putting Mike through.

Danny grinned as he bolted for the counter. His common sense was screaming no, but Danny wasn't listening to it. He intended to enjoy what was about to happen.

A high pitched "Whoopee!" exploded from Danny as he neared his mark. The big man jerked upright at the sound. The electronic key clattered to the floor. Danny dove for the falling key. But instead of catching it, Danny drove his shoulder into the back of the man's knee. The big man stumbled into the customer service desk and bounced off. At the instant the man's body impacted the desk, Danny slipped the fat wallet from the man's pocket.

With a soft grunt, Danny hit the floor, the wallet beneath him. Danny's left hand tucket the wallet into his clothing while his right hand grabbed the fallen key. Danny practically bounced to his feet and slapped the key on the counter in front of Mike.

The big man glared down at Danny. "Watch where the hell you're going, boy!"

Danny mumbled a quick sorry and then looked up at Mike. "Mommy says I get to buy a new screwdriver today. Where are they, please?"

The big man snarled. "It's not your turn, boy. Don't be such a brat. Get in line and wait your turn." Danny just stood there with a hurt expression on his face. Mike pointed off to the right without taking his eyes off the big man's face.

Danny smiled and took off, yelling a happy "thanks" to Mike. Danny couldn't remember ever having thus much fun in his whole life. The big man raised his voice again, but it didn't matter. He had already made the man pay for his rudeness.

The screwdrivers were right where Mike had pointed. There were so many different types of screwdrivers. It seemed kind of ridiculous. Danny ignored the fancy high-tech models. What he wanted was hanging down near the floor where he could reach it easily. A set of two craftsman steel screwdrivers. Simple, cheap, and designed to last forever. Danny didn't need a rachet screwdriver to pull a set of plates from a car.

The expensive screwdriver did make him think. He wouldn't mind having a small socket set with a speed rachet. Most tracking systems could be removed by loosening a few nuts. Danny turned a corner as he searched for what he wanted. That took him out of the two arguing men's line of sight.

Danny pulled the wallet from his shirt and looked inside. A stack of crisp new bills was tucked inside. The rude man had obviously just visited an ATM. Danny scanned the bills as he tucked them into his pocket. Fifties on the bottom and twenties un the top. It was a sweet haul. On a whim, Danny slid the annoying man's driver's license into his pocket as well.

Danny tossed the wallet behind a stack of socket sets and selected a set to purchase with his new supply of cash. It wasn't a large set, but it had a mix of U.S. and metric attachments. With it, he would have a greater selection of vehicles to choose from.

Danny was about to head to the front register when the big man slammed his hand on the counter again. The jerk was just so annoying. Danny looked at the place where he had tossed the man's wallet. Maybe leaving it there wasn't such a good idea. If he left it there, the obnoxious man would just accuse one of the store's employees of taking his money. With a grin, Danny picked up the wallet and tucked it under the socket set.

Danny began to skip back towards customer service with his treasures in hand. This time when Danny got there, he didn't stumble. But as little boys do, he had too many things in his small hands. He almost dropped his precious screwdriver set. Danny let go of the heavy socket set to catch the screwdriver before it hit the floor. With accuracy that could only be born of bad luck, the socket set came down on the toe of the man's leather Midas boots. Danny struggled to hide a grin as the small metal box left a scratch in the soft leather.

The marred boot retreated behind the man's other foot. With a grunt of pain, the man's reddened face turned from Danny to the blue metal box lying on the floor in front of him. Danny waited until the man bent to reach for the socket set before he moved. Danny's hand was much faster than the man's as he snatched the socket set away from the man's reaching fingers. "That's mine!" Danny cried in the man's ear as he slid the now lighter wallet back into the man's back pocket.

There was murder in the big man's eyes as he stood up. Danny glared right back at him. Danny shook his screw drivers at the socket thief. "Get your own tools!" Then Danny took his biggest risk yet. He turned his back on the angry man and looked up at Manager Mike. Holding both purchases up where Mike could see them, Danny shouted, "Thank you, thank you, thank you."

Before either man could act, Danny rushed back to the front of the store. He placed his purchases on the counter, laughing softly. Did life get any better than this? The young clerk rang up his tools. Anything else?" the young man asked. Danny nodded and grabbed a Coke from the cooler and a bag of Sunchips. He had earned a treat.

He got some smaller bills in change from the crisp new fifty he handed the clerk. Danny picked up the paper bag holding his new possessions and walked proudly out the door. He stood for a moment in front of Aubuchon and smiled at the silver Yukon sitting in the handicapped space. "I win," Danny whispered to it. Danny turned away from the SUV and walked around the corner of the store.

In the building's shadows, Danny knelt to repack his things. The screwdrivers came out of their package and were tucked into the front pocket of the backpack. The socket set joined the hoodie in the main pocket. Then Danny leaned against the wall to enjoy his Coke and bag of chips. He had one more stop to make before he went shopping for a new set of wheels.

The junk food brought back memories of college life. A pizza would be nice right now, too. But that would have to wait until later. Danny was stuffing his trash into the empty paper bag when a big engine roared to life in the parking lot. Danny peeked around the corner in time to see the silver SUV surge out of its parking space. With a squeal of its tires, the Yukon surged towards the street. It screeched to a stop at the edge of the road. The driver's window came down and the annoying man held his hand out the window in a one finger salute.

At the next break in traffic, the Yukon turned right and soon disappeared from sight. That man needed another lesson, Danny decided. And Danny knew just how to give it to him. Settling the backpack on his shoulders, Danny dropped his trash in the can by the door and headed down the street. Sunoco was only a short walk away.

The gas station didn't look that busy. He didn't see a tow truck, but they might still have what Danny needed. If not, there would be other service stations in town. Danny shifted two of his newly acquired twenties and the nasty man's driver's license to his right pocket. His plan should work as long as there was only one person working at the gas station right now. Danny stopped on the sidewalk to study the station.

An older Subaru was parked by the pumps. He watched as the young female attendant finished pumping gas for an elderly woman. She paused at the driver's window to chat. The two women laughed and carried on for longer than Danny would have expected. He assumed they knew each other well. Eventually, the Subaru drove off and the young woman went back inside the station. Danny ran to catch up. He followed her inside.

As the door closed behind them, she knelt down to meet his gaze. "And what can I do for you? You look a little young to be driving yet." She had a pleasant laugh and beautiful hazel eyes. Danny wished he could see her face behind her mask. But now wasn't the time to flirt with someone twice his height. He gave her his best imitation of puppy dog eyes and asked, "Do you have a slim jim?"

The young woman nodded and pointed over in the corner where a rack of snack foods sat beside a soda cooler.

Danny shook his head. "Not that kind. I need the kind that opens car doors."

The attendant pulled back and gazed at him thoughtfully. Her forehead furrowed as she asked, "Why do you need one of those? Are you planning to steal a car or something?" This time her chuckle didn't sound quite as friendly.

Danny shook his head furiously. She was getting suspicious and Danny didn't want that. "Not for me, silly. I'm too small to drive. The old man at the market needs to get into his car. He locked his keys in the car. Can you believe it? He has real keys for his car. I thought everybody just pushed the buttons. Anyway, he sent me here so he can watch his groceries."

The attendant sighed. "I'm sorry, little man. I can't go open it for him. There is no one else here to take care of my customers."

Danny pulled two twenties from his pocket. They were wrapped around the unpleasant man's driver's license. "He only wants to borrow it. He'll bring it back to trade for his license. He promised me another twenty if I brought it to him. Please?"

Danny saw her indecision, so he tried to push the money and license into her hand. "Pretty please? He's a nice old man." He would never know if it was kindness on her part or the two twenties, but she nodded and stood. He watched her go through a door into the back of the building.

She returned moments later with a long metal bar that Danny recognized. It wasn't as nice as his own, but it would do what he needed it to. He reached for it, but she held it just out of his reach. "Tell the old man that I will call the police if he doesn't return this in the next half hour. I have his license so they will know where to find him."

Danny swallowed his smile of elation. Calling the police was exactly what he wanted her to do. Danny nodded and replied, "I'll tell him."

She handed him the bar and Danny had no trouble being sincere as he accepted the precious tool. "Oh, thank you."

Danny ran from the station like he was on a mission from God. He headed back towards the market as another car pulled into the station. Danny continued to run until he was sure the young woman was distracted by her next customer. Danny rounded the corner onto Main Street and stopped to catch his breath. He wanted to lower the mask once more, but he doubted the people around him would approve.

Danny moved to stand next to the building on the corner. He quickly stuffed the business end of the slim jim into his backpack. It was too big by far, so a length of the bar stood well above Danny's head. He didn't mind. It would be easier to grab if he needed it.

With his latest acquisition secure, he was on the move, again. One block over and Danny turned north. He was fairly certain he had seen homes in this direction. Homes meant cars and minivans parked overnight in dark driveways. It was almost like being in a candy store. Pick the color and flavor you want and drive it away.

Fifteen minutes later, Danny was walking through a quiet neighborhood with pretty little homes on both sides of the street. The sun wasn't visible above the houses anymore. Danny guessed that he had less than an hour and a half until it was dark enough to start getting into any interesting cars. For now, he would just browse the neighborhood.

Danny studied the houses as well as the cars as he wandered from street to street. The homes didn't look like those of the rich people in Georgetown. They were just family homes with bicycles, swing sets, and children's toys lying on the grass. It was like the places he had grown up in. The cars were family cars and many of them were showing signs of age. There were no sportscars or fancy Yukons. These were not the kind of people Danny stole from. He wasn't sure any of these people could afford to lose their car to him.

Danny considered the two men he had stolen from that day. He didn't count the handful of paper masks he had taken from Dollar General. He had really enjoyed taking both men's wallets, just like he enjoyed stripping the cars of the rich people in Georgetown. Why was taking one of these cars any different? But Danny knew the answer even as he asked himself the question. In his mind, those he normally stole from deserved it. What Danny wasn't sure about was what that said about him.

He turned another corner and saw more of the same kind of houses. Could he treat these people the way he had Boboden or the dude at Aubuchon? He knew he could, but he wouldn't like it. The trouble was that he wasn't sure he had a choice if he wanted to remain free.

Danny was still arguing with himself when he looked up to see the mountains. Majestic, rocky peaks reaching up into a star filled sky. Traces of snow still frosted the surface of some of the higher outcrops. Tendrils of water flowing downhill to the right, merging into a raging flow that rushed over a cliff to disappear into the wheel well of the old panel van.

Danny whistled softly. He had heard tales of conversion vans painted like this, but he had never actually seen one. This had to be a relic of some long-lost age in automotive history. As far as Danny knew, Ford hadn't made the E-150 model 1 van in at least thirty years. And yet, this van looked almost new. The van wasn't just a work of art, it was an act of love. Even the porthole window was integrated into the paint job. The blue tinted glass was indistinguishable from the water cascading over the cliff. The tales that Danny had heard about conversion jobs didn't do this van justice.

Here was a vehicle Danny might even give up stealing to own. But possessing this dream was something that could never be. Before this moment, Danny couldn't imagine anything that would stand out on the highway more than the big Chevy farm truck. But he had been wrong. The vehicle he was yearning for was truly one of a kind.

He slowly circled the van. When he reached the front wheel well, Danny slipped his hand up inside it. There wasn't a trace of rust anywhere he touched. It was like the van had somehow been spared the ravages of New England winters. Danny continued examining the vehicle. The front grill of the van gleamed; Danny didn't find a single bug splat to mar its perfection.

A brand-new Celica, its glossy blue paint shamed by the beauty of the mountain scene, sat on the far side of the van nearest the small brick home. The only interesting feature on the Toyota was the wheelchair rack mounted on its back bumper. Danny turned his back on the insignificant sedan and looked up at this side of the van. Surprisingly, the view from this side wasn't just a mirror image of the waterfall. The unknown artist had transported Danny to the far side of the waterfall so he could experience that view as well. It was truly amazing work.

Danny finished his tour at the rear of the van. There he found the biggest surprise of all. The surprise wasn't the breathtaking representation of the water falling towards him, it was the sign in the back window of the van.

   *For Sale*
   *$5000*

For sale? Really? Danny couldn't wrap his mind around the idea. Why would anyone want to sell a classic like this? And for only five grand? It was insane.

Danny almost broke and ran when a proud voice spoke from right behind him, "She is beautiful, isn't she?"

The words eased the stab of guilt Danny felt. And that simple question drew his attention back to the van. "The mountains look so real."

"Thank you," the voice said. "I painted her myself when I was much younger. And they are real. Colorado Rockies. It was a beautiful drive."

"How did you keep her looking so nice?" Danny asked.

"Oh, I had to touch her up a few times over the years. The color faded in the sun. It wasn't easy, but it was worth it. She's still the sweetest ride in a thousand miles."

Danny turned to see an old man staring proudly at his van. The old man had to be in his seventies if he was a day. He leaned heavily on a plain wooden cane. Danny's mind was racing and words just spilled out of his mouth, "The Econoline was a great van. There can't be many that are still in such great shape."

The old man stared at him in surprise. "And there aren't many young boys your age that know that much about old cars."

Danny found himself liking the old man. He just couldn't lie to the old man, but he couldn't tell him the whole truth either. "I'm not as young as I look. I'm a college student." Danny gestured at his new body. "This is just…" Danny struggled for words that wouldn't sound mental. "This is just how I was made."

The old man just nodded. Danny liked that he didn't try to apologize for what Danny was. Instead, the old man's words were thoughtful. "None of us controls what we are, son. We only get to choose who we become in this life. I was born with a bad leg. Never let it stop me. Had a great life painting trucks and vans like this one. I have a beautiful wife. Never regretted anything. Hopefully, someday you can say the same."

Danny turned back to the van. "Why are you practically giving her away? I'd think you'd keep her for the memories if nothing else."

"Don't want to sell her, son. But sometimes we don't get what we want in this life." There was sadness in the old man's voice as he continued. "My wife has Parkinson's. She can't climb into the van anymore. The old girl's suspension won't support a lift for the wheelchair. So, I'm selling her."

Danny's "That sucks!" slipped out before he could shut it off. He tried to cover it up with a question. "Why so cheap? She has to be worth ten times as much as you're asking."

The man moved slowly past Danny to wipe away an imagined smudge of dirt. "Nobody wants a big old gas hog like this. It's not politically correct to drive her anymore. These days, you're supposed to drive one of those electric pieces of crap. I'll be lucky to get what little I'm asking for her."

The old man's cane lifted to point at the Celica. "My wife still enjoys riding through the countryside with the windows rolled down. I'll do what I must to make her happy even if it means spending all our savings on a lifeless car she can still get into. I also made sure I got the attachment so the dang wheelchair could ride along so she can use the bathroom when she needs to."

Then the stick pointed to the front porch. "The five thousand will pay for a ramp leading into the house and for a new shower she can get in and out of. Damned insurance paid for the fancy chair, but it doesn't help with much else."

There was a strange pressure building inside Danny. He wasn't used to caring about other people's problems or feeling their pain. Especially not about people he really didn't know. He looked up as the old man turned to face him. "I wish I could help." Before the old man could answer, Danny found himself running down the street. There was something wet on his cheeks and he didn't know why. What he did know was that he couldn't steal from someone like the old man. Not now and maybe not ever.

Darkness claimed the streets as the sun finally set. Danny was angry with himself. Why was he letting the old man's tale get to him. He needed to be what he was, a thief. He needed to steal something to regain his sense of himself. A pick-up sat in the next driveway. Danny used one of his new screwdrivers to remove its front plate. He rubbed the remains of two dead bugs off before stowing it in his backpack.

Stealing the plate wasn't enough though. Danny still felt like he had lost a piece of himself back at the old man's house. Danny stared up the street looking for another target for his frustration.

Not far ahead, Danny saw a minivan sitting in a driveway on the edge of a park. Danny pulled the slim jim out. He was determined to open the vehicle and take what he needed from it. But the slim jim wasn't necessary, the van wasn't even locked. The side door opened without a sound and Danny cursed the owners for being so trusting. The first thing Danny saw was a booster seat on the far side of the middle seat.

Danny forced himself to ignore the booster seat. So what if the family had children. At least that was what Danny tried to tell himself as he climbed into the van. If this van met his needs, they would take it. But it turned out that 'mini' was an apt description. Geoff would never fit in the back even if they pulled out the rear seat. Geoff was just too big. Danny told himself to take something, anything, just to prove that he could. Maybe that would teach the family not to leave their car unlocked. But what? One of the many toys stuffed into the compartments?

He looked for anything else he could take. But the contents of the van were useless. He shoved an old road atlas into his backpack, but he doubted the family would even notice it was missing. Danny climbed back out of the minivan with a grunt of disgust. As he stared at his rather unsatisfying robbery attempt, Danny noticed a pink lump under the middle seat. He hooked it with the slim jim and pulled it closer.

It was a child's hoodie. Danny held it up in the light of the streetlamps and groaned. Elmo stared back at him with that stupid grin on his face. Danny thought about tossing it back into the van, but it was big enough for Ruth and she really needed to hide that hair of hers. Danny stuffed it in his backpack and congratulated himself for stealing from a little kid. Danny pretended not to notice when his right hand dropped the twenty on the floor near where the hoodie had been. He closed the minivan's door and walked away.

There was another street leading away from the park. Danny considered it. But what was the use? His heart wasn't in it tonight. Giving up, Danny turned and headed into the park. The streetlights disappeared from sight as Danny headed deeper into the park. Strangely, the darkness he was expecting never came. Danny's vision, which had always been good at night, remained sharp and clear. Only it wasn't quite the same, Danny realized.

He paused to study his surroundings. Trees, grass, and the dirt trails were all clearly visible. But some areas seemed a bit redder than they should be. Others had a touch too much blue in them. Red and blue grass was just wrong as far as Danny was concerned. It took Danny a moment to see the pattern. The blue color was concentrated beneath the trees and in places that would have been shaded. The reds were in spots that would have been warmed by the sun. It was almost like having a superpower.

Danny considered what he had become. It was kind of exciting in a way. He could steal practically anything and now he could see better than a cat. Maybe he should start thinking about designing a costume. But, he wondered, would he be a superhero or the villain?

Danny surveyed the park with renewed interest. What could he see with his new eyesight? The park stretched out before him, trees around the edges and soccer fields in the center. The park appeared to be deserted except for a lone couple pushing a baby stroller along one of the paths. Might not hurt to stay close to them, Danny thought. That way anyone who saw him wouldn't start worrying about the "lost" little boy. Danny ran to get closer to them.

The couple walked slowly along a circular trail that followed the trees line. The stands of trees were so thick that Danny could not see out the far side. The couple ambled slowly along the path. They walked like they had all the time in the world, and yet, the man kept checking his watch. That some people are strange was all Danny could come up with.

Danny tensed as a dark form stepped from the trees. It was a man dressed in a dark leather coat with a bandana tied loosely around his neck. His face was dirty and unshaven. Danny shivered as the man raised a cigar to his lips. The tip glowed suddenly orange igniting Danny's sense of danger. Was the couple about to be mugged? Danny wasn't so much worried about the couple; they had chosen to be out here at night. But he didn't want to see the baby get hurt. Danny began to creep forward. He had no idea how he could help but he had to try. Then the man he had been following waved and greeted the stranger.

The two men whispered for several minutes before the new man handed something to the man Danny had been following. The man

Danny thought of as the Dad walked back and handed what he had been given to the woman. She bent to place the object in the diaper bag while her partner took a package from the stroller and handed it to the stranger. The man took the package and disappeared back into the trees. With a quick exchange of words and another check of the watch, the couple moved on.

Danny followed them. He didn't know what had just happened, but the need to know burned in him. Like his enhanced vision, the overwhelming curiosity was new to Danny. It was an exhilarating feeling, but also one that could get him as dead as the cat in that old saying. And, Danny knew, he didn't have nine lives to risk. Despite the danger, he got closer so he could watch.

The couple's next stop was just a little further down the path. This time it was a woman that came out of the trees. Danny didn't like the looks of her either. Danny snuck close enough to see everything that happened. This time when the woman pushing the stroller reached for the diaper bag, Danny could see the stack of bills she placed in the bag. The woman from the woods retreated with a similar package to the man's in the leather coat. The people coming out of the trees weren't a threat, Danny realized. They were customers.

Danny was still puzzled though. He had lived in a college town for a while now. He had seen pushers and dealers many times. But most pushers were small time. They sold a sandwich bag with some pot in it or a dime bag of something harder. Most of their sales could be hidden in the palm of their hands. Danny couldn't imagine them selling anything as large as the packages this couple was dealing.

It took three more sales before Danny figured it out. The small-time dealers were this couple's customers. The couple were in the big league, distributing drugs on a much larger scale. With that realization, Danny began to calculate how much money was actually in that diaper bag. There was enough to solve not only his own problems, but maybe to do something truly worthwhile.

Danny cursed himself for being a fool, but he knew it was already too late. Danny wanted this. The decision to take what was in that bag restored whatever Danny had lost at the old man's house. He was alive again. Danny's fingers began to twitch as he studied the way the bag hung on the stroller. That diaper bag was begging for someone's fingers to slip in and… Danny chuckled softly as he realized just how wrong that analogy sounded.

He continued to follow the couple closely. The only chance he saw to get away with this heist was to make his move during a sale. The couple would be focused on their customer. Maybe if he timed it just right. But the parking lot wasn't that far away. He needed one more buyer. Just one.

There turned out to be two. A man and a woman came out of the trees together. Danny used their arrival to move to within a few yards of the couple. Danny wanted to rush forward, but something made him wait. Something wasn't quite right about the two customers. They walked differently than the other customers. They didn't slouch as they stood there waiting to make their purchase. Danny wasn't sure what was about to happen, but he knew this would be the only chance he would get. So, he watched and waited.

The man with the stroller moved forward. But there was no friendly wave this time. He seemed tense. The woman actually moved to stand between the stroller and the new customers. He had an open path to the diaper bag. Danny saw her hand slip into one of her tall black boots. He sucked in his breath as she pulled a six-inch blade out of the boot and held it behind her back.

Danny's eyes moved back to the two men. They were arguing about something. It was now or never Danny decided. He darted forward and leaned over the side of the stroller yelling excitedly. "I want to hold the baby. Please?"

The argument between the two men died. Danny's left hand dipped into the stroller and snatched the thin baby blanket that lay across the seat. Two more packages had been hidden by the blanket. At the same time, his right hand slipped into the diaper back and his fingers closed on the thick envelope that lay on top of a pile of disposable diapers.

All four of the adults turned to stare at him. Shock showed on every face. Danny straightened and asked with all the innocence he could muster, "Where did the baby go?"

Stroller man turned and yelled, "Get the hell away from there!" Stroller woman spun and pointed the knife at him.

Danny slid the envelope he held in his right hand under the baby blanket as he backed behind the stroller. With the envelope out of view, Danny screamed a child-like scream. "Don't hurt me. Pleasssssse!"

Danny spun and began to run into a darkness that wasn't dark to him. A woman's voice yelled from behind him. "Police! Drop the knife. On your knees now!" There was a gunshot. Danny felt a strong urge to pee, but he refused to embarrass himself now. Instead, he ran on. Sirens began to blare and headlights crisscrossed the park. But none of them fell on Danny's small form. More voices began to yell as Danny ran between two trees.

He passed dozens of trees before he found one with a nice thick trunk. Danny wasn't sure when he had dropped the blanket, but he bit down hard on the envelope so his hands would be free. Danny had never been one for climbing trees, but tonight his fingers and toes found an endless supply of places to grab and pull himself up on. In only a few breaths, Danny found himself on a hid, wide branch where he sat huddled against the trunk of the tree.

The sound of his own ragged breathing seemed to echo in Danny's ears. His chest felt like it was being squeezed by his ribs. It wasn't fear so much as being out of shape that was causing him to pant. As the adrenalin rush faded, his breathing began to ease. Danny decided he would put a little more effort into Geoff's exercises. Or, maybe not.

Danny sat on his perch and waited. No one even came near his hiding place. As long as they didn't have dogs, Danny was fairly sure he had gotten away with his little heist. As the minutes dragged by, the headlights and the flashes of red and blue began to disappear one by one. Danny estimated he had been in the tree an hour before the park was silent once more. Danny's cocky grin was back in place as he slid back down the tree with the envelope safely tucked into his backpack.

He retraced his steps to the edge of the trees. A lone squad car sat in the parking lot. Two officers leaned against the side of their car talking. It was all over. The realization brought a sudden sense of loss. Would he ever have that much fun again?

This trip back through the park was farther than Danny remembered. He didn't hurry as he made his way back to the old man's house. The park and the streets beyond were empty. Most of the homes he passed were dark, the people in them already in bed. Danny stopped only once on the way to the old man's house. Under one particularly bright streetlight, Danny pulled out the envelope and examined his haul.

There were stacks of bills held together with rubber bands and paper clips. Nothing smaller than a twenty was in any of the bundles. Most of the bundles were filled with hundred-dollar bills. Danny whistled softly. He had at least fifteen thousand dollars in cash. More than his friends needed, but not more than the old man needed. Danny counted out four thousand dollars and slid it into the small pocket at the front of the backpack. He stuffed the rest back into the envelope. There was a bounce in his step as he continued.

When he reached the old man's driveway. Danny ran his fingers lovingly along the paint job as he walked to the front door. "Soon, baby, soon." He muttered to her.

The house was dark. Danny wasn't sure how late it was, but he rang the doorbell anyway. After a minute, he rang it a second time. He could hear movement inside and he saw a light come on through the narrow window beside the door. A tired "I'm coming," came from inside. The door opened about three inches before a short chain brought the door to a stop. An eye stared at him through the opening. "Kind of late isn't it, son? We were already in bed."

Danny reached up and took off his mask. "My name is Danny. My friends and I want to help. Will you listen?"

It felt like the old man studied him for a million years, but the door closed and Danny heard the chain rattling. The doorknob turned again and the door opened all the way this time.

The old man stood there in a faded bathrobe. He stared down at Danny with a questioning look on his face. "It's almost eleven and my wife needs her sleep. What can I do for you, Danny?"

A woman's voice echoed from inside. The voice wavered a bit as it asked, "Is everything all right, Edwin?"

Edwin studied him for a long time. His wife called "Edwin?" again and then he answered her. "It's all right dear. Danny didn't realize it was so late. Go to sleep while I find out what he needs."

The old man stepped aside and motioned Danny towards the lit room where a small table and two chairs stood. Danny took a seat and waited for Edwin.

The old man sat. "I hope you don't mind if I don't offer you tea or coffee. I would prefer to keep this brief."

Danny shrugged. "I'm more of a soda man myself. Coffee was never my thing." Danny reached under his shirt and pulled out the yellow envelope. He dropped it on the table. "My friends and I want to buy the van."

Edwin looked at the thick envelope but did not reach for it. "Couldn't this have waited until morning?"

Danny shook his head. "We need to be moving on. Our truck broke down and your van is big enough to carry all of us."

Edwin still ignored the envelope. "I am not a fool boy. Who is going to be looking for that?" Edwin's chin gestured towards the envelope.

Danny sighed. "No one. I swear. I wouldn't bring trouble to your door. More importantly, I won't bring trouble to her door."

They were both silent as a mantle clock began to ring somewhere in the house. Danny counted each of the eleven chimes. "What kind of trouble are you in, Danny?"

Danny wasn't sure how to answer at first. In the end, he decided on a version of the truth. "I won't lie to you. Someone is after us. But we didn't hurt anyone. We didn't do anything. But the government is searching for us. I know it's hard to believe, but it's true."

Edwin smiled then. He pointed to the backpack that Danny had set on the floor beside his chair. "There is no doubt in my mind about what that piece of metal sticking out of your pack is Danny. I recognized it when you came here this afternoon. I figured you would steal her tonight and I would get what money I could out of the insurance. Now, you are here looking to pay for my van. I can believe a lot right now."

Edwin's hand reached out and dumped the envelope in front of Danny. At the sight of the money. Edwin shook his head. Danny saw stubborn pride in the old man's eyes. "That's too damn much."

Danny shook his head. "Not half of what that van is worth. This money was supposed to do bad things. Use it. Take care of your wife. Take it for her."

A tear leaked from the old man's right eye as Danny watched. Edwin finally asked, "What do you want me to do?"

Danny grinned. "Sign the title, give me the keys, hide the money and go to bed. The van will be gone by morning. Then, just forget about me."

Danny felt a moment of panic as the old man shook his head. "No, Danny. I won't forget about you. Not after this. But I will promise to tell everyone about the 6'2" rich college boy that bought my van for less than I asked for it. Edwin winked and reached out a hand.

Danny took Edwin's hand in his own and shook it. Twenty minutes later he locked the atlas and the license plate he had taken in the van. Then he headed for the market. It was time to collect his friends. Danny began to whistle as he headed for the market. He was feeling pretty good about himself. Maybe, he thought, there is more than one kind of thief.

## Chapter 15
## A Gnoment of Inspiration

*Enterprise News*
*King Richard's Faire returning to Carver this fall for its 40th season ...*
*Apr 5, 2021 — The Faire will run from Saturdays through Mondays beginning Sept. 4 through Oct. 24 during its anniversary season after being canceled last year due to the Virus-C ...*

Ruth slipped into the passenger seat as the Professor drove the van along Interstate 90 into the rising sun. As she buckled in, she asked him, "Are you feeling better, Professor?"

Professor Dror turned his head briefly to meet her gaze. After another day and night of rest and freedom, his eyes were bright and untroubled. His smile was almost as welcoming as the one he had given her long ago on her first night of class. There was hope in his voice as he replied, "Better than you could imagine, Ruth. Herrera and I were locked in that lab for a long time." His eyes went back to watching the traffic flowing into the outskirts of Boston.

Cars and trucks flew past them every few seconds. They were all in such a hurry even though the sun was just beginning to reflect off the skyscrapers far ahead. In her opinion, there were far too many vehicles on the road for this hour of the morning. Then again, Ruth had never cared for interstate traffic in New York either. The professor's voice interrupted her musings. "How are you adjusting, Ruth?"

Ruth shrugged. "I'm not really sure, Professor. A part of me wants to run home to Mother. But another part of me never wants to go home again. For the first time in my life, I am free to do what I want to do. Father isn't picking schools for me or trying to plan out my future. I can make my own choices now. And then, there is what we can do with the old tongue. I like the feeling of power it gives me. It's kind of strange how the freedom and the power are exciting and scary at the same time."

The Professor chuckled softly. "You are growing up, Ruth. Life is exciting and power should be scary. What you're feeling is perfectly normal."

Ruth stared at him; her eyes drawn once more to his pointed ears. "Are you sure, Professor? Nothing feels normal anymore."

"Ruth," he said in a serious tone. "I think we need to get past the whole Professor thing. You aren't that young girl that needed to impress me anymore. And I am not the old man who continued to teach so he wouldn't be alone. I don't really know who or what any of us are now, but the old professor and his star pupil don't really exist anymore. I think the new Jacob would be happier with Ruth as his friend."

The part of Ruth that was reaching for her newfound independence really wanted what he was offering her. Her voice was tentative at first, but it grew bolder with each word. "That means a lot to me… Jacob. But I still need your lessons. I don't know enough of the old tongue yet."

"The lessons are yours," he replied, "for as long as you want them."

The van trembled slightly as another semi shot past them on the left. The Professor … No, Jacob, was keeping the van just under the speed limit. They couldn't afford an awkward discussion with a state trooper about how fast they had been going. Even if they could explain the strange way each of them looked, none of them had any form of ID, let alone a driver's license. She grinned suddenly as she wondered how Jacob would explain his ears to the officer. "Yes, officer, I know they are a bit unusual, but we are in a hurry to get to the Star Trek convention."

With that image in her mind, Ruth relaxed into the comfort of the bucket seat. The van was such an improvement over the farm truck they had started their escape in. She still didn't understand how they had gotten the van. Or, to be more accurate, what Danny had done to acquire it. Finally, she gave her curiosity free reign and asked, "This van is really nice. Are you sure Danny didn't steal it?"

Jacob began to laugh. His right hand came off the steering wheel and pointed at the dash in front of her. "Take a look in the glove box."

Ruth leaned forward and lifted the latch. The small door dropped open revealing its unexpected contents. Ruth gasped as she recognized the neat bundles for what they were, stacks of money. Ruth only hesitated a second before she grabbed the top bundle on the pile. Her fingers fanned out the bills. Her voice cracked as she blurted out, "This one has a thousand dollars in it!"

Jacob nodded as he lowered the visor to block the morning sun. "There are four more bundles just like it. Thanks to Danny we have enough cash to make our escape. But the answer to your question is under that pile of money. Look at the folded piece of paper at the bottom of the pile."

Ruth tugged the stiff parchment out from under the stack of bills and unfolded it. It was the title to the van. She turned over. The seller block at the bottom was signed by an Edwin Rousseau. The purchaser line was blank. Questions swirled in Ruth's mind as she considered what Danny had accomplished in just one night. Then she carefully folded the title and slid it and the money back in the glovebox. As she closed the door, she asked, "Is this why he was so pleased with himself yesterday?"

"That would be my guess," Jacob replied.

"Did he tell you how he pulled it off? Did he rob a bank?" Ruth asked.

Jacob shook his head. "All he would tell me is that Williamstown will be a safer place thanks to him."

Ruth sighed and then grumbled, "If he could do all that, why couldn't he get me a hoodie with a little more dignity? Elmo? Really? And why pink?"

Ruth liked the rich sound of Jacob's laughter as he ran his fingers over his own hoodie. "Better you than me, Ruth."

They sat in companionable silence for the next half hour as soft snores rose and fell in the back of the van. Jacob turned south at the 495 interchange and followed I-495 to exit 2. Route 58 would bring them right into Carver. Just outside of town, they stopped for gas. Jacob filled the van's large tank and then parked around the side of the station. Behind the bulk of the van, they took turns sneaking into the restroom. By the time Ruth came out, Danny was loading a six-pack of water and a dozen muffins into the back of the van.

The food and water disappeared quickly. Geoff finished off everything that was left in a few bites. Then Jacob started the van and got back on the road. There was no need for Ruth to remember the way to the massive park where the Faire was held. Signs led them right to the parking lot.

Traffic was stop and go and they missed more traffic lights than they made. Ruth turned on the radio and spun the dial until she caught the end of a news broadcast. The announcer was complaining about the only NFL game from the day before. Ruth switched off the radio and asked, "One football game? That means yesterday was Monday, right?"

Danny's voice echoed from the back of the van, "Or Thursday. Don't girls know anything about football?"

Before Ruth had a chance to tell Danny off, Jacob reached over and patted her on the arm, "Ignore him. John planned the escape for a Sunday. That would mean the day we spent in the rest area was Monday. So, today should be Tuesday. Is that important somehow?"

Ruth couldn't keep the excitement from her voice. "Yes! It means no crowds and no one to gawk at us when we arrive at the Faire. Even most of the vendors will be gone. King Richards is only open from Saturday through Monday each week. Only the Rennies will be there today. If the Faire was open, no one would have time to talk to us."

Jacob began to speak, but Ruth cut him off with a shriek of happiness. "There!" Her tiny finger stabbed out to point at the sign for King Richard's parking.

The main parking lot was empty. Jacob turned left onto the grass covered field. He brought the van to a stop so he could study the tall pine trees on the far side of the unpaved lot. Ruth's finger shifted to point at a path that led up to the gate. A line of porta potties stood like medieval soldiers guarding either side of that path.

A number of orange traffic cones sectioned off the area to the far right of the path. String ran between the cones. Cardboard signs hung from the strings at random intervals. From a distance, the faded handicap symbols looked like tiny toilet sets. It was like having dedicated parking for people who needed to use the porta potties.

The van began to creep forward. Jacob guided it across the mix of grass and gravel dotted by tiny tufts of bright yellow dandelions. He brought the van to a stop on the edge of the field just outside the handicapped parking. He put the van in park and turned off the engine.

The silence was overwhelming as each of them waited for a sign as to what came next. The tension was shattered by a loud click as Jacob unbuckled his seat belt. Ruth felt the weight of responsibility settle on her young shoulders when Jacob asked, "What next, Ruth? And for heaven's sake, what is a Rennie?"

Ruth released her own seat belt and stood on the floor in front of her seat. She stared out the front window as she struggled for an answer to that first question. Nothing came to her. The second question was simple, so Ruth focused on that. "Rennies are the people of the Faires. You could say they come in two flavors. There are the vendors and staff who just dress up to sell things and do odd jobs around the Faire. Then there are 'The Folk.' They are the ones who would live in character if they could. It's a way of life for many of them."

Jacob's tone was playful as he teased her, "I don't need three guesses to figure out where you fall on that scale, Ruth. I can hear the longing in your voice."

Ruth turned to face him. "Who wouldn't want to live that kind of life? It's like a non-stop magic show with none of the problems of the real world."

Ruth felt a pang of disappointment that Jacob face didn't mirror her own excitement. She had hoped his love of the past would extend to faires. Ruth knew she wasn't being fair to him. Jacob had never been to a Ren before. How could he ever understand what he was missing?

Jacob's hand came up and pointed towards the gate. Ruth turned to see two youngish men running a cable into the ticket area. They seemed to be arguing about how to hide the cable.

Jacob winked at her and asked. "Some of your mysterious Rennies sullying themselves with technology? Do you have a plan?"

Ruth reached back behind her head and pulled that awful pink hood up over her hair. She truly hated what she was wearing, but she wasn't ready to answer questions about her appearance yet. Pulling the strings to tighten it on her unruly hair, she reached for the door. "We go ask about work. You should do the talking, Jacob. You look more like an adult than the rest of us do."

"All of us?" Jacob asked.

Ruth nodded. "They're going to get a look at us sooner or later. We might as well get the gawking over with and see how they react."

Jacob nodded and pulled up his own hood. "Alright, everyone. Let's go. Try not to act like we are fugitives, okay?"

Ruth shook her head at Danny's snort of amusement. This was not going to be easy.

Six bodies tumbled out of the van and into the parking lot. The last to exit the van was Geoff who had to work his way out the back. The tiny form of Coon scrambled up his clothing to perch on the big man's shoulder. As soon as everyone was out, Jacob led the way to the ticket booth.

The two men continued to dig a small trench to bury the cable they were feeding into the booth. A dark-haired man with his back to them spoke as they approached, "Sorry, folks. We're closed. Come back on Saturday. We still have five weeks left in the season."

Jacob stopped not far behind him. "We're actually here looking for work."

The second man had red hair and freckles. He looked up and Ruth watched as surprise and then amusement crossed his face. "Nice makeup kids, but your costumes need a lot of work."

The dark-haired man stood and faced them. He had a neatly trimmed goatee. Ruth guessed that this was a rare out-of-costume event for him. The man gave Jacob a harsh stare before looking down at the three smaller forms clustered around Jacob. "I'm really sorry, kids. I know working here looks like a lot of fun. It is actually. But we aren't allowed to hire children. Perhaps when you are older. Keep working on your roles. Your makeup does look great."

Ruth was about to respond when Geoff walked up and stood behind Jacob. Jacob might have been twice her size, but the top of his hood didn't even reach Geoff's chest. The red-headed boy stared up at him from where he was kneeling. "Holy shit, Dave!"

The dark-haired man snapped. "Watch your mouth in front of the kids!" But he was also staring intently up at Geoff with a look of awe. Ruth grinned as Dave's eyes traveled down Geoff's body and came to rest on the big man's feet. Dave's eyes widened even more when he saw Geoff's sockless ankles where he had expected the stilts to be. There wasn't a sound as Dave's mouth spasmed open and closed, but Ruth had no trouble reading his silent "Wow!"

Before either man could regain their composure, Ruth stepped in front of Jacob. "Yes, he really is that big. And, despite my size, I am not a child and don't like being treated like one."

Dave raised a placating hand. "I am sorry, young lady. You are very smart for a... six-year-old? I do like your Elmo shirt though."

Danny began to snicker and Ruth shot him a look of promised retribution. She reached up and began to tug the hoodie over her head. It was a struggle to keep her t-shirt from coming off with the hoodie. The last thing Ruth wanted was to expose her breasts in front of either her friends or the two Rennies.

With great difficulty, the stupid hoodie finally came off. Ruth felt her strange new hair stand up and begin to rearrange itself as she rolled the offensive hoodie into a ball. Ruth threw the damn thing at Danny's face, but the annoying little man snagged it effortlessly out of the air.

In the blink of an eye, the hoodie was folded and tucked under Danny's arm. The obnoxious smirk never left his face.

Ruth glared at her not quite friend as she asked, "How would you like to spend a day looking like Elmo? I can make you…"

"Enough, Ruth," Jacob interrupted. "You're just encouraging him."

Ruth's hands rose to check that her white locks weren't doing anything strange before turning to face Dave. The man was staring down at her in with the same wide-eyed look he had given Geoff. Ruth placed her hands on her hips as she gave him her best death stare. Dave began to shake his head. "No, definitely not a child. Is that hair real?" Then Dave turned his gaze to Herrera. "That beard is real too, isn't it?"

Herrera didn't answer, but his toothy smile showed through his beard.

Ruth took a deep breath before speaking as calmly as she could. "Yes, this is how we look. It's not makeup or stage props. We know we need costumes. We lost all of our gear at our last stop. And for the record, we really are looking for work."

Dave shook his head. "Sorry, lady. It was an honest mistake. As for jobs, I don't make hiring decisions. Just a sec." Ruth watched him pull a cell phone out of his back pocket. His fingers dance across the phone before he lifted it to his ear. "Sir John, I have some playtrons at the gate looking for work. I know, but you really have to see this bunch. One of them is exactly what Wesley needs for his new act. Okay. Of course. We'll wait here."

Ruth frowned at him as he took the phone away from his ear. "I am NOT a playtron!"

Dave shrugged. "Maybe or maybe not, Lady. I'll let Sir John make that call too." He stared down at the cell phone for a moment before slipping it back in his pocket. "Hate that thing, but they are easier to hide than a walkie-talkie. Sir John will be here in a bit."

They stood waiting while the two men finished hiding the cable. The wait was longer than the promised couple of minutes. Ruth suspected the Rennies were just trying to brush them off. In frustration, she did something she hated, she dropped a name like one of the court snobs she despised. "Is Lady Aimée here today? She normally checks in after a busy weekend."

A cultured voice came from the far side of the gate as a well-groomed man in a courtier costume came into view. "And how would you know what is normal for the Lady? And Dave said you were looking for work. You are full of surprises, aren't you?"

His posture was near perfect as he strode forward. Ruth didn't recognize him, but from his clothing she guessed he was a member of the King's Court. "If you are going to drop names, why not ask for Queen Anne herself?"

Ruth knew she had gone too far, but she refused to back down. "Because Elizabeth likes to go back home to Rhode Island for a few days after a weekend of court."

The man nodded and his eyes grew a bit warmer. Ruth realized he was ceding her a point in their duel. "Apparently you are not just any noob. My name is Sir John. Might I enquire who you are, Milady?"

Ruth fumbled for an answer. She wasn't ready to admit to who she really was. That would be too dangerous. Worse, it might bring Father into the game. "You can call me Enchantrix. I am a friend and colleague of Ruth Starling."

Sur John shook his head. "Unlikely, young woman. Ruth works alone. And she hasn't done a stage performance since her debut on the King's Stage three years ago."

Ruth grinned back at him. "Ruth wasn't on the King's stage. Her debut was on a small stage on the Tournament Grounds. And, it was only two years ago. Six of your knights thrust their swords through that basket while she was inside it. She designed the entire illusion herself."

Sir John gave her a curious look but did not seem convinced. "Anyone in the audience that night could tell the same tale. Your information doesn't prove anything."

Ruth's grin spread across her face at the challenge in his tone. "Then how about a demonstration?"

Ruth felt Jacob's hand on her shoulder. She could feel the tension in him as he gently squeezed. Ruth reached up and patted his hand. "I know, Jacob. You need to trust me. This is important." She felt him squeeze one more time and then let go.

Sir John watched the byplay between them before asking, "What kind of demonstration?"

Ruth studied the gate area and the empty parking lot. There really wasn't much to work with. But when her eyes fastening the line of porta potties, she found her inspiration. A plan that began to form in her mind would definitely be original. She just wished she understood exactly what the runes blazing in her mind actually did.

Ruth didn't give herself time to get cold feet. She began to walk the thirty or so feet to the closest of the porta potties. The red-headed youth muttered something about losing her nerve. Ruth ignored his rudeness and focused on the illusion she wanted to create. When she reached the first porta potty, Ruth opened it to reveal its sparce interior. With a theatrical gesture, Ruth demonstrated that the stall was quite empty.

Ruth turned and grinned at the three Rennies before stepping back into the greenish-blue toilet. The glowing runes began to pulse and press against the boundaries of her mind. As she pulled the door closed, Ruth released the phrase loud enough for them all to hear, "PAw-sas!"

The word echoed, seeming to gain intensity in the confines of the stall. As the strange reverberations died away, Ruth heard a cacophony of sounds from beyond the door. She gave the door a gentle push, swinging it open again. The view beyond was more entertaining that even the illusion she was attempted to pull off. Or it would have been if not for the frown on Jacob's face.

All three Rennies were frantically digging in their pockets trying for their cell phones. The phone in the red-headed young man's hand was quacking like an insane duck. The dark-haired man's back pocket was backfiring like a badly tuned car. Sir John stared helplessly at his own phone as it cried out like a cat with its tail caught beneath a rocking chair. It took all of Ruth's self-control not to burst out laughing at their confusion. But the laughter would have to wait until later, she needed to hide while they were thoroughly distracted. The illusion would be complete if she could just hide in at least a few porta potties further down the line.

Ruth tried to step down onto the ground outside the stall. But that short step seemed to go on forever. Ruth became disoriented and almost fell. Her foot was missing. For that matter, so was her leg. She made a desperate grab for the door frame, but her hand and arm were also missing. It was only by chance that fingers she couldn't see encountered the heavy plastic of the wall. Ruth braced herself against that solid surface as a wave of vertigo washed over her.

The beat of her racing heart thundered in her ears. But if her heart was still beating then she must still have a body, right? Ruth ran her left hand up across her body. Waist, stomach, chest and head. Her fingertips found everything they searched for. Better yet, her body could feel those fingers as they moved up the length of her body. Nothing appeared to be missing; she just couldn't see herself. Did that mean that no one else could see her either? Her mind struggled to accept the reality of what she had done. She was actually invisible.

How was that even possible? Real magic didn't exist. Or did it? Ruth hadn't stopped to consider what might happen when she spoke the ancient word for disappear. The results of speaking those two simple syllables were beyond anything she could have imagined. The showman in her grew excited. Think of the illusions that she could craft with just this one word. The possibilities were endless. But the screams of the malfunctioning phones quelled her excitement. There would be consequences any time she chose to use any of the ancient runes.

Still, the damage was done for now. She had to make the most of this opportunity. It was time to bring the performance to a dramatic conclusion. Closing her eyes, Ruth stepped out of the toilet. That step was easier when she didn't have to not see her foot. Ruth sighed in relief as her feet settled onto the path. You can do this, she told herself.

And if she did it right, the finale could guarantee them all a place at the Faire.

Instead of turning down the line of porta potties, Ruth faced the gate behind the three Rennies. Her plan was simple, focus straight ahead, looking at nothing except the path beyond the gate. Ruth fought the desire to look down every step of that endless journey. She barely noticed when she passed the men fighting with their phones. The only thing that mattered was the gate. Then she was there and past it. She was safe. Slowly, Ruth turned to watch the fun.

One after another, the phones went silent. The cat noises died first as Sir John simply turned his phone off. The backfiring and quacking came to an end several moments later. All three men looked up for the cause of their predicament. But Ruth wasn't there to be blamed for their problems. The bluish-green door hung open and the porta potty was empty. The redheaded young man ran towards the line of toilets. "She must have hidden in one of the others while we were distracted."

Sir John sighed. "Help him, Dave. I want to know what she did to my phone."

Ruth watched the two men move down the line opening door after door. They seemed so surprised they didn't find her. This had to be one of her best tricks ever. Dave ran around the back of the line to make sure she wasn't hiding on the far side. The less intelligent red-head returned to the toilet Ruth had entered. She almost giggled as he lifted the seat and stuck his head inside the capture tank to look for her. As if she would ever be THAT desperate to make an illusion work. His face was more than a bit green when he pulled his head back out. Ruth thought the shade went well with his red hair and freckles.

But now the time had come to end the show; time for the master magician to reveal herself. If she could. Ruth remembered how Jacob had helped to undo her first use of one of the words. As he had coached her, she closed her eyes and visualized the runes she had uttered. But it was different this time. The runes she had spoken were shrouded in mist. She could not make out the individual characters within the mist. On a whim, she mentally pursed her lips and blew gently across the runes. The mist swirled away on her breath revealing the runes once more.

Ruth opened her eyes to see her body once more where it was supposed to be. It was nice to be whole again. Even the body the lab had changed hers into was better than no body at all. Ruth felt a smile of relief spread across her face. Then she raised two fingers to her lips and let out a piercing whistle. All three men spun to face her. The astonishment on their faces was very, very satisfying.

Ruth walked over to stand by Sir John just as his phone finished rebooting. Sir John turned the screen so that Ruth could see that it was back to normal. His voice was more curious than angry as he asked, "I don't suppose you would be willing to explain?" At Ruth's raised eyebrows, he shook his head. "Stupid question. Forget I asked."

Ruth laughed as he put away his phone. "Jobs? A meeting with Lady A? All of the above?"

Sir john actually broke into a smile at that. "I will pass your request on to Lady Aimée when I see her. As for jobs…. If Wesley can use your big friend, he has a job. Your talents appear to be at least on par with Ruth Starling's. We have work for you as well. Unless your friends have talents they haven't displayed, they will have to see if any of the Guilds need help. That's the best I can do."

Danny gave a loud whoop of joy and tossed the pink hoodie at the still green looking young man. Danny's was positively cheerful as he quipped. "Use that if you are going to get sick. Apparently, no one else wants it anymore."

Sir John turned and gave Danny's slipper clad feet a look of disgust. "That offer assumes that you can all acquire appropriate clothing. No one works the Faire looking like that."

Jacob snorted in amusement. "I guess we do look rather shabby and out of place. We really can afford proper costumes. Where do you suggest we get them?"

Sir John pinched his bottom lip as he considered his response. "There is a small green and blue tent on the far side of Peasant's Pass. The shop is called Ancient Attire. Mistress Tara is one of the best seamstresses I know. She can take care of you and she can use the business more than most. The virus hit the Faire folk harder than most.

Too many of our venues have been canceled." The Courtier's face grew stern. "Tara has a good heart, but she is raising a young daughter on her own. If you haggle over her prices, your stay here will be a short one."

Sir John started to turn away, but paused. He pointed towards the van. "Nice work. But it needs to be moved from the patron lot. Dave can move it for you to save time. I suggest you get started right away. Unusual sizes take time." Sir John walked back through the gate. As he passed Ruth he said. "I assume you know your way around. Stop by the admin building before the end of the day and we will discuss a contract."

Ruth nodded politely and waited until the courtier had disappeared from sight. Then she grinned at her friends. "We did it. Let's go shopping for some real clothes."

Jacob held up a finger. "Give me a second." Ruth watched him go for the passenger side of the van. Jacob didn't take long. When he returned, Ruth saw the bulge in his hoodie pocket. Their supply of cash, she realized, suddenly feeling foolish for not thinking of it. Jacob winked at her and then tossed the keys to Dave. "Lead on, Milady."

Ruth led them through the gate and up a broad, tree-lined lane. The smell of the pine trees filled the air. "This place is huge, about eighty acres. There are lots of streets and seven or eight permanent structures. When it's open, these streets are packed with performers and carts selling things. It really is incredible. The bigger vendors set up fancy pavilions to draw people in. A lot of them work here through the week as well, trying to fill customer orders before the next Faire weekend."

Danny, who had been skipping along just ahead of Ruth, came to a stop. "Wait. I know this place. I… It's crazy, but it's just like the dream when I first woke up. There is a large stage at the end of this path. There's a cart that sells funnel cakes too. And the shoemaker…" Danny looked down at his feet with a look of longing. The slippers he had been wearing since waking up were falling apart. The streets of Williamstown had ruined them.

Danny looked up at Jacob. "I want shoes. Real shoes. Or better yet, boots. And for Geoff too. We have all that money because of… Well, me."

Jacob looked down at his own ill-fitting sneakers. "I think we could all do with better shoes or even boots, Danny. And not just to get the jobs. Whatever we get needs to last a long time. When we make it to Canada, we are going to need to keep a low profile. Let's see if your cobbler can come up with something that will fit well. We just need to make sure we save enough for the rest of our costumes."

Danny gave another whoop and danced off ahead of them. Ruth groaned as Danny turned up King's Way. "These are some of the most expensive shops in the Faire," she warned the others. There was no chance to discuss it further as Danny quickened his pace. Soon they were all running to keep up with the tiny man. Danny didn't slow down until they were near the top of the street where a red and gold pavilion rested on the right side of the street. An ornate wooded sign hung outside the entrance.

*Legendary Leather*
*Footwear for All Ages*

One of the pavilion's side panels was open and a rather overweight man of about fifty was leaning over a table cutting leather. Beyond the worktable were dozens of wire shelves and large wooden chests. The tops of each chest and every shelf were filled to capacity with leather shoes and boots. One whole wall held nothing but modern dress shoes and fancy boots. Ruth even saw cowboy boots on one of the shelves. Apparently, the term "All Ages" didn't just refer to the age of the customer. Ruth could only hope the merchant had a reasonable selection of medieval footwear to choose from.

The heavy-set man put down his tools as Danny led the way into the pavilion. "How may I serve you, Lords and Lady?"

Danny's voice was filled with excitement as he announced. "Boots for everyone! I need something better than these ratty old things." Danny gestured down at what was left of his slippers.

The merchant looked down at Danny's feet with disdain. "Indeed, you do, young master. But boots like these aren't cheap. Are you sure your father can afford them?"

Jacob answered before Danny's less than tactful mouth could get them in trouble. "None of them are children. And, within reason… Yes, we can afford new boots. Our own gear was lost in an accident."

The merchants nodded as he scanned their feet and then their faces. His gaze lingered longest on Geoff and Danny. "Three of you I can take care of with minor adjustments to existing stock. The young master's feet are a tad wide. Depending on which of my wonderous boots he chooses, I may be able to modify something to fit him. The big man's boots will need to be sewn from scratch. It might be weeks before I can get to them though. I have taken so many orders already this season."

Ruth spun to locate Danny at her friend's overly excited response, "Nice!" Danny was holding a well-polished courtier's boot up to his nose. Danny had a curious look on his face as he muttered, "These even smell good."

The merchant's response was almost immediate. "An excellent choice, young master." Ruth could see the gleam of greed in the merchant's eyes. The merchant was already calculating how much he could soak them for. Sadly, Ruth realized, her friends were just a bunch of noobs looking to be taken advantage of. "Put it down, Danny," Ruth ordered a bit more harshly than she intended.

Then she turned on the merchant with a growl, "We are staff, not rich patrons. We need boots to replace our stolen gear so we can work. If you try to fleece us, I doubt many of the Folk will do business with you ever again."

Ruth saw a spark of anger on the merchant's face, but he hid it rather quickly. All of the merchants understood that the Faire Folk stuck together. Ruth nodded and continued. We will pay a fair price, but not for the fancy playtron footwear. We need sturdy boots appropriate for our roles. Clear?"

The man studied her for what felt like a long time before he nodded. Then he glanced over at Jacob. "Next time, leave her behind and I will give you a discount." Then he turned back to Ruth, his expression hardening. "You don't have to be so crabby about it. Can't blame me for trying to make a profit. Sheesh, you act like you are the royalty or something."

Ruth ignored the merchant's complaints. She looked around at her friends and considered their likely personas. Then she pointed to Herrera. "Blacksmith. Something that won't show burns." Then she pointed at Geoff. "Armsman. Nothing fancy. He is a low-ranking soldier. Unless, maybe hobnail? The rest of us need simple woodsman's boots. Water resistant and no fancy shines. Maybe age them a little so they don't look new. I assume you have the appropriate dyes."

The heavy-set merchant stood suddenly taller. "Young woman, I know my craft. I have been taking care of The Folk since before you were born."

It was nearly three hours later that they left Legendary Leather. Jacob, Ruth, and Herrera were wearing soft boots that came up to mid-thigh. Although they were all new, they looked well-worn like a peasants should. Hans Sachs, Ruth was certain that was just his period name, had promised that Danny and Geoff would have their boots before the Faire reopened on Saturday. Ruth was well satisfied with the man's work.

Under Ruth's uncompromising glare, the merchant had dealt with them fairly. But the bill had still been nearly $1,800 for the five pair of boots. The largest chunk of that had been the "fee" for placing Geoff and Danny's boots ahead of the orders the merchant was already behind on. Ruth had done her best to talk the merchant down, but Hans had refused to budge. At this rate, Ruth thought, they would be broke long before they even got to Canada.

The afternoon was warm and squirrels scampered through the pines. Ruth envied the tiny creature's carefree lives. There had been a time when her life at seemed just as worry free. But that had all changed the day she caught the virus.

The turn onto Peasant's Pass reminded Ruth of how much she loved the Faire. This tiny cross street was linked to so many of her most cherished memories. The Pass was home to many of the small vendors who often sold unique items that could be found nowhere else in any of the realms. She had spent countless hours here wandering from one table to the next, seeing treasures and wonders that only a lonely young child could truly appreciate. Ruth wondered if it would ever be that simple again.

She was so lost in her memories, that Ruth almost led them past the small green and blue tent tucked back under two of the larger pines. If not for Jacob's light touch on her shoulder, Ruth would have continued to wander through times long past. His touch brought the present rushing back and she turned to study the somewhat faded panels of the tent.

Despite the beauty of the day, the panels were all rolled down. To all appearances it was abandoned or, at the very least, closed for the season. Then a small child's voice began to chatter somewhere inside. The conversation sounded very one-sided, but it meant at least someone was inside. Ruth motioned for Jacob to take the lead.

Her old teacher stepped up to the flap that covered a door sized opening in the front of the tent. He lifted the flap and called into the tent, "Is there a Mistress Tara here? Sir John suggested that you might be able to help us."

Ruth heard an older voice shushing someone named Tuula. Moments later, the flap bulged outward forcing Jacob to step back. The woman that stepped into the sunshine was far from the middle-aged matron that Ruth had expecting to meet. The woman was nothing that Ruth could ever have imagined as the best seamstress around. Mistress Tara of Ancient Attire was both young and beautiful. Her dirty-blond hair was twisted into a tight bun at the back of her head. Her linen tunic was appropriate to her station, but it was also well tailored to accent the lines of her petite form.

But it was the woman's bright blue eyes that caused Ruth to suck in her breath. They were a different shade than Ruth's new eyes, but they were no less striking. Those brilliant orbs widened noticeably as they took in her remarkable guests. But there was no trace of that surprise in her melodious voice when she introduced herself. "I am Tara Helleväara, Mistress of Ancient Attire. How may I serve you, honored guests?"

Ruth immediately liked this woman. Tara took her role seriously. Many in the merchant class didn't bother with a persona even when the Faire was open. Mistress Tara didn't just use the Faire for profit. Instead, she was a part of what King Richard's was meant to be. The Faire might be closed and her customers might look like homeless refugees, but Tara remained steadfast in her role as a medieval seamstress. Ruth would have staked her reputation on Tara being of The Folk.

Mistress Tara looked at each of them, waiting for someone to speak up.

Ruth looked up at Jacob. Once again, the often-verbose professor was at a loss for words. Only this time, he was standing there with his mouth half open. But his eyes locked on Mistress Tara like she was one of the changed and not him. Ruth sighed in frustration. One would think that a man who studied ancient languages would have less trouble finding words when he needed them.

Ruth gave up on him and stepped forward. "We are in need of attire for the Faire, Mistress Tara. All of our belongings were recently lost. We need appropriate period clothing before we can assume our new duties in the realm. Can you help us?"

Tara dropped to a knee before Ruth, placing their heads at nearly the same height. "Well spoken, Milady." Then Tara glanced up at Jacob's awe-struck face. Her mock whisper was loud enough for them all to hear. "I heard that the King was looking for a new fool. Is your friend applying for the position?" They all began to laugh as Jacob's pale face turned a bright shade of red. Ruth could only hope that Tara's teasing would help Jacob regain his wits.

As the laughter died down, Tara continued, "Milady, Ancient Attire does not carry clothing for Lords or Ladies of the Realm. My tunics are designed for the common folk. I make tunics for soldiers, guild members, and, of course, for the peasant folk. I have little skill at embroidery for Ladies such as yourself. If my wares are what you require, I would be pleased to assist you and your friends." With a wink, she added. "Especially the nice-looking man who doesn't speak much. Such men are far too rare."

Jacob finally seemed to regain his power of speech. "We are not Lords or Ladies. Simple attire appropriate for commoners is all we ask, My Lady."

Tara and Ruth both broke out in laughter. The others all stared at them in confusion. Tara gave Ruth a knowing grin. "He's a noob, isn't he?"

Ruth whispered back, "And how! Can you help us?"

Tara nodded. "Considering what you are wearing now, I assume this is a rush order." Without waiting for an answer, Tara motioned for Ruth to turn around. "Too well endowed for a child's tunic. We will have to cut down an adult Tunic." One by one, Tara had Danny, Jacob and Herrera spin in place for her. "For the four of you, I can have a single tunic set ready by the end of the day. I assume you will need several changes if you are going to work here."

Tara pointed a thumb at Jacob and smirked. "He of few words can take his pick from the rack." Then Tara rose and walked over to Geoff. Geoff gave her a friendly smile as she stared up at him. She walked slowly around him muttering to herself. "I don't even have a pattern that big. It has been a while since I have had a good challenge like this. It might just be fun." Turning back to Ruth, Tara said, "I do have several Guild orders on my plate already. I am not sure how quickly I can finish something that big."

Jacob's voice was almost normal again as he asked, "What if you had another set of hands to do some of the sewing?"

Tara turned to give him an appraising stare. "Are you trained as a tailor?"

Jacob shook his head. "No, but I learned to repair tents in the army. I also hemmed and repaired my own uniforms." His voice grew softer then, "And later, I learned how to take in my wife's clothes after she got sick. She wouldn't let me buy her anything new. She couldn't see spending a lot of money on things she would only wear a few times."

There was a moment of uncomfortable silence as the meaning of Jacob's words became clear to them all. Tara's voice was like a soothing breeze as she asked, "Can you still take orders, soldier? Do the stitches exactly as I show you? I will not have my reputation damaged by sloppy work." At Jacob's nod, she motioned for Geoff to help her roll up one side of the tent. "Then let's get started. I will give you a good discount for your help, good sir."

Protests of "No discounts," came from several mouths at once.

Tara sighed. "Sir John has been meddling again, hasn't he? I told that man to stop interfering. I am more than capable of running Ancient Attire without his help." Wisely, everyone, including Danny, kept their mouths shut.

Geoff came forward as requested. When he saw what she wanted his help with, he stepped in front of Tara and began to roll up the tent panel without her help. He followed Tara's directions with a smile. Sunlight spilled into the tent revealing its contents to everyone.

Long clothing racks lined the right and back walls. Tunics of all sizes hung from the racks. Ruth saw white, grey, tan, brown and black among the tunics. All the colors allowed to the peasant class were on display in Tara's shop. Along the left wall were two tables covered in material and half-finished projects. Just past those tables was a pile of large fluffy pillows. A strawberry blond head with large blue eyes peeked out from within that soft nest.

Those eyes shifted from one member of the group to the next. Ruth swore they got larger as the little girl examined each of her friends. Ruth tried to meet the child's gaze to smile at her. But each time their eyes met, the girl looked away. Their strange dance puzzled Ruth.

As Tara waved them inside, an urgent whisper called across the tent, "Mother!" Tara walked over and crouched beside the pillows. "What is it, Tuula? I need to work right now. Can you entertain yourself while I am helping these people? Maybe you could draw in your sketchbook while I work?"

The young girl's voice dropped to an urgent whisper, but it was still loud in Ruth's ears. "Mother, do you know what they are?"

Tara's tone became stern as she replied. "They are customers, Tuula. And they are here to buy our tunics. Remember the rule…"

"Be polite to customers," the two intoned together.

There were several snorts of mirth when Tuula continued on in the same sing-song pattern, "Don't blame me if one them eats you, Mother." Her voice was filled with exasperation as she whispered, "You can't say I didn't warn you."

Tara shook her head. "Then you should get your sketchbook so you can document my demise. Please, Tuula. Mother has a lot to do. Okay?"

Ruth watched the child consider the request and then nod. The small girl, no more than six, scooted to the back of the tent and pulled a large sketch pad out of a backpack that Ruth hadn't noticed lying on the floor. Tuula also dug a tattered box of colored pencils from the pack before she returned to the pillows.

Tara turned back to the face them. "Please forgive her wording. She has a rather active imagination. She likes the fantasy scene much more than medieval culture."

Moving back to the tables, Tara's hand darted into a pile of scrap material piled where the two tables came together. It emerged a moment later sporting a long white tail. Tara pulled the rest of the tape measure from its hiding place among the scraps. Looking around the group, Tara asked, "Who's first?" Ruth stepped forward and the work began. The woman's skill was soon clear as each of them, except Coon, was carefully measured.

As the others took their turns being measured, Coon occupied herself by checking out the pillows and the child nestled within them. Ruth smiled as Coon rose up on her hind feet to see what little Tuula was up to. The little girl stared back. Ruth was momentarily jealous as Coon did something Ruth had not been able to. Racoon and girl stared deep into each other's eyes. That steady gaze seemed to go on forever before Tuula patted the pillow beside her. As Ruth watched, Coon climbed into Tuula's haven and snuggled in beside the child. Ruth wasn't sure which of them began the happy crooning sound that filled the tent.

Ruth turned from Coon and Tuula to see Jacob staring at the clothing racks with a look of confusion. The poor man had no idea what colors to select. Were all men this helpless? She wasn't sure. She considered what she knew of him. Jacob really had no medieval skill other than scholar. She briefly considered the black of a priest, but something told her that wasn't right for him. Ruth walked over to stand beside him. "All white," she insisted.

Jacob looked down at her in surprise. "Why? Won't they be harder to keep clean?"

Ruth just shrugged, "Maybe, but I think it's a better match for who you are about to become." She left him there to find something that fit him well.

Time passed as things were tried on and altered some more. Ruth's outfit was the first to be finished. Tara had made the alterations quickly while demonstrating the stitches to Jacob. Ruth no longer had any doubts about Sir John's appraisal of Ancient Attire or its Mistress.

With her new clothes in hand, Ruth slipped behind a curtain hanging behind the clothing racks. Ruth felt no regret as she stripped away what she considered her prison uniform. The tunic Tara had crafted for her was surprisingly soft for such thick material. In Ruth's mind, it was perfect. The material and tailoring were better than anything a peasant should have worn, but Ruth wasn't about to complain. She was simply grateful to have something that was really hers again. With a smile of satisfaction, Ruth tossed the clothes from the lab into Tara's trash can. Nothing could make her wear those things ever again.

When she came out from behind the curtain, Ruth realized that almost everyone was working to help Tara. Only Coon appeared to be napping. Coon's furry body was pressed up against Tuula's leg and her chin rested on the little girl's knee. No one seemed to notice as Ruth slipped out of Ancient Attire. With her new clothing, she was ready for her meeting with Sir John. Ruth felt her confidence grow as she walked towards the front of the park where the admin building waited for her.

The door to the admin building was clearly marked "Staff Only." Ruth assumed the job offer that morning qualified her as staff, so she opened the door. Once inside, Ruth found herself in a medieval antechamber.

Plain wooden benches lined the side walls of the room. These were for commoners like herself. Three wooden chairs with thick pads occupied the center of the room. Those would be reserved for Lords and Ladies or perhaps important merchants.

Across from the door, a wooden desk blocked access to a hallway lined with doors. Sir John sat on the corner of that desk looking for all the world like he had known she was on her way.

He smiled politely and rose to greet her. "Good, I was hoping you would decide to accept my offer." His arm came up to indicate the hallway behind him. "This way, please."

Ruth followed the courtier down the short hall to the door at its end. Sir John opened the door and stepped politely aside to allow Ruth to enter first. Ruth stepped into an elegantly furnished room. A forest green carpet covered the floor, its thick shag almost looking like grass. Intricate tapestries depicting knights in battle covered the walls of the room. A large desk of richly stained hardwood dominated the center of the room. A thick slab of black marble formed the desktop. It was a desk fit for royalty.

The only thing that didn't really match the décor of the room was the high-backed leather chair on the far side of the desk. The back of the ultra-modern office chair was turned towards Ruth. Its front was turned to face out a large picture window that looked out onto the Faire. Ruth assumed that was how Sir John knew she was coming.

Ruth stiffened as the door closed behind her. She turned slowly around to find that Sir John had not followed her into the room. "What…" was all that went through Ruth's mind before a familiar female voice came from behind her. "I understand that was quite a show you put on this morning. Is it one that you can repeat for our patrons? Preferably somewhere other than in the public toilets, of course."

Ruth turned back around. "Maybe? Although it might be tough on their cell phones."

An amused chuckle filled the room as the chair spun slowly around to reveal Lady Aimée enthroned behind the desk. The Lady hadn't changed much since Father had introduced her to Ruth three years earlier. Ruth felt herself almost come to attention in response to this woman's presence. Lady Aimée might not play the Queen of the Faire, but she wore the mantle of authority as if she did. The Lady stood and walked around the desk, holding out her hand to Ruth. "It is nice to make your acquaintance, Enchantrix."

The Lady bent low so Ruth could shake her hand without standing on tiptoe. Ruth felt suddenly vulnerable under the Lady's appraising gaze. Those intelligent eyes seemed to strip away the new, confident Ruth to expose the little girl that she had once been. Lady Aimée released her hand and stood tall once more. "I understand that you are one of Ruth Starling's contemporaries. Do you only do your own illusions, or can you handle some of Ruth's as well?"

Ruth knew that seemingly innocent question was like a steel trap waiting to close on her. The problem was that she could not see where the trap lay hidden. Which response would trigger the trap? Should she play timid or be bold? Or, could she avoid the danger by being vague? Non-committal was the best she could do until she figured out where Lady Aimée was going with her question. "Ruth and I have discussed some of her illusions. It depends on what you have in mind?"

Lady Aimée sat on one of the two guest chairs that stood in front of the desk. Both were antique wooden chairs without a pad. They weren't designed for comfort, especially not for someone as short as Ruth now was.

Lady Aimée motioned to the second chair. Ruth climbed up onto it with as much dignity as she could manage. Lady Aimée seemed not to notice the effort it took for Ruth to reach the seat of the chair. Her right hand came up and she twirled her index finger slowly in her long brown hair before inquiring. "I was wondering if you could manage the 'Trial of Swords' illusion that Ruth performed for our guests a few years back. It was quite popular with our patrons."

Ruth tasted fear as she remembered her first live performance. She had spent months constructing the wicker basket with the trap door at the bottom. Father had paid someone to construct a small stage with just enough space underneath it for Ruth to hide in. She had trained six of King Richard's most famous knights on exactly where to thrust their swords into the wicker. She had planned for everything. Well, almost everything. The illusion had gone off perfectly except for the blood-curdling scream that sounded as the last sword was thrust through the basket.

The crowd had gone wild at that scream. Only a few people knew that the scream hadn't been part of the act. No, the scream had come from a frightened young girl who suddenly had creepy-crawly things running up her arms and across her face as she hid there in the tiny prison below the stage. Somehow, Ruth had managed to control her fear enough to stay in her hideaway until the knights had each stomped their boot as they withdrew their swords. At the sixth stomp, Ruth had climbed back into the basket. She tried desperately to brush her assailants off her face and arms as she waited for the basket to be opened.

That had been the longest minute in Ruth's life. When the lid was finally lifted, Ruth stood and bowed to her adoring audience. But inside, a frightened child was vowing never to do this illusion ever again.

It had taken everything she had to walk back to the Winnebago Father had rented. Once inside, she had stripped and climbed into the tiny shower. The water was cold long before she finished trying to wash away the tiny creatures that still existed to this day in her mind. Ruth had abandoned the stage and basket after that one performance, never wanting to see either again.

Awareness of where she was came creeping back. Ruth wasn't sure how long she had been lost in the memory. Lady Aimée was smiling knowingly at her. "We still have the stage and wicker basket. I am sure you will fit inside them. If you wish to practice, we can move the stage to an appropriate place on the Tournament Grounds tomorrow. What do you think, Enchantrix?"

Ruth wanted to scream as she had that night three years ago. Asking her to go through that again was so unfair. She wasn't even aware of what she was doing as the words tumbled from between her lips, "No more centipedes. Please, anything but that."

The aristocratic woman leaned forward. "Hello, Ruth."

Ruth was startled out of her nightmare when she heard her name. Looking up, she met Lady Aimée's curious brown eyes. Ruth managed to squeak out, "No! I'm not…"

The Lady chuckled. "You never were a very good liar, Ruth. Too many tells. One would expect a master illusionist would be better at deceiving people."

Ruth felt her face muscles tighten at the insult. Lady Aimée's chuckle transformed into laughter. "And that is what made Sir John suspicious this morning. You never could back down from a challenge, girl. Our Ruth was always ready to prove herself capable of anything."

Ruth's anger faded under the gentle teasing of the Lady. It was almost humiliating how easily she had been caught in her own lies. But there was one piece of the puzzle that Ruth knew she was still missing. "Sir John was only suspicious. Somehow, you knew. What gave me away?"

The Lady held up her hand with her thumb and index finger about an inch apart. "Centipedes, Ruth. Tiny little centipedes."

Ruth shook her head. "I never told anyone about them, not even Father. It was my secret."

Lady Aimée leaned back in her chair. "Your scream that night wasn't some last-minute inspiration. That scream was real. There was real fear in your voice. No one who knew you could have missed it. Besides, you were pale and shaking when you came out of that basket. We didn't know why until the next morning when my crew removed the stage. The centipedes swarmed as soon as we moved the stage. We must have disturbed their nest when we set the stage up."

"Oh," was all that Ruth could think to say. She had convinced herself that no one knew how scared she had been that night.

Ruth was still trying to regain her equilibrium when the Lady changed subjects again. Gesturing at Ruth's new body, she asked, "What did you do, child? No cosmetic surgery I have ever heard of changes a person like that. You are shorter and more muscular than the girl I remember. Your hair is… interesting. And I don't think contacts can make your eyes that shade of blue." The Lady studied Ruth's face as she spoke. Then she gave a soft gasp as her eyes flashed in anger.

"Bloody hell! This wasn't your choice, was it? Who did this to you and why?"

The wall that Ruth had built around her emotions could have withstood any assault, but it crumbled at the sound of real concern in Lady Aimée's voice. Tears began to flow down Ruth's cheeks. Suddenly the Lady was kneeling before her, gentle hands pulled Ruth into a tight embrace. Ruth let herself be comforted as only her mother had done before.

Finally, Ruth controlled her tears and the Lady leaned back. "Tell me what happened, Ruth."

Ruth wasn't sure where to start. "I had the virus. I think I was dying. There was a doctor. He gave me something to kill the virus. This," Ruth ran her hand over her body, "is what his cure did to me. He knew what it was going to do and he gave it to me anyway. I… We were his guinea pigs. My friends were changed too. We managed to escape their lab. Now, we are trying to hide."

The Lady's eyes flashed. Ruth saw something dangerous in her gaze. But the Lady's voice remained calm as she asked, "Why haven't you returned home now that you are free?"

Ruth looked down at herself. "Go home? Looking like this? I can't do that to Mother. And then there is Father. He was already trying to run my life. Can you imagine how he is going to react to this?"

The Lady eased back onto her chair. "Your father loves you, Ruth. It might not look like love to you, but then again, love doesn't always look like balloons and birthday cake."

"What," Ruth blurted out, "the heck is that supposed to mean?"

Lady Aimée's face took on that same look that Mother's did when she thought Ruth was being childish. Ruth hated that look, but she had learned to listen when she saw it on Mother's face. "What it means, Ruth, is that real love is much more complicated than just doing fun things that make people love us. Sometimes, love means doing hard things that the people we care about don't appreciate. Parties and presents are the easy way to show someone you love them. Sadly, that is often the only kind of love young people recognize."

Ruth considered the older woman's words and then asked, "What other kind of love is there."

Lady Aimée smiled in triumph at Ruth's question. "True love is doing the things that aren't any fun, Ruth. Doing things you don't like just because you know they need to be done. It's doing those things even if the person you love gets angry at you. For example, a father who pushes his incredibly intelligent but very innocent daughter to learn things she isn't interested in so she can face the world without him by her side. Or, a father who brings his daughter to a Ren Faire year after year even though he hates them. A father who arranges his daughter's first stage performance at that Ren Faire even though he can't stand the idea of her going into the entertainment industry."

Ruth's protests about Father suddenly seemed silly. She had never realized that Father had made so many sacrifices for her. She had never realized that Father was the reason she had been offered the chance to perform at King Richard's. There was so much she hadn't known. But there was one question that bothered her more than all of the rest, so she asked, "Why doesn't he want me to perform my illusions?"

Lady Aimée face grew serious. "That is a question you should have asked him a long time ago, Ruth. But if you want my opinion… As an investigative reporter, your father has seen just how ugly the entertainment industry can be. He either wanted to protect you from the sharks who eat talented young people or he just wanted to make sure than none of that ugliness rubbed off on his little girl. Which answer would you rather be angry with him for?"

Ruth shook her head. "Neither."

Silence filled the room, the Lady seemed lost in thought. Ruth waited until she continued, "One more thing that I think you need to know, Ruth. The hard kind of love is also a father who hires a dozen private investigators to search for his missing daughter because he refuses to accept that she is dead. It's a father who has harassed every law enforcement agency on the east coast trying to make them locate his daughter. It's a father who has been banned from visiting homeland security or the FBI because he has made such a nuisance of himself. And it is a father that has been to visit me three times since we opened hoping that his beloved daughter would show up at her favorite place on earth."

Ruth's tears began to flow again. She hadn't known. But even knowing, she could not go home now. But the Lady did not understand that, so she probed the open wound in Ruth's heart one more time, "Is there any reason you won't go home now?"

Ruth's tear-filled gaze rose to meet the Lady's. "Yes! They will be looking for me at home. Even Father can't protect us from the kind of people who are after us. They have Army helicopters and I don't know what else. I think that they killed the man who helped us escape. I can't bring that kind of trouble against my parents."

There was a sad smile on Lady Aimée's lips. "Even for you, dear Ruth, real love isn't all about balloons and birthday cake. Why did you come here then, Ruth?"

Ruth shrugged. "We were betrayed by one of the other prisoners. We had planned to go to Canada, but now they are waiting for us at the border. We needed a place to hide until we could come up with a plan. I thought we might blend in here. The Faire was the only place I could think of."

Lady Aimée's piercing eyes seemed to look into Ruth's heart. "And what of the danger to the Folk?"

Realization hit Ruth at that moment like one of the big rigs that had passed them on the interstate. She hadn't intended to, but she had still placed the Rennies and the Folk in the same danger that she was trying to protect her parents from. "I'm sorry. I didn't think anyone would look for us here. I thought we could just blend in. But you're right. We might get even more people hurt here. I will explain to my friends. We'll leave as soon as it's dark."

Tension seemed to leave the Lady at Ruth's confession. That dangerous gleam came back into her eyes again as she spoke, "No, I think not. The Folk do not send their own into exile simply for seeking our protection."

Lady Aimée stood and walked back around the desk. She pulled open a drawer and began to rummage around inside. Ruth blinked in surprise as a composition book landed on the desk near her. Several pens bounced and came to rest beside the book.

Lady Aimée sat down on the leather chair with her queen's face back on. "You have been officially retained by the King. Your service to the Realm begins immediately. Neither the King nor the Folk recognize the authority of those who are after you. Our rules and code of conduct supersede their laws. The most important of our rules is that WE protect our own. You were adopted by the Folk that night you stood your ground despite your fear. That night, you proved yourself to be one of us. We will protect you, Ruth, and your friends as well."

The Lady locked gazes with Ruth. "You will not leave until you have completed the duties for which you were retained. There will be no contract as there can be no record of your time with us. Instead of pay, you will work for room and board. A tent is being set up on the back lot for you and your friends. Your first duty in my service will be to record everything you know about this doctor for your father. He and your mother need to know you are safe. Your father also needs to know what he is up against. Understood?"

Ruth nodded and the Lady continued. "You will also work with my show crews to improve their acts. Your talents with illusion should make our performances more realistic. Your friends will either help the performers or the Guilds. When I deem it time for you to leave, you will do so fully outfitted with gear and supplies. Do you agree to serve as I require?"

A tiny smile came to Ruth's face as she nodded her agreement.

With uncanny timing, Sir John opened the door at that moment. The Lady rose, towering over Ruth. Ruth slid down from the chair and curtseyed.

The Lady's voice lost its imperious tone as she announced, "Welcome home, Ruth."

**Chapter 16
Raccoon Rumbles**

Soft pillows cradled her body. This was a sensation she could become quite fond of. Coon released a rumble of contentment as she leaned against the warmth of the young girl's leg. For the first time since she had gotten sick, Coon felt safe enough to relax. Her jaws stretched impossibly wide in a tail-straightening yawn. Coon let her eyes drift closed as she contemplated a nap. It was tempting, but dozing off probably wasn't fair. Her companions wouldn't be able to rest any time soon. They were too busy getting measured and fitted with "appropriate" clothing.

Coon's raccoon lips peeled back in what she imagined was a rather frightening grin. She didn't care though. She would never have to suffer the indignity of finding "appropriate" clothing ever again. Shopping for school had been a never-ending nightmare. Designers didn't make trendy clothes for over-weight young girls like she had been. Even if she had been able to afford the "in" fashions, they either didn't fit or they accentuated her weight problem. She had been self-conscious enough without adding insult to the injury of her own body.

Never again, she promised herself. The change had eliminated her need for clothes. Her only worry now was keeping her fur clean. The rest was easy. She wouldn't even have to worry about the change of seasons. Her fur would always be fashionable and it would thicken or thin as the weather dictated. What more could a girl ask for?

The scritchity-scratch of pencils on the artist pad made a nap impossible. The sounds never stopped or even slowed. To Coon's ears, the pencils seemed to move too quickly. Was the girl just scribbling?

As her half-closed eyes focused on the pad, Coon was surprised to see how talented young Tuula was. The pencil danced across the page. With the swiftness of a striking snake, Tuula's hand would dart into her lap and return to the pad with a different color. Coon was mesmerized as random lines and curves began to take on a recognizable form as she watched.

Tuula brought up a red pencil and began to sketch in the lines and curls of what could only be hair and a beard. Coon rested her head on Tuula's knee as the image of Herrera came to life. Tuula's fingers dipped into her lap again and again as Herrera's bushy facial hair filled in. Except, this version of Herrera's beard wasn't the fuzzy tangle Coon was used to. This version of her friend's beard was braided in an intricate pattern that exuded dignity and power. Above the beard, Herrera's face and eyes had an intensity that Coon had only seen when Herrera was working on that set of chainmail he had made back in the lab.

Coon leaned closer as Tuula changed colors again. A grey pencil dropped into the empty outline of Herrera's body. Silver and black alternated with the grey as a pattern began to take shape. If anything, little Tuula's pace grew even more frantic. Lines, circles and dots began to spread from the beard towards the figure's arms and legs. As Coon watched, chainmail like the set Herrera had crafted, began to cover her friend's body.

Coon lost track of time as color spread outward from the red of Herrera's beard. Pants, shirt sleeves, boots - even Herrera's ruddy complexion perfectly rendered - were drawn with precision. Only this wasn't the lost boy from the lab that Coon knew. This Herrera was much, much more.

The almost magical pencils moved back up to Herrera's arms which were raised over his head. Lines of browns began to spring from Herrera's clenched hands to form what looked like a baseball bat. The pencil in Tuula's talented left hand transformed to the silver and then grey as a silver flower blossomed on the end of that wooden shaft. Coon realized the wood wasn't a bat she was seeing; it was the haft of an axe. It was an axe unlike any that Coon had ever seen with two broad blades, each inscribed with intricate designs and strange characters. It was an axe for a warrior.

With an abruptness that caught Coon off guard, Tuula was done and the pencils fell silently into the little girl's lap. Tuula's left hand came up to caress Coon's ears. It felt so good that Coon's head dropped back to the child's knee as another rumble of contentment escaped from Coon's chest. Coon wanted to cry out in protest when that hand left her sensitive ears to reach up and tap the image it had drawn.

Tuula's voice was filled with conviction as she explained, "He is a dwarf and a warrior like in my books. He just doesn't know it yet."

Childhood memories surfaced at Tuula's proclamation. Coon wanted to laugh as she imagined a line of seven Herreras marching through the forest. Walt Disney's cute and cuddly dwarves were the only ones Coon had ever seen. With a silent snort of mirth, she wondered which of Snow White's friends Herrera would be? Definitely Grumpy, she decided. Coon glanced once more at the masterpiece that Tuula had drawn. As she studied the warrior in the image, Coon had to wonder if old Walt had seriously misjudged the entire dwarven race.

Tuula laid her pad on the pillow in front of her crossed legs. An old-fashioned pencil sharpener appeared from somewhere in the pillows and the young girl began to sharpen each of the pencils she had used. Coon listened to Tuula's quiet monologue as the young girl critiqued each pencil's point. Many emerged only briefly before being subjected to another round of sharpening. Coon thought the process seemed quite an ordeal, but eventually all of the stubborn pencils met Tuula's exacting standards. Drawing the artist's pad back into her lap, Tuula turned to a clean page to begin her next masterpiece.

The scritchity-scratch of the pencils became a familiar part of life in the tent. Coon's own thoughts chased the sound from her mind. And then, sleep chased away the thoughts as well. Coon dozed with her head resting on the girl's soft thigh. Her dreams were only disturbed on those rare occasions when Tuula shifted positions. Coon had no idea how much time had passed when Tuula's talented fingers returned to caress her ears. Coon roused fully to press against those fingers, increasing the pleasure for them both.

When both girl and raccoon had finally gotten their fill of the ear rub, Tuula raised the pad to show Coon what she had created. Coon marveled at the realism of each picture. Each of her friends was featured on their own page of the pad. As Tuula flipped through the pages, she proclaimed the identity of each of her subjects.

On one page, Ruth stood proudly as a swirling mist rolled from her hands. Tuula's voice was filled with wonder as she whispered, "Forest gnome." The next page featured Geoff with a large sword in his hands. Geoff's armor wasn't chainmail. Instead of links, it was formed from many small overlapping metal squares. Tuula announced "Ogre" as Coon studied the drawing. On the next page, Jacob was dressed in a long white robe. The robe's hood was thrown back to reveal Jacob's pointed ears. A lightning bolt erupted from this version of what Tuula called an elf's hands. The next page showed a small form that was obscured in shadow. The image could only be Danny. For the first time, Tuula seemed less certain about her naming. "Hobbit. But not quite. He is different from the ones in my books."

It was the final page of Tuula's artistry that took Coon's breath away. That disturbing image left her naked and exposed. The where, why, and especially how of it swirled in Coon's mind. The drawing was fantasy and reality rolled into one. And, it frightened Coon.

Centered low on the page was a fierce-looking raccoon. Its teeth were bared in a snarl and one front paw was raised as if to strike. She had no doubt that this was her new body, but it wasn't her. Not the Coon she knew anyway. She had never believed herself capable of that kind of courage. She could not accept that she had that kind of strength. And she wouldn't have if not for the ghostly form that emanated from somewhere in the raccoon's chest. The spirit hovering over the raccoon was both separate and a part of her new body. The dual nature of what Tuula had drawn shook Coon to her core.

Coon wanted and needed to deny what that image showed her, but the features of the ethereal form could not be refuted. There could be no question as to the identity of that ghost. Its face was one that Coon had both hated and loved her whole life. It was the face of a slightly overweight Hispanic girl named Conchia Alimara. It was her face.

It was a face that little Tuula had never seen, but one the child had rendered perfectly.

Coon tried to close her eyes and block out the image, but her eyes refused to obey. Questions swirled in her mind. The world seemed to shift all around her. And then, the soft, gentle arms of a child pulled her close and anchored her. Tuula whispered to her like a mother might comfort a new born, "You are the first. There are none like you in any of my books. That makes you very special. What will you accomplish in this world now that you are here?"

Coon had no way to answer. Not for herself and not for the child. At that moment, any response was beyond her. Coon escaped to the only place she could, the mindless oblivion of sleep.

Tuula closed the book and settled down, cuddling Coon close. She whispered one last time before she too drifted off to sleep. "There are other raccoons here in the park. They live in the trees behind the Queen's Stage."

The sound of laughter cut through the emotional fatigue that had sucked Coon into a deep and dreamless sleep. Voices from her past, voices that had tormented her in her youth, taunted her anew. They warned her to stay in that dark place; nothing good would come of crawling back into the light. Coon ignored them. She had to believe that the voices outside her head would not betray her as so many others had in the past.

Coon's eyes opened. Tuula's soft breathing tickled the fur on her left ear. Coon slipped from between the little girl's arms and climbed out of Tuula's sanctuary. It was time to face the world once more. Reality seemed unaware that she had escaped its clutches for a time. The sun still shone through the open tent panel, but the bright orb sat much lower in the sky than it had when she had joined Tuula among the pillows.

And yet, something had changed during her absence. The melancholy that had overwhelmed her companions for weeks now, had been defeated in the span of one short nap. Coon scanned the tent, looking for anything that might explain the sudden change.

The smiles on the faces of her companions were accompanied by many other changes. The cast-off clothing they had been provided with at the lab had been replaced by the elegantly simple tunics of Ancient Attire. Well, except for the sweatpants that Geoff still wore. Apparently even Tara could only do so much in such a short time. While she slept, they had been transformed from homeless vagabonds to refugees from an age long past. Coon liked what she saw both on their bodies and in their eyes.

Coon quickly found the cause for the laughter that had woken her. Geoff stood before the open panel with a look of utter concentration on his face. He struggled to grasp buttons that seemed so tiny in his large fingers. He was having no luck fitting those tiny dots through the holes in the tunic. Coon wanted to be angry with the others, but she quickly realized that they were laughing with the big man and not at him.

Coon wished that she could help Geoff, but she wasn't sure if her new hands could manage the buttons either. The problem was solved when Tara walked up and began to button the tunic for him. Geoff grinned at her appreciatively. Tara patted him playfully on the chest. "That's just not going to work. Is it, Geoff? Give me a day or two and I will take care of you. That work for you?" Geoff nodded with a shy smile.

The smiles everyone had on their faces chased away the last of the darkness in Coon's heart. But the face Coon wanted to see smiling more than any other wasn't in the tent. Ruth wasn't there. Before Coon could begin to worry, Ruth's cheerful voice called from outside the tent, "Quit showing off your new muscles, Geoff. You're blocking both lanes of traffic. I can't get back in the tent."

Geoff giggled like a small child as he backed out of the way, revealing the figure that had been hidden behind his great bulk. Ruth stood in the tent opening with a grin on her face. Her strange white hair shifted with a life of its own, seeming to draw the sunlight into itself with each movement. Ruth had changed like the others; Coon noted. It wasn't just her new tunic or the composition book she clutched in her hands. The tension of the past weeks had lost its grip on her friend. Coon hadn't seen Ruth look this relaxed since their first days at GU. Coon realized how much she had missed that look on Ruth's face.

Ruth seemed to vibrate with excitement as she entered the tent. It was obvious that she had something important to tell them. The sparkle in Ruth's eyes could only mean that it was good news. Or, so Coon hoped. And that was when the show began.

Coon wanted to laugh when Ruth clambered up to stand on an empty chair, still unable to tower over her expectant audience. Ruth compensated for her small stature with pure bravado. With the cunning of a corrupt politician, she looked from face to face as the suspense built. Ruth's performance had everyone captivated until her gaze met Danny's. Danny waited for that precise moment to steal the show with a sarcastic dig. "Do you want a drum roll or do you just have a bad case of gas? If it's gas, please take it back outside."

The room erupted in laughter. Even Ruth couldn't keep her composure. Geoff scooted over to sit protectively beside Ruth's chair. The big man shook a finger at Danny. "Be nice."

Ruth smiled and winked at Geoff. "It's okay. Danny can't help being an Elmo."

There was more laughter at that, but Danny seemed unphased. He waited until the laughter died down before asking, "Where did you sneak off to? Change your mind about that pink hoodie? I can help you search for it if you ask nice."

Coon wandered over and climbed up on Geoff's knee. She wanted a front row seat if Ruth decided to clobber Danny. Regretfully, Ruth only gave Danny a condescending smile. "No, I'm good. That Elmo can stay lost. One short, annoying male in the tent is enough, thank you very much."

Jacob allowed the next round of laughter to pass before ending the verbal duel. "Best to quit before the hole you're digging gets any deeper, Danny. So, where did you go, Ruth?"

"I went to see about getting a job. Sir John did ask me to come by his office." Ruth answered.

Coon jumped as her seat blurted out, "Get job?"

Ruth's face lit up. "Yes, Geoff. The job and much more." Then the spillway opened and the tale practically burst out of Ruth. "The Folk have agreed to let us stay until the end of the season. You aren't going to believe this. They asked me to work with the different acts as an advisor. They want me to make the shows more realistic. It's like a dream come true."

"And the rest of us?" Herrera asked. "Do we have jobs too?"

Ruth nodded. "They want Geoff to play a hero in one of the new acts opening this season."

Coon ducked her head as Geoff began to clap his hands at the news. Ruth continued, "They would like everyone else to work with the Guilds. Almost all of the Guilds are shorthanded this year."

"Sir John mentioned these Guilds, too. What are they?"

It was Tara who answered Jacob's question. "We are the men and women who make the Faires possible. We are the craftsmen and women who make all of the props and most of the trade goods sold at the Faire. Only the best are invited to be members of a Guild. The main Guilds here at King Richard's are the Clothiers, the Tanners, the Bakers, the Merchants, and the Blacksmiths. We are subject to the King's law, but we also set standards for the products sold here. Those who don't measure up are encouraged not to return next season."

Herrera's "I can learn to be a blacksmith?" blurted out at the same instant as Danny's "How much do we get paid?"

Tara looked first to Herrera. "We have several good blacksmiths. I can introduce you if you want to learn." Then she turned to Danny. "Most Guild members aren't rich, Danny. We eke out a living doing what we love. I'm afraid we can't afford much."

All eyes returned to Ruth. Coon saw her friend fight off a moment of panic before Ruth announced, "The Folk are taking us in. They are giving us a place to stay. It's only a tent, but it's in the back lot. We don't have to worry about prying eyes there." Ruth paused as she decided what to say next.

Geoff used that pause to ask, "Eat?"

Ruth gave him a quick nod. "Everyone that contributes to the Faire will be fed at the Dragon Tavern. The menu is somewhat limited, but the food is really good. And there will be lots of it for you, Geoff."

"Why not pay us and let us buy our own food?" Danny asked.

Coon could smell Ruth's nervousness as she replied. "If they pay us, Danny, there will be a record of our being here. Our names would show up on tax documents. We don't want that and neither do the Folk. They also agreed to supply us with things we will need in Canada. It's the best we could come up with."

Danny started to protest, but Jacob rose from his seat. "Later, Danny. Ruth, you appear to have told them a lot about us. I am curious why. Our freedom and maybe even our lives depend on no one knowing about us."

Ruth slumped into the chair. Coon scrambled up onto the chair to place herself between Ruth and the others. Ruth wrapped her small arms around Coon. "It's okay, Coon. It's a fair question." Ruth met Jacob's gaze then. "My interview wasn't with Sir John. Lady Aimée was waiting for me. She outsmarted me, Jacob. She figured out who I was. She knew I am Ruth Starling. All I had left after was the truth. After that, I didn't want to lie to her. She used to be my friend. Besides, apparently, I am a terrible liar."

Jacob sat back down. His expression was thoughtful as he studied Ruth. "There are worse things in life than being a bad liar. The question now, Ruth, is can we trust them? None of us want to go back to that place."

Again, it was Tara that spoke up. "If the Lady offered you sanctuary, then all of the Folk are bound by that offer. I don't expect you to understand this, but the Faire is more than a game to us. We have our own rules and laws. If one of us breaks those laws, we face banishment from this Realm and probably all others. None of us would willingly risk that, Jacob."

Coon watched Jacob stare at Tara with a strange expression on his face. Then he nodded. "Thank you, Tara. Okay, my young friends, we have a home for the next month. We need to make some plans."

Coon climbed down from the chair as the discussion began. Raccoons didn't have jobs so there wasn't any reason for her to listen. Coon moved into what was left of the sunlight and let it warm her fur. Eventually, the laughter returned to the tent as everyone began suggesting jobs for Danny. Coon lost track of the conversation as she thought about her own future.

Did raccoons even have futures? Everything she had ever read about them indicated they lived each day as its own adventure. That way of life had appealed to a young girl who saw her own future as rather bleak. Now that she had achieved the impossible, she wanted more than to just exist. It was strange how dreams and wishes didn't work out the way you expected them to. She had to figure out what to do with this new life now that she had it. Even she needed a plan.

She hadn't come up with anything when she spotted a lone man walking up the path. It was one of the men from the front gate. Coon was pretty sure his name was Dave. She backed into the tent as Dave turned towards the Tara's tent.

Dave stopped outside the open panel, a set of keys dangling in his hand. Dave tossed the keys to Jacob before he turned to face Ruth. Bowing deeply, he recited, "Lady Ruth, I have come to escort you to your demesnes." Ruth tried to argue that she wasn't a lady, but the man just shook his head. "I do not question the decrees of the Lord Steward, Milady. Nor should you."

At his urging, they quickly took their leave of Ancient Attire. Everyone had to promise Tuula that they would visit her the next day. Dave then led them through several twists and turns until they reached the King's Stage. A smaller path led from there deep into the pines. Even Coon's eyes didn't notice the mottled green and brown tent until they were practically on top of it. Dave left them there after promising Lady Ruth that someone would bring their dinner.

Coon watched as the others went in to explore their new home. Coon couldn't bring herself to join them. Her sensitive nose didn't approve of the tent. She sniffed and then gave a raccoon's sneeze of protest. The tent stank of dust and mold. Unless it was raining, she saw no need to seek shelter inside. She could sleep more comfortably and probably more safely up in one of the pine trees.

Voices mingled with the sounds of things being moved as her friends argued about who would sleep where. Finding a place to sleep didn't seem like a bad idea. Coon picked an older pine with a good view of the tent. She hesitated only a moment before she began to climb her first tree. The claws on the ends of her fingers sank through the bark to grip the trunk. For a time, it became a game as she learned to go up and down the tree. She was having a great time, when a noise alerted her to the fact that someone was coming up the path.

A young woman was carrying two pizza boxes through the trees. Coon's stomach rumbled at the sight. The pizza's disappeared into the tent and the delivery service ran back down the path like someone was chasing her. The stink of the tent warred with the aroma of pizza. The battle of smells was resolved moments later when Ruth brought a slice of pizza out on a paper plate for Coon to enjoy. Coon chittered her thanks as Ruth sat down beside her.

Coon had always loved pizza, but eating it as a raccoon was almost impossible. Her hands were too small to pick up the slice. The melted cheese stuck to her fur like glue. Ruth had to break chunks off for Coon to eat. Coon placed the first small piece in her mouth and almost gagged. Her raccoon taste buds did not appreciate her dinner as much as her nose did. In the end, Ruth helped her to pick the "stuff" from the top of the pizza. Coon decided raccoons did like pepperoni, but not soggy mushrooms or green peppers that tasted of tomato sauce and cheese. With regret, Coon scratched pizza off her favorite food list.

Ruth went back into the tent when Coon gave up on the pizza. The conversation inside turned to the morning and then to sleep. As goodnights echoed through the tent, Coon headed back to the Faire. She wasn't tired after her nap, so she decided to explore. The darkness didn't hinder her ability to check out the stages, tents, or even some of the permanent buildings. She even found a stash of granola bars in one of the tents. They were even better than she remembered. Granola and especially Honey and Oat bars were now one of her favorites.

By morning, Coon knew her way around the Faire. She had a mental map of where to find both food and water. She should be able to fend for herself until the Faire closed for the season. Coon liked the feeling of independence that gave her. At the same time though, there were lines she was unwilling to cross in name of self-reliance. The biggest of those lines were trash cans. Despite how good some of them smelled to her new nose, she would starve before she sampled that cuisine.

As the sun began to shine through the pines, Coon returned to Ancient Attire and crawled into Tuula's nest of pillows.

Coon's life fell into a strange new pattern after that night. By day, she dozed among the pillows. Tuula could talk for hours and often did. Sometimes, Tuula read to Coon from her favorite book. Coon had never read Tolkien's The Hobbit. The book wasn't bad, but it also wasn't an easy read. That a six-year-old read it at all amazed Coon. Tuula did more than just read it, she performed it with different voices for all of the main characters. Thus began Coon's education on dwarves and elves and strange little creatures called hobbits.

By night, Coon roamed the grounds of "Queen Coon's" Faire. She watched the security guards on their rounds and entertained herself by getting into places she wasn't supposed to. Danny's lessons on picking locks were turning out to be quite useful. Coon had always had a weakness for junk food. Her new ability to get into almost anything provided her with an endless supply of goodies. Apparently, raccoons were as fond of treats as she had been as a young girl. Except for chocolate. That was a definite no-no. Coon quickly learned that chocolate went right through raccoons.

A day passed and then two and then three. Coon stayed away from the tent and especially Ruth. She wasn't sure if she had a place in the life they were planning. Tuula provided the companionship Coon needed. She liked the fact that Tuula had no expectations. The child didn't ask her to be anything more than someone to talk to. The nights were peaceful and quiet. That solitude was also something Coon needed. In the darkness, there were no demands that she do anything other than exist. For a time, Coon was content.

All good things do come to an end, though. The Faire reopened. Coon hated it. There were too many people and way too much noise. Coon did the only thing she could. She retreated into the trees as far from the crowds as she could get. She hid there through the day and into the night, not even visiting Tuula. She stayed apart until the mass of people were gone. Then she would sneak back into the tents to eat and drink.

The quiet never seemed to last long enough. For three days, Coon suffered and then her world returned to normal. But in her heart, she knew it was only a short reprieve before the crowds descended on her domain again.

That period of peace was even shorter than Coon expected. Didn't she deserve more than a few hours respite? Coon had just torn open an Oats and Honey granola bar when the silence was shattered by a crash of metal. The harsh clatter startled her so badly that her claws sank deep into the brittle bar. Her meal disintegrated into hundreds of tasty chunks, most of which now lay in the dirt. As Coon stared down at her ruined dinner, anger and resentment over the last three days consumed her. She was going to make someone pay for this indignity.

Coon shoved the last small piece of honey-covered oats into her mouth and headed towards the source of the noise. The sane part of her knew she was being foolish, but she was too angry to care. Whether this was a guest or a thief, she intended to chase them away. After hours, the Faire belonged to her.

She expected the noises to fade away. What kind of trespasser would continue to call attention to themselves? But the silence she longed for didn't return. A new and more annoying sound came out of the darkness to fray her nerves. A steady pattern of rattle-thumps led her directly to the Canterbury Kitchen. Whoever the intruder was, they were hiding behind one of Coon's favorite snack stops.

Coon slowed her pace, creeping around the Kitchen instead of charging directly into battle. The grating sound of metal on metal continued as she made her way to the back of the building. Coon had little more than vague ideas running through her head. Whoever these people were, she wanted to scare them as badly as they had startled her. As she peeked around the final corner, Coon discovered a fatal flaw in her half-formed plan. There was absolutely no one behind the building to scare.

The source of her rapidly growing headache was a large aluminum trash can. The lidless can lay on its side with the opening facing away from her. The can rocked slowly back and forth, apparently of its own volition. Each time the haunted can changed direction, the two handles would clang and rattle against the side of the can. After a half rotation, the descending handle would slam into the ground with a thump bringing the can to a halt before it reversed direction again. The rattle thump now made sense even if the self-moving can did not.

Coon came around the corner scanning behind the kitchen for anything that might explain the animated trash can. She moved forward slowly, but still triggered the motion sensor on a single security light mounted high on the back wall. In its dim light, she could now see three more trash cans near the back door. The other cans were all chained together in a tight cluster. Only the haunted can appeared free to roam around freely. Coon froze as something else moved in the light. This form was darker and it emitted a soft rustling noise as it bulged and squirmed like some creature formed of shadow. It took her a moment to recognize the black shape of a black trash bag. But no trash bag Coon had ever seen convulsed the way this one did. An uncertain chitter escaped from Coon's throat. She wasn't sure if it was driven from her by curiosity or fear.

At her outburst, both bag and can stopped their strange motion. Those responsible for the noise and for ruining her meal were suddenly revealed. Coon discovered that there were indeed thieves at work here, but they were not the kind of thieves that Coon had imagined. The plastic of the trash bag parted without warning. Gleaming eyes stared at her from within a masked face. A second masked face peered at her from the open end of the can. Chittering noises much like her own burst from both raccoons. Coon had no clue if those sounds were meant to welcome her or warn her to stay away from their feast.

More than anything, Coon wanted to rush forward to greet both raccoons. This was her chance to fulfill all her adolescent dreams. Everything she had ever desired stood before her in a trash bag and an oversized trash can. Acceptance and friendship could be hers. She might never have to be alone again. She was one of their kind, but would they welcome her among them? Not knowing the answer to that question, she hesitated, letting the closer raccoon come to her. It… no, she realized as it rose on its hind feet to study her… he seemed as hesitant as she felt. The second raccoon watched them both from the safety of its aluminum shelter.

The male dropped back to all four of its legs. Its body elongated as it stretched its snout closer to Coon; its small black nose twitching in an effort to draw in her essence. Coon's anticipation grew as the distance between them shrank. And then, as it had so many times in the past, her hopes and dreams were assassinated by someone else's thoughtless response. As the male drew in her scent, he jerked away from her like he had been slapped. He gave an angry hiss as his lips pulled back to reveal sharp-looking teeth. Coon stared in surprise at the raccoon's stiff-legged stance. Its tail began to lash from side to side as it backed away from her. The second raccoon gave a frightened squeak as its head disappeared back into the trash can.

This rejection stung more than any she had ever suffered as a human. Did she have a place in this world if even the raccoons didn't want her? Coon reacted as she always had in the past, she turned and ran. She rushed into the darkness without thinking and without a destination in mind other than away from where she was. She needed to escape as much from herself as from the two raccoons. Coon ran until her legs sank into the cold embrace of mud. The wet slime clung to her, sinking through her fur to coat her skin. Her headlong flight came to an abrupt end as the mud gripped her legs. She panted, out of breath, as she stared around her. It was long moments before she recognized where she was. The Mud Pit stretched out before her, beckoning her to sink beneath its surface.

But Coon wasn't ready to die, and definitely didn't want to die that way. So, she backed out of the Pit. It was a struggle to pull her legs free. It took time and effort to save herself. She used that time to shove this latest hurt into a mental box. That box joined thousands of others containing the countless indignities she has suffered in life. She would survive this pain too as long as she followed the rule. "Never reopen the boxes!"

With the events of the night carefully locked away, Coon stared down at her own body. She snarled in disgust at the slumps of mud that hung from her legs and underbelly. How was she ever going to get clean. An image of her grandmother's cat cleaning itself flashed into her mind. Coon shuddered. There was no way she was going to try to lick the muck off. Yuck!

She sat there in the darkness, wet and miserable. There were too many things swirling through her thoughts for her to latch on to even one of them. But she had to try. She needed to understand why the male raccoon had reacted the way it had. Something in her scent had repelled it. Coon sniffed herself. The mud stank, but the rest of her fur smelled nice. A touch of the pine mingled with the scent of Tuula overlay the rich aroma of her own fur. She smelled nothing like the disagreeable male whose unwashed body stank of trash and rotted food. Coon had kept herself fastidiously clean since she found herself in this form. What could the other raccoon have possibly found offensive about the way she smelled? She didn't understand and that just made the events of the night even more painful.

A warm, familiar presence intruded on the edge of Coon's mind. It was no surprise when Ruth knelt on the ground a few feet away. Her only friend from her life before the change knelt there with her arms open. Coon considered the offer of comfort but could not let go of the misery. The fire burning inside her was warmer than her friend's love. Besides, she was covered in mud that would stain Ruth's new clothes.

Ruth slowly lowered her arms. The pain Coon saw in Ruth's eyes was nothing compared to what Coon felt. Ruth's words only made Coon want to run again, but she knew Ruth would just follow her, so she might as well listen.

"What happened, Coon?" Ruth asked. "I felt your unhappiness. I came as quickly as I could. I'm sorry that it took me so long to find you."

Emotions swirled within Coon. She didn't want to admit that she had been rejected again. It hurt too much. What Coon wanted to do at that moment was cry. But she couldn't. Apparently, this new body did not make tears. So even that comfort was denied her. That loss was just another log to add to the fire of her anger.

Ruth's right hand came to rest on Coon's back. "Coon, I want to help, but your emotions are overwhelming me too."

Coon's body shuddered as she buried this new pain deep inside. How many more boxes could she fit in the dark place where she hid them all? And what would happen to her when that place finally overflowed?

Ruth soft voice seemed to croon its next question, "Who hurt you, Coon?"

Coon felt a wave of love wrap itself around her mind, sheltering it. Ruth had been able to sense Coon's emotions since the change. Now, it appeared she had learned to share her own emotions as well. Coon had lost even the ability to speak. It seemed so unfair. If they were going to have this talk that Ruth was insisting on, Coon would have to improvise. Raising her a mud-covered hand, Coon pointed at herself. Then she raised two fingers and held them where Ruth could see them.

Ruth stared at her as if trying to see into her mind, then a look of understanding came to her face. "You met a couple of raccoons tonight? Isn't that good news, Coon?"

Coon shook her head and bared her teeth the way the male had. Her own pain made it easy to imitate his reaction to her.

Sympathy that Coon didn't want shone in Ruth's eyes. Of course, her friend asked the question that Coon still did not really understand. "Why, Coon? Why didn't they like you? You are a beautiful female raccoon."

Coon thought but could not think of any way to pantomime her answer. The raccoon's body was just too limited. But her human mind wasn't that limited. There were other ways to communicate. Coon lowered her muddy claw to the damp ground, dragging them through the soft, wet soil. Her fingers left crude letters in the mud. "SMELL BAD! WRONG!"

Ruth stared down at the message in surprise. Her voice was little more than a whisper as she said, "I am so sorry, Coon."

Coon wrote one more message before retreating back to the nearest tree. "ALONE AGAIN FOREVER."

When Ruth spun to face her, there was anger on her friend's face now. Coon wasn't sure she liked that look, but it was better than Ruth feeling sorry for her.

Ruth's voice was uncompromising as she hissed, "You have never been alone since we became roommates. I was your friend whether you were Conchia or Coon. There were others that wanted to be your friend, too. But you never let them in."

Coon shook her head knowing in her heart that the people Ruth was talking about had only felt sorry for her. But Ruth raised a hand and began to shake her index finger at Coon. "No, we did not feel sorry for you. You only felt sorry for yourself."

Those words stung. She couldn't be to blame. It had never been her fault. Why didn't Ruth understand or was she just being mean? Coon began to edge back towards the trees.

Ruth's face softened and she lowered her hand. "I am your friend, Coon, and I am not the only one. We care about you even if you can't see it. Danny, Herrera, Geoff, Jacob and Tuula. Especially that little girl. You will only be alone in this world if you choose to be that way."

Coon turned and scrambled up the tree. For the second time that night she ran, leaping from branch to branch without looking back. She had to get away. Ruth's words hurt as much as the raccoon's rejection. Being around others just hurt too much.

That night, the part of her that was Coon retreated into the far recesses of her mind. As she withdrew into herself, Coon discovered that she wasn't alone in the uncharted depths of her mind. Another presence played and frolicked in that endless space. Her unexpected companion seemed quite content rummaging through Coon's half-forgotten memories. The raccoon, her raccoon, watched her as Coon sought refuge from the outside world. There was a confused look on its masked face that seemed to ask why Coon was here instead of being in charge. Coon had no answer that her raccoon would understand. So, she did the only thing that made sense to her at that moment, she surrendered control and sent her other self out to face the world in her stead.

Free from all responsibility now, Coon huddled alone in the darkness. The raccoon turned out to be more than capable of running Coon's life. It slept when it was tired, it drank when it was thirsty, and it ate when it was hungry. Coon would have objected to some of its meal choices, especially when it began to eat from trash cans, but it took too much effort to protest. Coon just let her raccoon do what it thought best. The only times Coon felt any urge to rise to the surface of her mind was when she heard the sad voice of a little girl calling her name. Coon did her best to ignore that voice, but not so her raccoon. It seemed drawn by the girl's lonely cries. Her raccoon watched over the girl whenever Tuula wandered among the trees.

A day came when the tone of those cries Coon refused to acknowledge changed. Instead of sounding sad, that small voice was filled with anger. Her raccoon, agitated in a way that Coon had never experienced, came down from the high branches where it normally watched the girl. Coon would have turned her back on them both, but her raccoon's angry chittering reverberated through the mental barriers she had erected. Coon knew that if she wanted peace, she would have to venture out of her sanctuary one last time. A quick peek, she decided, was all she would give her raccoon. Enough to calm her and no more. Then Coon would close the door to that other world forever.

Her resolve was quickly forgotten when she saw what was happening below the tree. A large teenage boy strode through the trees, dragging a much smaller form behind him. That small form, a young girl, struggled to pull free but she did not stand a chance against the boy's greater strength. Tuula's angry voice demanded he let her go. Not once did little Tuula beg or plead. Instead, she fought with everything she had. In a fit of anger, Tuula tried to bite the hand wrapped tightly around her small wrist. Coon had no idea how the boy sensed the attack, but he spun on Tuula with his left hand outstretched. There was a loud crack when the boy's palm connected with child's cheek.

"Tuula!" Coon screamed in her mind as her friend fell to her knees. Coon tore control of her body from her raccoon. It seemed as if an eternity passed before her body responded to her desire to move. She had no idea how much time really passed, but neither of the figures below moved in those untold centuries it took Coon to regain control. Coon raced out on a limb barely strong enough to hold her weight. When she reached the boy, Coon threw herself at him. Her descent lasted far longer than she expected. She might have been higher than she had realized when she jumped.

When it came, the impact was brutal; driving the air from Coon's lungs. She felt the boy stagger as she scrabbled to hold on to his head. But there was nothing for her small hands to grip. The ear she managed to snag was shredded by her claws. Her hand slid down his neck, leaving deep furrows where it passed. Even the t-shirt the boy wore came apart in her grasp. Coon hit the ground almost as hard as she had hit the boy. She lay there helpless as the bleeding boy spun on her.

Coon tried to crawl away, but the boy kicked out catching her in the haunch. There was another flare of pain as Coon found herself flying through the air a second time. The boy came at her again, but Coon hurt too much to move. The boy raised his foot over her. Coon could only stare up at the Nike Air logo as she waited for the boy to stomp on her head. But his foot never came down. Instead, the boy stumbled to the side as a long stick connected with the back of his head.

Coon wasn't sure where she came from, but Tuula was suddenly beside her. Like a guardian angel, the child assumed a protective stance over Coon, a large stick grasped in both her hands. The boy, unwilling to give up his prey, came at Tuula once more. His voice was filled with pain and anger as he cursed, "You little …" His words broke off when the stick lashed out. Tuula swung the stick with the ease of a seasoned swordswoman. The boy became confused as the stick lashed out twice in rapid succession, first striking his undamaged ear and then hitting his temple with a solid thunk. Before he could recover his wits, Coon rose and snapped at his ankle.

Now facing two opponents, the boy turned and ran.

Tuula knelt then and gathered Coon into her arms. The reality of what Tuula had done was impossible to deny. Tuula had risked her life to save Coon just as Coon had risked her own to save Tuula. To question their friendship now seemed rather foolish. Coon was just beginning to realize that she might have been foolish for a very long time. Sirens began to wail in the distance, coming closer as she sheltered in Tuula's arms.

Tuula released her and leaned back. A bright red handprint marred the child's face where the boy had slapped her. Coon could also see bruises forming on the girl's arm where the larger boy had dragged her into the trees. Coon wanted to go after him, but Tuula just shook her head. Then Tuula whispered softly in a voice far too mature for such a young girl. "Let him go. You must hide now. The dark riders are coming and you must not let them find you or all will be for naught."

Coon rubbed her furry cheek against Tuula's before backing away. The climb up the pine tree was painful but not unbearably so. She found a place high in one of the branches of a nearby tree. She hid there to watch over Tuula as her raccoon had always done.

Tuula seemed so small and helpless as she stood alone in that small clearing. Coon could only pray that someone came for her soon.

The sirens were much closer now. It was a relief when their undulating cry finally came to an end. For a short time, silence reigned in the small clearing where Tuula waited. Coon understood that the silence was just a prelude for the storm to come. She could already feel the first gentle breeze of the tempest that might mean her death. Ruth was that breeze and she was almost here. Her warm presence growing ever closer. The scary question was… Who would be coming next to deal with the mad raccoon?

Ruth's footsteps announced her arrival. Her roommate glanced up at Coon with unerring precision. Coon's hiding place was not proof against the bond that connected the two of them. Coon nodded down at her friend. It was a relief to finally accept that Ruth really was her friend. And maybe, just maybe, Ruth's last conversation with her had not been mean so much as brutally honest. Ruth gave her a brief smile before turning to Tuula.

Tuula stiffened when Ruth got close and opened her arms. Ruth studied the girl and her obvious injuries. Lowering her arms, Ruth gave Tuula her space. Coon heard Ruth whisper, "Friends?" At Tuula's nod, Ruth took up a protective position at the child's side. Coon signed in relief when she saw Tuula take the hand Ruth offered her.

Discordant voices began to filter through the trees and from up the small game trail. The storm was about to break. Coon could hear people arguing while more authoritarian voices ordered people to stay back. She had no idea who was winning the argument, but there seemed to be a large crowd gathering in the vicinity of the stage. Coon doubted the crowd was gathering for one of the performances.

Footsteps pounded up the game trail. Coon went perfectly still as three police officers burst into the clearing, their pistols swinging back and forth as they scanned the underbrush and the trees. Not one of the officers even looked at either Ruth or Tuula. Coon had a sinking suspicion she knew who and what they were searching for. And if they found her, she wasn't likely to last long.

The officers were still searching the trees when Tara ran into the clearing with Jacob right on her heels. One of the officers reached for Tara's arm but somehow Jacob stepped between them. Tara was past him in that instant and sank to her knees beside her daughter. Tuula's fierce look of independence fell away as a frightened little girl fell into her mother's arms.

Coon could see Tuula whispering in her mother's ear. She couldn't make out what Tuula was saying over the blustering of the officer that was glaring at Jacob. "We told you there was a dangerous animal out here. You should have waited until we said it was safe. That beast already attacked a teenage boy."

Jacob looked ready to argue, but Tara's angry voice had both men turning to face her. "That animal, as you call it, was trying to defend my daughter. Just let it be."

The officer met Tara's gaze as if he was about to lecture her, but whatever he saw in her eyes made him look away.

Then, the officer's day went from bad to worse. An older man in expensive clothing erupted from the game trail. The man took an authoritative stance in front of the officer and demanded, "Well? Have you shot that damn thing yet? That pet of hers hurt my son. It practically chewed his ear off. Now what are you going to do about it?"

Coon tasted bile in the back of her mouth at the mere thought of eating someone's ear. But the older man's tirade wasn't done yet. "I demand that you hunt that damn raccoon down and shoot it. Bring in dogs if you have to. It's a menace. Well, what are you waiting for?"

The officer's face hardened at the man's tone. Apparently, he had no intention of backing down a second time. "Please calm down, Mr

Trombettista. We will search for the animal once everyone else here is safe."

The older man began to sputter in anger, but the three officers ignored him as Coon's remaining friends stomped out of the trees, literally blazing their own trail to join the party. Coon saw all three officers step back as Geoff led the charge into the now crowded clearing. The big man stood behind Ruth with his arms crossed over his massive chest. Herrera and Danny circled around to flank the three officers. In the confusion, Jacob moved to stand beside Tara with his hand on her shoulder.

But it was the figure that followed her three friends out of the trees that really surprised Coon. The bossy man from the front gate, now dressed in full court finery, paused on the edge of the trees. The man, Sir John, if Coon remembered correctly, turned to face the officer that appeared to be in charge. "Sergeant, I assume you had good reason for denying the Court's legal counsel access to a member of our staff?"

The officer holstered his gun and raised a placating hand. "We are just trying to keep everyone safe, Sir."

The loud man raised his voice again. "If you want to keep everyone safe, kill that deranged rodent. And ask that little girl why she tricked my boy into coming out here where it could attack him."

The man was going to continue but Tuula pulled herself free from her mother. She may have only been six, but Tuula matched the older man glare for glare. Her index finger shot out and she began to shake it at him as she lectured, "I did not trick him. And raccoons are not rodents. They are actually more closely related to bears. And, for your information, Coon is not a pet. She is my friend. She is not deranged either."

As Tuula faced down the older man, the bright red handprint on her cheek became visible to everyone. It stood out like a beacon on her normally pale skin.

Before anyone else could react, the fancy-pants man was suddenly kneeling in front of Tuula. He whispered softly to her, "I am sorry for this, Tuula. But it is necessary to protect us all." His phone appeared from somewhere in his court robes. He quickly snapped several pictures of Tuula's face. Her hand came up to cover the mark, revealing the bruises on her wrist. Coon heard the camera's shutter trigger several more times as Tuula held her hand in front of her face.

Sir John stood as his thumbs danced across the phones small screen. One of the officers leaned in to see what Sir John was doing. The officer sounded worried as he asked, "What are you doing, Sir?"

The defiant look on the courtier's face dared the officer to object. "I just forwarded evidence of an assault on one of our people to my legal team. I suspect that your Captain will be getting a phone call any minute now. As the victim is a minor, her identity is to be protected at all costs."

Coon tensed as Sir John stepped back and Jacob got his first view of the marks on little Tuula. His face darkened and Coon's fur began to stand on end. Whatever the strange power was that Jacob now controlled, Coon sensed that it was about to break free. Coon saw fear in Ruth's eyes as she stared up a Jacob. One of the officers cried out in pain as the taser on his belt began to emit bright blue sparks. Sir John shook his head as the screen on his cell phone flashed brightly and went dead. The radios the officers wore all gave a burst of static and then went silent. Coon wondered if any of them would survive what was about to happen.

Then little Tuula reached up and placed her small hand in Jacob's. Jacob closed his hand gently around hers as he looked into her eyes. Tuula simply shook her head. They stood like that for far too long while Coon wondered if the world was about to end. Then Jacob nodded and anger faded from his face. Coon's fur lay back down as quickly as it had risen. She had no idea what Jacob had almost done, but she was very, very glad that Tuula had stopped him.

No one spoke as Jacob and Tuula continued to stare at each other. The officers all looked confused. At Jacob's nod, Sir John once again took control of the situation. "Mr Trombettista, you and your son are banished from King Richard's Faire. You are never to return. I would like to add on pain of death, but that is no longer under the Crown's purview."

The older man's face turned a bright red. "You have no right. My son was the victim here. We have done nothing wrong."

Sir John shook his head and indicated Tuula's face. "I am sure that the officers can perform a DNA test to determine if those marks were inflicted by your son. Do you really want to contest my ruling?"

The policeman stared back and forth between the two men. Sir John turned his gaze to Tara. "Mistress Helleväara. Do you petition the Crown for redress on behalf of your daughter? We will provide you with a lawyer if you choose to press charges. It would be a pleasure to represent you myself. But, I would be remiss if I did not warn you that filing charges will mean that young Tuula may have to testify in court."

Tara stood up and placed a hand on her daughter's head. "Thank you, Lord Steward, but if they accept banishment from this Faire and all others… I will let the matter rest."

Trombettista turned to the officers for support, but the looks they gave him were cold and unyielding. He tried one last desperate plea, "Sergeant, you are still going to shoot that damn raccoon, aren't you? It attacked my son. It isn't safe to let a crazed animal like that live."

The chorus of outraged protests soothed a pain deep inside Coon that she hadn't even realized was there. She had never had so many people defending her at the same time. But it was the words of the Lord Steward that she least expected. "Officers, I suggest that you check with your superiors before you respond to Mr Trombettista's question. The raccoon known as Coon is a member in good standing of the Folk. If you do not understand what that means, I am sure your chain of command does. Coon acted in defense of a six-year-old child. She is innocent of any and all wrong doing in this matter."

The annoying man started to complain but the officers moved in to surround him. "Come with us please, Mr Trombettista. You and your son are now trespassing on private property. More importantly, the District Attorney's office may have some questions to ask you and your son. If you have a lawyer, I suggest you contact him."

Two of the officers placed gentle but insistent hands on the angry man's arms. They lead him back down the game trail, ignoring his many protests. The final officer turned back to face Tara. "Ma'am, will you be available for questioning if that fool tries to press charges?" At Tara's nod, he added, "I know you want to protect your daughter, but pressing charges is the only way to ensure the boy doesn't do something like this again." When Tara's face did not relent, he turned and walked away.

The group waited until the officer was well down the trail. Then Tara picked up her daughter. "Thank you, Sir John." Without looking back, she marched back down the trail with her four bodyguards close behind.

Sir John turned and looked down at Ruth. "Ruth, I am truly sorry about this. Can you find your pet?"

Ruth stared up at Coon's hiding place with an inquisitive look on her face. Then she turned and took the courtier's hand, pulling him towards the trail. There was a smile on Ruth's face as she explained, "Coon is my friend, not my pet. She will return when she is good and ready. Thank you for what you did just now." She paused briefly to stare up at him with an evil looking grin. "If you are not careful, Sir John, the King might saddle you with an ugly job like Lord Regent. Then where will you be?"

The courtier began to laugh as they continued up the trail. Coon only caught part of his response. "In deep…"

The two chuckled as they walked from the clearing.

Coon sat on her perch and considered everything that had happened. Her universe had shifted in the last hour. What exactly did it mean to be one of Ruth's Folk? It was hard enough to imagine having so many friends, and now there were people she barely knew willing to come to her defense. It felt strange to be a part such a close-knit group. More than a group, she amended. It was a community and they welcomed her.

Ruth's words at the Mud Pit sounded much different today than they had that dark night. Had there always been a place for her? Had there really been people who wanted Conchia to be their friend? As Conchia, she had always felt so isolated, so alone. Becoming Coon had helped for a while. For a short time, she had felt a part of something big. But once her novelty had worn off, those new friends and fallen away. She ended up alone again despite becoming exactly what they said they wanted her to be. It had all been so unfair.

Where would she be today if she had figured this all out sooner? What would she be right now if she had learned to accept herself, to love herself back when she was Conchia. Would she be human right now? Would she be living happily at home? Maybe, but she could not find it in her to regret what she was or where she was right now. She couldn't change what the lab had done to her, but she could accept it and live this new life that she had found. She had friends and people she could trust now. They even loved her as a raccoon. She had found her place among a group of misfits and she was happy. Only, perhaps, they really weren't the misfits after all. Perhaps the real misfits were the people who had tried to convince her that her old self wasn't good enough.

For now, she was content with who she was. She would be Coon. Someday, she might try to reclaim that lost little girl that she had once been. Who would she become then? Coonchia? Coon giggled at that sound of that name. The giggle came out of her throat sounded like a chihuahua bringing up a hairball. She would have to work on a better laugh. And, she would need to find ways to communicate with her new friends. She had no intention of ever being alone again.

## Chapter 17
## Forged Anew

Herrera stood on the edge of the Tournament Grounds watching Geoff practice for his debut in tomorrow's show. It was his turn to "escort" the big man and make sure he didn't get into trouble. Geoff might be one of the most capable warriors at the Faire, but his innocence made him vulnerable. Babysitting Geoff wasn't a bad gig. He got to watch the shows and glare at anyone who tried to take advantage of his large friend. Herrera found that he was actually quite good at glaring these days. It was one of the many perks that came with his new body.

The hard part of the duty was looking interested as the cast went through the routine for the umpteenth time. Geoff's role was pretty simple, but it seemed to take his friend a lot of repetitions to get it right. And, to tell the truth, Herrera thought the act was kind of lame. The Princess Bride had been a great movie. Heck, even gang bangers like him had seen it more than once. But that didn't mean it made a good act for the Faire. The Rennies apparently didn't share his opinion. They were all very excited to be playing a part from their favorite movie. Maybe the problem was that he just didn't get the whole sword swing hero mindset.

The crash of steel on steel pulled Herrera back out of his head. He was more interested in the swords themselves than the idiots trying to brain each other with them. The man playing Wesley had a particularly fine-looking rapier. Its steel sang with perfect pitch each time Wesley parried one of the three blades his opponents swung at him with such vigor. Not that the man wielding the blade was bad. The handsome young hero made swinging that heavy sword look easy, even against three opponents. Wesley was apparently very serious about his swordplay. Then again, so were the other Rennies. Most of them spent hours each day practicing simply for the joy of being a swashbuckling hero for a few hours each month. Most, but not all. The man to Wesley's far left had a mean streak in him. Herrera didn't like the man at all. Sir Gilles got too much pleasure out of playing the villain.

And, as one would expect of any good Hollywood drama, the script required an unarmed Geoff to go toe-to-toe with Gilles and his sword. It was a recipe for disaster. Even Sir Gilles' unsharpened blade would hurt when it hit. And Herrera knew that eventually, it would hit. Sir Gilles wasn't going to go easy on the new "star" of the show. The errant knight wasn't going to miss a chance to embarrass the man who had replaced him in the limelight. And how hard could that be? Geoff had barely had a week to learn the routine. It had been a rough week until Danny had explained to Geoff that this was just another Kata form. Now, the big man seemed to have the routine down, or so Herrera hoped. The only problem they had not been unable to solve yet was getting Geoff to remember that he was playing Fezzik.

The mock battle grew more intense as the three villains pressed their attacks. Wesley slapped aside all three of his opponents' swords at once and spun to face the brightly colored pavilion behind him. "Fezzik," he called. "I have need of your great strength!" Geoff stepped away from the silk wall of the pavilion where he had been waiting. Geoff's face was a mask of confusion. Sadly, Herrera knew that look wasn't an act. Then a young girl, the daughter of one of the Rennies, ran up and grabbed Geoff by the finger. His big friend smiled down at the child as she pulled him towards the battle. In his head, Herrera filled in the missing line that Geoff had been waiting for, "Hurry, Fezzik! Wesley needs you!"

Herrera grinned as Geoff rushed across the field to aid the brave young swordsman. Two of the knights spun to face Geoff leaving Wesley to battle a single opponent. The fight went off exactly as it was choreographed. Geoff slapping aside sword swing after sword swing. Then Gilles broke the rehearsed pattern. Instead of the lunge that was supposed to come next, Gilles brought his sword up for an overhead chop. The blow came down hard and fast, aimed for Geoff's unarmored shoulder.

Herrera's hiss of anger turned into a whistle of appreciation. In a move that seemed too fast for such a big man, Geoff stepped in close to Gilles. Geoff's left hand came across in a hard chop that caught Sir Gilles' wrist. The unsharpened longsword flew across the lists. All of Geoff's forward momentum seemed to transfer into his right arm as it shot forward. The big man's open palm slammed into the center of Sir Gilles' breast plate. The clang of that hammer-like blow rang across the field. Every eye on the practice field watched as Sir Gilles was launched through the air to land at least a dozen feet away. The impact with the ground was no less spectacular as the knight's breath exploded from his lungs. Herrera could not hold back a chuckle as the defeated warrior tried to suck air back into his lungs. Herrera turned away from the fallen knight to check on his friend.

Geoff was staring at Gilles with a worried look on his face. Figures, Herrera thought. The jerk finally gets what he deserves and Herrera's kind-hearted friend felt bad about it. Herrera hurried over and placed a restraining hand on Geoff's arm. When Geoff looked down at him there were tears in his eyes. Geoff's whisper was loud enough that half the training field probably heard it. "Accident. No time think. Just do. Boom!"

To Herrera's relief, no one except the medical team seemed overly concerned about Gilles. In fact, almost every warrior on the practice field was gathering around Geoff. Instead of anger, there was awe on most of their faces. Herrera could actually see several of them mouthing the word "Boom" with smiles on their faces. The silence was finally broken when Wesley asked, "Are you okay, Geoff? I couldn't tell if he hit you or not. It all happened so fast."

Geoff refused to meet Wesley's gaze. "Not hurt. Did I break him?"

That question brought peels of laugher from the gathered warriors. Someone muttered quite loudly, "Serves him right if you did. He'll be lucky not to get banned from the lists for a move like that."

Another voice from the circle of admirers asked, "What did you do to him? I could use a few moves like that."

Geoff gave Herrera a pleading look. Herrera patted him on the arm and then explained. "Geoff may not be much for words, but he is damned good at judo. He's also a pretty good teacher. I know he's taught me a lot."

Suddenly, the practice field was like a candy store full of starving children. Except, these children wore battle armor and carried big swords. And, the treat of the day was a judo lesson instead of a lollipop. Every man and woman on that field wanted in on the fun. They all wanted Geoff to teach them. Everyone except Sir Gilles who was now being helped off the field. The rest of the knights were stripping off their armor and weapons.

Geoff's shy uncertainty melted away. Judo was the one subject the big man felt confident about. Herrera knew from personal experience that Geoff could handle teaching a lesson, even to such a large crowd. Of course, Herrera thought with a smile, most of Geoff's lessons involved someone landing on your back at the big man's feet. Herrera seriously doubted any of Geoff's new students would complain about being tossed around like a rag doll. As the new class bowed to their instructor, Herrera backed away and let Geoff play Sensei.

With Geoff safely occupied, Herrera decided he could indulge his own curiosity. He headed across the field to the displays being set up for tomorrow's show. Racks containing all manner of medieval weapons alternated with tables holding various types of armor. This would be his opportunity to put his hands on things he had only touched in his dreams. The only question was… where to start? In the end, he chose a rack containing three swords. None of the weapons had an edge, so he was allowed to touch them.

The display was labeled long, short, and bastard sword. Herrera reached out to touch the blade of the large bastard sword. As his fingers caressed the bright steel, a simple melody began to play through his mind. When he lifted his fingers, the faint music faded away. Touching the blade again, the song returned. He placed his palm against the sun-warmed steel and the music rose up, becoming clear and vibrant. Herrera listened to it, hearing the sword's voice as it sang to him of its forging. Its story was short and incomplete like the blade itself. The sword did not understand why it had never been given an edge. The lyrics of the song were filled with longing. Its desire to be used in battle felt overwhelming as the song reached its finale.

Herrera stood before the rack of weapons reliving the swords sad existence. It was hard to separate his own emotions from those of the blade. He realized that there was a danger in allowing himself to become a part of the symphony of the steel. He would have to learn to control himself and the steel. If he was to become a smith, he would have to master the steel both with his hands and with his mind. He studied the two remaining swords. He needed to try again.

Like the bastard sword, the long sword was too large for him to use as a weapon. For this experiment, it would have to be the short sword. Wrapping his fingers around its hilt, Herrera lifted it from the rack. Music again sprang into his mind. It seemed so much more powerful with the hilt locked in his grasp. There was a brief battle of wills, man versus blade. But in the end, the iron of Herrera's will was stronger than that from which the sword had been made. The sword continued to sing its song, but the smith-to-be now controlled the volume of that music. Never again would the song of the steel overwhelm him. Herrera returned the short sword to its place. Even without an edge, it was a solid weapon. It had even been used to spar from time to time. It could be content with that.

Herrera turned away from the swords. The next display contained three pieces of armor. A gauntlet whose articulation looked too modern sat between a chainmail coif and a buckler. Herrera began with the coif, lifting it and running the weave between his fingers and thumb. Once again, the steel sang its story to him. But unlike the swords, this melody was imperfect. His fingers found the mistakes in the weave as parts of the song played off-key. The weaver had attempted to repair the errors, but Herrera could feel the weakness in those malformed links. Herrera lowered the coif to the table. It was far heavier than it needed to be. The weave from his dreams would have provided better protection at half of the weight. Someday, he would make real armor using that weave and not just a child's plaything.

The gauntlets were next. Something about their design repelled him. With an effort of will, Herrera pushed aside his feeling and lifted the piece from the table. The steel was smooth and well-formed. There were no obvious errors. There also was no song. The gauntlet was dead. Lifeless. The exacting perfection of each joint was obviously the product of machines. The technology used in its making had stolen its soul. The gauntlet was incapable of bonding with its wearer. It would never be one with the warrior who wore it. Herrera dropped it on the table with a frown of distaste. He would prefer a poorly forged piece created by a smith to the feel of dead steel.

The final piece, the buckler, intrigued him. Bands of metal crisscrossed its surface in an intricate pattern. It was significantly more complicated than a solid steel buckler, but he could see how the design would add strength without increasing the weight. Herrera lifted the buckler from the table. He could not help himself; he slid his left arm into the straps on the underside. The music of its crafting came to him like a balm after the silence of the gauntlet. Herrera listened carefully to the song, learning about the layering that went into its creation. And yet, the song was somehow wrong. There were no obvious flaws in the music as there had been with the coif. He was no music expert, but the song seemed to be slightly off key. It would have sounded better if it had been played on the deeper notes of a keyboard.

Herrera stepped away from the table and began one of the defensive routines Geoff had taught him. He swung the buckler in a series of blocks to see how it felt. At each point in the routine, Herrera found his arm just out of place. Was it the weight of the armor or was it something more? He listened again to the music of its story. There, in the middle of the song, was the answer he sought. The buckler remembered the fumble-fingered apprentice who had helped in its creation.

A man's voice jarred Herrera from his thoughts. The curious voice came from behind Herrera's right shoulder. "Well?"

Herrera didn't turn to face the voice. He slid the buckler off his arm and stared at it. Understanding came to him slowly. Shifting the buckler from side to side, he muttered more to himself than to the presence he felt at his side. "It's off."

A scarred yet muscular hand reached over Herrera's shoulder to caress the buckler's boss. The voice sounded interested now, "How so?"

As the hand withdrew, Herrera's own fingers traced the pattern of the buckler's surface. With growing confidence in his conclusion, Herrera placed the buckler boss down on the table. Grasping an edge with each hand, Herrera spun the buckler like a top. The arm straps actually blurred from the speed of the buckler's rotation. Unlike a well-balanced top, the buckler did not spin smoothly. It began to wobble almost immediately. The imbalance grew more and more pronounced until the buckler's edge hit the table and it flipped.

The voice in his ear simply muttered, "I see."

Herrera turned around. A powerfully built man with salt and pepper hair stood thoughtfully at the table. By human standards, the man wasn't tall, but he towered over Herrera. The man's arms were immense; easily the thickness of most men's thighs. His grey tunic and trousers were covered by a leather apron. Pockets of different sizes and shapes decorated the apron. Herrera wasn't sure if there were more burn marks or pockets on the heavy, black leather. An array of tools protruded from the pockets of the apron, a different tool in each pocket. More tools hung from the leather belt at the man's waist. The most impressive of tools was the massive hammer that hung by the man's right hand.

"Smith?" the man asked. He seemed unconcerned that Herrera was staring at him.

Herrera was beginning to wonder if the man only spoke in one and two-word sentences. "Not yet," Herrera replied. "But I will be a great smith one day."

"Maybe, maybe not," the man said. The man reached out and grasped Herrera's forearm. When the man squeezed, it felt like a vise closing on his arm. Herrera refused to pull away and the man just grunted. Then the man turned Herrera's hand palm up as he studied the callouses on Herrera's hand. He shook his head at what he saw there. The man released his hand and stepped back. He stared at the buckler for a moment before turning and walking away. "Come along," the older man commanded.

"Where?" Herrera asked, uncertain of what was going on.

The man turned back with a sigh. "I must certify a weapon before it can be used in the lists. You shall assist me." The older man seemed unhappy about needing to explain himself.

Herrera looked back at Geoff and his judo class. Could he just leave Geoff here without someone to watch over him?

The older man turned and began to walk away. "Be what you are or learn what you can be. Choose!"

Those words hit home like a blow from the older man's hammer. What was he meant to be in life? Herrera had been searching for an answer to that question his whole life. What the lab had changed him into had only intensified his desire to find his place in this world. And now, without warning, a virtual stranger made it sound like finding his answer was as simple as taking a walk across the field. The old man had baited his hook with the one thing in life that Herrera could not resist. With only a small pang of guilt, he ran after the man who seemed to know more about Herrera's future than Herrera himself did.

The man's pace was unhurried as he walked towards a blue and gold pavilion. Herrera followed along, uncertain what he was getting himself into. He had no idea what it meant to certify a sword. For all he knew, they were going to see if it was sharp enough to make him bleed.

A young boy ran from the pavilion. The boy was out of breath by the time he reached them. Still, he managed to ask, "Master Smith, shall I tell father… I mean, tell Sir Garand that you are here to examine his new sword and armor?"

Herrera almost stumbled at the boy's words. Master Smith? This was one of the men he had been hoping to meet? And now he was following him around like a lost puppy?

At the Smith's nod, the boy sprinted for the pavilion. Herrera watched the boy dart inside. Moments later, a large, blond-haired man stepped out into the sunshine. The man stood casually with his arms crossed over his broad chest. Based on the cut of his silk tunic, Herrera assumed this was Sir Garand. The Smith seemed unimpressed by the man or his fancy clothing. As they reached the tent, the big man exclaimed, "Steven, welcome!"

At the Smith's frown, Herrera saw the skin around the blond man's eyes tighten. Then the big man bowed his head. "My pardon,

Master Smith. I forget myself in my excitement. But you are indeed most welcome. All has been unpacked in anticipation of your visit. Everything is ready for your inspection."

The Smith nodded his head in return. "Very well, Lord Knight. Let's see what you have acquired this time."

The knight stepped back, holding out his arm to indicate that the Master Smith should enter first. Herrera hesitated, unsure if the invitation included him or not. Apparently, the Smith didn't care if Herrera was invited or not. He snapped his fingers and crooked a finger for Herrera to follow him. Herrera stepped up beside the Smith and they entered the pavilion together.

Herrera was unprepared for what lay inside. To the right of the entrance was what looked like a reception area. A large wooden chair that almost qualified as a throne dominated that corner of the pavilion. A colorful banner hung over the ornate chair. Although interesting, neither throne nor banner held his attention once he noticed the armored figure staring at him from the center of the pavilion. The man wore a set of full plate armor, polished mirror bright. Herrera could see his own reflection on the warrior's breast plate. Herrera had never dreamed that such armor could exist. This could only be the man destined to sit on that throne.

Herrera raised his eyes to stare at the warrior's face. Should he bow or kneel? The warriors face gave him no clue. It was hidden beneath the golden visor of his helm. The helm's dark eye slits seemed locked on him and him alone. Golden wings flowed back on each side of the warrior's head like those of a hunting bird preparing to strike. This was a warrior that could not be vanquished. Nothing could stand against the man encased in such armor. Herrera lowered his eyes as a servant before his master. But his eyes continued to scan the exquisite armor. From across the room, he could not even detect the seams where the armor fitted together. It was exquisite.

Herrera's thoughts faltered as he realized the warrior had no hands. Empty holes reached for him from the ends of the warrior's extended arms. No, it was not a god or even a man that stood before him. It was merely the shell of a man that hung before him on a simple armor stand. That realization was almost a relief. He could accept that such armor might exist, especially without the fallibility of a man within it. Herrera glanced at the Lord Knight, realizing that he was destined to wear this suit of armor. Was he deserving of such a forging? Herrera wasn't at all sure that he was.

To the left of the armor sat a small table. On it rested a set of gauntlets like those he had seen in the demonstration area. Herrera grimaced at their machined perfection.

To the armor's right was a weapon rack of dark, polished wood. The luster of the wood was insignificant in comparison to either item that it held. On the lower rungs was a large, jeweled scabbard. The jewels sparkled even in the light of the pavilion. Their colors were the same as those on the banner over the throne-like chair. It was the scabbard of a king. But it was no less wondrous than the sword that rested above it.

Herrera studied this sword with interest. The Lord Knight's sword was even longer that the bastard sword he had examined earlier that day. The blade alone had to be close to his own four-foot height. Its hilt had room for both of the Lord Knight's large hands. Unlike the other swords he had seen, this blade had a slight curve to it. The curve was more pronounced near its tip. The blade seemed to glow with an internal light. As he stared at the sword, memories of the Bible stories his mother used to read to him came back to him. This was the blade of an Archangel. What mortal would dare to wield such a blade?

Was it surprise or insult that Herrera saw in Sir Garand's eyes when the Smith motioned for Herrera to examine the armor. Herrera didn't wait for the Lord Knight to object. At that moment, he wanted to hear the song of that armor more than he wanted to breathe. The fingers of both hands came up to explore the plate. It wasn't a song that came to him, it was a symphony. The armor wasn't just a lone instrument, it was an orchestra. The music was the tide and it almost washed him away. Again, Herrera pitted his will against that of the steel and, again, he won that duel. The armor, it appeared, was as proud and overbearing as the Lord Knight himself. It boasted of the Master Smith who had crafted it. It knew beyond all doubt that it was superior to all other armor in existence.

Herrera wasn't so sure the armor's vanity was justified. It was truly exceptional work, but his questing fingers found places where machines had aided in its crafting. The spots touched by technology were dead and lifeless. Herrera knew them to be a weakness and it was one that the armor itself was unaware of. Like him, the armor could not feel the things made by machines. The armor and the knight who wore it could be attacked at those points. Was what he sensed important enough to mention? He wasn't sure. Herrera didn't know enough to judge how dangerous these vulnerabilities were.

The Smith gave Herrera an inquisitive look. Herrera considered his words. What should he possibly say that wouldn't sound insane? He couldn't very well tell the Master Smith or the Lord Knight that the armor sang to him. Who would believe him? And what of his distrust of the pieces fashioned by a machine? Was that feeling even credible? In the end, Herrera just shrugged. The Smith seemed disappointed as he stepped forward to do his own evaluation. Herrera watched the older man reach into one of his many pockets and pull out a tuning fork. Striking the instrument against his hammer, the Smith placed the base of the tuning fork against the armor's breast plate.

The hum of the turning fork was picked up and magnified by the armor. Herrera could hear pieces of the complex melody that the armor had sung for him in the vibrations induced by the Smith. Other parts of the song played out as the Smith placed the tuning fork against different parts of the armor. It became clear to Herrera that the Master Smith did indeed know the Song of the Steel. The Smith just couldn't hear the music in his head the way Herrera did. The Smith finished his inspection and the tuning fork disappeared back into its pocket. The Master Smith's conclusion was simple and direct. "It will do."

Sir Grand frowned. "For what I paid for that suit, it damn well better do more than 'just do!'"

The Smith ignored him and pointed to the gauntlets. Herrera did as he was asked. He picked up first one and then the other. He felt no connection to either of them. It was as if they did not exist to him. Handling them was like picking up dead worms on the pavement after a rainstorm. With a shudder, he returned them to the table. Once again, he was at a loss for words. There was no valid reason for the distaste he felt for the gauntlets. But when he turned to meet the Smith's gaze, there was a mischievous grin on the man's face. He had been played.

The Smith had somehow known what Herrera's reaction would be before he even asked him to evaluate them. Herrera began to feel like the Smith was more interested in studying him than the armor and sword.

The Smith gestured towards the sword and scabbard. The grin was gone from his face as he ordered, "Finish!"

Herrera felt his pulse quicken at the thought of handling the blade. The suspense came to an abrupt end when Sir Garand barked out a challenge, "I protest, Master Smith. That is an expensive blade. The techniques used to forge it are beyond a mere apprentice's ability to understand."

The Master Smith turned from the armor and sword and began to walk away with the same measured step he had used on the way to the pavilion. "Then we are done here."

Herrera saw outrage flicker across the Lord Knight's face. Herrera could see the effort it took the man to suppress his anger and speak respectfully to the Master Smith. "I apologize again, Master Smith. Please continue."

The Smith's face showed no emotion as he turned and motioned Herrera forward. "Proceed."

Herrera nodded and stepped closer to the weapon rack. He stared at the blade. Now that he was closer, he could see runes had been etched into the blade near the hilt. He did not recognize the characters so he had no idea what they meant. Other lines and shapes ran down the blade to its curved point. Herrera would love to ask how the blade had been marked without weakening it. He leaned closer. The lines and shapes that ran down the blade were flames. Those flames had somehow been tinted a realistic-looking red.

His eyes followed the lines of fire back to the decorative crossguard. Wings, very similar to those on the helm, angled forward. The fragile guard was very deceptive. Those wings had been forged of a single piece of steel, far thicker than even the blade itself. They would serve well to stop and bind an opponent's blade. Again, the vision of an Archangel came to mind. But this time the divine power wielded a sword of flame. Past those angelic wings was a hilt that seemed out of place. Unadorned, wrapped in dark leather and wire, the hilt could only be described as functional. There was nothing about the hilt's rather plain surface that would betray a warrior's grip.

His need to touch the blade became irresistible. Despite his desire, warning bells went off inside him as he reached to touch the steel. Before he could, a hand towel hit him in the beard. Sir Garand's gruff voice demanded, "At least wipe the oil and dirt from your fingers before you sully the blade."

Herrera did as the man ordered. As he wiped his hands, Herrera realized that he was sweating. Anticipation was like having a fever on a hot summer day. His body sweated profusely to dissipate the heat. The towel was damp by the time his hands were clean and dry. Dropping the towel, he once again reached out his hand to touch the blade. He felt the spirit of the blade long inches before he brushed his fingers across its decorative runes. A sense of unease rose within him, but he dismissed it. What harm could there be in listening to such a sword?

Then he touched the blade. His fingers burned and yet froze in the instant of that contact. The sword held the fire of its intense hatred within the icy grip of death. He wanted to snatch his hand away, but the need to understand drove him to run his fingers down the blade.

There was no melody, only discordant notes filled his mind and raked at his senses. He did try to pull away then, but the sword clutched him in its grip, begging him to take it into his hands and use it as it intended. When he did not respond, it promised him victory over his enemies. Finally, it demanded that he strike out with it. Any target would satisfy its need to kill. The sword hated life. All life. It simply needed a tool to take it up so it could satisfy its desire.

Herrera was stunned. Why? The other swords had not demanded blood as this one did. He reached deeper into the steel, seeking an answer. What he found there was pain. The sword was in pain. No, it was pain incarnate. Hidden within the bitter cries of the sword, something was broken. It wanted to share its pain and the sword was not picky about who suffered with it.

Herrera watched as his fingers moved towards the hilt at the sword's coaxing. He need only wrap his fingers around that dark leather and the sword would do the rest. It would even take Herrera's own pain away. He could finally find peace too. With an effort of will, Herrera pulled his fingers free. His own cry of pain echoed that of the sword. Herrera became aware that he was on his knees, the Master Smith's strong hands were the only thing that kept him from falling on his face.

The Smith waited patiently. Herrera's heart eventually stopped pounding in his ears. His lungs were finally able to draw in a deep breath. He tried to rise, but the Smith held him where he knelt. "Tell me," the Smith demanded in a gentle voice.

Herrera tried to speak, but his throat felt like he had been screaming for hours. Raspy words tumbled from his lips, "It hungers for pain and death. Only blood will satisfy it."

A voice boomed from somewhere behind the Master Smith. It was the Lord Knight. He sounded like a proud father as he mocked Herrera, "What else would it seek, apprentice? It's a sword. A good sword has but one purpose… to slay one's enemies."

The Master Smith's voice was filled with scorn as he answered the knight with a rare explosion of words. "Fool! The purpose of such a blade is to protect and serve!"

Sir Garand barked out a laugh. "It can serve me best by defeating my enemies."

Herrera wondered how any man could be so callous. Was the Lord Knight as damaged inside as the sword was? It didn't matter. He had to warn the man. "It is flawed. Broken. He who forged it made a terrible mistake. The sword will try to take you with it when it dies."

Sir Garand grew angry. "You're only an apprentice. What could you possibly know about that sword? It was forged by a master. I paid over 10,000 dollars for the sword alone. It was over two years in the making. That might be the finest sword ever forged. Its balance is like no other blade I have ever held. Now, after a few seconds of running your sweaty fingers over my sword, you tell me it is flawed? I think it is clear who the real fool is."

The Master Smith ignored the knight's bluster. He reached down and squeezed Herrera's shoulder in his powerful grip. "Where?"

Herrera rose to his feet. He understood what the Smith was asking of him. Slowly, he reached again for the blade, cringing inside at what was to come. This time, his hand closed around the unsharpened blade. The harsh cry of the steel assaulted him again. Opening his mind fully, he sought the source of the sword's pain. The search seemed to take an eternity, but his heart had only beaten a few times before he found the small crack in the heart of the blade. So small, at most a half inch long… but its location just in front of the crossguard meant that every blow the Lord Knight struck and every blow that he parried would put stress on the damaged steel. How long would it be before someone hit it in just the right spot and the blade shattered?

Herrera separated his mind from the blade. It took a moment longer to convince his hand to release its death grip on the blade. The Smith's soft voice cut through the remnants of the sword's assault. "Show me."

Herrera touched one of the strange runes, pointing to a diagonal line that had no meaning to him. "Along this, but not quite as long."

The Master Smith stared at the spot that Herrera had indicated. Herrera heard him mutter, "Just above the tang." The Smith placed his finger on a spot on the sword's spine and asked, "If I strike here?"

Herrera closed his eyes as he visualized what the Smith was suggesting. He flinched as the sword shattered in his mind. "Boom," he whispered in reply.

The Smith just grunted.

Herrera opened his eyes as a warm piece of wood was placed in his hand. His fingers closed reflexively around the sweat-stained haft if the Master Smith's hammer. A presence, more powerful than any he had ever known, wrapped itself protectively around his mind. A song of restoration and healing flowed into him. The music of the hammer merged with his thoughts. The hammer did not try to control him, it simply became an extension of his will. Together, they sought out the residue of the sword's corruption. As partners, they healed the damage to Herrera and made him stronger than he had been.

At peace now, Herrera opened his eyes to watch the Master Smith. A pair of heavy leather gloves, as scarred as the Smith's apron, appeared from one of the Smith's larger pockets. The Smith studied the sword as he pulled the gloves on. Grasping the hilt with both gloved hands, he lifted the sword from the weapon's rack. The Smith angled it towards the ground before ordering, "Strike where I showed you."

Herrera shook his head. "It will try to kill you."

The Smith winked at him. "My apron is armor enough. Strike, boy."

Garand's eyes darted back and forth between the two of them. With a final burst of bluster he growled, "You damage my sword, Smith, and I will…."

The Master Smith cut him off. "Watch and learn!"

Herrera lifted the hammer over the sword. The Smith nodded, but Herrera hesitated. He studied the downward angle of the blade. His mind tried to calculate the path of the shards. No, even the Smith's apron could not protect him from that many shards. He motioned for the Smith to cant the blade a touch to the side. Staring down at the blade, the Smith nodded in agreement. He angled the blade a few degrees to the left.

Herrera brought the hammer down as he had in thousands of his dreams. The sword screamed at him as he brought the hammer down. But its dark emotions could not penetrate the serenity of the hammer. His strike was true. At the hammer's urging, he struck the sword harder than he had intended. The sword screamed in pain and in triumph. The sword shattered. Fragments of metal shot from the point of impact. Dozens of tiny shards came seeking Herrera. None of them made it past the protection of the hammer. Hundreds if not thousands of bits and pieces attacked the Smith. Like drops of rain, they ran down the apron to fall at his feet.

It was done.

Garand strode over and stared in horror at the remains of his sword, some of which were still embedded in the Master Smith's apron. "Bloody hell!" he swore, "If that had happened in a duel…"

"Exactly," the Master Smith replied. Then he dropped the hilt to the floor and gently took his hammer from Herrera's hand. Looking up at Sir Garand he said, "Give them my name. They are at fault." With that pronouncement, he walked out of the pavilion without looking back. Herrera wasted no time before following him.

The Smith's shadow led the way back across the field. The warmth of the afternoon sun felt good after the events within the pavilion. Herrera could just make out Geoff demonstrating a block to his enthusiastic students. The Smith stopped abruptly, He spoke without turning to face Herrera, "Blackthorne Forge. One hour after dawn."

The Smith left him without waiting for a response. Herrera realized with a sardonic grin that was all the invitation he was going to get. Then again, it was really all that was needed. Herrera hurried across the field and joined the class as Geoff the Sensei began to demonstrate the first kata form. Herrera lost himself in the mindless repetition.

His dream that night wasn't pleasant. He relived the death of the sword over and over through the night. His dream self tried again and again to save the sword. Each time, the end was the same. The lesson he learned was a harsh one. It just wasn't possible to save something or someone who didn't want to be saved. The sword has stubbornly clung to its hatred even when it knew that road led to destruction. He had met people like that back in the Boroughs. Their lives had been as lonely as the sword's.

Herrera rose in the early hours before dawn. He slipped out of the tent without waking his friends. He watched the last stars fade from the sky as dawn chased away the darkness. The simple beauty of the sunrise erased the stress of his dreams. As the pinks of dawn fled before the light of day, Herrera realized that he had no idea where to find Blackstone Forge. With a grin of anticipation, he began to wander the streets of the Faire.

Vendors were already setting up for another busy weekend. Herrera soon found himself walking along Royal Way. Colorful pavilions and fancy carts lined both sides of the broad street. He expected to find the Forge here among the most expensive shops at the Faire. Surprisingly, none of the colorful attractions were what he was searching for. Wouldn't the Master Smith of the Faire be found among the elite businesses? Blackstone Forge was indeed located on Royal Way, but it was nothing like he expected it to be.

Blackstone Forge was anything but colorful. Compared to the other shops on Royal Way, it was an eye-sore, the ugly duckling of King Richard's Faire. Rough-hewn wooden posts marked out the boundary of the Master Smith's domain. The enclosed area was utilitarian at best. One look told customers that this was a place where real work was done. Herrera grinned as he imagined warnings signs all around the venue, "Enter here and get your hands dirty!" Instead of fancy display tables, the centerpiece of Blackstone was a portable forge and two large propane tanks. Arrayed around the forge were three anvils of varying sizes. Tools and incomplete projects were scattered around each of the anvils like litter.

Other than the enticing smell of eggs and bacon coming from somewhere within, the only attempt the Smith made to appeal to customers were his wares. Armor hung from an array of mismatched racks throughout the enclosure. Not fancy armor like the plate mail Sir Garand had been so proud of. The pieces of armor here were solid, practical pieces like Blackstone and its Master Smith. This was armor meant to protect a warrior in battle. It might not gleam in the sunlight, but it would not fail in battle. Scattered among the racks were leather covered tables with weapons of all types. Herrera could see swords, maces, war hammers, and even a double-bladed axe that his fingers itched to caress. Some of the weapons even held an edge.

He was still admiring the axe when the man walked out from behind the forge with two metal platters in his hand. Before Herrera could speak to him, the Smith thrust one of the two platters into Herrera's hands. It was piled high with eggs, bacon, peppers, and onions. The mix was crowned by a large chunk of corn bread. The steam rising from the food carried the scent of garlic and other spices. Herrera's stomach awoke with a growl. The Smith turned his back on Herrera, walking over to one of the wooden posts. The Smith sat on the ground and leaned back against the bark covered post. The older man began to scoop food into his mouth with his fingers.

Herrera stared at him in shock. This interview wasn't going anything like he expected. The Smith pointed a greasy finger at the ground beside him. "Smiths and forges require food. Eat."

Herrera didn't argue. He sat beside the Smith and ate with his own fingers. The food was spicy and filling.

When they had both finished, the Smith handed Herrera his own empty platter and pointed to a bucket of water. Herrera got the hint and cleaned the platters. When he returned from the bucket, the Smith handed him a roll of leather, a pattern, thread, heavy sheers, and a needle. The smith left him there without a word. Herrera studied the pattern. It showed how to make an apron. Herrera got to work. The Smith appeared whenever Herrera was unsure how to complete a step. The Smith would demonstrate a fold or a stitch and then disappear until the next time Herrera needed guidance. How the older man knew when to appear mystified Herrera. There were no words, only busy hands. The morning passed and Herrera found himself wearing an apron like the Smith's only without pockets or burn marks.

Lunch was also cooked on the forge. Meat and beans and a piece of heavy bread. The Smith seemed to anticipate everything and everything was there when it was needed, not before. Customers came and went, and orders were taken. There were even a few demonstrations for the children. The rest was work.

After lunch, the Smith set up a large manual bellows behind the forge. He demonstrated the proper speed and rhythm, all without speaking a single word. Herrera watched the man set out his own tools. From one of his many pockets, he produced a half-finished dagger which he set in the flames. With a single word, "Begin," they did. Herrera was pleased to note that he could see the Smith work from his position beside the bellows.

The dagger began to glow in the heat of the flames. The Smith would lift it from time to time with a large set of tongs in order to evaluate its color. Most of the time it went right back into the forge. The bellows never slowed during those brief inspections. Maintaining the proper rhythm on the bellows wasn't as easy as it looked. His breaks, when they came, seldom lasted long. When the dagger rested on the anvil, he could rest. If he was lucky, the Smith might bring his hammer down three or four times before placing the dagger back in the forge. When he was less fortunate, the dagger would ring out but a single time before his labor resumed. Not that the breaks did him any good, Herrera wasted those rare opportunities. Instead of stretching his tired shoulders, he stared intently at each meeting of hammer and steel.

Eventually, the Smith plunged the dagger into a bucket of water that rested at his feet. No single word that Herrera had ever heard was as welcome as when the Smith said, "Enough."

The Smith walked away and returned with two large jugs of water. Handing one to Herrera, the Smith proceeded to drain his own jug. Herrera had not realized how thirsty he was until the warm wetness entered his mouth. He still craved more when he lowered the empty jug from his lips. The Smith reached into one of his almost magical pockets. The card he pulled out was a voucher for a meal at Canterbury Kitchen. The Smith dismissed him with the longest string of words Herrera had heard all day. "If you still want to be a smith, comeback tomorrow for more of the same."

Herrera hardly remembered what he ate that evening. Hunger battled exhaustion as he sat in the Kitchen eating the sandwich he had ordered. He could not remember if he finished it or not before stumbling back to the tent. He fell onto his cot without undressing and was asleep instantly. His body rested that night, but not his mind. The dream, never far from him, returned as soon as his eyes closed. Thankfully, the screams of the dying sword were gone. In the sword's place, Herrera found a bellows. The assault on his mind had merely been replaced by physical torture. The Smith's voice echoed through his mind, "Begin!"

It was dark in the tent when he woke the next morning. During the night, his body had learned to become a part of the bellows instead of fighting it. The pain from his dream lessons was gone as was only a dim memory. Even the soreness from the day before had faded away. Never again would he struggle to maintain the rhythm or speed that the Smith demanded; they had become a part of what he was. With a grin, Herrera slipped out of the tent again. He did want to be a smith, and if he was lucky, that lesson included another of the Smith's breakfast platters.

The days ran together in the heat of the forge. Customers or no customers, he worked beside the Smith. Each morning, he had to show that he had mastered the lesson of the day before. Each afternoon, he was taught a new skill. Each night, he practiced what he had been taught in the dream. The Smith did not coddle him. Within days, he was doing simple forging on his own. From pulling nails to forging a letter opener, the Smith soon had him doing demonstrations for the Faire-goers. Each and every activity was an opportunity to learn.

Herrera's favorite lessons were those that involved mastering new tools. He was never quite sure if it was his love of learning that motivated him or the Smith's simple but effective reward system. His successes were always marked by the appearance of a new pocket on his own apron. Then, like some medieval version of Santa Claus, the Smith would fill that pocket with the tool Herrera had just mastered. At the rate he was progressing, Herrera might soon have all the knowledge and tools he would need to become a smith. All of the tools he needed, except for the most important one.

Apparently, that too was a part of the Smith's plan. Herrera's first unsupervised forging took place over the four days that the Faire was closed. Herrera was set the task of making a hammer. By morning, he worked at the forge shaping and then hardening the hammer's head. By the heat of the afternoon, he worked to carve and shape the handle for the hammer. It took most of the four days to complete. On Friday afternoon, he placed the fruit of his efforts on a table before the Smith. As was the way of Blackstone, it was not a showy piece. But it had good weight and near perfect balance. The hammer might be smaller than the Smith's, but Herrera liked the feel of it in his hand.

Near bursting with pride, Herrera waited for the older man's appraisal of his work. The Smith glanced at the hammer and then pushed it back across the table to Herrera. Herrera was crushed. He hadn't expected many words of praise, but also hadn't expected his work to be dismissed so casually. Herrera looked up to see a quizzical expression on the Smith's stoic face. Then the Smith smiled and picked up the hammer. He placed it in Herrera's hand. The Smith spoke only two words and they went far beyond mere praise for the hammer. "Yours, Journeyman."

Gratitude swelled Herrera's heart. "My thanks. I will use it as you have taught me."

The taciturn Smith pushed aside his plate. To Herrera's utter surprise, the Smith gifted him with an explanation, "Steel must be heated many times before you can begin to shape it into a blade. The same is true of turning a boy into a man. Both require repeated use of the hammer to form them into their desired shape. Usually, the boy requires more hammering than the steel."

The Smith pointed at the hammer in Herrera's had. "That is a proper tool for the shaping of steel. Experience is the tool for the shaping of the boy. Hardening the blade and the man is a labor of love. It takes much time to do the job right. Even then, both must be tempered. If the process is rushed, both man and blade may be damaged. Patience is the key. Even when all is done properly, no smith can know the quality of blade or the man until each is quenched. Then each must undergo the test."

Herrera was fascinated by the Smith's words. As much by their wisdom as by the fact that the Smith could actually speak in complete sentences. Herrera sensed there was more to the Smith's lesson, so he asked, "What test, Sir?"

The Smith used the last of his heavy bread to wipe the remaining food from his plate. He shoved the bread in his mouth and chewed while Herrera waited for an answer. Herrera began to think the Smith wasn't going to answer him. Then, as if reaching a decision, the Smith said, "Blackstone closes in two days. I have taken enough orders for the next season. It is time to go home."

Herrera felt the world shift beneath his feet. The Faire had two weeks left until it closed. He had counted on using that time to learn all that he could from this man. And now, it was over just like that. Herrera hated the longing he heard in his voice as he asked, "And me?"

The Smith met his gaze without emotion. "Stay or come. Choose, as a man."

He could go with the Smith, but not really. Life and obligations stood in his way. The Master Smith made it sound so simple, but Herrera knew in his heart that it wasn't. He and his friends were refugees. All they had in this world was each other. What if the others ran into trouble? What if they needed him and he had deserted them? Herrera looked away from the Smith's steady gaze and murmured, "My friends…"

The Smith shook his head as he rose and picked up his own plate. "Who can help them more? The boy you were or the man that you can be?" The Smith took his empty plate and walked away, once again not waiting for Herrera to answer him.

Herrera knew what his decision was as soon as the Smith walked away. But that didn't prevent the guilt from eating at him. He felt that he owed a debt to each of his friends and to Jacob most of all. Jacob was the who had kept him sane during the change. In some ways, Jacob had become the father he had never had. Leaving was a terrible way to repay that debt. Deep down, Herrera knew the Smith was right. If he wanted to help his friends, he needed to become what he was meant to be. And even if the Smith had been wrong, would the dream let him walk away from the Smith's offer? He knew it wouldn't.

Herrera hung his new hammer from his belt and approached the Smith as he cleaned his plate in the bucket. "May I have one of your cards so they know where to find me?"

The Smith pointed with a wet finger at a white card sitting on the ground beside the bucket. Herrera picked up the stark black and white business card. The Master Smith had known his answer before he did.

Herrera nodded his thanks and went in search of Jacob. He knew where to find his friend, but the pretense of a search was supposed to give him time to find the words to tell Jacob he was leaving. He still had no idea what to say when he arrived at Ancient Attire.

## Chapter 18
## Ogreisms

Geoff leaned against the tent support with a smile of contentment on his face. Many days had passed since the bad people had tried to hurt little Tuula. The fear he had felt for his friends was finally under control. Everyone was where he could keep them safe except for Herrera. Geoff was pretty sure his missing friend would be okay even without Geoff to watch over him. Herrera had gone with the nice man who made things out of metal. That seemed to make Herrera happy even if Geoff didn't like it very much.

Tuula's voice suddenly became much deeper and Geoff realized he was lost in his head again. He looked around the tent one more time, checking on all the people he was responsible for. And, of course, not everyone was still in the tent. As usual, Danny was missing. His small friend seemed unable to stay in one place for long. The only way he could keep Danny close would be to sit on him and Geoff wasn't sure even that would work.

Tara and Jacob were still sitting at the table talking while they sewed. Ruth was no longer at the table with them. Somehow, he had missed it when she left, but she should be okay out among the crowd. Ruth had the knights to protect her and at least two of them followed her everywhere. Besides, to be honest, Ruth could be kind of scary sometimes. That only left his two smallest friends to take care of and they were the closest of all. Coon was sleeping on a pillow right beside him and little Tuula was perched happily on his knee. Both small ones seemed to have forgotten the danger of that day. Geoff hadn't forgotten. His small world had been badly shaken by the near loss of his two smallest friends.

Geoff still blamed himself for what happened that day. He had not been ready when trouble had come to his new family. Despite all his training, he had not been there when Tuula had needed him. Instead of watching over her, Geoff had been wasting time watching the men on horses try to hit each other with long sticks. It was a silly game, but Geoff found it exciting. He just knew one of them was going to get hurt falling off one of the horses. But the knights liked the game anyway and so did all the people who came to see them.

The knights' game was almost over when the loud wailing noise had sounded from the far side of the faire grounds. The noise hurt his ears and Geoff didn't like it. He was looking for a way to make it stop when he saw Ruth and Danny running from the field where the men always played their games. Ruth had looked really scared, so Geoff had run after her. More people joined the chase as they ran.

Ruth led them to a narrow path that disappeared into the trees. Geoff hadn't bothered with the path. He just pushed his way through the trees, ignoring the branches that got in his way. What they found in the middle of the forest was not what Geoff expected. Tuula stood alone among the trees, her young face bore the mark of someone's hand. Suddenly, everyone that had followed Ruth was angry. The people, even Jacob, were trying to pick fights with each other.

Geoff could not understand what the yelling was all about. He only knew two things: someone had hit Tuula and some of the strangers wanted to hurt Coon. Both of those thoughts had made him angry too. Thankfully, Coon wasn't there to be hurt. Sadly, the person who had hurt Tuula wasn't there either. For the first time in his life, Geoff had actually wanted to hurt someone. Did that make him bad too? Was it wrong to hurt someone who hurt little girls? He still did not know the answer to those questions. With no one to punish, Geoff had simply scooped Tuula up and carried her to safety.

Geoff had spent that night sitting on the ground beside Tuula's pile of pillows. No one was going to get past him to hurt her ever again. Only one person had even tried to enter the tent that night, but even Coon could not sneak past him. Geoff's large hand had shot out, lifting the raccoon up where he could see it clearly. The only sound Coon made was a mewl of pain. At her cry, Geoff had gently lowered her to the pillows. He watched as Coon curled up beside Tuula. He kept them both safe until the sun came up. He did not rest until Jacob returned to take his turn as protector.

He had not been able to relax until the crowds went away. Then, suddenly, he was too busy to worry about anything. Geoff was given a job. It was a simple job, all he had to do was pretend to fight. Somehow, that had led to giving judo lessons to all of the knights. The lessons made the knights happy and now he had many new friends. The lessons made Geoff happy too. Now everyone was happy, especially Tuula. She now had Geoff to read her favorite book to.

Geoff finally noticed the small finger poking him in the ribs. "You aren't paying attention, Fezzik. This is a very important part of the book." Tuula had a very stern expression on her small face as she stared up at him.

Geoff gave her his best 'I'm sorry' smile and she went back to reading out loud. Geoff really didn't understand the book. What were dwarves and elves? And why didn't they get along with each other? If they were all supposed to be the good guys, why were they fighting with each other? Geoff realized he wasn't paying attention again when Tuula stopped reading. "Sorry," he muttered, "not understand."

Tuula nodded and gave him the same look his teachers had when they tried to explain how to do numbers in school. That expression was very cute on a six-year-old's face. Tuula carefully put her book down and ran over to pick up her sketch pad. She brought it back and sat down on his knee again. She flipped through a number of pages before she held the pad up where he could see it.

The page was filled with drawings of his friend Herrera. Tuula pointed at one of the drawings and said, "Dwarf." This Herrera was dressed in heavy armor like the knights wore. But instead of a sword, Herrera carried a huge axe. Tuula had drawn his friend in many different battle poses. His friend looked very, very brave in all of her drawings. The fighting pictures were nice, but Geoff's favorites were three small sketches at the bottom of the page. In them, Herrera wore an apron with many pockets on the front. In two of the pictures, Herrera was making something with a hammer. It was the final picture that Geoff liked the most. Herrera was fixing the wing on a shiny owl. Geoff hadn't known that his friend was a bird doctor.

Tuula lowered the pad. She flipped several pages before she found what she was looking for. When she held the pad up again, the new page was filled with pictures of Jacob. In some of the drawings, fire shot from Jacob's hands. In others, it was lightning. The pictures were all a bit frightening. Geoff had not known Jacob could do those things. The picture in the upper corner was more like the Jacob he knew. In that drawing, Jacob stood holding both of Tara's hands. Jacob was dressed nice, but Tara wore the most beautiful white dress that Geoff had ever seen. Geoff wasn't sure why, but he knew that picture was very important.

Tuula placed a finger on one of Jacob's pointed ears as she explained, "Elf. Elves have ears like that." She then touched her own rounded ear and sighed, "Only human."

Geoff raised a finger and touched his own round ear. "Human?" he asked.

Tuula quickly flipped several more pages and then lifted the pad to show him a single large drawing. The picture showed a knight in plate armor. The knight's right hand held a really big sword. Tuula had made the sword glow with golden light. In the knight's other hand was a white shield. A golden cup had been painted in the center of the shield. The face of the knight was very familiar. Geoff wondered if he had ever met this knight. The knight had two large front teeth just like he did.

Tuula tapped a fingernail on her knight's chest. "You are an ogre, Fezzik. A very special ogre. You will be the first ogre ever knighted. Tolkien didn't know about you when he wrote his books. I would write him a letter to tell him about you, but he's dead. Now there is no one left who understands to write your story. Someone needs to, though."

Geoff could not keep the smile from his face. He liked the way Tuula saw him. He wanted to be a knight like Wesley and his other friends. Right now, he was only an armsman. But that was just for now. Someday, if he was good, he might be more.

Tuula looked up at him then and asked. "Do you understand now?"

Geoff shook his head. "Why do elf and dwarf and human fight? They should help each other."

Tuula's face became very serious. "Because they are adults, Fezzik. Adults do dumb things. They forget the important things, even when the important things are right in front of them. Even Mama and Jacob won't talk about the important things. Promise not to grow up, Fezzik. I don't want you to forget the important things… like me. Promise?"

Fezzik nodded somberly, "Me promise."

Tuula's smile returned with those two words. She stood and gathered her things. Geoff watched as she placed the pad and her book on the table. How long would it be until she was grown up? Would she forget about him too? The thought of losing her friendship made him sad.

Geoff was still thinking about Tuula growing up when Danny burst into the tent. Danny's excited chatter scattered Geoff's worries like squirrels in the morning sun. It was hard to be sad when Danny was so happy about life. His friend scampered up a chair to sit on the edge of the table. Danny's face had a broad grin on it as he announced, "It's almost show time, Big Guy. Why aren't you dressed?"

Geoff looked down at himself. He was wearing his normal clothes. What was his Danny talking about? "Me got clothes on."

"Not all of them," Danny shot back at him. Since everyone seemed to be staring at him, Geoff looked down to make sure he had his socks on too. The socks were both there and they were even the same color. Danny just laughed as Geoff got more confused.

Tara stood and grabbed a half-finished tunic from the pile on the table. She balled it up and threw it at Danny. Her voice held a note of warning, "Stop picking on him, Daniel."

Danny snagged the tunic out of the air without a backward glance. His voice was thoughtful as he announced, "My mother used to call me Daniel when I was in trouble. It never worked for her." With a shrug, Danny hung the shirt over the back of the chair before asking, "Haven't you given it to him yet?"

Tara shook her head. "No, Tuula was reading and I didn't want to interrupt."

Geoff had no idea what either of them were talking about. He looked at Tuula for a hint, but she just gave him a mischievous grin.

Then Jacob lifted a box up onto the table and Tara reached inside it. Geoff heard the crinkle of paper as Tara lifted something out of the box. It was a package of some kind. When Geoff saw the colorful paper, he realized that it wasn't just a package, it was a gift. He held his breath as Tara walked around the table and placed it in his lap.

Geoff stared down at the brightly wrapped bundle sitting on his legs. The paper was covered in butterflies. Some were flying and others rested on flowers. There were butterflies with orange and black wings, Others had yellow wings. Butterflies with red and green wings floated across the paper. And, in the center of the paper wrapping paper, was a large butterfly with blue wings on top and brown on the bottom. The breath that Geoff had been holding whooshed out as he exclaimed, "Beautiful!" The paper crinkled again as he ran his fingers over the butterflies. "Thank you," he whispered. "Keeps this fer eber. Best present in the whole world."

Geoff looked up from his gift at Tuula's sigh of frustration. She was shaking her head at him like he had done something terribly wrong. "You have to open it, silly. That is the rule. You are supposed to rip the paper so you can see what is inside."

Geoff's eyes widened in horror at her suggestion. "Not posed to hurt beautiful butterfly!"

Laughter came from all around the tent. Tuula placed his hands on her hips as she fussed at him, "It's the rule, Fezzik! You have to tear open the paper so you can see your present."

Geoff didn't want to rip the pretty paper. Tara smiled down at him, speaking in a reassuring voice, "It's okay, Geoff. I have more of the paper in the truck. I will give you another piece to keep."

Geoff looked around the room. Danny just sat there grinning, but Jacob gave him a solemn nod. Geoff tried to carefully tear the paper along one edge, but his big fingers were not made for such delicate work. The paper split in several directions and the large butterfly lost one wing. "Bery sorry," he whispered to it.

Geoff felt something soft beneath the paper. Folded neatly within the paper was what looked like a coat without sleeves. The outside of the coat was a mix of blue and black with red markings stitched below one shoulder. The inside of the coat was white and even softer than the outside. Geoff recognized the white insides as fur from one of the shepherd's fuzzy pets. It was beautiful, too, but not nearly as nice as the butterfly had been. Geoff lifted it from the paper and rubbed the coat against his cheek. He liked the way it felt.

Underneath the coat was another piece of black cloth. It looked like one of the coat's missing sleeves. But if it was a sleeve, it was only the part that went under his arm. Geoff touched the second piece of cloth and asked, "Not finish?"

Jacob chuckled as he replied, "That is a sling bag. I will show you what it's for after you try on the vest."

Geoff moved the torn butterfly paper to the side where it would be safe. Then he stood up. Tara helped him put the new coat on. She smoothed it over his broad chest and touched the red lines that now rested over his heart. "This means that you serve the King. Wear it proudly."

"Thank you," he told her again.

Jacob came over next and helped him put the thing called a sling bag over his head and under one arm. It hung there limply. Geoff tugged at it gently. "What it for?" he asked.

Jacob went back to the box and pulled out a large bag of candy. He watched Jacob pour the candy into the sling bag until it was very full. As he poured, Jacob explained, "There will be many kids at the show today, Geoff. The Boston Children's Hospital brought two buses full of children to see the show. Even more children came in special vans. The knights want all the kids to have a good time. Give candy to as many of them as you can. And try to have fun."

Danny stood by the tent flap, but Geoff was so overwhelmed by the thought of so many children to protect that he just stood there. Tara pulled one of the chairs over beside him. She climbed up onto the seat, but still could not look him in the eyes. "You look like a hero now, Geoff. These kids need heroes almost as much as they need doctors. They need a Fezzik even more than Wesley does. Go be their hero." Then she pulled his head down and she kissed his forehead like his mother had long, long ago. He was still blinking in surprise when Tuula's hand closed around one of his fingers. She pulled him to the tent opening and then sent him on his way.

The streets were even busier than normal, but the crowds parted before him as they always did. Little Danny stayed right in front of him keeping Geoff safe from all of the strangers. They arrived at the show early. Geoff took his place beside the big tent. Then he stared out at the crowd. There were so many people. And children were everywhere. Many of the children wore bandages or seemed pale and thin. Geoff didn't like that. He was so busy watching the children that he never saw Wesley or the others move out onto the field.

A van was parked behind where the children all stood. Geoff had never seen a vehicle on the field before. The knights didn't like them much. They preferred horses. The van wasn't like the one his friends had. This one had a large white bowl on the roof. The side door of the van stood open. There was a large box sat on a stand beside the door. The box had something round sticking out of it. Geoff stared at it for a long time. The word "camera" finally came to him. That thought made him uneasy, but he didn't really know why.

Geoff was startled when a small hand grasped a finger of his right hand. Geoff glanced back at the field to find Wesley and the other knights waiting patiently for him. Once again, he had been lost in his head. Geoff looked down only to find two children waiting to lead him to the field instead of one. Neither of them was what Geoff would have expected.

The taller child was a girl a bit older than Tuula. But unlike Tuula, this child had no hair. Where her hair should have been, the girl had tied a large red ribbon. Pink flowers decorated most of the ribbon. The girl stared back up at Geoff with an obvious challenge in her young eyes. Geoff did the only thing he could, he smiled warmly at her and gave her small hand a gentle squeeze. At her nod of approval, he turned to study the second child.

The second child was a young boy. Geoff realized as he studied the boy that he really wasn't shorter than the girl. He only looked shorter because he was sitting in a strange chair with wheels. The boy's hand seemed to tremble as it gripped a nob on the arm of the chair. Geoff didn't understand what was wrong, but he smiled at the boy. The boy appeared to concentrate very hard as he stared up at Geoff. Finally, two words passed his lips, "Hurry... Help!"

Geoff nodded and the boy's hand twisted a nob on the arm of the chair. The chair spun in place and then began to move out onto the field. The moving chair was fascinating. Geoff could have watched it for a long time, but the girl tugged on his finger. Geoff followed the two children to lead him out onto the field where Wesley waited for his help. Tara's words came back to him as he followed the boy in his chair. She had called him a hero. But seeing these children, Geoff did not feel like a hero. All of these children were much braver than he was.

As the children led him through the crowd, the cheering began. Cries for "Fezzik" seemed to come from every person in the crowd. It was exciting, but it was also very distracting. Somewhere along the way to Wesley's side, the girl and boy stopped to watch. Geoff was determined to do his best for them. His body began the first moves of the new kata that he had learned. Thoughts of the children and the van slipped away as he became a part of the routine. Soon, Geoff was no more. There was only Fezzik and the dance. They were one. Swords came at him and he slapped them away. He dodged and attacked in perfect harmony with the other knights. And then, it was done. He was only Geoff once more. His lungs burned for air, so he breathed deeply. Suddenly tired, he sat on the grass. Then, the children came to him.

Small forms swarmed over him. They touched him and climbed on him. He handed out candy until there was no more. Wesley gave him another bag of candy and that too disappeared into tiny hands. Children chattered and smiled. Geoff had no words, so he gave them his smiles and the gentle hugs so many seemed to need. He gave them fist bumps and was taught something called a "dap." He sat there and was one of them. Their favorite game was when he raised his hand high overhead for a high five. It became a challenge to see who could reach that lofty target. They loved it and they loved him. Geoff found that he was happier than he had ever been.

The children disappeared in ones and twos. The weapon and armor displays called to them. There were other things to touch, explore, and captured their attention. After a time, only a single child remained at his side. The little girl with the red ribbon and pink flowers stared at him expectantly. He looked into her eyes, but her gaze was so intense that he had to look away. When she began to speak, her voice was soft and low. And yet, her words cut through the sound of the other children as if they were meant for his ears alone. "Oh, to have the faith of a child once more! How will you use that gift, gentle giant? If faith the size of a mustard seed can move mountains, then what will you accomplish with what you have been given?"

Geoff lowered his eyes, the wisdom he saw in her eyes should have been impossible for one so young. It made him feel small. Worse, he had no idea how to answer her questions. Her words felt like a referee's command to begin. But begin what? What should he do? Who was he to battle? As he asked himself that last question, the painful wailing began again. This time, there were many dangers crying out a warning. When he looked back at her, the girl was gone.

He surged to his feet. Tuula, was she safe? He wanted to rush to her side, but what about all the other children who might need him too? Some of those children already looked scared by while others just seemed curious. He searched the crowd for Danny. Danny would know what to do. But his small friend was not to be found.

Geoff only recognized one face in that mass of people, the boy in the chair with wheels. The boy sat in his chair near the white van. The men in the van seemed unaware of the boy as they struggled to get the camera back into the van. The side door finally closed and the van began to move off the field. It moved slowly towards the bad noise. The children followed like chicks behind a mother hen. Only the boy sat there in his chair. Geoff wondered if the boy needed his help. Should he stay here to keep the boy safe? At that thought, the boy smiled at him. The boy's lips began to move.

Again, soft words cut through the noise of the crowd. To Geoff's surprise, words came easily to the boy this time, "The Code of the Knight is simple. To those whom much is given, much is expected. To be a knight is to serve."

Those words sank deep into Geoff's heart. He looked down at his large hands and powerful arms. He had been given much. Making children happy was not a bad way to live, but was it enough? Did it balance the scales for what he had been given? Unlike his friends, Geoff had no regrets about what had become. Most of the time he didn't even mind how hard it was to think in this new body. This one time though, he wished he could think more clearly, that he could know what he was meant to do.

There was no answer in his head, or at least not one that Geoff could find. He looked to the boy hoping for an answer or maybe a clue. The boy's smile grew wider as he whispered, "Protect those who are smaller than you. That will be your burden to bear in this life." The boy's arm came up and he pointed to his right. This time, his arm did not tremble as it had before.

The wailing cries seemed to be gathering in one place. They were close. Geoff looked to see what the boy pointed at. He saw the bright red ribbon with its pink flowers moving through the crowd. Geoff hurried to catch up with the girl who knew too much. The girl moved with ease through the crowd. But there were children everywhere and Geoff could not catch her without trampling the small forms all around him. He saw the girl turn onto a street that led to the front gate. He followed her, praying not to lose sight of her as he worked his way past the children.

## Chapter 19
## Magical Moments

The Paths and Ways of King Richards Faire grew more and more crowded as he meandered through the throngs of those the Tennies called patrons. As often as not, the currents of moving people carried him where they would. It wasn't that he was lost. Jacob could find his way to the green and blue of Ancient Attire with his eyes closed. Nor was he searching for anything among the many vendor carts and displays that lined every pathway of the Faire. What Jacob sought could not be manufactured by even the most skilled of craftsman, and even if it could be, it could never be purchased with mere money. What exactly was the price of happiness in a world as crazy as this one had become?

If only he had more time, maybe he could find a path that would take him where he wanted to go. But there were only two weekends left before King Richard's closed for the season. And, as fate would have it, this was one of those weekends. Life moved too fast and things changed too quickly for an old man like him. Or, at least for the old man he had been just a few short months ago. So many things had happened. Getting sick, the lab, their escape, and now the Faire. Even he was different, inside and out. He was young and sported pointy ears. How could anyone adjust to all of those changes. And, on top of all his other problems, there was a woman. That was a complication he had never expected to deal with again. Go figure.

Jacob turned another corner as the crowd thickened and his thoughts bogged down. The future wasn't looking any less complicated than what he had been through already. He and his young charges had to try for Canada as soon as the Faire ended. Somehow, they needed to slip across the border and disappear into the northern wilderness. The odds weren't in their favor, especially since he didn't even have a plan yet. He would be a lot more confident about the whole idea if Herrera still had his back. But Herrera had already left in search of his own destiny. Who would have thought a good Jewish boy could become so dependent on a gangbanger from the Boroughs? He had though. And now, his best friend in decades was gone. Jacob had no doubt that Herrera would soon be a master smith. The boy was too talented not to achieve his dreams. Jacob would just have to manage without his friend, something he should have learned to do a long time ago. He would get the four kids into Canada even if he had to leave what he wanted most in life behind.

And that brought up the reason he was wandering aimlessly instead of going to the place he really wanted to be… with Tara. What was he going to do about her? What could he even tell her? Damn it, he thought, he was almost sixty-three years old. He should be long past this kind of nonsense. But he wasn't, was he? His new body showed no sign of the decades he had lived. At this moment, he felt more alive than he had when he joined the Army at eighteen. Hell, he didn't even know if this body aged like a normal human or not. He had been rejuvenated somehow and now there was Tara. And Tuula. What could he offer either of them except a life on the run? What was he thinking?

The problem was, Jacob realized, he wasn't thinking. He was feeling. Every part of him seemed more alive than ever before. His body, his mind, and his heart had all been reborn. Even his senses seemed more acute. Jacob swore he could feel the sap moving through the trees, He could sense birds, squirrels, and even field mice as they went about their daily lives. Sometimes he even thought he could hear the grass growing. He was intensely aware of the life force that flowed through every living thing.

And that was how Tara had captured him. Her spirit had overwhelmed his senses the moment he had seen her. Jacob was a logical man. He didn't believe in love at first sight. But what else could he call it? More than any person he had met since the change, Tara Helleväara glowed like a beacon on a dark, moonless night. He wanted nothing more than to remain at her side for as long as she would let him.

It was a beautiful dream. But that was all it would ever be. He was a fugitive. She had a beautiful daughter that he also loved. What kind of man would put them in danger by staying at their side? Not the kind of man he wanted to be. Even if he mastered all of the ancient words that filled his mind, he doubted he could protect them from the kind of people who made him what he was. He would not put them in that kind of danger. But he also could not just disappear without an explanation. He had to tell her the truth, now, before the Faire ended. They both deserved that much.

Jacob found himself standing on Peasant's Pass. Tara's small blue and green tent stood before him; its front panel open as if in invitation. He needed to get inside before he lost his nerve. Besides, he was supposed to help Geoff get ready for his big show later this morning. The buses from the Children's Hospital had already arrived. It would not do for one of the stars of the show to be late. It took all of his willpower to approach the tent. Even then, Jacob paused just outside the tent to listen as Tuula read her book. The voices she had developed for each of the characters were quite amazing. Jacob smiled as an elf and a dwarf began arguing over who deserved the dragon's treasure more. That conversation was as fraught with peril as the one he needed to have with Tara.

He didn't speak as he entered the tent. Geoff and Coon appeared to be dozing as they listened to Tuula's performance. Tara had no customers, so she was sitting at the table hemming a sleeve. Jacob took the chair across from her and picked up his unfinished work from the day before. All was suddenly right in his world when Tara beamed a smile at him. They worked in companionable silence as the voices of children moved past Ancient Attire. Apparently, the kids weren't interested in looking for new clothes today.

That peaceful interlude came to an abrupt end when Danny arrived to escort Geoff. Tara had wrapped Geoff's show costume, but the giving of that gift did not go as she had planned. Child-like protests soon erupted from Geoff and Tuula as Danny did his best to stir things up. Even Tara lost her patience with Danny's antics. The flurry of protests ended with Geoff wearing his new vest and carrying a bag full of candy to hand out to the children after his show. Danny led Geoff away and peace crept back into the tent. Somehow, Coon still slept on one of the pillows, oblivious to all the excitement. Jacob finally had a moment alone with Tara. Well, alone except for Tuula and the sleeping raccoon. It was now or never, he told himself. He wasn't likely to get a smaller audience than that.

Jacob followed Tara back to the table. He sat staring at her as her fingers ran a needle back and forth through the material in her own intricate stitching pattern. He was still trying to decide where to start when she placed her work back on the table. With a shake of her head, Tara asked, "Why are you here, Jacob?"

The question caught him by surprise. None of the Folk had pried into why he and his friends had come here. That lack of prying was one of the big reasons they all felt safe here at King Richard's. But her question was as good a starting point as any other. Jacob looked her in the eyes, trying not to be distracted by the warm glow that seemed to radiate from her. "Because we are fugitives, Tara. We are hiding from our own government until the border reopens."

"Why would your government want to capture you?" She asked. "Are you guilty of some crime?"

"We did nothing wrong," he replied. Then he paused to find the right words.

"Then, why?" she pressed.

Jacob slowly lifted a hand to his ear. With his index finger, he traced the soft point at the top. "This is not some vain bit of cosmetic surgery, Tara. This is one of the more visible signs of what they did to me. Ruth has her hair and Geoff is a giant now. Each of us bears the marks of what they did to us, both inside and out."

Jacob could see the confusion on her face as she asked, "Did to you?"

Jacob let out a deep sigh. "It's hard to know where to begin. A year ago, I was a 62-year-old man. A large part of me was just waiting to die. I lived alone in a small apartment in New York City."

Tara smiled mischievously. "You seem rather spry for such an old man. What's your secret?"

Jacob shook his head. "It isn't my secret. It belongs to my government. I caught the virus. I was dying, Tara. They experimented on me. On all six of us. Yes, even Coon. The bodies you see are what came out of their laboratory."

Tara looked from Jacob to Coon. The now awake raccoon looked her in the eye and nodded its head. Tara gasped and turned back to Jacob. "What kind of experimentation can change a person into a raccoon, Jacob? I don't understand."

Jacob shrugged. "I don't really understand it myself. Some kind of genetic manipulation. It kills some people. Others, like the six of us, become something that I am not sure is even human anymore."

Shock showed on her face. "Others?"

Jacob forced a stern look onto his face. "I have already told you more than it's safe for you to know, Tara. I don't want to put you or Tuula in any more danger than I already have. As soon as the Faire is over, we are heading north to Canada."

Tara gave him a strange look before saying, "So, you will bring your problems to my country?"

Jacob realized he hadn't really thought of how their presence might impact Canada. "We thought, but maybe didn't think it through, that we could disappear into the wilderness of your country. There are places in the north where we hoped no one would look for us."

Tara nodded sagely. "There are many places to just disappear, especially in the Territories."

Jacob stared down at the table and whispered, "We just want to be left to live out our lives in peace. Is freedom too much to ask?"

There was silence between them for a long time. Then Tara asked again. "So, why are you here, Jacob?"

At his look of confusion, Tara laughed. "You didn't answer my question, Jacob."

"I just explained why we were here," he sputtered in indignation.

Tara gave him a sympathetic smile. "I didn't ask why your group came to the Faire. There are as many reasons for choosing to live in the past as there are Folk. It's considered quite rude to even ask why someone chooses to be one of us."

Jacob started to argue, "But you…"

Tara shook her head. "I asked, Jacob, why you were here. Why Jacob Dror keeps coming to Ancient Attire. Why would a man of your intelligence sit here day after day stitching tunics? You are capable of so much more."

They both jumped as the heavy copy of The Hobbit dropped on the end of the table. The chair beside the book slid back and Tuula climbed up to stand on the seat. Disappointment battled with impatience on her young face as her eyes darted between Jacob and her mother. Her tone was that of a frustrated adult as she began to lecture them both. "Why can't adults just ask the question they really want an answer to? Or say the things they really need to say? It's always 'What are you doing, Tuula?' when you already know what I am doing and you just want me to stop. Is it so hard to say what you mean?" Tuula crossed her arms over her chest and glared at Tara. "Mother, I thought that I taught you better than this. Surely you can come up with a better question to ask. It's quite obvious why Jacob is here."

Jacob felt himself losing the struggle to keep a smile off his face. As he lost the battle, he brought his right hand up to cover the evidence of his defeat. But Tara just took it all in stride as if she was used to being lectured by six-year-old. Tara gave her daughter a solemn nod and then said, "Very well, daughter. Give me a moment to think of a more appropriate question."

Jacob waited with as much anticipation as Tuula did as her mother stared at him thoughtfully. An intelligent man would have run when that devilish grin appeared on Tara's lips. But he couldn't run. Some part of him had to know what put that playful gleam in her eyes, even if it meant his own undoing. Tara leaned towards Tuula, speaking in a mock whisper, "Let's see if this one meets with your approval."

The playful look faded from Tara's face as she sat up straight on the chair. Her features became stern like those of a Rabbi about to perform his first circumcision. Her voice took on a formal tone that Jacob had never heard her use before. "Exactly what are your intentions with respect to my daughter, good sir?"

Jacob's thoughts came to a screeching halt at the unexpected change of direction. Whether it was the look on his face or a shared sense of humor between mother and daughter, Tuula fell into her chair giggling and clapping her hands. Apparently, thought Jacob, that qualified as a good question in the young girl's mind. Jacob could not allow himself to be outdone. His answer had to be at least as entertaining as Tara's unexpected question.

As Tuula's mirth died down, Jacob realized there was only one possible answer to the question posed. Bowing his head towards Tara and waving his hand in Tuula's direction, Jacob assumed the same formal tone that Tara had used, "My dear Lady, it would be my great honor to assist your effort to raise your daughter as a proper Lady of the King's Court."

A loud and wet sounding "Thhhbbbbbbfftftttt!" ensured that Jacob could not elaborate on his plans for the girl's future. Tuula's raspberry couldn't have been more unladylike. This time, Jacob couldn't keep the smile from his face. With an air of utter disbelief, he turned to Tuula and asked, "What? You don't want to be a Lady of the Court?"

Tuula stood back up and held her fist over her head like she was holding a weapon. "Ladies of the Court are soooooo boring. I am going to be a knight. The King's most trusted knight. Maybe even the King's champion."

"I see," Jacob replied. Then he looked into Tara's eyes. Despite the attitude Tuula was giving him, he saw approval there. With a shrug, he told her, "I know little of swords beyond the fact that one end is sharp and the other is not. That said, perhaps there are other skills that I could teach the next Champion of the Realm."

Tuula grinned at him then and gave him a wink. "It's okay. Mages aren't supposed to use swords. Maybe you can be my Merlin."

Jacob blinked in surprise and Tara snickered softly. "Mage?" he asked.

"Of course," Tuula replied, "you just haven't figured it out yet." Before Jacob could come up with a response, Tuula took charge of the conversation once more. "It's your turn now. What did you really come here to say?"

Jacob searched for the right words, but there weren't any. The words that spilled out came from somewhere deep inside, but they came more easily than he would have anticipated. "I have spent too many years content with being alone. My books and my classes were enough for an old man. I was biding my time until my time was done. I am not old anymore, Tara. I want to live my life now and I don't want to be alone anymore. I want to be with someone whose spirit matches the one that is growing within me. I want to be with you."

At her warm smile, he shook his head. "The problem is that I don't know how to do that without putting both of you in danger. I can't be responsible for leading my enemies to your door."

Tara's face grew serious at that. "Then I ask a third time, Jacob. Why are you here?"

The look of exasperation returned to Tuula's face. But Jacob reached out to lightly caress her cheek. "It is the right question this time, Tuula." Then, without turning to face Tara, he answered her, "Because I could not disappear from either of your lives without an explanation. You both deserved more than that. And, perhaps, so do I."

A warm glow the color of sunshine suddenly filled the tent. It was as if the sun had suddenly risen within the cloth walls of Ancient Attire. Jacob turned to the source of that light, Tara. The radiance that sprang from within her was no less blinding than the smile on her face. Her voice was a soft invitation as she asked, "If there was a place where we could all be safe, what then, Jacob?"

Before Jacob could reply, chaos erupted outside the tent. Cries of indignation mingled with the sound of running feet grew louder and closer. Through the open panel, Jacob saw Danny pushing his way through the crowd. The little man ran straight for Ancient Attire with Ruth right on his heels. They both stumbled into the tent, out of breath but still struggling to speak. Through their ragged breaths,

Jacob managed to make out, "Geoff… show… television… cameras… live…"

Their words made no sense. Jacob rose to his feet. "Slow down, both of you. Please. What are you talking about."

Another voice, also out of breath, but calmer, answered Jacob from just outside the tent. Jacob looked over to see Sir John standing by the tent's entrance. The courtier wasn't nearly as winded as Danny and Ruth, but his face appeared even more concerned. Sir John sucked in another deep breath and began to speak. "We are truly sorry, Jacob. When Channel 5 asked to film the Children's Hospital visit, we didn't really think about the consequences. We never expected them to film Geoff and Wesley. And, we definitely didn't expect the story to be picked up by the network. Our gentle giant was just too good with the children."

Icy fingers of dread clawed at Jacob as he realized the implications of what had happened. But that fear was brushed aside by the place in his mind where the ancient tongue resided. That part of his mind told him to have faith, that this was meant to be. With a calm that surprised even him, Jacob asked, "How long ago did the broadcast go live? Any idea how long I have to get us out of here?"

"The broadcast started about half an hour ago when Wesley's act went on. I didn't learn it was a live feed to the network until a couple minutes ago when people called to congratulate us for being famous."

Without turning, Jacob snapped, "Danny! Where is Geoff now?"

Danny's voice sounded frightened. "I assume he is still with Wesley. Geoff was fighting beside him when I realized they were filming Geoff and not the kids. I came to get you as fast as I could. I literally ran into Ruth about halfway here."

Jacob looked back at the courtier, but Sir John was busily typing on his cell phone. Jacob winced when the man muttered an angry, "Damn it!"

"Now what?" Jacob asked.

Sir John's thumbs continued to tap the phone's screen as he replied, "How the hell do you lose a ten-foot-tall man in a crowd of children?"

Glancing up, Sir John muttered, "I have security looking for him. We'll find him. In the meantime, your things are being packed and Dave has already removed your van from the lot. We just need to get you off the grounds without anyone noticing."

Jacob glanced over at Ruth, "I think we can help with that."

"Sir John sighed and put his phone away. "How are you doing for money? You spent a lot on your gear. Is there anything left? You have wages coming, but I doubt a check is going to help right now."

Jacob shrugged "Danny?"

Danny moved forward and reached under his tunic shirt. The hand-tooled leather wallet he pulled out seemed too big not to have been hidden under his clothing. He thumbed through the contents of the wallet and then nodded. "We are good as far as travel expenses go. But if we need more gear, I will need to supplement our funds."

Jacob frowned at Danny. "I have a feeling I am not going to like your ideas on supplementing our cash."

Danny smiled up at him innocently. "Probably not." But that smile faded as sirens began to scream in the distance. As their warning cries came closer, Ruth's face hardened. "I won't let them take me, Jacob."

Jacob could not find it in him to argue. "None of us will, Ruth. But we can't endanger the children."

Sir John pulled out his phone and swiped the screen. "Security reports police cars at both the main parking lot and the employee lot. Still no sign of Geoff."

Jacob glanced around the tent. Everyone was staring at him as if he had all the answers. He didn't, but it really didn't matter anymore. Stepping through the open panel, he motioned for everyone to follow. "Okay, Ruth. We have to slow them down until we find Geoff. Then, we disappear." No one spoke as they followed him, but everyone seemed more at ease.

Jacob turned left towards the front gate. There seemed to be even more people on the path now that the sirens filled the air. For whatever reason, everyone seemed to be heading for the exit gate. The song of the police cars was like a true sirens' call summoning all who heard them into danger. His hope that they could stay out of the public eye was being dashed on the rocks. There would be no way to keep secret what he and Ruth were about to do.

He had gone no more than a few steps when Tara's work-roughened fingers slipped into his right hand. Her strong grip slowed him only long enough for a much smaller hand to link with his left. Together they pushed their way through the crowd. Danny darted ahead followed by Ruth and Coon; their smaller forms finding more openings through the mass of people.

Runes began to take shape in Jacob's mind as they moved like cows in a herd. "Turn off your cell phone, Sir John." Jacob warned. But there was no answer. When Jacob looked around, the courtier was gone. Both Tuula and Tara squeezed his hand at the same time. That encouragement would have to do. The battle for their freedom was upon them.

# Part IV
# Epidemic

## Chapter 20
## The Siege at Carver

By the time they reached the path leading to the gate, the exit was blocked by the Channel 5 news van. How the driver had maneuvered it through the crowd was beyond Jacob's understanding. The news team already had their cameras out and focused on the parking lot. Jacob could just make out a man in a blue blazer standing in front of the camera with a microphone in his hand.

Jacob was sorely tempted to use one of the words that was trying to push its way out of his head to fry every piece of equipment in the van. That part of him wanted to blame all of their current problems on the reporter and his team. He knew he was being petty, but shutting them down would feel really good right now. But could he afford to waste even one word on revenge? He suspected that he would need every precious word in order to get them out of this mess.

Ruth was standing just a few yards ahead of him. Her hands were on her hips as she glared at the camera crew. Coon crouched protectively at Ruth's feet. There was no sign of Danny, but he wasn't the problem at the moment. Ruth was. The power she was gathering felt like a static charge dancing over Jacob's skin. Reluctantly, he let go of Tuula and Tara's hands. Stepping up behind Ruth, he rested his hands on Ruth's shoulders. "Don't waste it, Ruth. They aren't the ones we need to be worried about." It took a moment before his skin stopped tingling from the power she had called.

Looking back at Tara, he asked, "Can the Folk keep the crowd back? I don't want anyone to get hurt. And Tara, I'm sorry. I thought I would have more time."

She nodded and pulled a phone from her tunic pocket. Tuula stood at her mother's side, staring up at him. The confidence he saw in the young girl's eyes was unnerving. He knew he was not the hero she thought him to be. With a last look at them both, Jacob turned to face his future. As if sensing that something important was about to happen, the crowd parted, clearing a path to the van. Jacob began to walk with Ruth at his side. The sound of the people gathered around the exit faded from his mind. Only the sirens and the annoying voice of the reporter still intruded on his thoughts. Jacob paused by the camera.

The parking lot was deathly still. No one moved in the lot nor did a single engine appear to be running. Even the reporter went silent as Jacob surveyed the potential battlefield. The opposing army's location was clearly marked by the line of flashing red and blue lights. Jacob counted eight police cars. Two black and whites bearing the Carver PD logo blocked both the entrance to and exit from the lot. Six blue and white cruisers from the Massachusetts State Police were lined up on the street. Jacob shook his head. This was not going to end well no matter what he and Ruth did. So be it! He would rather die here than go back to that lab or to the prison that John had warned him about. He would not be a victim ever again.

Jacob led the way out beyond the edges of the crowd. He stopped just shy of the handicapped parking. He made sure that the police officers could see them both clearly. Better that the police were focused on the two of them and not the children. He felt Ruth's shoulder brush against his leg as she stood beside him.

"What do we do now, Professor?" Ruth asked.

Despite the sense of hopelessness, a smile found its way to Jacob's lips. "I thought we agreed you would call me Jacob?" he asked in reply.

Ruth leaned against him a little harder. "I'm scared, Jacob. Really scared. Right now, I need you to be more than just a friend. I'd go so far as to call you Master if you could make them all go away."

He began to chuckle. "So, if I am to be the Master, what am I to call you? Padawan?"

Her laughter joined his. "Wow! Never would have pegged you for a Star Wars geek." The laughter died away as she stared out at the flashing lights. "You do realize that you're mixing up your genres? I think Tuula would tell you to call me apprentice."

Jacob sighed as one of the black and whites backed up, clearing a path into the parking lot. "Then apprentice it is. Here are the rules of engagement. Those officers are just doing their duty. We do NOT hurt them. I don't want there to be any children without a parent tonight."

Ruth nodded. "And when the people calling the shots show up?"

Jacob's eyes were cold when he looked down at her. "Then you do whatever you need to do to make sure we don't go back to that lab."

Ruth looked up at him and nodded. Anger smoldered in her eyes in a way that Jacob didn't like. No, Jacob realized, he could not leave Ruth that much latitude when things got bad. "Ruth, you are not to do what you did to John Boboden ever again. If you do, our lessons are over."

"Yes, Master," was her simple reply.

Things began to happen out on the street. Two of the blue and whites turned into the parking lot. Jacob had to assume that he and Ruth had been recognized. The black and whites rolled back into place as the state troopers sped down the lines of parked cars.

"Take the lead car, Ruth. I will handle the next one." Jacob ordered as he moved to the side and focused on the word that was demanding its release.

---

Danny carefully studied the battle lines the police had set up out on the street. There were at least a dozen places where he could slip past them unnoticed. He saw exactly zero ways he could get the whole group through without getting them all shot or captured. And why did all the cops look like they were here for a pitched battle? Machine guns and body armor? Sheesh. He and his friends weren't even armed. Geoff was the only one trained to fight and his big friend didn't even have a sword. This was a car thief's nightmare and Danny was ready to panic.

Then Jacob and Ruth walked out of the crowed as if nothing unusual was going on. Neither of them seemed at all concerned as they stood in plain sight of the armed officers. What did they know that he didn't? Danny realized he was about to find out when four officers piled into two of the blue and white cruisers. The squad car blocking the entrance pulled back. With a squeal of tires, the two cruisers sped into the parking lot.

The two police cars raced into the lot with lights flashing and sirens blazing. Danny crouched even lower beneath the SUV he was hiding under. He practically hugged the front tire as he watched the cruisers head for his friends. Holy crud, he thought. What was Jacob thinking? As the speeding vehicles fishtailed into the first lane between the rows of parked cars, Danny saw Ruth step forward. She reached out towards the first cop car. Somehow, he heard her words over the blaring sirens. "meK-o-lAW ore!" Ruth shouted. Those words made no sense at all. It was just gibberish, and yet, the harsh sounds invaded his thoughts. Then, they were gone as quickly as they had come. Try as he might, Danny could not remember a single syllable that Ruth had spoken.

Then Danny stopped caring about the words. There were more entertaining things to watch. Light and color seemed to explode within the squad car. It was like watching fireworks without the painful booms. Through the side windows, Danny could see red, blue, green, brown, and a host of other colors. The colors flashed and strobed and swirled in a nauseating pattern. Danny wanted to look away, but he could not tear his eyes from the show.

The squad car swerved to one side and then the other. Instead of heading for Ruth and Jacob, it sped towards the line of porta potties. Too late, the driver hit the brakes hard. Instead of slowing, the cruiser slid. It was still moving fast when it plowed into the third and fourth porta potty. Both greenish-blue containers went over releasing their contents on the blue and white car. White joined the other colors exploding within the car's interior as the airbag inflated. The blue and white's slide came to an abrupt halt with the porta potty half under the vehicle. That had to hurt, Danny thought as the car listed hard to the right. The only sign of the officers inside was a lone arm pinned to the window by the white wall of the airbag.

Danny had no idea what Ruth had done, but this was the best magic show he had ever seen in his life. Did she have more illusions like this? If so, maybe he and his friends could get away after all. Danny hoped so. He would feel pretty bad if he had to disappear into the city without them.

---

Ruth felt a sense of exhilaration as the language of the ancient civilization flowed from her lips. As she uttered them, the words became infused with power.

The pressure in her skull eased as one set of glowing runes disappeared. At the same moment the rune faded away, light flared within the police car. Ruth grinned as the car rammed into the public toilets. She wondered if there was an acceptable way to include a porta potty into a professional magic show. It would certainly make for a unique act. As she considered the possibilities, Ruth turned to watch what her teacher would do to the second car.

The car Jacob had chosen came down the outside edge of the parking lot. There was nothing before it except the stand of trees that separated the parking lot from the Mud Pit. Jacob waited until the car neared the end of the line before speaking a phrase he had used once inside the lab. As his hand clenched into a fist, she heard. "tAR-dAY-maw."

Ruth knew that word from her lessons. It meant sleep, but it was a phrase she seemed unable to use. That rune pattern refused to stick in her mind no matter how many times she practiced it. Jacob obviously did not share her limitations. As Ruth watched, both officers in the car slumped in their seats. The cruiser's siren warbled and died. The vehicle barely slowed as it headed for a pine tree at the edge of the lot.

There was a sharp crack when the front bumper hit the tree. The eight-inch trunk didn't snap, but the tree's roots were not as sturdy. They tore from the soft ground and the tree toppled over. The proud tree got its revenge as the roots came up under the tire, lifting it and the passenger side of the car into the air.

Ruth winced as the car leaned hard to one side. There was a brief moment where she thought it might right itself, but then the undercarriage hit the downed tree and the car rolled on its side and slid forward. The good news for the two officers was that, on its side, the car fit between two other large pines. Ruth would have clapped for joy if not for the somber look on Jacob's face.

---

Jacob frowned as he watched the slowly rotating front tire on the second police car. He could only pray that the officers inside weren't badly hurt because there was nothing he could do to help them right now. The crash into the tree had surprised the crowd almost as much as it had him. The laughter that had broken out when the first police car hit the porta potties had come to an abrupt end when the second cruiser had flipped on its side. Jaccob hoped that at least some of the people watching had figured out that this wasn't just a new act at the Faire.

A more important question was, how were the other officers taking the loss of four of their finest. Jacob turned from the damage he had caused to see what was happening out on the main road. The state troopers stood motionless behind their vehicles, apparently stunned by what had happened. He would have considered that a victory if things hadn't already gotten much, much worse.

Their real enemy had arrived while he and Ruth had been distracted by the two cruisers. The threat had come in the form of a large black SUV. The FBI, or so Jacob guessed them to be, was parked alongside the remaining blue and whites. Four men in black body armor jumped out of the SUV. One of them moved at a trot towards what appeared to be an ad-hoc command post. The other three men began to pull large crates out the back of the SUV.

Jacob sighed and looked down at Ruth. "The calvary is here. They are about to take off the kid gloves."

Ruth glanced at the two wrecked cars and asked, "Um, Jacob? Two police cars are kid's gloves? What's next? A tank?" Ruth gestured towards the crate the men had placed on the ground behind the SUV. "Any idea what that is?"

"No," Jacob replied. "I doubt we'll like whatever it is."

They both watched with interest as the three men pried the lid from the crate. The men lifted a large metal tripod out of the crate. Jacob had a sinking feeling in the pit of his stomach as he studied its green paint marred in various places by spots of rust. Jacob prayed that he was wrong, but his enemies had no honor. Two of the men slid the long green tube out of the back of the SUV. Jacob watch in horror as they attached it to the tripod, its sinister black opening pointed towards the parking lot. "They wouldn't dare!" Jacob hissed. "Not with all these people standing so close."

Jacob spun around to stare at the small exit gate. Hundreds of people had already come through it to see what was going on. In a few more seconds, they would all be trapped here. The outer edge of that crowd was mostly kids from the Children's Hospital, each and every one of whom was captivated by the wonderous new show. In his mind, Jacob saw their small bodies being trampled when the first shells landed near the crowd. Jacob turned back to the street, unwilling to watch what he knew was coming.

Ruth was yelling at him. Jacob barely comprehended Ruth's repeated question. "Dare what?" How could he explain the evil that was about to be unleashed. A loud 'whoosh' followed closely by another ended the time for frivolous contemplation. He had to act, but he had no idea what to do. Before he could hope to react, two silver cylinders clanked and clattered on the gravel covered parking lot. Thankfully, both shells fell short, landing in front of him instead of behind him were the children stood. As they bounced haphazardly across the ground, both canisters began to hiss, spraying a white mist into the air.

Ruth grabbed his hand. "Jacob! What is that?" she cried out.

"Tear gas, damn them!" Jacob yelled.

Another series of whooshing noises sounded from the street. Absently, Jacob's mind counted three more inbound canisters. He had run out of time to do anything.

The fine hairs near Jacob's ears shifted as a light breeze began to blow from the heart of King Richard's. Its touch was oddly familiar, although that was an insane thought. How could a breeze be familiar? As that breeze caressed his skin, time seemed to slow. The mist now hung in the air, unmoving. The inbound canisters seemed to hesitate at the top of their arcs. The whole world somehow paused while Jacob's mind raced on.

A voice that he knew, and yet did not, spoke with the voice of that breeze, "Save them, Jacob. Save all of my children. And then, bring them unto me."

Then the breeze entered his thoughts as it wafted across his suddenly overheated skin. The glowing runes that had become a part of him when he was changed, began to shift and alter. No, he realized, it was more subtle than that. The runes weren't changing so much as they were being rearranged by those currents of air. The new combinations were more complex and so much more powerful. The potential of what pulsed within his mind was staggering. Were mere mortals intended to wield such power? Did that question even matter if this was the only way to save the children? He would gladly bear the burden of those words and their use if he could save even a single life.

Jacob examined each of the patterns that the breeze had given him. One of them pulsed more brightly than all of the others. He read the ancient runes and the answer to his problem became clear. He finally understood what he had to do. Jacob took a step forward and then another. With each step, time flowed a little faster. By his sixth step it had returned to normal and it was time to speak. The pulsating words leapt from his tongue in a roar of victory, both of them rejoicing as he cried out, "Tay-Kah ROO aKH!"

———————

Ruth stared in horror at the white mist as it crawled across the ground towards her. Tear gas! It would leave her helpless and that was something she never wanted to be ever again. What could she do? None of the words in her mind would affect it. It was a thing and she could not fool it with her illusions. To make matters worse, there was nowhere to run. She was trapped. And even if she could run, it would mean abandoning the children. How could she live with herself if she did that? Ruth turned to Jacob, hoping against all odds, that he had some idea what to do.

The Jacob she knew no longer stood beside her. She took one look at the man who had taken his place and her fear gave way to a new emotion, one she had never expected to feel... awe. The kindly old man who had transitioned from teacher to friend was suddenly gone. Standing in his place was an angry warrior wrapped in a nimbus of power. Ruth actually had to step away from him; the power that surrounded him burned her skin and tore at her mind. When Jacob shouted, the whole world seemed to suddenly stop to listen. Ruth listened too, but she could not comprehend the meaning of his words.

Then a new sound thrummed all around Jacob. It took her a moment to recognize the sound of air rushing past. What began as a breeze quickly became a strong wind and then a storm and finally a tempest. Jacob stood in the center of that maelstrom, his long hair caught up by the storm, but otherwise he was untouched by what he had wrought. But the world was not untouched!

The first to flee before Jacob's anger was the mist. Rather than face him, it dissipated long before the storm reached full strength. That victory was not enough to satisfy the wind or its master. They both demanded more. Pine needles and twigs followed the mist, leaving the battlefield before they could suffer Jacob's wrath. The two canisters, recognizing their impending doom, scampered back to their masters as Jacob's temper flared. Even the inbound canisters had the sense to return the way they had come. They were unwilling to face Jacob's fury. As his ire reached its peak, even the loose gravel panicked and fled before him. Routed, hundreds of small stones pelted the vehicles parked in the street in a vain attempt to flee the battlefield. For a time, it seemed there was no such thing as a haven from the storm. And yet, through it all, the crowd remained untouched by the hurricane named Jacob, not one hair on their heads was ruffled by what Jacob had called. As far as Ruth could tell, no stone had so much as touched any patron's car. Only their enemies felt Jacob's wrath.

Silence returned and the winds were suddenly gone. Ruth had no idea if this was the eye or if the storm was truly over. The sudden stillness made the whole experience seem unreal. But there was no questioning the reality of what had been unleashed. Out on the street, police officers and FBI agents huddled behind vehicles that now bore the scars of battle. Windows were cracked and shattered. Lights were busted out. Paint was scratched and the metal pock-marked by so many impacts that it was hard to imagine. Even the tripod and tube had fled before the storm. Despite the damage, their enemy seemed undeterred. If anything, the men and women that they faced seemed more determined than ever to press the attack. That should have worried her, but it didn't.

Ruth glanced up at her friend and mentor. Their foe had awakened something in Jacob. The harsh set of his face was reassuring. He wasn't uncertain anymore. Just a short time ago, she had teased Jacob about calling him 'Master.' Her words didn't feel like a joke anymore.

Ruth was still staring at Jacob when a new sound rose to consume the silence. She tensed, waiting for the onslaught to resume. But the winds did not return as the sound of human voices washed over her. The crowd, the people of the Faire, were cheering. Ruth looked back to see people yelling, clapping, and even whistling their approval. Whether they understood that Jacob had saved them, or whether they just liked the show, their voices left little doubt about how the people of King Richard's Faire felt about their new hero. Then Ruth noticed the gestures of the man in the blue blazer. A small camera was focused on the reporter while the larger camera was trained on Jacob. What Jacob had done wasn't just being viewed by the people here, it had been broadcast on network television. Ruth scanned the crowd. It was amazing how many people held their cell phones up, cameras pointed at Jacob. No, Ruth amended, what Jacob had done was being broadcast to the world. How long would it take to go viral? Five minutes or ten?

---

Danny hissed in annoyance as the second "statey" car barreled past his chosen hiding place. The cruiser's lights were flashing and the siren warbled incessantly. Danny sang softly to himself in time with the siren, "We're coming to take you away, ha ha! We're coming just for you, Dan-ny!" This time the ditty did nothing to relieve the tension he felt. Danny just wasn't liking the way this whole scene was playing out. They had gotten lucky once, but how many cruisers were going to just self-destruct like the first one had? And how had Ruth pulled that off anyway? Looking at the line of police cars still sitting on the street didn't make Danny feel any better about their prospects.

Then the statey's siren began to malfunction. It sounded like a teenage boy hitting puberty, one second it was three octaves too high and the next it was singing baritone. The sudden changes actually startled him and he cursed softly as his head introduced itself to the driver's side tie rod. The pain was an unfortunate reminder of just how vulnerable he was out here in the parking lot. Why had he come out here anyway? Had that initial rush of adrenaline made him stupid?

Danny's eyes were drawn back to the speeding cruiser as the siren began a death spiral down into silence. That definitely qualified as "not normal," and Danny had a sneaking suspicion that his friends had something to do with it. Sure enough, Jacob stood there with his fist extended towards the oncoming vehicle. Except that it wasn't really coming at Jacob anymore. The driver ignored the turn at the end of the lot and continued on, directly towards a large pine tree. There was something intensely satisfying about the crunch of steel when the cruiser hit the tree. Danny actually felt bad for the tree that now lay on the ground, but he had no sympathy at all for the cruiser as it flipped on its side. It was too bad he didn't have time to strip it while its underbelly was exposed. Maybe there would be time later, but he didn't think it was likely.

Things were getting weird. Two cruisers and two freak accidents. Danny wasn't one to complain about a little good luck. Was there any chance the police would just give up now? He doubted it even though he would have cut his losses and run by now. Speaking of running, wasn't it about time to find the van and get the flock out of this town? Danny was about to crawl out from under the SUV when he heard the crunch of footsteps on the gravel. "Not good, Danny Boy," he whispered softly. Laying his cheek on the ground, Danny peered under the line of cars the SUV was parked in. There, only three cars away, stood a pair of black combat boots. Ever cautious, Danny rolled his head over to check the line of cars behind his hiding place. Another set of boots was moving slowly closer on that row too. Talk about a game of monkey in the middle, and he didn't even have a tree to hide in this time.

As the footsteps came ever closer, Danny looked above the tire. It wasn't a tree, but was there room in the wheel well for him to hide? No, even he wasn't that small. There was little he could do besides hug the tire again and hope he wasn't seen. Waiting, Danny found, was neither easy nor fun.

The nearest set of footsteps were headed directly for Danny's hiding place. He listened as they paused behind each vehicle in the line. Too soon, they were standing on the other side of his new best friend, the all-weather Michelin tire. Danny's heart began to pound when the boots stepped in front of the SUV. The boots now had legs growing out of them, legs wearing black pants heavy with padding and armor. Those pants were tucked carefully into the boots. Danny's breath caught in his chest as the boots and legs moved along the front bumper. The officer never even looked under the SUV, so Danny's hiding place remained safe. Danny just didn't feel safe. The threat posed by those legs and boots kept growing in Danny's mind. Imagination could be a terrible thing sometimes.

The nightmare could have ended then. All the officer had to do was move on. But no, he had to stop on the far corner of the SUV. Danny wanted to scream at them, "Keep going!" He didn't scream so, of course, the boots and legs didn't just stop, they decided to kneel. As the officer dropped to one knee, more of his body was revealed to Danny and his overactive imagination. The armored pants curved up to the officer's waist where they met an even more heavily armored vest. There, riding low on the officers hips, was a thick belt with two holsters that dangled just above the ground. The dark black pistol grips were disturbing enough, but when the wooden stock of a heavy shotgun thudded against the ground beside the officer's boot, Danny imagination went wild. The polished wood gleamed with dark menace. Views of Ruth's bloody corpse appeared to flicker across its surface. Danny closed his eyes to the horrifying images.

Danny was still trying to purge those images from his thoughts when he felt his body shifting forward, somehow without disturbing a single rock as he moved closer to the officer. "What the hell are you doing?" his common sense screamed at him. "It's not me." Danny groused back at it. "Do I look like I'm that stupid?" His body apparently wasn't concerned about the argument he was having with himself. It just kept inching closer to his doom. Danny found himself crouched within easy reach of the officer and his deadly arsenal. Throughout the eternal seconds of Danny's movement, the officer remained oblivious to Danny's presence.

Apparently, the officer had more interesting things to pay attention to than the three-foot tall midget sneaking up behind him. Instead of watching his back, the officer kept leaning forward to peer around the SUV. The only things in that direction were Ruth and Jacob. Again, Danny fought off images of dead friends. When Danny's heart finally stopped its frantic beating, he heard the officer whispering softly to himself or perhaps into some kind of radio. Danny leaned closer, but he just couldn't make out what the officer was saying.

A sense of helplessness consumed Danny. He wasn't a black belt like Geoff. What was he supposed to do against an armored man with three guns? He was a thief and nothing more. Oh, he might get away with taking one of the guns, but for what? It wasn't like he knew how to use one. He actually despised the damn things. There were no winners when you pulled out a gun and started shooting. Even if you survived it, they put you away for a long, long time. That left Danny with no options other than screaming, "Shoot me instead!" And that was an option he wasn't very fond of.

Danny frowned as he noticed movement near the holster riding over the officer's butt. Now what, he wondered. There was an almost undetectable pop and the leather strap that held the weapon in the holster sprang up and away from the weapon's grip. Danny stared in shock at the small and oh so clever hand that hovered over the weapon's grip. "NO!" his mind cried out. It was one thing when his talented fingers lifted a wallet without conscious thought. It was quite another to steal a police officer's sidearm. Danny's complaint fell on deft fingers. The cool, rough surface of the grip was already nestled in his hand. With the greatest of ease, the weapon slid out of the holster.

Danny glowered down at his own traitorous hand. What it held wasn't even a gun. It was a taser much like those the guards at the lab had carried. Great! He had stolen something that was completely useless. He had no idea how to use a taser. And even if he did, what was it going to do against a man in body armor. He would be lucky to get even one hair on the officer's head to stand up and notice. His right hand didn't seem to care though. It gripped the weapon tightly as his index finger explored what had to be the trigger.

Danny's internal debate ended when a new sound triggered his sense of self-preservation. The sound began with a distant whoosh, but soon the parking lot was filled with the sounds of a strong wind. Within moments, the wind began to howl like the world was coming to an end. Did they have tornadoes in Massachusetts? Danny didn't know, but he also didn't feel even a whisp of a breeze under the SUV. How weird was that? Something had to be going on though. The officers hand had crept under the car to latch onto the underside of the bumper. The man's grip was so tight that his knuckles were turning white. Danny had no idea what was going on and he couldn't risk sticking his head out to see what was happening.

The wind continued to blow, but not on him, for a few minutes. As the howling faded, the officer released his death grip on the bumper and began whispering once more. Then the man did the one thing Danny couldn't allow, the office picked up the shotgun. Danny heard the slide on the gun pump once. With a calm he couldn't explain, Danny slid from under the SUV to stand behind the officer. Danny's eyes traveled from the barrel of the shotgun, now braced on the hood of the SUV, down the mans armored body. Where could he aim? The officer's helmet even protected his neck. There was no place to aim the taser.

Then Danny noticed one -oh so small- opening in the officer's defenses. The officer's stance, leaning over the hood, had created an opening in his protective covering. There where the pants and vest met was a tiny white stripe of t-shirt material. And just below the telltale white flag was an even smaller strip of bare skin. Danny's lips twitched in an almost smile as he thought of the hundreds of plumber jokes he had heard in his life. But there was no time for humor when this man was aiming at one of his friends.

Danny raised the taser, pointing it at the officer. No, he decided. He did not trust even those magical fingers not to miss. He stretched out his hand until the taser was barely an inch from the flesh that begged for his attention. There was resistance as he pulled the trigger, but only for a heartbeat and then it was gone. There was no bang, no thunderclap. It was so unsatisfying. Out of spite, Danny squeezed again. Time slowed for Danny as the officer's back suddenly arched. Danny dropped the taser and stepped back. Time resumed its normal flow and then some as the officer began to spasm. The shotgun, no longer clamped against his shoulder, fell against the hood. With a crack of metal on metal, the shotgun fell from the hood to bounce off the bumper before clattering to the ground. The officer's erratic movements ceased and he slumped against the SUV. His helmeted head bounced off the SUV before he too hit the ground.

Danny was already moving before the officer came to rest on the ground. The taser lay forgotten by the man's unmoving right hand. Danny was already two cars over when a new voice, this one much louder, began to call, "Bob? Bob! Are you alright?" Footsteps ran towards the fallen officer. Danny huddled under a much smaller car as they move past him. The voice resumed; this time filled with panic. "Code three! I say again, code Three! Officer Quartz is down." There was a pause and the new voice got angry. "I haven't a clue what happened to him. I need a medical team! Now!"

The rest of the officer's conversation got lost in a burst of applause from the other side of the porta potties. Cheers erupted from what sounded like every person in attendance at King Richard's Faire. Danny had no idea who they were cheering for, but he was fairly certain it had nothing to do with him stopping the officer from shooting one of his friends. It really didn't matter right now. All Danny cared about was disappearing into that sea of voices. If he was lucky, no one would ever connect him with what happened to the cop named Bob.

---

Jacob stared across the street, waiting to see how the FBI would react to what he had just done. They would try again; Jacob was sure of that. They would never let someone who could control the wind get away from them. Did the new combinations filling his head have the power to thwart their plans? They probably did, but only if he had the sense to use them properly. Only time would tell. Jacob turned slowly to make sure the children and everyone else were safe. To his surprise, everyone, even the news team, was cheering.

Ruth's voice came from beside him. "They understand that you saved them, Jacob. They may not understand how and, by tomorrow, most of them won't believe it ever happened. But they are grateful and so am I."

Jacob nodded silently. He raised his hand and pointed at the small figure coming around the line of blue-green stalls at a dead run.

Ruth grinned and asked, "Do we want to know why he looks so guilty?"

"Probably not," he replied as he turned back towards the street. The FBI's next move was coming up the road from the interstate and it was much worse than he expected. The weight of the world felt like it was settling on his shoulders as he stared at the force being sent against them. Would that foe care about the innocent lives standing behind him? Not likely, he decided. "Ruth, do you have any words left?"

"Only a few. Why?" As Ruth turned to see what he was looking at, Jacob pointed at the six armored SUVs coming down the road and what looked like a tank leading the way. Jacob could barely make out her words as Ruth whispered, "Oh my God!"

"Oh my God, indeed," Jacob agreed.

## Chapter 21
## Battle Lines

So many people, small bodies so easily broken, surrounded him on all sides. Each step was another opportunity to hurt one of them because none of them were in as big a hurry as he was. Geoff wanted to run, to chase after the girl with the red ribbon and pink flowers. But it just wasn't possible. Those small bodies darted into every opening as soon as he spotted it. He was hemmed in, trapped by the ebb and flow of the swarm. Somehow, he had to get free to find the girl. She had the answers he needed. Only she could tell me how to save all of the people here. Saving them was the only way he could become a knight.

Snails moved faster than the crowd did. Eventually though, he reached the spot where he had seen the girl smile at him. But, of course, she wasn't there anymore. Geoff scanned the crowd. Finding that bright red ribbon should be easy for someone as tall as he was, but it wasn't easy at all. His dream of becoming a knight had nearly died when something red emerged from the shadow of one of the tents. It was her! Geoff watched the girl drop to her knees and begin to dig in the dirt. He strained to see what she was after, but he was too far away. Abruptly, she looked directly at him, giving him that same knowing smile once more. Then she stood. Something fluttered from her fingers and a flicker of pink disappeared into the hole she had dug.

Without warning, the crush of bodies against his right leg melted away. The pressure against his left leg increased, pushing Geoff towards an opening he sensed more than saw. He didn't hesitate. Geoff began to wind his way through the previously impenetrable wall of tiny people. His progress was maddeningly slow, but it was better than anything he had managed since the return of the painful wailing noise. Geoff risked a glance up from the people he was moving past, but he could not see the girl anymore. She had disappeared again. He groaned in frustration. At that grumble of annoyance, the crowd pulled back leaving him a path to the tent where the girl had stood.

Finally, he was able to run, dodging those people who withdrew too slowly. He reached the tent, but there was no sign of the girl or her red ribbon. He looked down into the hole, hoping she had left him some clue about what he needed to do. If there was a clue, he wasn't smart enough to figure it out. All that lay in the hole was a small pink flower. Kneeling, Geoff reached down and snatched it up, banging his knuckles on something hard that lay beneath it. Geoff slid the flower's plastic stem into his own hair before studying the bottom of the hole.

What had the girl been digging for? Certainly not the flower. His fingers brushed aside some of the loose dirt at the bottom of the hole. Beneath that thin layer of dirt, his fingers found a half-buried rock about the size of his fist. Geoff pulled it from the ground and brushed away the dirt that still clung to it. The rock was smooth and well-balanced. Why would the girl care about a rock? He didn't know, but it must be important to her. He placed it in the empty sling bag. He would ask her when he found her.

Standing, he checked the front of the tent. She wasn't there. Then he looked around the back. Two tents over, there was a smaller path that ran from one side of the Faire to the other. The girl was skipping along that path with that same smile that was really beginning to annoy him. Geoff called out for her to wait. The girl paused and motioned for him to hurry. Then she continued whatever game she had been playing. Whether they were playing chase or hide and seek, Geoff knew he was losing when the girl disappeared from view.

Geoff wanted to run after her. This time, it was tent ropes that slowed him down instead of people. By the time he made it to the side path, she was far ahead, standing beneath a tall pine tree. Again, she motioned for him to hurry. He would catch her this time. Geoff lowered his head and ran. The carts along the path seemed to fly by as his longer legs carried him the length of the path. But when he reached the tree, panting for breath, she was gone again. The only sign that she had been there was another pink flower sitting on top of a rock that was identical to the one he carried in his bag.

He slipped the flower into his hair beside its twin. Then he placed the second rock in his bag. With both treasures safely tucked away, he looked around for the girl. There were only two ways to go at this intersection. To his left, the street was empty except for two merchants guarding their large tents. He spun back to the right, afraid of losing her again. He need not have worried. She was waiting for him to catch up. There, far ahead, near the front of the Faire, the girl leaned against a big wooden sign. How had she gone so far? Was she really that much faster than he was? Geoff walked towards her, not taking his eyes off her this time. As he watched, she reached up to the red ribbon and pulled something from it. Another flash of pink fluttered to the ground.

The girl motioned a third time for him to hurry before she turned and walked away. Geoff knew he didn't need to hurry this time. The way she had gone was a dead end. She had entered the place of mud and there wasn't another path leading out of it. This time, she was trapped. He grinned in triumph. He would win the game of hide and seek. He would have the answer to his question.

The sign with the markings he could no longer read waited for him. His fingers traced the symbols, "The Mud Pit," that had been carved into the wood. Once he had cared about reading those markings, but they didn't seem important anymore. At the base of the sign was another pink plastic flower. It had landed atop another fist-sized rock. Geoff wasn't surprised, somehow this was part of her game. The flower joined the other two and his bag was now full with the three rocks inside it. Geoff walked after the girl, not wanting to frighten her.

To his surprise, the girl was not in the place of mud, no one was. Well, almost no one. At least nothing living was there. A dead beast, blue and white in coloring, lay on its side in the mud. An old memory that was fading from his mind tried to tell him this was a thing that had never lived. But how could that be? Things did not eat people. Only monsters did. In this beast's half open mouth, Geoff could see the bodies of two men. The beast's large white tongue still pulsed as it tried to pull the bodies into its stomach. He had been too late to save these men; he must not fail to save the other people that had come to see him.

Behind the blue and white creature was a tree that had been knocked over by the beast's death throes. The only tracks in the mud were those made by the now dead beast. Could the girl have come this way without leaving tracks? She was much smaller than the creature. Geoff stepped out onto the mud. His feet sank into the mud's sucking grip. It wasn't easy to pull them free and when he did, his new boots left large wounds in the mud's smooth surface. No, the girl could not have come this way without leaving signs of her passing. Had she led him here only to disappear? It made no sense. Why bring him here if it did not help him save the children?

The answer to his question came from the far side of the trees. A monstrous roar momentarily drowned out all other sounds. That call to battle had barely faded when Geoff heard the terrified cries of the people he was supposed to save. He hurried to the stump of the fallen tree. As he stood in the gap its destruction had created, the place called parking lot opened up before him. Many things became clear to him as he stared into the eyes of the monsters gathering there. The girl had known where he needed to be. She had been leading him here all along. Thanks to her, he would meet his destiny. His years of training as a warrior would now be tested. Now, the future was up to him.

Two black beasts with eyes that glowed like demons waited for him. Their dark, hungry maws hung open as they began to move towards him. Geoff reached into the sling bag, the comforting weight of one of a large stone filled his hand.

---

As if in anticipation of the devastation to come, both black and whites retreated into the protective line formed by the other police cars. Then, one by one, the sirens ceased their strident calls leaving only the restless muttering of the crowd to compete with the rumble of the enemy convoy. Like some mythical beast, the metal behemoth and its serpent-like body of black SUVs slithered to a halt just outside the parking lot. The beast appeared to flick its tail and two of its black offspring shot forward to infest the line of police cars sitting across the street. That done, the beast turned its head to face the entrance to the lot. Its diesel engine roared out its challenge as the beast invaded the Faire.

Ruth and Jacob could only watch as their enemy crawled closer, its strange rotating feet ripping up the ground to cast gravel and dirt in an arc behind it. The SUVs that formed its tail held their place on the pavement, narrowly avoiding the vicious spray. The metallic beast ignored the first path through the crowded lot as it crept towards the wider second lane in the center of the parking lot. On reaching that aisle, it firmly planted its closest foot and ponderously turned to face them. Inching forward just enough to clear a path behind it, the beast paused to scowl at them.

"What is that thing?" Ruth managed to squeak out as she stared into the barrels of the twin machineguns mounted on its upper surface.

"Some kind of armored personnel carrier," Jacob replied without taking his eyes off the enemy he must somehow defeat.

"Can you stop it?" Ruth asked hopefully.

Jacob shrugged. "I don't really have a choice, do I?" he murmured. "I just don't know if I can do it without killing the people inside."

As if to show him the futility of defying them, the four SUVs chose that moment to surge into the lot. The first two darted behind the carrier to block the third and final aisle. The last two turned into the first aisle. Their enemy was now poised to attack on three fronts. Both of them knew that no matter what they did, one part of the enemy force would get through. Ruth looked to her mentor for reassurance.

The new Jacob faced their foe with his head held high as if unwilling to admit to the possibility of defeat. There was a trace of contempt in his voice as he said, "The dogs of war have arrived."

The phrase meant nothing to Ruth. She wanted to ask him what it meant, but the crowd suddenly broke into cheers again. Through their whoops of joy, Ruth heard someone cry out, "It's Fezzik! He's come to save us!"

They both turned to see Geoff walking out of the trees that bordered the Mud Pit. He moved to take up a position near the first lane through the parking lot. "Reinforcements," Ruth uttered with a grin. Then she pointed at the third lane. "There are still a couple words running around in my head. Stop that big thing and I will see what I can do to slow the last two down."

———————————

Geoff felt a pang of uncertainty as he stared at the mighty foes arrayed against them, huge beasts that they must somehow defeat. He and his friends were being asked to fight way above their weight classes. The shiny dragon that Jacob faced was enormous. It was hardly a fair fight. Even little Ruth needed to slay two of the black demons. But what choice did they have? Helpless children stood behind them. If any of them failed, the children would pay the price. Becoming a knight, Geoff realized, wasn't going to be an easy job. He squeezed the rock to calm his nerves.

The rock was comforting, but a sword would have been better. With a sword, he could strike for the demons' hearts. What could he do with an ordinary rock? But the girl had not given him a sword. She had given him rocks and flowers. The roar of the crowd swelled up, wrapping itself around him. The people were chanting something. At first, he did not understand. Who were they calling for? "Fezzik!" sounded over and over. Then he understood. He wasn't just Geoff anymore. He was Fezzik, too. Fezzik was a hero. Together Geoff and Fezzik could save the children just like they had saved Wesley. He only had to believe.

He focused once more on the demon before him. Its shining eyes lay below the dark opening of its mouth. Geoff's arm shot forward, his hand releasing the rock at the exact point where he would have struck a judo opponent. The rock sailed towards his dark enemy. His aim was true. The rock struck it between those glowing eyes. There was a strange crunching noise and greenish goo began to drip between its front feet. It wasn't enough to kill it, but another blow like that would surely kill it.

Fezzik's hand was already in the bag, a rock cradled in his palm. Again, he stepped into his throw, trying once more to strike it between its eyes. But the demon surged forward and his rock flew high, straight for the dark opening of its toothless mouth. The rock did not go down its throat as he expected. Instead, it bounced away as if the opening was somehow protected. Disappointment at his failure replaced the thrill of his first hit. He had but one rock left to defeat his two opponents.

Then something strange happened. Spiderwebs began to form in the demon's mouth. Small white circles appeared at the point where the rock had bounced. Larger circles wove themselves around the smaller ones. The pattern grew and grew filling the demon's mouth. Long jagged strands of web reached out to anchor the circles to the edges of its mouth. Geoff wasn't sure what was happening, but the demon was clearly disoriented. It twisted to the side, heading for the dead things that lined the path. There was a loud crash as the demon and the dead things collided. A cloud of white mist shot into the air over the demon's head.

It was dead, but the second black demon didn't care. It was coming for him even faster than the first demon had. His hand slipped into the bag, but there was only one rock left.

---

Ruth walked around the last porta potty to take her place at the end of the last path through the parking lot. Two black, armored SUVs sat at the far end of the lot like they had been waiting just for her. It was kind of creepy. And why did their windows have to be so heavily tinted? She could practically see her reflection in the windshield. Were these men so afraid of her that they could not look her in the eye? Either way, she had news for them. It would be a cold day in hell before she let anyone control her ever again. She would not be enslaved.

She also had no intention of waiting for them to run her down. Ruth strode purposefully down the aisle to prove that she wasn't afraid. The SUVs began to move as she passed the first parked car. The absurdity of what she was doing made her chuckle. This was like starring in an old-fashioned spaghetti western. It was time for the shoot-out. The hero and the bad guy were facing off on Main Street. Who would be the first to reach for their gun? Who had the fastest draw? The thought of guns sent a shiver down her spine. Maybe that wasn't the best analogy since they had guns and she didn't.

But the thought of old movies did give her an idea. What would her hero have done in a situation like this? Ruth shook her head. Harry Houdini would never have gotten himself into a trap that he didn't have a way out of. Harry had always been at least one step ahead of those who thought they could outsmart him. A Houdini-like idea began to wiggle around in her brain as the distance to the SUVs shrank. In 1918, Harry had pulled off the ultimate illusion. He had made a live elephant disappear in front of a large crowd. Could she one up her idol?

The worm began to grow in her mind. Soon, it was the size of an elephant. But it could not be just any elephant. Houdini had always done things with style. Ruth could do no less. The devil was indeed in the details and this would be the most detailed illusion she had ever tried.

This had to be about justice. She wanted it to be more than just revenge for what had been done to her and her friends. This was her chance to address the wrongs of a world that had lost its way. She had an opportunity to challenge those who viewed heart-warming animated classics as vile and racist. She would chastise people like the ones who had driven the world's greatest circus out of business with absurd claims of animal cruelty. There were so many victims in this world and no one recognized the real culprits. The things that had made ordinary people happy weren't bad. No, evil was forcing others to change into your own version of reality, coercing others into becoming something they didn't want to be. She had never really understood what evil was until she woke up in that lab. Ruth grinned as the final pieces of her creation slid into place in her mind.

Ruth stopped between the two lines of parked cars. It was finally high noon. Her hand didn't reach for her six-gun, but it did stretch out before her. There was no gunshot to signal that the duel had begun, but the words she spoke were harsh and guttural. "kis-sAY teM-OO-Naw khoZ-Kaw!" she shouted. The image Ruth had so carefully crafted flowed out on the tide of those ancient syllables. Light blossomed before her. Brakes locked as the leading SUV slid in the gravel. The grinding noise was punctuated by a loud thump when the second driver failed to react quickly enough.

The child of her mind came into being among the weeds that decorated the gravel lot. Its inauspicious birthplace did not diminish the grandeur of what she had conceived. Excitement ran through Ruth as she stared at the leathery gray wall of the elephant's posterior. Her child was at least a dozen feet tall, easily a match for one of the SUVs. Its tiny snake-like tail hung there limply. Now she just needed to animate it. Ruth raised her left hand towards the elephant. She flicked her pinky finger. The elephant's tail came to life, striking repeatedly at imaginary flies. It was so life-like, she had to see more of it.

It took over twenty of her short strides to reach the elephant's side. Her eyes traveled up its massive leg to the shiny circus blanket that covered in broad back. A red field of satin hung low on the elephant's side. Bright yellow tassels dangled from its lower edge to swing between those tree trunk legs. In the midst of that satin field, large golden letters spelled out her protest against those who wanted to cancel out the world she loved: "Mrs Jumbo's Revenge." Smaller golden letters, a memorial to one of the victims of the culture war, flowed across the bottom of the blanket just above the tassels. They declared, "In memory of the Greatest Show on Earth: 1882-2017." Even if no one understood, she had proclaimed her message.

The SUVs began to creep forward again. It was time for the performance to begin. Ruth flicked the index finger of her left hand. The elephant's long trunk swayed between her pearl white tusks. The elephant tossed her head and her small eyes came to rest on the lead SUV. Mrs Jumbo didn't look happy to see their guest. As the two five-foot-long tusks lined up with the driver's side door, the lead SUV came to an abrupt halt. Ruth smiled; this was going to be fun.

Ruth blew the elephant a kiss and motioned with her right hand towards their unwelcome pests. The elephant gave her a sassy wink with its right eye and took her first lumbering steps. Synchronizing the movement of four legs took a great deal more concentration that Ruth would have expected, but she quickly found a menacing gait that brought the elephant ever closer to the lead SUV.

On a whim, Ruth raised all four fingers of her right hand. In true circus elephant fashion, Mrs Jumbo reared on her hind legs, bringing her massive front feet up higher than the hood of the SUVs. She held that position for several heartbeats before bringing both legs down in a hammer blow that could crush even an armored SUV. No one but Ruth seemed to notice the dandelion sticking up between the elephant's toes. The impact of her landing didn't so much as bend its stem.

The ground hadn't even shaken when the elephant landed, but the driver of the lead SUV was clearly rattled by the implied threat. Tires spun and rocks flew as he slammed the vehicle into reverse. There was the sound of breaking glass as he backed and spun to the right, hitting the second SUV. An angry horn blared as the lead driver executed a tight three-point turn that had him heading back the way he had come. Mrs Jumbo tossed her head giving the second SUV a clear view of her long white tusks. That was all it took.

Within moments, both SUVs were headed back towards the safety of the main road. Ruth's only regret was that she never saw the look on the men's faces. Mrs Jumbo raised her trunk in victory and then she faded from view.

---

To his left, Jacob felt the power of Ruth's… well, magic. He had no other word for what they could do except the one little Tuula had given it. From his right came a bellow of rage that Jacob assumed was Geoff's battle cry. Both of those fights were distractions he couldn't afford, not with their greatest challenge facing off against him. The engine of the FBI's armored personnel carrier roared to life again as its air brakes gave an evil hiss. With a groan of grinding gears, the metal monstrosity began to advance.

Ancient runes still swirled in his head. Sorting them out was like trying to herd hungry cats away from a food bowl. All he would get for his efforts was a nasty scratch or two. There were too many new combinations that he had no time to figure out. Which sequence held the key to stopping or at least slowing down the APC heading his way? He just didn't know, but the runes thought they did. How far could he trust this power he now called magic? He didn't know that either. But, as he had told Ruth, he really didn't have a choice. Jacob gave in to the inevitable. He lowered the barriers he had created in his mind and let the cat-like runes do what they would.

The surge of understanding he had hoped for didn't come, but he became certain about what the runes wanted him to do. In his mind, glowing runes stepped back like soldiers avoiding an unpleasant detail. Only one combination remained at the forefront of his thoughts. Those words pulsed softly signaling their readiness. Jacob read the runes. Then he read them again, disbelieving what they said. No one could control that kind of energy and live. And even if he did survive, could it even affect an armored vehicle? His foe was halfway down the lane already. It was now or never. Jacob stretched out one hand. With far less confidence than he had felt when he called the wind to his service, Jacob spoke the words that flared white hot in his mind, "Baw-rAWk."

Even having read the words, Jacob was caught off guard by the power that leapt from his fingertips. The world paused around him, or was that just the speed of what he had unleashed. Harsh white light reflected off every car between him and the APC and every shadow in the lot was devoured by the intensity of the blast. Thunder rumbled in the same instant that the bolt of lightning raced away from him. His heart didn't have time to beat before the APC was bathed in dripping plasma while fingers of light arced from one protrusion to the next. The light show went on forever and yet was gone in the blink of an eye. The great diesel engine spurted once and then roared in renewed fury.

The breath Jacob had been holding escaped in a soft moan. It had been beautiful, but the magic had failed. The APC had shrugged off one of the primal forces of nature without a care. It still came for him, seeking vengeance for his audacity. Ten feet and then another fifteen disappeared under its treads. Jacob should have had more faith. The APC was a thing of technology and such creations weren't compatible with the power Jacob wielded. The engine faltered a second time. Something thick and viscous gushed from the underbelly of the beast. Dark fluids, red and green and black, coated the ground beneath the APC like the lifeblood of some great leviathan. The APC shuddered and came to a halt as it bled out. The magic had not been wrong after all.

With a sigh of relief, Jacob turned to check on his friends. Ruth was walking towards him with a dreamy smile on her face. There was no sign of the two SUVs she had gone to deal with. He could only assume that she had done well. With a smile and a wave in Ruth's direction, Jacob turned to see how the FBI had fared against the powerful young man. It turned out there was no time to assess that part of the battle. A black SUV fishtailed around the corner with a large rock embedded in its windshield. Jacob froze, his mind went blank, and the words darkened as the driver aimed the armored SUV at him and stomped on the gas. He was incapable of doing anything but watch as Geoff charged into the lot.

Jacob had never been a big fan of football, not even as a college professor. But he had seen enough games to know a good block when he saw one. Geoff's form was almost perfect as the big man lowered his right shoulder and drove it into the driver's door. The SUV literally skipped sideways. White waves exploded within the vehicle as the air bag inflated. The SUV slowed. But what was really impressive was seeing Geoff reach down to grip the running board in both hands. His arms and thighs bulged as the SUV's left wheels left the ground. Geoff stepped in close as he pushed the vehicle over even farther. Jacob could only gape when the SUV rolled on its side, ending the war for their freedom.

But it wasn't the end of the war, only the end of a single battle and their respite was short lived. A voice cried from somewhere in the crowd, "Soldiers! Look out!"

Jacob turned back to the APC. Apparently, he hadn't killed the occupants after all. Men and women in body armor were pushing their way out of the APC. A man that was clearly in charge was shouting orders and organizing the twenty or so armored agents staggering away from the crippled vehicle. The runes that had been so dim as the SUV hurdled towards him flared to life, one set glowed more brightly than all the others. There wasn't time to argue with them, so he just gave those words their freedom, "awash awB!"

Wisps of greenish-yellow mist began to ooze from the gravel where the squad was forming up. The mist's slow trickle quickly grew into a torrent, billowing up to engulf the entire force. Jacob heard men and women gagging and then someone retched within the cloud. Could it really end so easily? He could only hope. Then a dark form emerged from the cloud. The squad's commander stepped into the open wearing a gas mask. More shapes made their way clear in his wake. In moments, a dozen masked forms stood at their commander's side, ready for battle.

The commander motioned towards Jacob. Four of the faceless agents broke ranks, heading for Jacob. The commander uttered only one phrase, but it was an order that made Jacob's blood run cold. "Alive!" the man snarled. Jacob begged the words for a non-lethal option, but the magic hesitated. The runes may have wavered, but Geoff did not. He was among the four agents before they had a chance to react. Geoff's hand shot out, his open palm striking the largest agent in the chest. The man's arms pinwheeled helplessly as he flew through the air to land at his commander's feet. Two impossibly fast strikes later, two more agents lay doubled over on the ground. Only the smallest form, a woman Jacob thought, reacted quickly enough. Several of her punches and kicks actually connected, but none seemed to have an effect on his big friend. Then Geoff caught one of her strikes in his hand. He pulled her in close, her back against his stomach. Jacob watched in horror as Geoff's forearm came across her throat.

Loud, rhythmic thumping filled Jacob's ears; his heart seemed to pound too hard as he watched Geoff strangle the female agent. Jacob screamed out, "No!" but Geoff had already lowered her unconscious form to the ground. The thumping was interrupted by a loud crackling sound. Geoff stood suddenly stiff. A look of annoyance crossed his face as he slapped at his own chest. Jacob looked up to see the commander holding a taser in his extended hand. Geof stepped towards his tormentor. Two more agents stepped forward and the crackling was louder this time. Geoff seemed confused as he reached for the wires now sprouting from his chest. More agents stepped forward. The crackling sounds were drowned out by a loud groan as Geoff dropped to his knees. The commander stepped in front of Geoff, aiming his taser at Geoff once more. This time Geoff toppled forward like a fallen tree, his body spasming from time to time.

Runes glowed in Jacob's mind. He knew at that moment that he could kill this man with a soft whisper, but was that the kind of man he wanted to be? The commander pulled the mask from his face. The smile on his face angered Jacob. He stared into the man's hazel eyes, memorizing his face. The commander dropped his discharged taser and pulled a second one from his belt. He winked at Jacob as he pointed the weapon at Jacob. The thumping that seemed to fill the air grew louder. Suddenly something long and white stuck the man in the chest. The commander staggered backwards, his taser discharging harmlessly into the ground. Jacob stared, uncomprehending, at the crossbow bolt that now hung from the man's shirt. It hadn't penetrated his armor, but it had done its job quite well. More bolts whizzed through the air, some striking armor and others flying past to bounce off parked cars.

The thumping that had not been his heart came up behind Jacob, mingling with the clanking of what could only be medieval armor. As the agents began to drag Geoff's body away, two lines of armored men and women marched past Jacob, one to his right and one to his left, their booted feet striking the ground in perfect unison. Unlike the agents, the armor these warriors wore did not match. This army, for that was what it was, wore equipment from dozens of cultures that had thrived over the course of thousands of years. The heroes of King Richard's Faire now controlled the field of battle.

A small hand slid into his own. Ruth's voice was filled with grief as she whispered, "They have Geoff."

"They won't keep him!" Jacob promised.

They both watched as the Knights of the Faire formed a battle line before them. Swords, maces, axes and a score of weapons Jacob didn't recognize were raised in defiance. The agents fled before that show of force. The Siege of Carver was broken, but not without losses. Jacob wondered how he would keep that promise to Ruth. Especially since he had no idea where Geoff would be taken.

## Chapter 22
## The Folk

Jacob and Ruth watched as the line of knights overlapped their shields, forming the first shield wall in nearly nine centuries. Smaller clusters of knights scoured the parking lot in an effort to harass their retreating foes. Here and there, cries of victory rang out as the invaders from a far distant future fled the field of battle. A force that they should never have been able to defeat had been routed. Pride suffused the Folk as they stood shoulder to shoulder; not one man or woman wavered in their defense of the realm. No matter what came next, this day belonged to the Folk.

"My friends, it is time for you to go," a cultured voice spoke from right behind them. Jacob and Ruth turned to see a sight that neither could have imagined in their wildest dreams. Sir John stood behind them in an impeccably tailored pin-stripe suit. Peeking from his breast pocket was a red silk handkerchief that matched the tie double-knotted around his neck. The look of shock on their faces brought a smile to the courtier's lips, but that smile did not reach his eyes. His tone was grave as he explained, "In addition to my other duties, I also serve as senior legal counsel for the realm. Some of our more unwelcome guests find this look more intimidating than my court attire."

Despite his explanation, Ruth's mouth hung open. Jacob wasn't doing much better, but he managed to point at the line of knights and ask, "Why?"

Sir John's expression relaxed just a bit. "Take note, Jacob Dror, and understand. The Folk take care of their own. That duty is more than just a matter of honor to us; it is the essence of who we are. And, it is a matter of pride among us."

Jacob shook his head. "But I am not really one of you. As Ruth likes to point out, I'm just a noob."

Sir John pulled at the sleeves of his suitcoat, unconsciously adjusting the fit of clothing that seemed foreign to the man Jacob knew. But his demeanor was that of a seasoned lawyer addressing the courtroom. "The Folk decide who they claim and who they banish, Sir. This day, you stood against our enemies, risking your freedom to protect our patrons. I do not know how you did the things you did today, but you became one of us the moment you saved the children from that tear gas. For good or ill, you are now one of us and so are your friends. Much will be expected of each of you, but in the performance of those duties, you will never be alone."

To not be alone. That was a feeling Jacob hadn't known in more years than he cared to admit. Moisture gathered at the corners of his eyes and his throat felt too tight for even his breath to pass. He forced the words past that unwelcome obstruction, "I thank you, but I would trade that honor to get Geoff back."

Sir John nodded as if he had expected no less. "And that is one of the reasons why we claim you, Jacob. Know this, we will help you find him. He too, is one of us. However, I suspect that freeing him will fall to you, your friends, and your…shall we say… unusual talents." Turning, Sir John pointed towards the crowd. Come and say your goodbyes. Your presence here is a danger to us all. We have to get you to your van before the Feds close off the only remaining escape route."

Jacob and Ruth walked beside Sir John as they reentered the Faire. The reporter started to step forward, but froze at the glare Sir John gave him. Ruth giggled, but only for a second before regaining her composure. A line of strangers blocked their way. None of the faces she expected to see were there. "Where are Danny and Coon?" she blurted out.

"They are already gone. They are waiting for you at your van," Sir John replied. Then he gestured and the crowd parted. Standing in that newly opened space were Tara and Tuula. Tara's face beamed with pride as she watched them approach. But Tuula's face was troubled and the tracks of her tears still glistened on her cheeks.

Jacob knelt before the distraught little girl. He didn't need to be told; Jacob knew who those tears were for. "Somehow, Tuula, I will find him. I will get him back. I promise. Just give me time."

Tuula threw herself into his arms and Jacob felt her body shudder with silent sobs. Her trembling voice was warm against his chest. "Wizards always have to keep their promises. It's a rule."

"I will always keep my promises to you, Tuula," he whispered into her hair. Then Jacob gave her one last squeeze before releasing her and getting to his feet. Then he turned to face her mother. "Tara, I… I wish that…"

That was as far as he got before she silenced him with a kiss. "Shut up and listen carefully. Take Interstate 87 north to the Canadian border. You have to get into Canada somehow. My parents have a place up on the Hudson Bay. We'll be safe there." Jacob watched her brow furrow in concentration. "There is a place just across the border called Park Safari. It's a wildlife refuge. Find the boardwalk. Follow it around to the end where you feed the giraffes. Tuula loves the giraffes. Meet us there in eight days. Don't you dare let us down!"

Jacob was still trying to absorb it all when she kissed him again and then shoved him away. She pointed to a young man in jeans and a t-shirt. "Go! Quickly!"

With Ruth tugging at his hand, Jacob stumbled away.

---

It was just before dawn a week later when Jacob brought the van to a stop on the shoulder of US-9. The interchange for I-87 North was less than a mile ahead. Jacob turned off the headlights and waited as his eyes adjusted to the darkness. He was coming to appreciate his new body's ability to see in the dark. The colors took some getting used to, but it was better than being blind.

Jacob stared out the passenger window. Off to his right, he could just make out the skeletal shape of an electrical pylon. Its metallic frame appeared as pale blue lines against the night sky. Nestled in its core were four bright red trash can shaped objects. Those should be the transformers that powered everything at the border crossing. If he could short them out, it might create enough chaos that one van could slip across the border undetected. Especially if that van happened to be invisible.

Jacob hated ifs, but this was the best plan that he and Ruth had been able to come up with in the six days since their escape from Carver. It should work, but they would only get this one chance. He had to be sure. Jacob turned his attention to the small man standing beside him. "Are you positive, Danny?"

He could hear the frustration in the young man's voice. Jacob couldn't blame him; it was at least the tenth time Jacob had asked that same question. Jacob had to accept the mild rebuke in Danny's voice. "Come on, Jacob. I spent the last three days running through the woods tracking cables. These are the last transformers between here and the border station."

"I'm sorry, Danny," Jacob replied. "I know how hard you worked. But we have to be sure before we fry that tower. They won't be fooled this way twice."

Apparently, they were all getting edgy, even Ruth. Her tone was overly harsh as she snapped at them both, "Then let's do this. I am tired of hiding in rest areas and eating trail mix. Danny keeps stealing all the peanut M&Ms."

"I do not!" Danny protested.

Jacob grinned as he watched them bicker in the rear-view mirror. This was as good a way as any for them to blow off steam. Besides, Jacob knew he was the one who had been eating all the M&Ms.

Jacob eased the van along the shoulder until he came to a small service road that led back to the pylon. The "road" was hardly more than a dirt path between the trees. According to Danny, the service road was only a couple hundred yards long. It ended at a security fence that was supposed to keep both curious and stupid people from getting hurt.

Jacob had his doubts. It probably worked great for those who were curious, but stupid always seemed to find a way to get into trouble.

Jacob backed the van onto the dirt road, stopping just inside the tree line. He placed the van in park and turned the engine off. For a time, he sat listening to the sounds of the night. The drone of countless insects returned intermingled with the occasional pops or pings of the engine as it cooled. Those simple sounds were somehow transformed into a hymn of peace as Jacob listened. Or, they were until the insistent tapping of fingers on the back of his seat was added to the melody. With a sigh, Jacob asked, "Yes, Danny?"

Now it was Danny's turn to get snippy. "Are you sure this isn't going to screw up my van? She's irreplaceable, Jacob."

"Your van is old, Danny. I doubt there is a computer chip in it. Once you disconnect the battery cables, she's little more than inert metal. I don't think that what Ruth and I have planned will do any damage, but I can't make any promises. This is new to us too."

"Fine, but I don't have to like it," Danny grumbled. "Pop the hood so I can get started."

Jacob pulled a lever on the left side of the steering wheel. There was a loud thunk from the front of the van. He watched Danny climb out of the van with a screwdriver in one hand and a small stepladder in the other.

The sky began to lighten as the hood went up. There was hardly a sound as Danny went to work on his beloved van.

Jacob felt Ruth's hand on his shoulder. "Are you sure you don't need my help?"

"No, not this time," he replied, "I'm just worried about who else is going to lose power."

Ruth's blue eyes shone in the darkness. "I'm sure everyone will be fine, Jacob. With the border so close, they will need to repair this quickly."

He nodded and opened his door. Jacob began to walk, the cool air felt good on his face after days of being stuck in the van. Ahead, through the trees, he could see the cold blue of a chain link fence. Looking up, Jacob studied the transformers suspended well out of reach, their rounded forms glowing like overheated coals in the center of a fire. Fire, Jacob realized suddenly, was the solution he had been searching for. Any of the words flitting around in his head could short out the transformers. He needed a solution that didn't make it obvious who was responsible for their failure. And, since shorts did tend to cause fires…

Jacob raised his right arm, pointing his index finger at the cluster of transformers. The sounds of birds and insects died as if they sensed what was coming. "aySH shED-ay-Faw" he whispered into the sudden silence.

A tiny spark, barely noticeable against the glow of the transformers, rose into the air. Its movements were like those of a feather caught up by a wandering breeze. But its path never wavered as it followed the line of Jacob's extended finger. It seemed innocuous until it reached those red-hot cylinders. That touch was no more than a soft caress. The blaze that gentle embrace ignited ripped away Jacob's night vision. It didn't matter though as the resulting ball of flame lit the world like the midday sun. The transformers blackened, their paint bubbling away as they began to burn.

His mission complete, Jacob headed back to the van. Everyone was on their feet when Jacob climbed into the driver's seat. "What the hell was that?" Danny demanded.

"Later!" Jacob commanded. "The battery?"

Danny scowled but answered, "Disconnected and everything is fully discharged."

Jacob felt the tension mounting as the moment of truth approached. But his voice was calm as he said, "As we practiced it, Ruth."

"Yes, Master," she replied as she sank to the floor in the back of the van. Ruth pressed her hands into the shag carpet and waited.

Jacob reached out, placing both his hands on the dashboard. Energy danced across his skin as he contemplated the words that now fought for their freedom. Jacob held those ancient syllables prisoner until he was sure Ruth's power matched his own. And then they spoke in perfect unison, "kheb-YONE!" and the power that they had called surged into the van.

The first rays of sunlight fell on the shiny silver stepstool that stood alone out in the middle of the dirt road.

Jacob grinned, or he thought he did anyway, at the emptiness that surrounded him.

Danny gave a hiss of surprise. "Where's my van?" Danny's voice dropped to a whisper, "Wait! Where am I? Oh hell, this is sweet. Can you teach me how to do this?"

Coon merely growled in annoyance. Jacob could only assume she didn't approve of the change.

The tension in Jacob's neck and shoulders disappeared into the same nothingness that had taken the van. The magic had worked. The only question was, would the van still run. "Battery, Danny! Move it! We need to get to the border before they get themselves organized," Jacob ordered.

"Uh, right," came from the back of the van. A door that no one could see opened and Danny whispered softly. "How do you walk without feet?"

Things began to rattle and bang somewhere in front of them. Danny's normally talented hands seemed to struggle with the connectors the little man couldn't see. The hood slammed down, harder than necessary. Then the stepladder floated to the side of the road and flew behind a tree. Moments later, the rear door closed and Danny's voice whispered, "It's done."

Jacob fastened his seatbelt before reaching for the ignition. His hand moved too far and he jammed his fingers into the dash. The flash of pain reminded him that he needed to be more careful. Jacob tried again. This time his outstretched fingers found the keys dangling above his right knee. Jacob pumped the gas once before turning the key. The van protested everything it had endured with a sharp clicking cry of refusal. Danny began to curse. Ignoring him, Jacob reached out with his new senses.

Remnants of the power he and Ruth had expended drifted all around him. One by one, Jacob began to draw that energy into himself. Each tendril of power that he absorbed revitalized him. He hungrily reached for everything he could find. When the air was clear, Jacob turned the key again. This time the engine only whined once before it turned over. A cheer went up behind him. Jacob counted four clicks as he shifted into drive.

The van began to move. It was more like crawling than driving at first. Controlling a vehicle that you couldn't see took some getting used to. Eventually Jacob realized he just needed to focus further ahead and stop trying to anticipate where the van was on the road. Confidence restored, he turned smoothly onto the onramp and began to accelerate.

Traffic on the Interstate was light so early in the morning. Two semis were approaching in the right lane while a couple of cars passed them on the left. Jacob accelerated trying to match speeds without the benefit of a speedometer. He was about to slip in between the two big rigs when the enormity of his mistake hit him. How could he safely merge into traffic when no one on the road could see him? Jacob's foot eased off the gas.

The van slowed and the second semi sped past. More cars and another semi weren't far behind it though. Getting into the flow of traffic would be insane, Jacob decided. So, at the end of the ramp, he stayed to the right, driving in the breakdown lane at a speed that kept in the gap between the two traffic clusters. It was nerve wracking. Thankfully, it wasn't far from Exit 43 where they got on to the Canadian border. Jacob could only imagine how white his knuckles were from gripping the steering wheel.

More traffic lanes appeared as they approached the border. The additional lanes didn't really help as they were all backed up with cars waiting for them to reopen. The border agents were all standing around behind traffic cones looking helpless. This was exactly the kind of confusion Jacob had been hoping for. Now they just needed a little luck. Jacob stayed to the right, following the two lanes designated for oversized. A half dozen trucks and a Winnebago were already waiting in line.

To the right of that growing line of trucks was what Jacob had been hoping for, a single lane marked for official use. That lane would have been their ticket to freedom if not for the two agents standing in the middle of the lane. Neither man seemed to have anything better to do than talk and point. So, they sat there with the van. Their conversation seemed to go on forever and Jacob was starting to think about running them down. But then the lights began to come back on at the individual stations. The two agents finally found something else to do.

As soon as they stepped out of his way, Jacob pressed the gas pedal to the floor. The engine roared and the tires may have spun just a bit, but Jacob did not care. The agents' heads jerked around, but there was nothing to see. And then there was nothing but open road ahead of them. They sped past a large sign that read "Bienvenue au Canada." His passengers began to cheer as Jacob announced, "You are officially in Canada!" When the excitement finally settled down, Jacob asked, "Can someone figure out where I need to go next?"

Someone crawled into the passenger seat. He knew it was Ruth when she began to giggle. "I would love to help," Ruth managed to choke out, "but the map is a little hard to read right now."

They both began to laugh.

---

It was an hour after Park Safari's opening on the eighth day after their hurried departure from King Richard's Faire. The chill of the morning breeze didn't penetrate the cloak that Jacob had found waiting for him in the van during their escape. The heavy wool was soft and the deep hood was lined with an even softer material. Jacob recognized the stitching. Tara had made this for him and he treasured it.

He stood alone on the boardwalk with three boxes of food in his hands. The food was for the giraffes that were now wandering in his direction. Their stride was a strange mix of awkwardness and grace as their long legs brought them closer to the high boardwalk. The first of the enchanting creatures reached the rail and leaned its head in his direction. Jacob stared into its brown eyes. He had only seen pictures of giraffes before, never a living one. Who could have imagined that his first encounter would be face to face with a fourteen-foot-tall specimen?

His left hand came up to stroke the giraffe's neck. The giraffe was a female, although he had no idea how he knew that. Her short fur was much softer than he expected. His fingers were drawn to caress the horns at the top of her head. She did not protest his exploration. Instead, she turned her head, snuffling at the food in his other hand. She was hungry and he couldn't deny her. So, he set two of the boxes behind him for Tuula. Opening the last box, he poured some of the pellets into his palm.

Jacob extended his right hand to her, offering what he hoped was a tasty treat. Jacob wasn't sure what he expected, but it definitely wasn't the long tongue that stretched out to wrap itself around his wrist. He watched, stunned, as her talented tongue slid down his hand leaving behind a thick coat of saliva. With amazing dexterity, it scooped the pellets from his hand as it slid back into her mouth. Somehow, she avoided dropping even one of the precious morsels.

The giraffe was magnificent. Jacob was so focused on the beauty of his God's handiwork that he didn't notice that he wasn't alone anymore. His first clue that he had company came when a familiar voice began to lecture him. "Their tongues are really strong. They can strip an entire branch of leaves with one swipe. But don't worry, they almost never hurt people who feed them."

Jacob lowered his now wet hand and felt tiny fingers curl around his own. "And, did you know that a giraffe's drool can hang from their mouth all the way to the ground? Just imagine it! An eighteen-foot-long string of drool!"

He smiled then. "I've missed you too, Tuula."

Tuula's fingers squeezed his own tightly. Then an arm came around his waist from the other side. A woman's voice whispered in his left ear. "I was worried. I didn't see your van anywhere."

In that instant, his world contained everything he would ever want in life. He was content. "I parked it out of sight while the youngsters went looking for pizza."

"Pizza is not a breakfast food," Tuula replied in a deadpan voice that brooked no argument. When no one argued with her, she grabbed one of the boxes of food from where Jacob had set it.

The two adults leaned together and watched their extraordinary child feed the giraffes.

## Chapter 23
## Web of Deceit

### CNN
*President's son still unwilling to discuss "the laptop"...*
Dec 2, 2021 — President Robin Bendi's son is still dodging any and all questions about the laptop seized by the FBI. The White House press secretary states the computer was planted as part of a Russian dis-information ploy to discredit...

### Centers for Disease Control and Prevention (.gov)
https://www.cdc.gov
*New Virus-C variant confirmed on https://www.cdc.gov*
Dec 17, 2021 — 529 cases of the Omicron variant confirmed in the United States. The figure shown is a map indicating locations reporting at least one confirmed case...

### Washington Post
*Bendi's first year in office marred by legal battles and social unrest*
Dec 21, 2021 — President Robin Bendi's presidency has been a roller coaster of legal challenges and social upheaval. His executive orders for vaccine mandates and masking have been challenged and struck down by the courts again and again. Protests and riots have become a a national pastime rivaling football in popularity. What will he say to the American people in his national address tonight? ...

### Boston Herald
*Bendi's approval rating plummets to new low*
Dec 21, 2021 — Amid rumors of scandals involving his son and a general dissatisfaction with his handling of Virus-C, President Bendi's approval has dropped below 43 percent. Tonight, he addresses the nation...

Anita Caufi stared out her window at the dark December night. Despite the late hour, a line of taillights marked the path out of the campus. Brake lights pulsed on and off in an orderly pattern as vehicles made their way to the red light that marked the boundary of her domain. If only all of her problems were that simple and orderly. Hell, at this point she would settle for just knowing if or when her plans would make things better and if they were about to blow up in her face.

She had been forced to use too many of the political favors owed her in setting up the operation to recapture the missing specimens. Once they were found, the FBI should have scooped them up like any other suspected terrorist group. The biggest problem should have been finding them. She had gotten lucky there. One of the specimens showed up on national television. The fool had been putting on a show for children. She couldn't have asked for a better break. Or so she had thought. But once again, reality had fallen so short of her expectations.

The FBI's Rapid Response Team had responded with the support of local law enforcement. It should have been easy. But the mission fell apart almost immediately. The first two squad cars on the scene had crashed. Her team was still trying to figure out what went wrong. So far, all anyone had been able to give her were pathetic excuses about mass hallucinations and officers passing out.

Then the Rapid Response Team had moved in that had assumed command. That was when everything went FUBAR. Some idiot had authorized the use of tear gas near a crowd of patients from Boston Children's Hospital. If that strange wind hadn't come up, she would have had a public relations nightmare on her hands. She still might since the whole debacle had played out on network television. The only positive spin on the media coverage was that it backed up some of Dr Morrall's wild tales. She was beginning to believe there might be more to his fear than simple paranoia.

There had to be a reason why four armored SUVs, an armored personnel carrier and thirty-one of the FBI's best trained combat operatives had been defeated in a matter of minutes. Elephants appearing out of nowhere. Freak lightning bolts striking out of a clear sky, and a man who could throw rocks through bullet proof glass. She wouldn't have believed any of it if she hadn't watched the broadcast over and over. Could Morrall's babbling be factual? Did these "changed" have powers and abilities that would redefine science as they knew it?

If what she was beginning to suspect was true, she wanted those specimens under her control, especially the blond specimen and the woman child that had controlled the elephant. But in true screw up fashion, the FBI had only managed to capture the one Morrall called an ogre. Even with all of their blunders, the FBI would have captured them all if not for the costumed clowns that had marched out of the crowd. Armor and swords? Really?

The specimen they recovered had already been delivered to the Moriah Shock facility. She had made it clear to Morrall that he was to get her answers one way or another. She didn't really care how many pieces the specimen was in when he finished. All that mattered was that he figure out how to control the results of the serum. The DoD would give her anything she wanted for soldiers who could do the things she had watched on that broadcast. And if not them, there were other countries that would.

And even if they didn't get what they needed from this specimen, Morrall had nearly 150 others to learn from. Specimens were expendable. Well, maybe not all of them. She had a use for any that manifested power like the two specimens she had lost. She had a feeling she would see those two again soon. And when she did, she would need a way to counter them. Morrall had his orders. She wanted…no…demanded an explanation for the changes. And it had better be something more scientific than the specimen's secret desire.

Damn it! Morrall's research had the potential to give her the power and prestige she deserved. Even if all Morrall did was decouple the Virus C cure from the genetic changes, she would be heralded as the savior of the world. If they could go a step further and control the genetic changes, she could market the serum world-wide. Black market sales alone would make her wealthy beyond even her wildest dreams. Morrall just needed to deliver. And he would, or, she would replace him. He wasn't the only mad genius in the world.

Anita glanced down at her watch. There were only a few minutes left until the President's broadcast. She doubted there was anything he could say that would help his approval rating. What was that old phrase? His numbers were in free-fall and he didn't have a working parachute. In reality, the best that any of them could hope for tonight was that he didn't trip on the stairs to the podium and end up with both feet in his mouth. And, if his staff was lucky, they would get him off the stage before he tried to answer any of the media's questions.

And if the President did make things worse, Anita wasn't responsible anymore. Bendi had a new Girl Friday running the CDC. The new CDC director was now responsible for all of the President's Virus C policies. Anita was rather proud of sticking the woman with the blame for all of Bendi's mandates. The woman had been a fool to take the job, but Anita was glad she had.

As for President Robin Bendi… When he hit rock bottom, Anita would be there to offer him solutions for all of America's problems. It would all start with a vaccine capable of improving the human race. If that wasn't enough to get his support, Bendi was old and going senile. What would he give for a younger, healthier body? And if eternal youth didn't sway him, even presidents get their Virus C boosters. Only the good doctor really knows what goes in that syringe.

Anita smiled as she considered her future. She poured herself another cup of hazelnut coffee and settled into her extremely comfortable desk chair. Hitting the controls for the flatscreen, she watched as Bendi stepped onto the stage. Not for the first time, she wondered what his staff was slipping into his coffee to make him actually look like a President. This wasn't the tired, old man she so often saw wandering around the White House like a lost puppy.

## Chapter 24
## Epilog

The darkness of the night was comforting. Even the moon and stars were hidden behind a thick bank of clouds. The only source of light to disturb the dark came from the headlights of the Lexus. Even the low beams were a constant irritation. The twin cones of light were not only painful to her new eyes, they literally destroyed the near perfect night vision that the change had given her. She was so tempted to just turn them off and race through the darkness. After all, how much risk was there really? There was almost no traffic on US-15 at two in the morning. But a part of her hesitated to call attention to the Lexus just yet. It was too useful.

Alicia liked the big, black Lexus. Its big engine leaped forward at the slightest pressure on the gas pedal. Driving the Lexus made her feel powerful, almost as powerful as she had felt when she snapped the neck of the fat fool who had owned it. The feel of his neck bones shattering in her hands had been intensely pleasurable. It was what he deserved after all. Had he really believed that whatever he had slipped into her drink would make her more pliant? Could he really have believed she would allow a weakling like him to violate her? She only wished she could have made him suffer a little longer for his arrogance. But the excitement of the moment had overwhelmed her and she had lost control. C'est la vie. It was time to go home anyway. It was time to face Mother.

The fool's body had gone into the dumpster out behind the bar where he had tried to pick her up. Well, everything except his wallet and the keys to the Lexus. She had needed both of those to get home. Mother didn't know she was coming yet. It would only take a few more hours. She could hardly wait to see the look of amazement on Mother's face when she revealed what she had become. How would Mother react to the changes in her "little darling?" The anticipation was almost more than Alicia could bear.

Alicia's right hand slid from the padded steering wheel to the passenger seat. The two pieces of paper she had stolen from the Jew's notebook rested safely beneath the dead man's wallet. She could not read them yet. But the voice had promised her that it would provide her a teacher. Once she could pronounce those strange characters, she would steal the Jew's power and, perhaps, even his life.

And when she had mastered those words of power, she would use them to control Mother. She would subjugate Mother's mind and will to her own. After years of being Mother's puppet, so many years of Mother pulling Alicia's strings for her own purposes, she would become the puppet master and Mother would be forced to do Alicia's bidding.

Alicia smiled as she wondered how many of Washington's elite she could draw into her web. Maniacal laughter echoed through the Lexus as the headlights went out. The black sedan surged forward into the night.

---

Clarance was humming along to with the radio as he drove up Route 7 towards the orchard. Things a Man Ought to Know was playing again. It was a catchy tune. Sadly, only old men like him seemed to take the time to listen to the words. If more of the youngsters in this crazy world could learn to listen, the world would be a better place. Clarance stopped thinking about the world and began to sing along as the old pickup entered the last long curve before arriving at his apple orchard.

He came out of the curve to find a hunched form lumbering down his side of the road towards him. Clarance's singing turned into a scream, "Aw, shiiiiiiiiitttttt!" He felt the brakes lock as he stomped down on the petal. At the same time, he spun the wheel to the left trying to get into the oncoming lane. But it didn't work the way Clarance hoped.

The old pickup slewed sideways and began to slide down the center of the road. The thump of the body against the side of the truck never came. When the truck finally came to a stop, Clarance spun to look out the rear window. The damn fool was standing no more than a couple feet from the bed of the truck. Clarance had never even gotten a parking ticket his whole life and today he almost killed a man.

Clarance kicked open the truck's door in his hurry to confront the man. He was on his feet with the bed of the truck between them. Angry words erupted from his mouth before his brain had time to engage. "Ya trying ta get us both killed, you damned id…" That was the moment his brain finally processed what he was seeing. The man looked like he should be dead except that he was walking down the road. The damned wrong side of the road, but he was walking. Clarance almost grinned as thoughts of that zombie show on HBO flashed through his mind. But none of that was real. Or so Clarance hoped.

The right side of the man's face was red and blistered. The ear on that side was blackened and most of the hair on that side of the man's head was little more than stubble. The suit jacket the man wore was badly scorched. It was even melted in a few places. It looked incredibly painful and that was the man's good side. The left side of his face had the worst case of road rash that Clarance had ever seen. The jacket sleeve on that side had been shredded as had the man's pants. Clarance could see small stones poking out of the man's bare skin. That whole side of his body was covered in dried on blood.

Clarance's anger was gone as quickly as it had come. It was rapidly replaced by concern for the injured man. Clarance reached into his jacket pocket for his old flip phone. "Hold on, mister! I'll get the police and an ambulance for you."

Clarance opened the phone and almost dropped it at the man's moan of terror, "Nooooo! No police."

Clarance didn't understand. He started to argue with the frightened man. "Mister, you're hurt real bad. You need a doctor."

The man practically collapsed against the side of the truck. "No, please. Government… kill me."

Clarance stared into the man's desperate eyes and then looked away. What he saw in the man's gaze was almost as disturbing and the damage to the man's face. Clarance didn't care much for the new President, but had things really gotten that bad? Maybe he ought to be paying more attention to the news. Except that most of the news wasn't worth listening to either.

Clarance lifted the phone once more. "Look, I know this retired doctor. Doc Smith is a good man. Can I call him?"

At the man's nod of resignation, Clarance brought up his contacts and scrolled down until he found James Smith. The phone rang 4 times before a deep male voice answered, "Hello."

"Doc? This is Clarance. I sort of need your help."

The voice on the other side of the line replied. "Is Penny all right, Clarance?"

Clarance took a deep breath and then the words kind of exploded out of him, "It's not my wife, Doc. I almost hit this guy out on Route 7. He's burnt bad. And he's got the worst case of road rash I have ever seen. He was just walking down the middle of my lane. I think he was in an accident."

"Did you call the police, Clarance?" the voice asked.

Clarance was shaking his head even though he was talking on the phone. "No, Doc. The guy is scared. He thinks they will try to kill him. I don't know what to do."

There was a moment's hesitation before the calm voice of the doctor asked, "Are you near your orchard, Clarance? Close to that crazy building they built in the hills above your farm?"

"Yeah, Doc," Clarance replied, "I was going to pick up a couple bushels of Macs. Penny wants to make applesauce. What does that have to do with anything?"

"Never you mind, Clarance. Can you get him in your truck?" the voice asked.

Clarance studied the injured man. "I'm not sure I can get him in the cab, Doc. He really is hurt bad."

The voice took on authority that Clarance had never heard from Doc Smith before. "Then lay him down in the bed, Clarance. And get him here as fast as you can. Then forget you ever saw him."

"In the bed, Doc? Are you sure?" was all Clarance could think to ask.

"Yes! Quickly!" The line went dead. Clarance closed his phone and slid it into his pocket. He walked around behind the truck and opened the tailgate. It took some effort to get the man into the bed of the truck. But even at 67 years old, Clarance was used to lifting bushel baskets full of apples into the back his truck.

The man rolled onto his back and closed his eyes as soon as Clarance got him into the truck. Closing the tailgate, Clarance headed for the open driver's door. Straightening the truck, he headed north once more. Two miles later, he passed the dirt road that headed up to the crazy building on the hilltop. There were soldiers at the gate this time. Clarance had never seen soldiers there before. He wondered what exactly was going on. But he didn't slow down.

In another mile or so, Clarance reached the gate into the orchard. He passed that by, too. He would be at Doc's place in another ten minutes if nothing else went wrong. Clarance said a silent prayer as he drove on.

# Cast of Characters

**Dr Anita Caufi** – Human female, M.D.
Anita is only the Chief Medical Advisor to the President of the United States and the Director of the National Institute of Allergy and Infectious Diseases (NIAID). Her ambitions go far beyond such insignificant titles. She's rather tired of working for and with people who are her intellectual inferiors. She has begun to branch out, seeking discoveries that will make her famous. When one of her unauthorized experiments gets loose, she winds up with a pandemic on her hands. The only way to stop the new virus appears to be another of her illicit projects, but which is worse, the virus or the cure. Doctor A. Morrall's genetic research has some unexpected side effects.

**John Boboden** – Human male, Development Team Leader
John had spent over a decade working his way up the corporate ladder, taking every undesirable project management job they threw at him. No job was too ugly. John had a reputation for getting things done, but it never seemed to get him one of the high-profile jobs he wanted. More often than not, it got him another ugly duckling. He was totally unprepared when Corporate offered the Virus C Rapid Response Program. It was a dream job with a huge budget. It might even save lives. He jumped at the opportunity. Then he met his chief scientist. The doctor was uncooperative and had his own agenda. That was just the beginning of John's headaches.

**Dr Alfred Morrall** – Human male, M.D.
Alfred is a genius. He tells himself that at least once each day. There wasn't a mind on the planet that understood human DNA the way he did. He had patented his first virus to resequence genetic defects before he had even finished medical school. It had been child's play to him. Alfred had his pick of jobs and he took many of them. But it seldom took long for him to get bored and move on. Alfred had his own ideas about how to employ his skills. Out of desperation, he took a job with NIAID. It was there that he finally found a sponsor, Dr Anita Caufi. She not only found him a place to play god, she gave him specimens to work his magic on.

**Chief Michel Barreau** – Human male, warrior
Ex-marine turned security specialist. The Chief was brought in after the death of the previous chief of security. Barreau is a true professional, competent in both combat and electronic warfare. He has

reorganized the security team to ensure there will be no containment breaches or staff losses under his watch. The Chief is divorced. His wife left him when he accepted a deployment to fight in the Gulf War. She could not understand that his honor demanded that he lead the men he trained in battle. He is still in touch with his young daughter.

**Jacob Dror** – Elf male, Mage
Jacob grew up in New York City. His first exposure to ancient languages was as a young boy reading in the Synagogue. Hebrew and later, Aramaic, became his passion. But some dreams can't be reached by a poor Jewish boy. So, Jacob joined the Army. He stayed in the service until he had his degree from NYU. Jacob fell in love and married while at NYU. Tragically, his wife died of cancer ten years later. Since that time, he has taught the languages he loves to anyone willing to learn. At 62, his only dream was to master the old tongues. Suddenly he finds himself young and full of life. He has pointed ears and the languages he loves are alive in his head.

**Miguel Sanchez (Herrera)** – Dwarf male, Blacksmith
Miguel was a Hispanic boy trying to survive in the inner city. Books and school seemed mostly a waste of time to him. What Miguel loved was using his hands to make things. The leader of the local gang recognized his skills and took him in. They made him their Herrera, maker of weapons and armor. As Herrera, he found a place where he belonged. He was no longer a burden to his single mother. His new family kept him safe. Now he is shorter than ever before. His scraggly, black mustache is now having a bushy red beard that hangs to his waist. The boy who only loved to build things is crafting the most incredible things from his dreams.

**Ruth Starling** – Gnome female, Illusionist
Daughter of one of the world's top investigative reporters and an island-born beauty from Jamaica, Ruth is a child prodigy. She was taking college classes at age 12 and graduated from high school at the tender age of 15. Ruth's dream was to be stage magician performing her own illusions. Her father wants much more for her than that. Ruth took classes to help her reach her dream, but her father insisted she be a full-time student at Georgetown University. Ruth is no longer a child, but she doesn't really know what she has become. Her magic is real now. As real as the new body she is trapped in.

**Conchia Alimara (Coon)** – Raccoon female
Being a teenager sucks. Being a bit overweight and not being able to afford the right clothes to fit in is infinitely worse. The teasing and bulling never stopped. Conchia dreamed of becoming a raccoon so she could disappear into the woods where she didn't need to fit in ever again. Some of the kids called her a "furry" and for a time she was accepted. But it didn't last. In the end, only her roommate, Ruth, stuck by her. Now she really is a raccoon and being furry isn't what she expected it to be.

**Danny Markos** – Halfling male, Acquisition specialist
Danny grew up poor. Actually, poor overstated the way he and his parents lived. But being poor didn't mean you had to do without. It just meant not getting caught or letting his parents know what he was up to. By the time he was sixteen, Danny had a lucrative business selling slightly used car parts. He could strip a car in under five minutes. He was smart too. Getting into Georgetown wasn't hard. And the selection of car parts around the school was incredible. Once he has his business degree, he plans to open his own parts store and keep all the profits from his work. Now, Danny finds himself too short to drive, but his fingers are magical.

**Geoff Harding** – Ogre male, Armsman
A hometown hero from the backroads of Tennessee, Geoff is good at two things, wrestling and judo. At eighteen, Geoff has already placed third at Nationals. Never more than a C student, he is smart enough to know that he can't fight forever. So, when Georgetown University offers him a four-year scholarship, he trades time on the mats for a degree. His future is looking up, but Geoff still has dreams of greater glory. No one cares who wins the 149-pound weight class. The crowd only watches the heavyweights. He would give anything to be bigger and stronger. He gets his dream, but that dream doesn't come free and neither is he.

**Alicia Octavia Condemn** – Drow female
Born into privilege, Alicia is the daughter of a US Congresswoman. She expects to step into her mother's place as soon as she is old enough. She is double majoring in Pre-Law and Liberal Studies. Capable of earning the perfect grades she gets; Alica only cares about "causes" that make her look good. After all, who would dare give the

Congresswoman's daughter less than an A. Her spring break beach party goes wrong and she comes down with that new virus. She goes to sleep in her private hospital room and wakes up changed. She's no longer Mother's little play toy or anyone else's for that fact. She will get the power she craves one way or another.

**Tara Helleväara** – Human female, Seamstress
Owner and proprietor of Ancient Attire, Tara is young, beautiful and very talented. She is a Master Seamstress who supports herself and her daughter by sewing tunics to sell at Renaissance Faires. Tara is the head of the Weaver's guild at King Richard's Faire. She, like most of the tradesmen and women, have fallen on hard times due to the virus that has shut down so many of their venues. Tara is a longtime member of The Folk.

**Tuula Helleväara** – Human female, Psychic
Tuula is only six-years old. She is autistic, but she functions at such a high level that most people just think she's a bit quirky. Tuula is an artist of rare skill. Her pictures often show strange insights into the people she chooses to draw. Some might call her images prophetic. Her mother says that Tuula just sees thingsthe way they are instead of seeing them the way she wants them to be. Tuula adores Tolkien and all of his stories. Through those tales, she sees the true potential in the newcomers to King Richard's Faire.

**Sir John** – Human male, Seneschal
Sir John is a senior member of The Folk. Sir John is a member of the King's Court and serves as a personal advisor to the King. His duties include solving any and all problems that impact the smooth operation of the Realm. That includes interviewing strange newcomers seeking employment. In his spare time, he is also the senior legal counsel for the Realms.

**Lady Aimée** – Human female, ElderLady Aimée and her mother are co-owners of King Richard's Faire. More importantly, she and her mother are the unofficial Elders of The Folk. As such, they are responsible for most of the behind-the-scenes activities that keep the faire functioning. She is also a member of the Council of Elders that connects the many realms within North America. Her authority is absolute if there is any threat to The Folk.

## About the Book

Where do stories and book ideas come from? I haven't a clue where most authors get their ideas. All of mine come from questions. Having taught middle school for eleven years, I just can't leave a question unanswered. The question gnaws at me until it's answered to the student's satisfaction.

So, there I am, playing AD&D online from the comfort of my home. My favorite good-natured and bumbling character is caught red-handed by the party. No, he wasn't stealing from them. He was distractedly talking to a squirrel and feeding it from his nut collection. Why, you ask? So did the rest of the party. Only they weren't quite as nice about it. That might have been because he was supposed to be on guard duty. But at least no one in the party died.

And there it was, an unanswered question. Why? Yes, it's his quirk. Every good character needs to have a quirk. But that wasn't a good answer as to why a 480 pound, 7' 8" half-ogre would be obsessed with squirrels. There was something just wrong about the ogre's interest in squirrels was the response of my friends. That led to the next question that had to be answered. What did the squirrels mean in Shorty's life?

It took a lot of thought. After a lot of self-examination …after all, where else would I look? Doesn't the main character always represent some aspect of the author? I found the answer. The squirrels represented Shorty's ability to choose his own destiny. They were in essence his right to be himself, the right to be free. And thus was born All Good Things come with Squirrels.

By now, I suspect you are asking what this has to do with the book, Virus-C? Everything and nothing at all. You see, Virus-C was never supposed to be written. I had a twenty-book plan for the Becoming Heroes series. Each step was carefully laid out. Short stories were my distractions whenever I needed to lock a piece of history into place. There was no plan to do anything that even resembled urban fantasy. Why would I write something like that? Magic and technology just don't play well together.

Then that old Bard in The Short Path to Becoming Heroes had to open his big mouth. He let the proverbial cat out of the bag. And before you ask the question… No, I had nothing to do with the orcs shooting him full of crossbow bolts. It was their idea from the start. Trust me, those orcs were a bad lot. And, when they were done, the Bard couldn't cause me any more problems by telling secrets.

But now what was I to do? The Bard told everyone that the Mages of Science were responsible for creating elves, dwarves, ogres, and all of the mortal races. More importantly, they somehow were to blame for magic leaking into the world. I tried to ignore him. Honest! I did. I went on to write several more books (sadly, out of order so they have to wait their turn to be published) and I thought no more about the dead Bard.

In the end, my efforts were to no avail. The question finally raised its very ugly head. And not just one, mind you. A whole slew of questions began hanging around me, muttering and whispering to me. They would not leave me alone. Yes, I am quite sane. Thank you very much for asking. 'Who were the mages?' tried to talk louder than 'What went wrong?' 'How did they do it?' and several of his buddies made rude comments in the background. All in all, they made more noise around the house that my 9, 13, and 17-year-old kids. At least the kids went to school and gave me peace for a few hours.

And so, in the end, the questions had to be answered as they always do. And Virus-C was born. My hope that the idea would go away after a few unsuccessful chapters was soon dashed and the book took on a life of its own. Not only did I want to find out how it ended, but I found that I really liked several of the characters. Along the way, I discovered the runes and pronunciation for the language of the Arcane. Going back to add that to each of the stories already finished was painful but fun. And the story continued to grow.

There was so much fun to be found in the story. Turning the world in which we live into the setting for the story was a blast. I could not believe how so many of the events that really happened in our world were the perfect backdrop to the story. Headlines from the internet were reworded to avoid plagiarism, but the media really was reporting stuff like this. Best of all, the .gov pieces are all real except for the names.

And then there were the names: twisting and turning names, creating new ones, pulling names from history to fill in the gaps. It was all out there to be a part of the story. And the crowning name of all (Nope, you have to find this one for yourself because I am not telling.) came from my beautiful wife. She is of Puerto Rican descent and has shared with me many of the tales of folklore of her family's homeland. In Puerto Rico, they tell the tales of the boy who always tried to be good and failed. He has a special place in my story. And so, the names almost all had meaning to me.

Not every part of my research for Virus-C was fun and games. Memories of the harsh realities of life during COVID came crashing back. As I reflected on the nearly five years of chaos that the people of this country endured, I found key trends within our society that would leave our society vulnerable to a "Great Change." That change would not create real orcs and trolls, but it could create evils that our world can't hope to survive. If the meandering path of this note has caused you to close the book, I ask you to bear with me a little longer while I explain.

I know, from personal experience, that all officers take an oath before they are commissioned in any branch of the military. It is an oath that binds us long past our time of service of our country. It is a lifetime obligation. The oath goes like this:

> *I, Ursa, having been appointed a Major in the United States Armed Forces, do solemnly swear that I will support and defend the Constitution of the United States against all enemies, foreign and domestic. That I take this obligation freely without mental reservation or purpose of evasion*

*and that I will well and faithfully discharge the duties of the office upon which I am about to enter, so help me God.*

Our elected officials in Washington, DC take similar oaths on entering office. Officer Candidates, at the service academies at least, are well trained on the meaning and the responsibilities of their oath. They need to be because it is the basis for every decision they must make for the rest of their career and beyond.

One would think that those elected officials, especially those who give orders to the soldiers, sailors, and airmen, would receive at least as much training. But they don't. Why not? Don't the people that our elected officials serve deserve that? Shouldn't Presidents and members of the Legislative Branch understand what their oaths mean?

To support and defend the Constitution of the United States of America is such a powerful phrase. It is both simple and more complicated than one can imagine. To keep that oath, one must understand what the Constitution really is. The easy answer to the question is that the Constitution is the supreme law of our country. And it is, but it is much, much more than that.

The founders of our county were incredibly intelligent people. Their mastery of the written word was nothing short of remarkable. They not only understood how to convey their ideas in writing, they knew how to put those words into the minds and hearts of the people. One of those basic rules of writing is to put the important ideas right up front. That is a rule I still struggle with as you might have guessed. But our early leaders didn't struggle with it. The most important part of our Constitution is the first three words, "WE THE PEOPLE."

That means that every officer and every one of our elected officials in Washington swear to support and defend "WE THE PEOPLE." Their oath says nothing about supporting their political party, their own political agenda, or even their own careers. It is all about the citizens of the United States and their needs, not the needs of the politicians or even the needs of millions of illegal immigrants.

My second concern, and I will keep this more brief, is very similar in nature. Medical professionals also take a binding oath, "To do no harm." The meaning of that oath appears to have been lost in recent decades. Medical integrity gets superseded by questionable treatments, surgeries, and drugs. The more profitable the treatment, the more likely it is to be performed even if the patient might suffer for decades. And why not? That patient will need costly medical treatments for the rest of their life. It is little different than designing a refrigerator that has a life expectancy of five years (or less).

In some ways, it sounds kind of hopeless. But, remember this. We don't have to get on that runaway train. "WE THE PEOPLE" still have a say. Our voices can and must be heard. Let it start with a few heroes who have the courage to say, "Not this time." How much better could things be if all of the "WE" in "THE PEOPLE" raised our voices to be heard. What could this country become…or even the world…if the vocal minority was drowned out by the millions of voices of reason. That is a dream I would love to experience in real life. Together, we can make that dream a reality. Just raise your voice and be heard!

# Author Bio

Major Ursa's love of fantasy and science fiction began as a child lost in the worlds created by Andre Norton. Her characters were true heroes. They walked the paths of honor even when it came at a price. That lesson became a part of Ursa's own life.

Major Ursa made his first forays into fantasy gaming in 1980. Soon, he was creating worlds and adventures to entertain friends and family. The games became stories to entertain his children and grandchildren. Somewhere along the way, entertainment turned into teaching about honor and sacrifice and ways to persevere when things were hard. Now, the old bear is putting his favorite tales in print. The world needs heroes, even fictional ones, that are willing to put the needs of others before their own desires.

To find out more about Major Ursa and his stories please visit his website at www.ursabooks.com and his Facebook page at Ursa Books.

Previous works:

    Tapestry of the World, a collection of short stories

    Short Path to Becoming Heroes

    Beautiful

Milton Keynes UK
Ingram Content Group UK Ltd.
UKHW040353111224
452348UK00001B/124